HEWLETT & MARTIN

TANK GIRL THREE

TITAN BOOKS

TANK GIRL THREE (REMASTERED)
ISBN: 9781845767617

Published by
Titan Books
A division of Titan Publishing Group Ltd.
144 Southwark St
London
SE1 0UP

First edition: 2009
10 9 8 7 6 5

A CIP catalogue record for this title is available from the British Library.

Cover illustration by Jamie Hewlett.

Printed in China.

Visit our website: www.titanbooks.com

Did you enjoy this book? We love to hear from our readers. Please email us at: readerfeedback@titanemail.com or write to us at the above address.
To receive advance information, news, competitions, and exclusive Titan offers online, please register by clicking the "Sign up" button on our website: www.titanbooks.com

Checkout the official website at:
WWW.TANK-GIRL.COM

THE COMPLETE CLASSIC TANK GIRL COLLECTION

CHAPTER INDEX

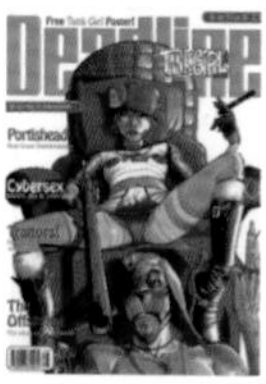
Deadline

EPISODE THIRTY-TWO: THE TASTE OF PARADISE – DECEMBER 1994/ JANUARY 1995

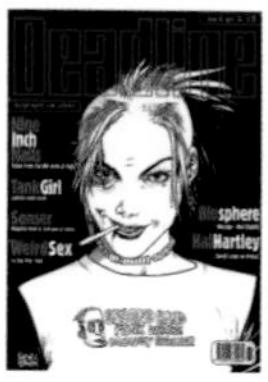
Deadline

EPISODE THIRY-THREE: BUSHMAN TUCKER – APRIL 1994

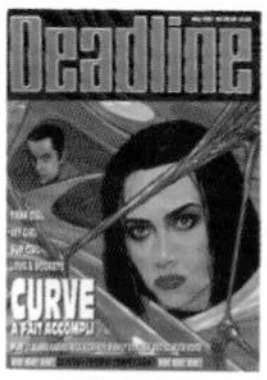
Deadline
CURVE

EPISODE THIRTY-FOUR: WHATEVER HAPPENED TO THE SMITHS – MAY 1992

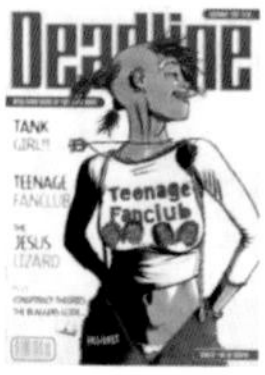
Deadline
Teenage
Fanclub

EPISODE THIRTY-FIVE: BALL HANGER – SEPTEMBER 1993

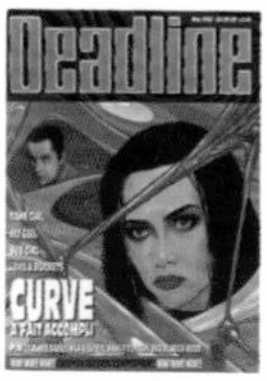
Deadline
CURVE

EPISODE THIRTY-SIX: THE ALL-NEW JET GIRL IN 'FUCK' – MAY 1992

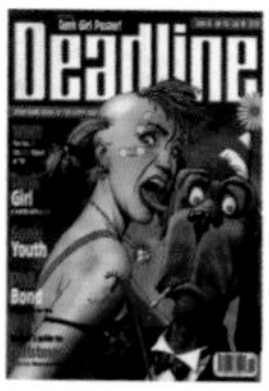
Deadline

EPISODE THIRTY-SEVEN: MORNING GLORY – DECEMBER 1993/ JANUARY 1994

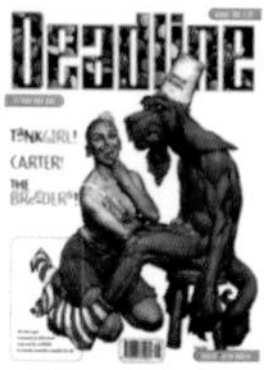
Deadline

EPISODE THIRTY-EIGHT: BURNING VACATION – OCTOBER 1993

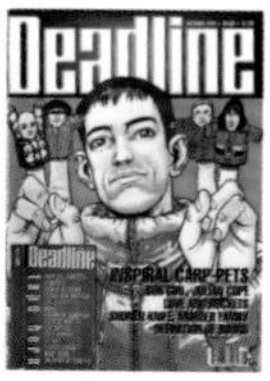
Deadline

EPISODE THIRTY-NINE: THE GOSPEL ACCORDING TO SUB GIRL – OCTOBER 1992

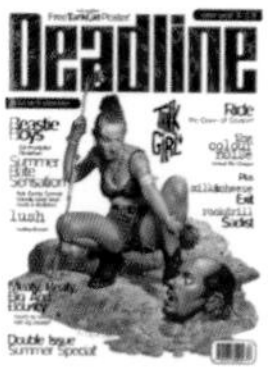
Deadline

EPISODE FORTY: THE MOUNT MUSHROOM MASSACRE – SUMMER SPECIAL 1994

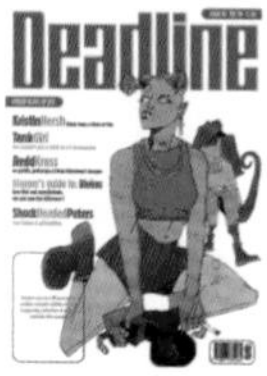
Deadline

ALMANAC – FEBRUARY 1994

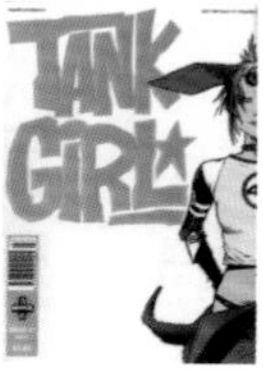
TANK
GIRL

BOOGA'S LUCK – JULY 1995

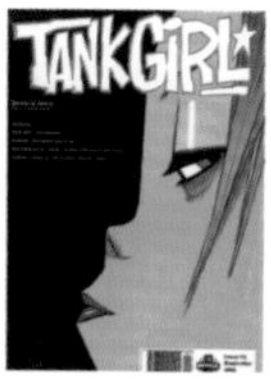
TANKGIRL

ONCE UPON A TIME IN THE EAST: COWBOY CHANG – SEPTEMBER 1995

INTRO

Hello good buddies. A warm welcome to this third and final compilation of classic Hewlett & Martin Tank Girl comic strips, as presented in their original printed form, straight from the pages of their mothership publication Deadline Magazine.

As a lot of you already know, the bulk of the material in this book was produced around the time of the controversial Hollywood movie version of Tank Girl. I'm going to try not to dwell on the movie for too long (if I start ranting, throw a pint over me), but it does need mentioning to help put this stuff in context.

This book centres around a moment in time when everything thing climaxed and collapsed simultaneously, much like a drunken shag. And, just like the morning after a drunken shag, all we were left with was a banging headache, an underlying feeling of guilt, an unsavoury taste in our mouths, and a long walk home.

Whether you love the film, hate the film, or haven't even seen the film, the fact remains that a lot of people have found their way to the comics by discovering the movie version first. And whether Jamie and I loved it or hated it, it's still very obvious that it had a palpable impact on the content of the comics. This was first noticeable in the strip "Tank Girl's Guide To Joy" (Tank Girl Book #2), where we were already predicting our own wobbly route to precarious worldwide infamy via Tinseltown – "A year later Hollywood sniffs out the Tank Girl trail, like a dog to another dog's arse. The offers come thick and thin. We were overcome and then asked to come over." From then on, snide references to Hollywood started to pepper all of our Tank Girl strips.

A master plan to cash in on the publicity generated by the movie was hatched. So as our work on *Deadline Magazine* started to wind down, production was cranked up on Tank Girl's own eponymously titled magazine that was to be published by

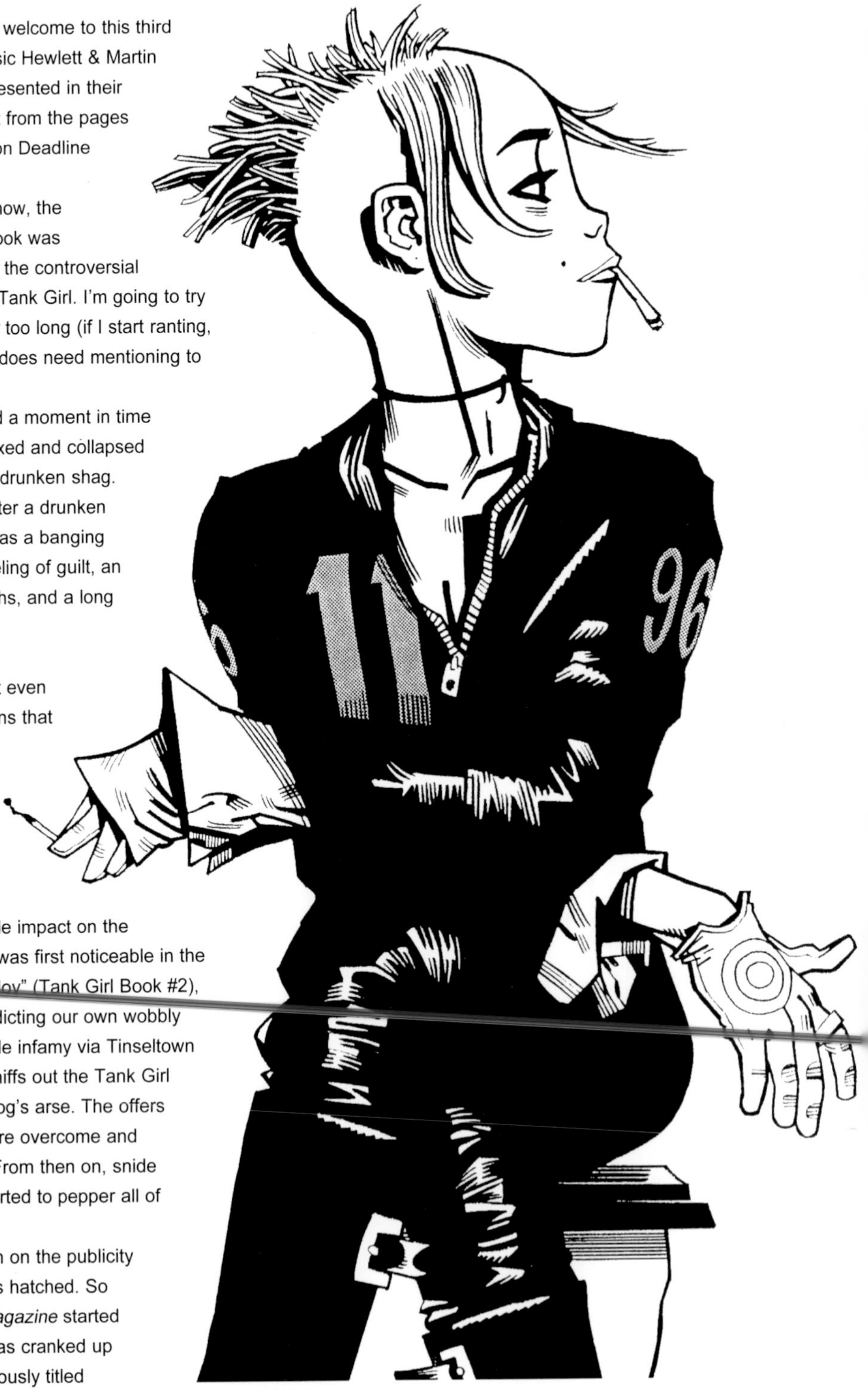

The uncoloured art for the cover of *Manga Tank Girl Magazine #3.*

ROLL over Mickey Mouse and Donald Duck, Tank Girl is coming to the big screen.

Britain's latest cult cartoon character has been bought up by a Hollywood film studio which aims to make her the next superhero of the silver screen.

But Tank Girl is different: she has *attitude*. Created by two 20-year-old art students in Worthing, West Sussex, five years ago, she has gained cult following in this country for her sexy, independent approach to life.

She is eternally 23, lives in a tank in the Australian outback with her half-man, half-kangaroo boyfriend Booga, and makes a point of always having a good time.

Her creator Jamie Hewlett, 25, says he based her on Clint Eastwood: "She is totally indestructible. She tries her hardest to be smart and be against everything. Everything she does is cool."

Hollywood heard of Tank Girl through Rachel Talalay, the American director, who was shown the cartoon by her English stepson. She got in touch with *Deadline*, the British comic which features the strip.

Tom Astor, the cartoon's publisher, went to America several times before striking a deal with Talalay, who has directed one of the *Nightmare on Elm Street* films, and MGM. They have commissioned writer, Tedi Sarafian, whose last film script was snapped up Stephen Spielberg. The script should be finished this autumn.

The success of Tank Girl has amused Hewlett and his co-creator, Alan Martin, 26. They say the purpose of the character was to parody other cartoons. "We just wanted to upset people," says Martin. "The strip has things that British comics don't have — drugs, alcohol and sex. Tank Girl belches, sweats and is always going to the toilet.

"Also, our stories never have endings. People realise we are taking the mickey but they also realise we are pushing the boundaries of comic art. She appeals to people not interested in comics."

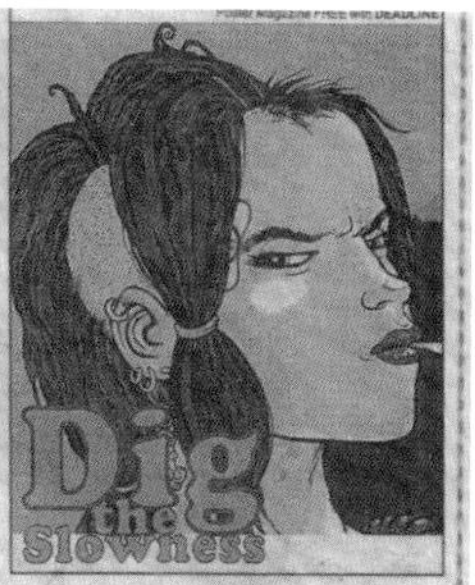
Dig the Slowness

Mean: the rebel cartoon character set for stardom

Hewlett says he deliberately baits his readers: "People used to come up to me and say 'That Tank Girl has a really wicked haircut'. So I'd change it."

The pair have been inundated by companies wanting Tank Girl to endorse their products. "We chose Wrangler," adds Hewlett, "because it is such rubbish."

Penguin has published a book of Tank Girl strips, reprinting it three times in three years. The cartoon has also been translated into seven different languages.

Tom Astor believes Tank Girl struck a chord with young people: "She is fanciable and intelligent. Also, living with the elements she appeals to grunge, traveller fashion.

"I hope MGM keep her humour and her links with British culture and don't turn her into a bald babe with a gun; the female Arnold Schwarzenegger."

Emma Peacock, who wrote a dissertation on Tank Girl for her Politics, French and European Studies degree at Sussex University, says the character is like a comic-strip Madonna (the controversial pop star). "She is cocky, feminist and aggressive. She has power through her sexuality, like any other superhero."

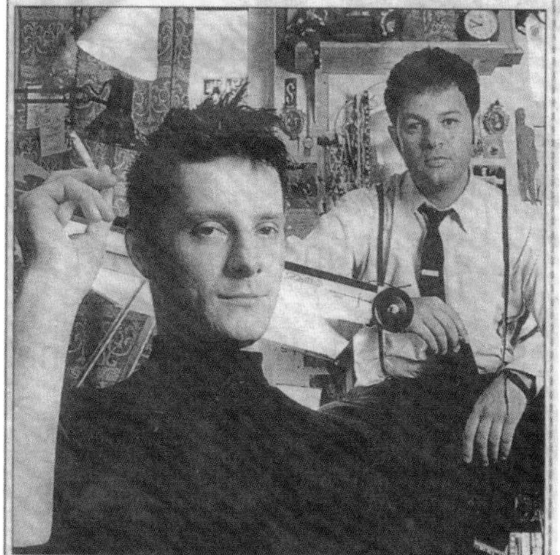

Team: Hewlett (left) and Martin created the cult

Hewlett and Martin in *The Sunday Telegraph* May 9th 1993.

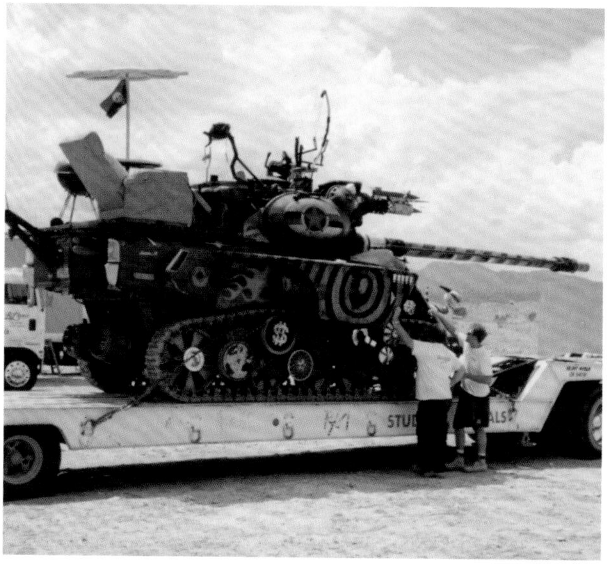

Taking delivery of the tank – on the set of *Tank Girl* the movie , Arizona 1994.

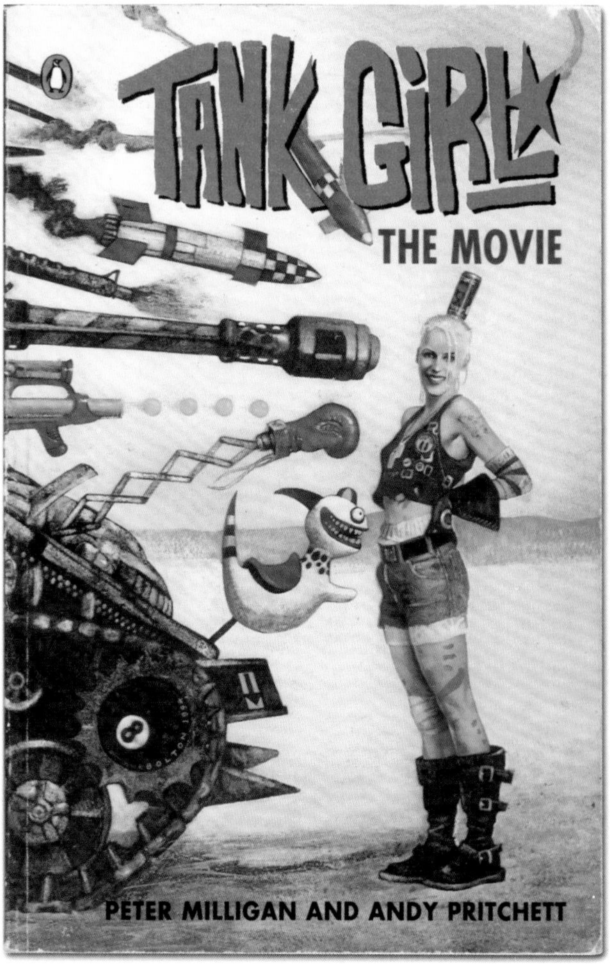
TANK GIRL
THE MOVIE
PETER MILLIGAN AND ANDY PRITCHETT

The graphic novelisation of *Tank Girl* the movie, currently fetching the princely sum of twenty-five pence on on-line auction sites.

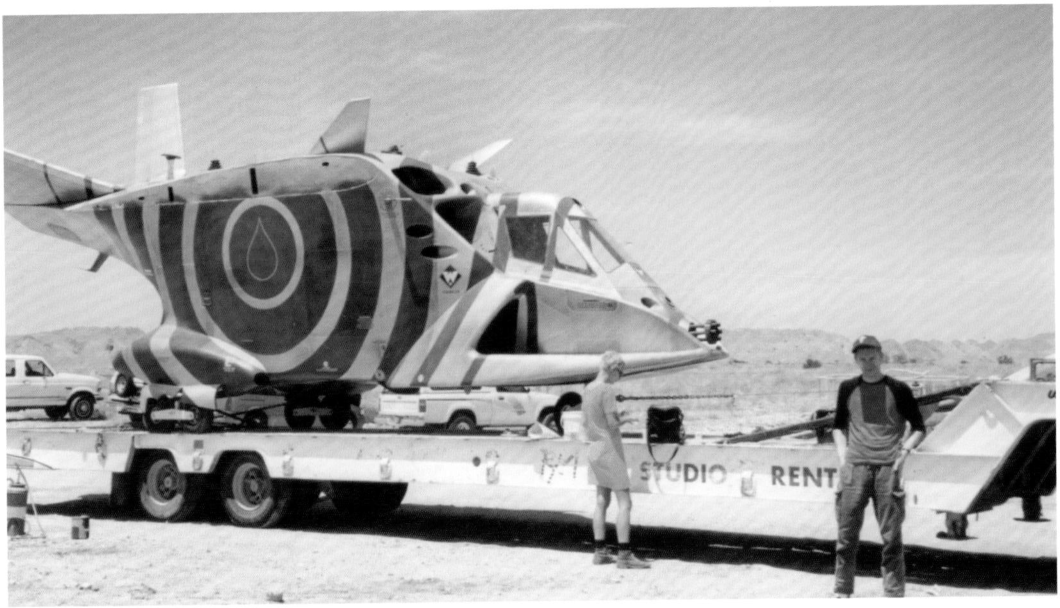
STUDIO
RENT

Jamie contemplates hijacking the jet and getting the fuck out of there.

Manga in the UK, with the main stories simultaneously being printed in classic comic format by DC Comics in the US. For the debut issue Peter Milligan was brought in to write *Tank Girl: The Odyssey* (the next remastered book in this series), a story that regularly pulled focus onto Tank Girl's emerging silver screen counterpart and all the bullshit Hollywood trappings that would have plagued her path to glory. That was swiftly followed by Alan Grant, Peter Bond and Andy Pritchett's graphic novel adaptation of the film, which has the movie tale book-ended with the superstar Tank Girl, bloated out to the size of a small whale, floating in her private luxury pool, recounting the movie plot as if it was all bullshine.

My work was relegated to the back of the Manga magazine as I turned in scripts for the solo Booga outing "Antidisestablishmentarianism" and the reckless art-fest "Tank Girl vs Cowboy Chan". These strips have never seen the light of day since their original printing in the Manga magazine, so I'm pretty chuffed that we've updated this volume with them in their rightful chronological place. The Manga mag also featured Booga in "Mind Control" (which can now be found in *The Cream Of Tank Girl*), the Hewlett and Bond drawn two-pagers that were reprinted from the US magazine Details (all of which can be seen in the new volume of *Tank Girl: The Odyssey*), and the epic "Picnic at Hanging Cock" (which is now a bonus feature in *Tank Girl: Apocalypse* – the final book of our remastered series).

With everything rolling along merrily, I bought myself a word processor set to work on writing my own epic to follow on from *The Odyssey* – *Tank Girl: The Soul Of The Ape*, a dark and murky tale that I had based loosely on Joseph Conrad's *Heart Of Darkness*. I submitted the first twenty-two-page script with pride and awaited the

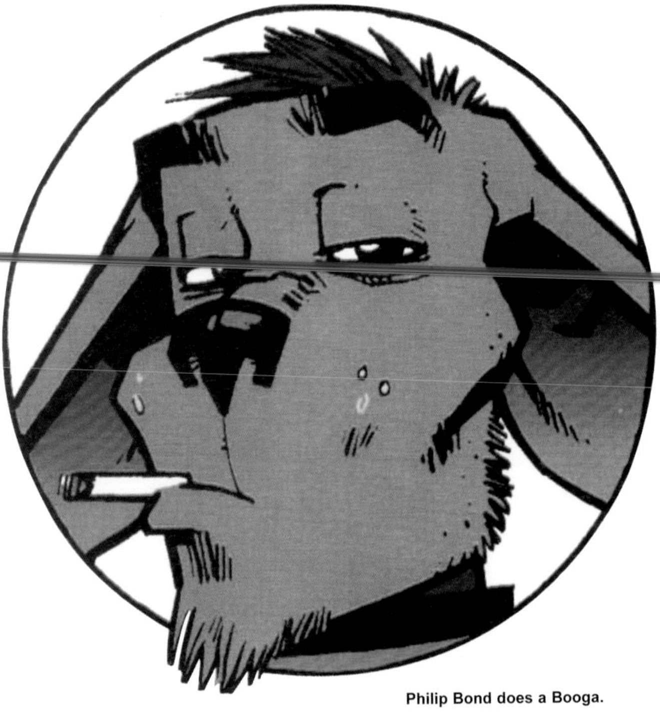

Philip Bond does a Booga.

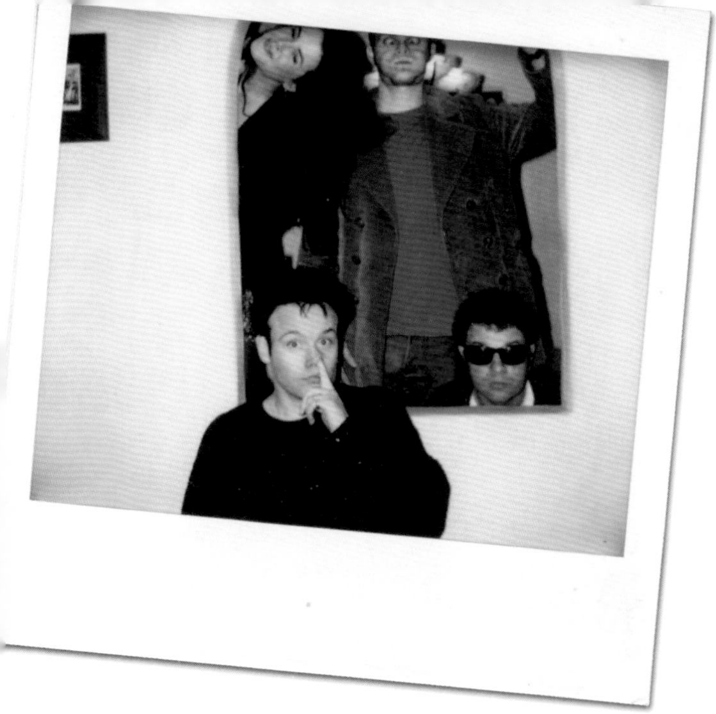

Ridicule is nothing to be scared of – Jamie and Alan goofing off round at Adam Ant's house, L.A. 1994.

editorial reaction while I got on with the next part. And I waited. After hearing nothing for a few weeks I gave them a nudge and was solemnly told that another four-part story had already been commissioned. I was incredulous. I already knew that the movie bore little resemblance to our beloved comics, so this was the final blow. I had totally lost what little control I had of Tank Girl. I could've argued the toss with publishers and editors but by then the will was gone, and I wasn't prepared to accept scraps from the table. Things just weren't fun anymore, and it's damned difficult to produce a funny comic when you're tired and pissed off. So I got the fuck out of there. And I didn't look back for a long time. And I burnt my unused scripts on an open fire in a cottage in Wales.

As you can probably tell, a rage still burns deep inside me from those days, and while I do understand that a lot of you hold the movie close to your hearts, I hope you can now appreciate that

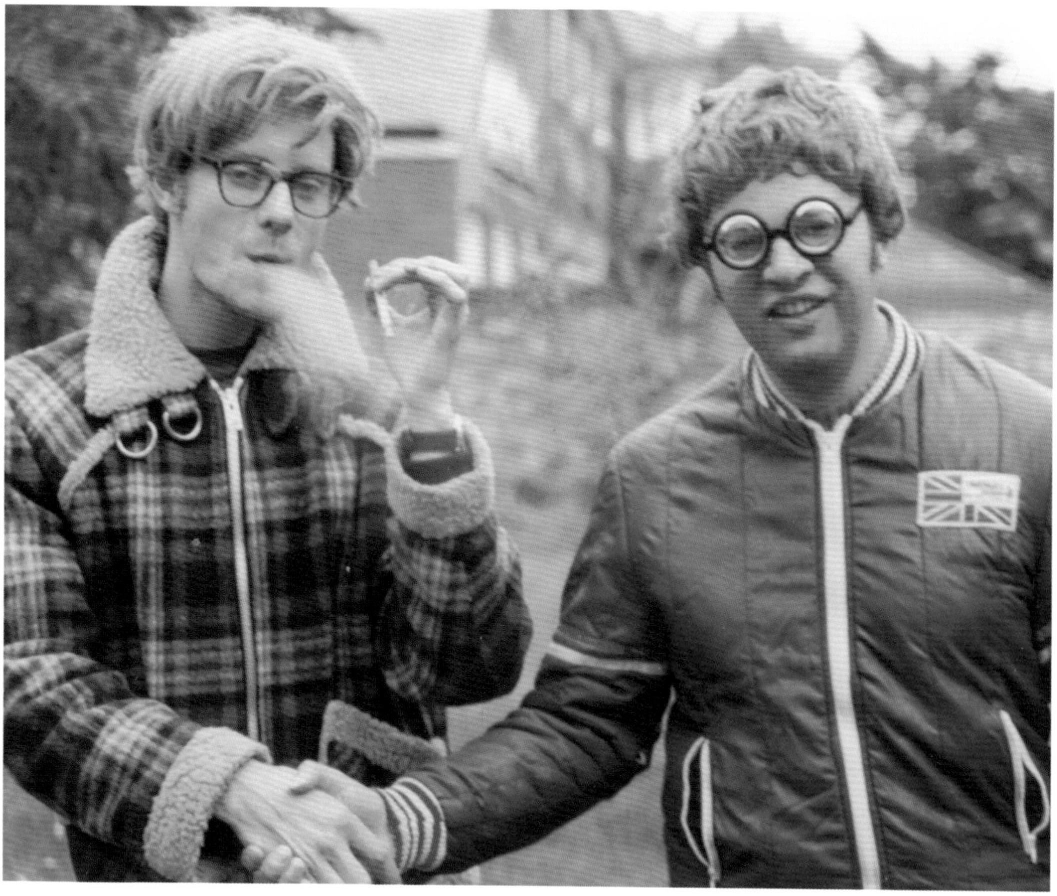

The real Hewlett and Martin congratulate themselves on being shafted by Hollywood.

my dislike for it goes way beyond simple aesthetics. This is personal.

Bad vibes aside, the lead up to the movie was still a premium period for classic Tank Girl comic strips, and this book holds some of my all time favourites: "Ball Hanger" – featuring Booga's dad, Kevin Kegan's afro, scotch eggs, and a yeti; "Morning Glory" (named years before the Oasis LP, you understand) – with the death of Sub Girl, The Undertones, and a Christmas pudding on Booga's knob; "Bushman Tucker" – had an all-star cast of The Buzzcocks, Ken Dodd, and Tucker Jenkins' poo poo; and "The Mount Mushroom Massacre" (in my opinion, the very pinnacle of Tank Girl's career) – which had our heroes raiding a theme park bank and making a getaway on a bouncy castle owned by Graham Coxon.

You just can't argue with stuff like that – cheap, sugary, low-grade enlightenment. That, to me, makes this volume priceless – a bible for modern times.

As you'll see from some of the pages in this book, we had a hard time sourcing as-good-as-new artwork to print from; mostly all we had to work with was the original publication in *Deadline Magazine*, which, in a few glaring cases, left a lot to be desired. So I can only apologise for these blips and hope that you can accept them as, erm, 'authentic and original period blemishes'. Perhaps one day when Jamie is in his dotage, he may have the time and inclination to redraw some of the panels. Meantime, if anyone owns or knows the whereabouts of the originals of said pages, could you please do us all a favour and contact either myself or the publishers and we'll re-instate the art at the next available opportunity.

Finally, before I sign off from this series, I just wanted to say a little thank you to all of the people who've followed and supported Tank Girl over the years. I hope that our efforts to bring a fresh look to the character – not just with these re-issues and *The Cream Of Tank Girl*, but with the new material too – meet with your approval.

I let Tank Girl get away from me once before, but believe me, I'm a right tight bastard with her now. Here's a little extract from my Tank Girl novel *Armadillo!* that just about sums those feelings up –

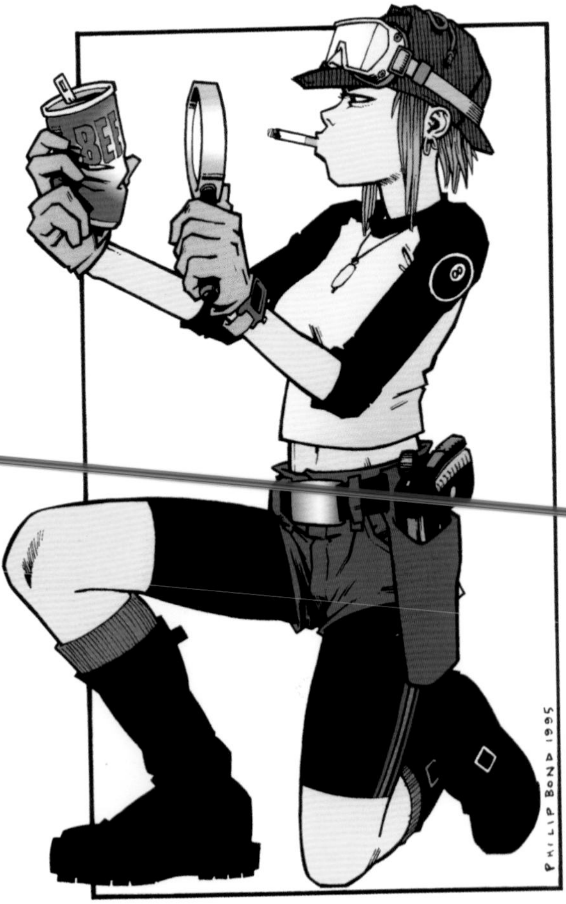
PHILIP BOND 1995

Philip Bond does a Tank Girl.

<u>MINE MINE MINE</u>

I lost you in the playground
I lost you near the swings
I was distracted by the Helter Skelter
and all the chaos that it brings

I lost you in a crowd of kids
too many faces, too many screams
you jumped out of my pocket like an errant glove
slipped from my hands like a melting ice-cream

but now I'm binding you to me with an idiot string
I'm pegging you by your ears to the washing line

and I'm sewing my name inside you

because you're mine
mine
mine

Peace brothers and sisters,

Alan C. Martin
Top of the World
Berwick upon Tweed
October 2008

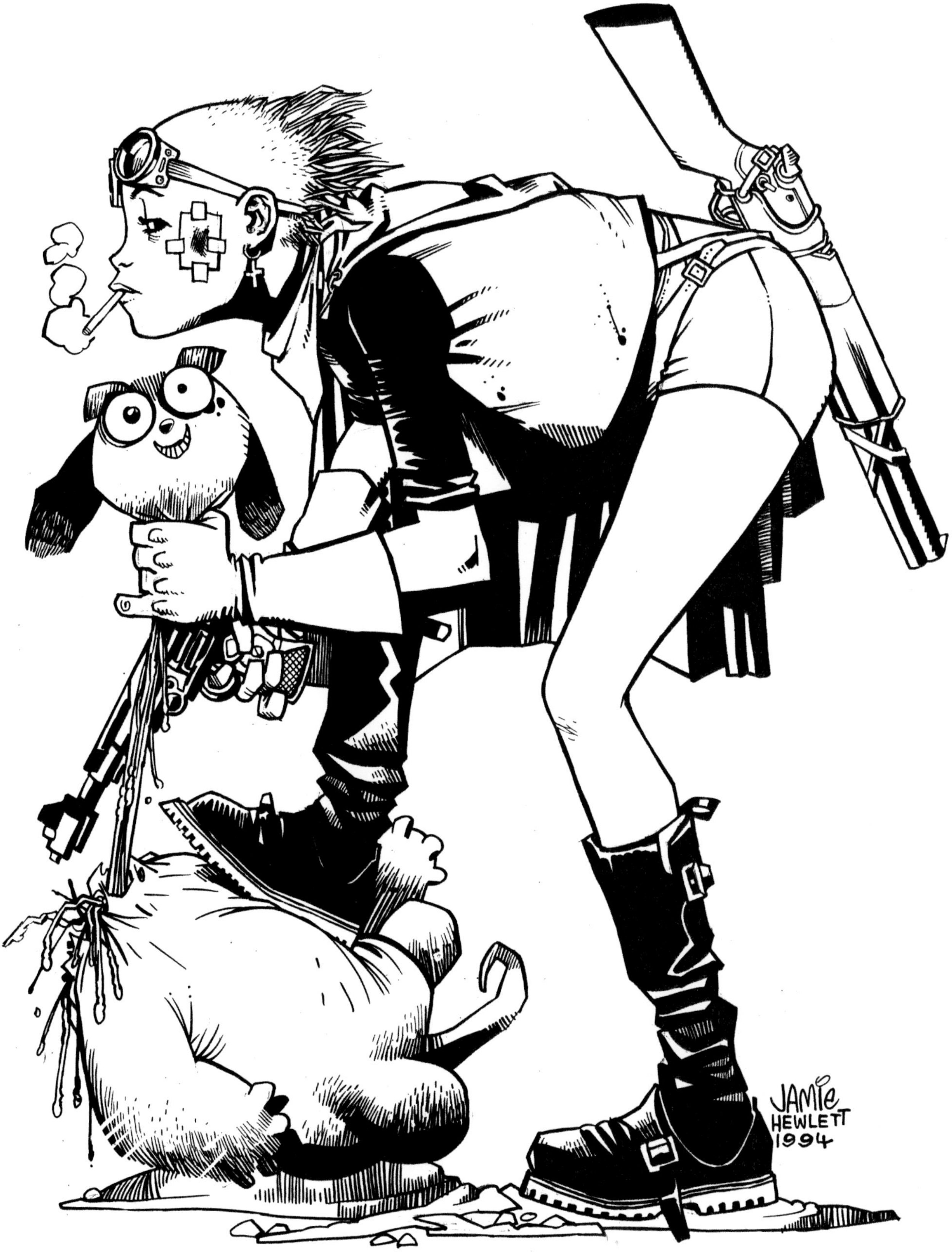
JAMIE HEWLETT 1994

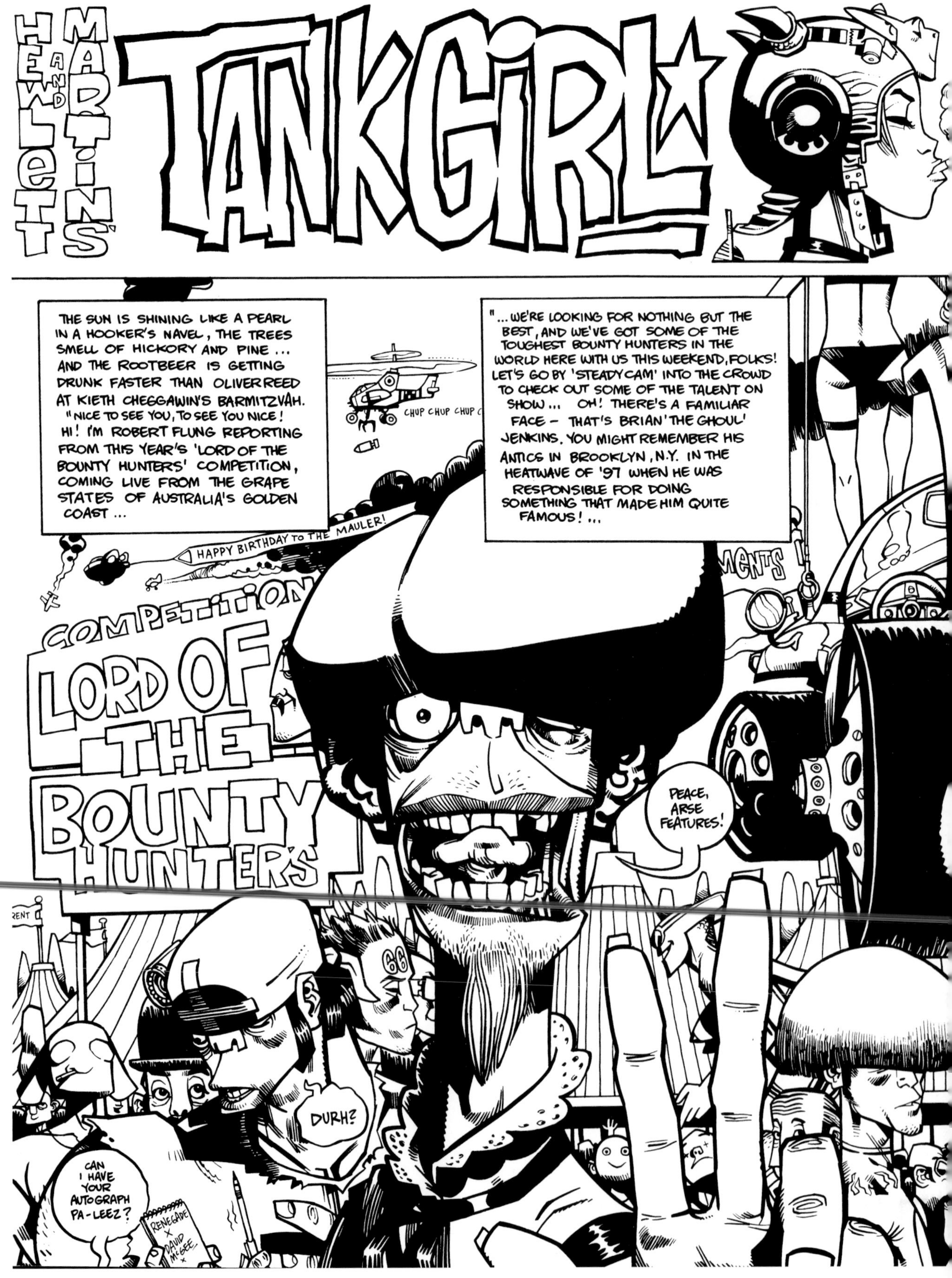
HEWLETT AND MARTIN'S
TANK GIRL
THE SUN IS SHINING LIKE A PEARL IN A HOOKER'S NAVEL, THE TREES SMELL OF HICKORY AND PINE ... AND THE ROOTBEER IS GETTING DRUNK FASTER THAN OLIVER REED AT KIETH CHEGGAWIN'S BARMITZVAH. "NICE TO SEE YOU, TO SEE YOU NICE! HI! I'M ROBERT FLUNG REPORTING FROM THIS YEAR'S 'LORD OF THE BOUNTY HUNTERS' COMPETITION, COMING LIVE FROM THE GRAPE STATES OF AUSTRALIA'S GOLDEN COAST ...
CHUP CHUP CHUP
"... WE'RE LOOKING FOR NOTHING BUT THE BEST, AND WE'VE GOT SOME OF THE TOUGHEST BOUNTY HUNTERS IN THE WORLD HERE WITH US THIS WEEKEND, FOLKS! LET'S GO BY 'STEADY CAM' INTO THE CROWD TO CHECK OUT SOME OF THE TALENT ON SHOW ... OH! THERE'S A FAMILIAR FACE - THAT'S BRIAN 'THE GHOUL' JENKINS. YOU MIGHT REMEMBER HIS ANTICS IN BROOKLYN, N.Y. IN THE HEATWAVE OF '97 WHEN HE WAS RESPONSIBLE FOR DOING SOMETHING THAT MADE HIM QUITE FAMOUS! ...
HAPPY BIRTHDAY TO THE MAULER!
COMPETITION
LORD OF THE BOUNTY HUNTERS
MENTS
PEACE, ARSE FEATURES!
DURH?
CAN I HAVE YOUR AUTOGRAPH PA-LEEZ?
RENEGADE X DAVID McGEE X

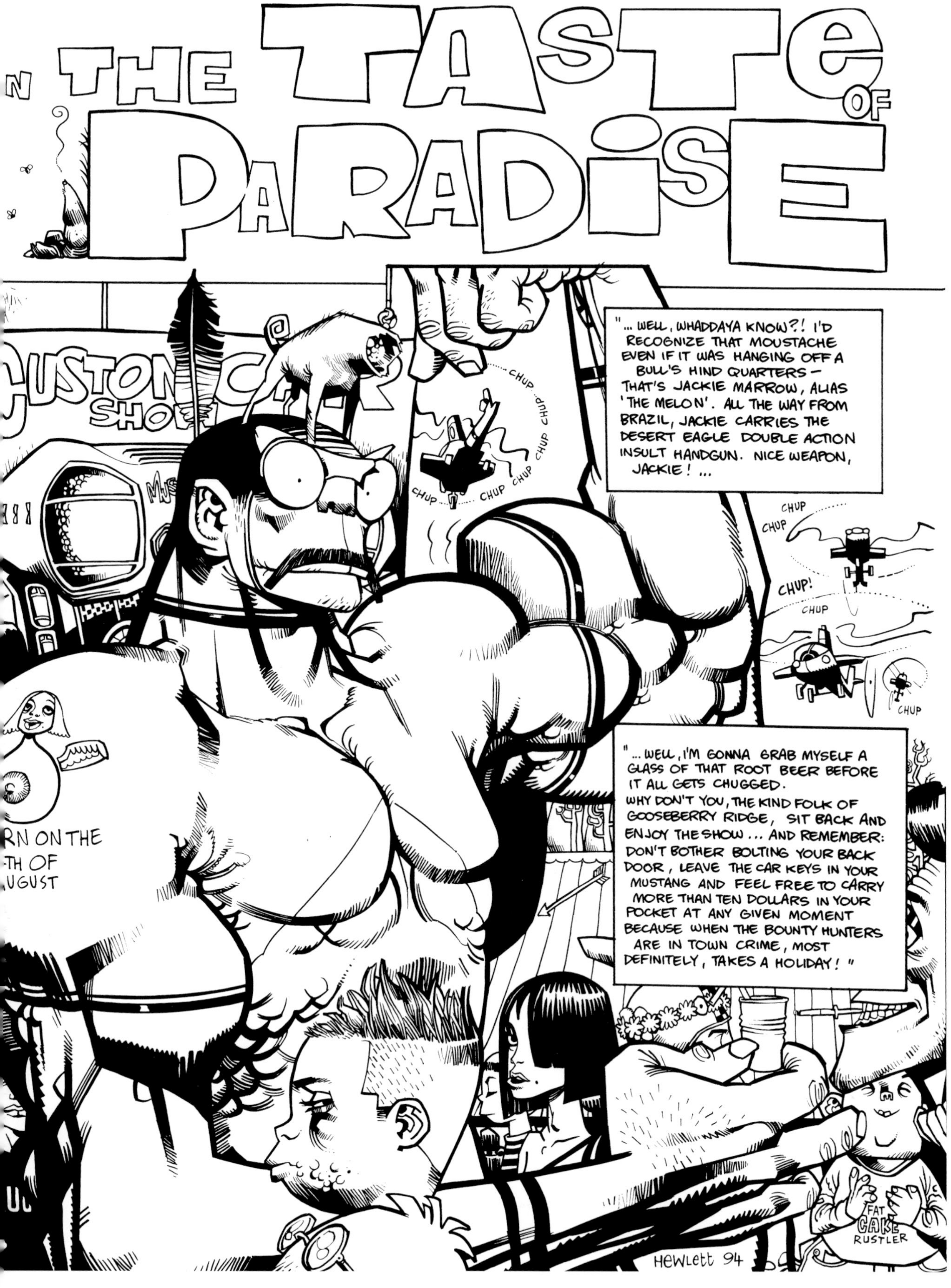
THE TASTE OF PARADISE
"... WELL, WHADDAYA KNOW?! I'D RECOGNIZE THAT MOUSTACHE EVEN IF IT WAS HANGING OFF A BULL'S HIND QUARTERS – THAT'S JACKIE MARROW, ALIAS 'THE MELON'. ALL THE WAY FROM BRAZIL, JACKIE CARRIES THE DESERT EAGLE DOUBLE ACTION INSULT HANDGUN. NICE WEAPON, JACKIE! ...
CHUP CHUP CHUP CHUP CHUP CHUP CHUP
CHUP CHUP CHUP! CHUP CHUP
"... WELL, I'M GONNA GRAB MYSELF A GLASS OF THAT ROOT BEER BEFORE IT ALL GETS CHUGGED. WHY DON'T YOU, THE KIND FOLK OF GOOSEBERRY RIDGE, SIT BACK AND ENJOY THE SHOW ... AND REMEMBER: DON'T BOTHER BOLTING YOUR BACK DOOR, LEAVE THE CAR KEYS IN YOUR MUSTANG AND FEEL FREE TO CARRY MORE THAN TEN DOLLARS IN YOUR POCKET AT ANY GIVEN MOMENT BECAUSE WHEN THE BOUNTY HUNTERS ARE IN TOWN CRIME, MOST DEFINITELY, TAKES A HOLIDAY!"
RN ON THE
TH OF
UGUST
FAT CAKE RUSTLER
HEWLETT 94

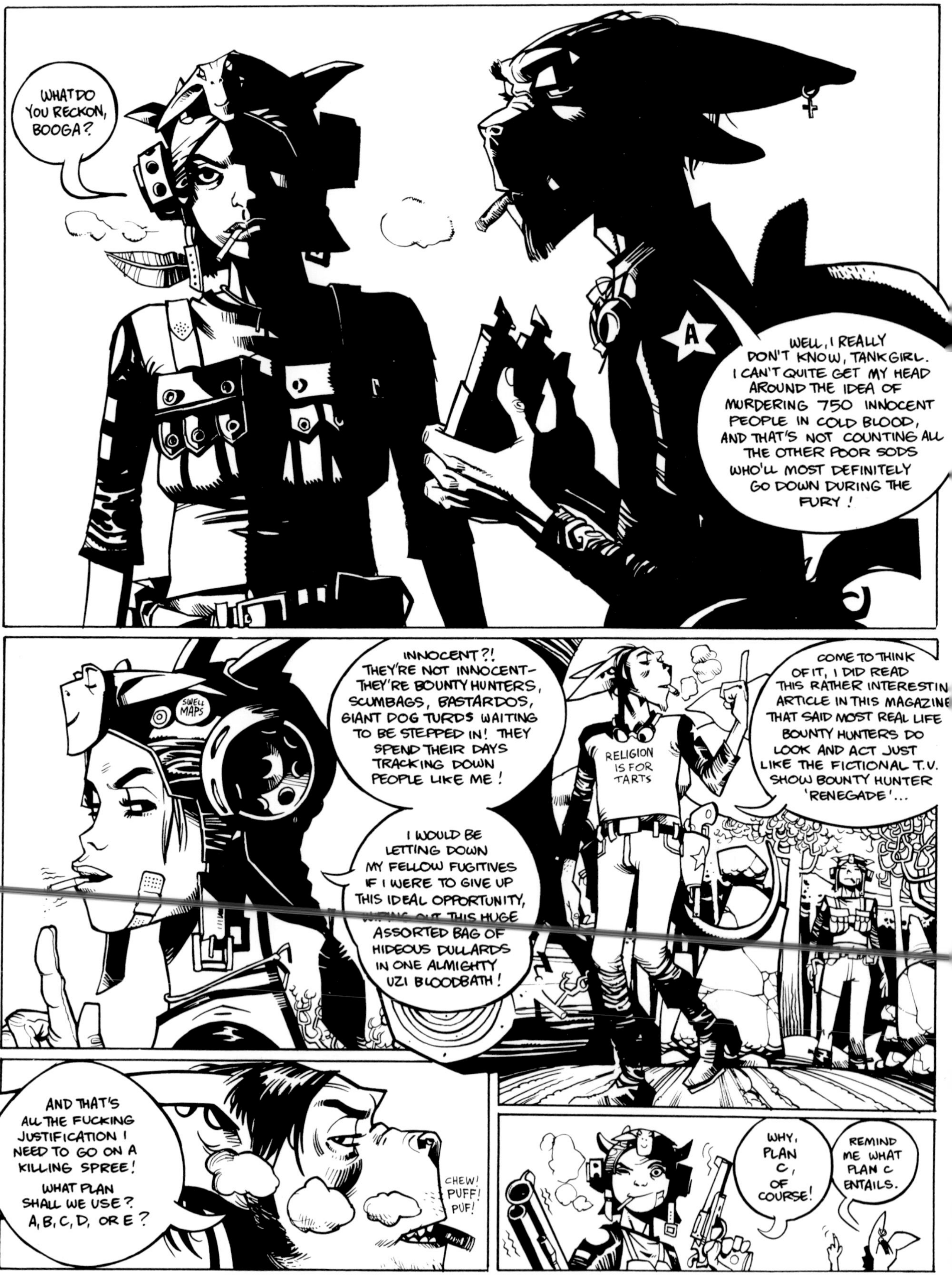
WHAT DO YOU RECKON, BOOGA?
WELL, I REALLY DON'T KNOW, TANKGIRL. I CAN'T QUITE GET MY HEAD AROUND THE IDEA OF MURDERING 750 INNOCENT PEOPLE IN COLD BLOOD, AND THAT'S NOT COUNTING ALL THE OTHER POOR SODS WHO'LL MOST DEFINITELY GO DOWN DURING THE FURY!
SWELL MAPS
INNOCENT?! THEY'RE NOT INNOCENT- THEY'RE BOUNTY HUNTERS, SCUMBAGS, BASTARDOS, GIANT DOG TURDS WAITING TO BE STEPPED IN! THEY SPEND THEIR DAYS TRACKING DOWN PEOPLE LIKE ME!
I WOULD BE LETTING DOWN MY FELLOW FUGITIVES IF I WERE TO GIVE UP THIS IDEAL OPPORTUNITY, WIPING OUT THIS HUGE ASSORTED BAG OF HIDEOUS DULLARDS IN ONE ALMIGHTY UZI BLOODBATH!
RELIGION IS FOR TARTS
COME TO THINK OF IT, I DID READ THIS RATHER INTERESTIN ARTICLE IN THIS MAGAZINE THAT SAID MOST REAL LIFE BOUNTY HUNTERS DO LOOK AND ACT JUST LIKE THE FICTIONAL T.V. SHOW BOUNTY HUNTER 'RENEGADE'...
AND THAT'S ALL THE FUCKING JUSTIFICATION I NEED TO GO ON A KILLING SPREE! WHAT PLAN SHALL WE USE? A, B, C, D, OR E?
CHEW! PUFF! PUF!
WHY, PLAN C, OF COURSE!
REMIND ME WHAT PLAN C ENTAILS.

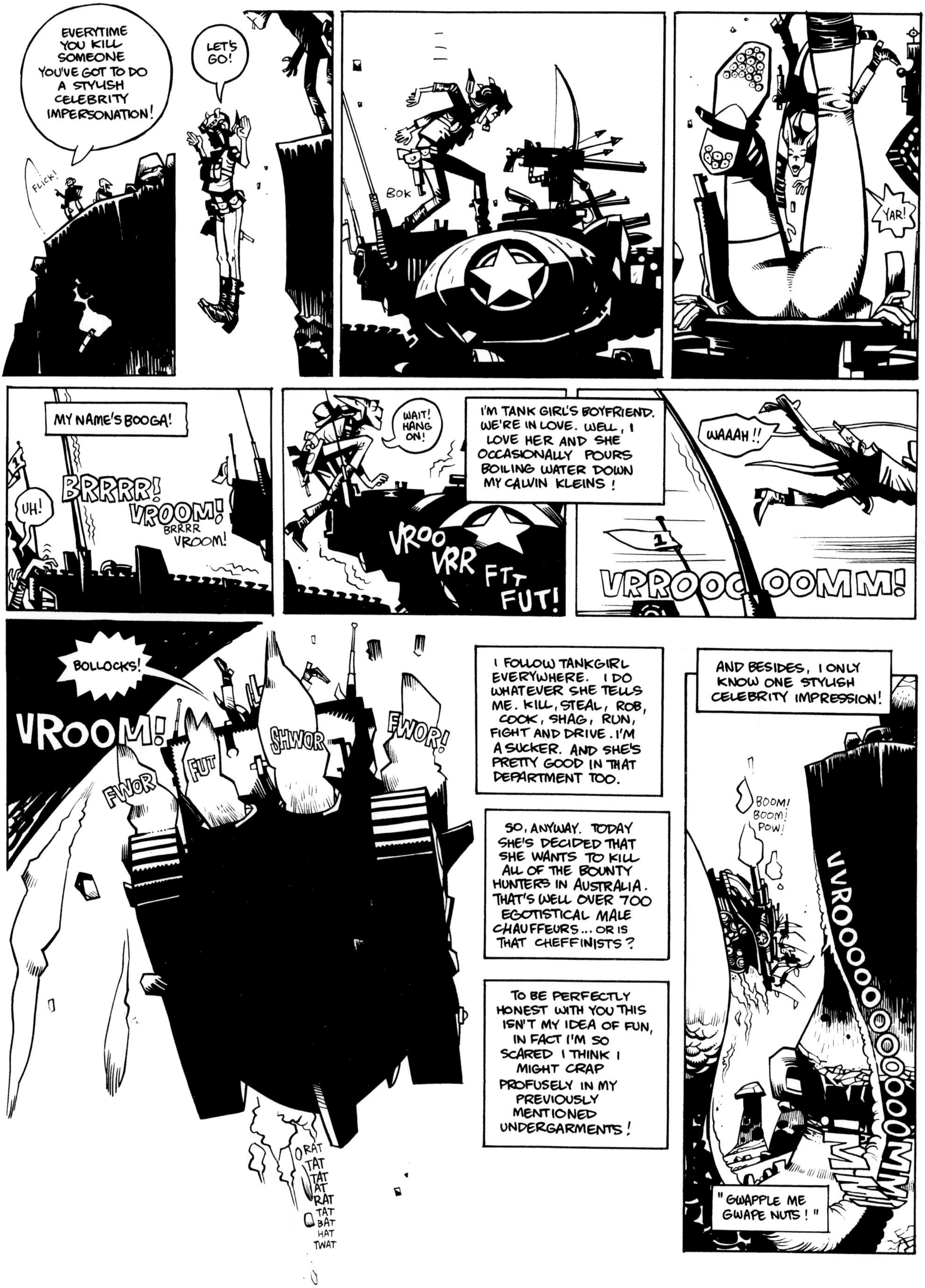

EVERYTIME YOU KILL SOMEONE YOU'VE GOT TO DO A STYLISH CELEBRITY IMPERSONATION!
FLICK!
LET'S GO!
BOK
YAR!
MY NAME'S BOOGA!
UH!
BRRRR! VROOM! BRRRR VROOM!
WAIT! HANG ON!
VROO VRR FTT FUT!
I'M TANK GIRL'S BOYFRIEND. WE'RE IN LOVE. WELL, I LOVE HER AND SHE OCCASIONALLY POURS BOILING WATER DOWN MY CALVIN KLEINS!
WAAAH!!
VRROOOOOMM!
BOLLOCKS!
VROOM!
FWOR
FUT
SHWOR
FWOR!
RAT TAT TAT AT RAT TAT BAT HAT TWAT
I FOLLOW TANKGIRL EVERYWHERE. I DO WHATEVER SHE TELLS ME. KILL, STEAL, ROB, COOK, SHAG, RUN, FIGHT AND DRIVE. I'M A SUCKER. AND SHE'S PRETTY GOOD IN THAT DEPARTMENT TOO.
SO, ANYWAY. TODAY SHE'S DECIDED THAT SHE WANTS TO KILL ALL OF THE BOUNTY HUNTERS IN AUSTRALIA. THAT'S WELL OVER 700 EGOTISTICAL MALE CHAUFFEURS... OR IS THAT CHEFFINISTS?
TO BE PERFECTLY HONEST WITH YOU THIS ISN'T MY IDEA OF FUN, IN FACT I'M SO SCARED I THINK I MIGHT CRAP PROFUSELY IN MY PREVIOUSLY MENTIONED UNDERGARMENTS!
AND BESIDES, I ONLY KNOW ONE STYLISH CELEBRITY IMPRESSION!
BOOM! BOOM! POW!
VVROOOOOOOOOOOMM
"GWAPPLE ME GWAPE NUTS!"

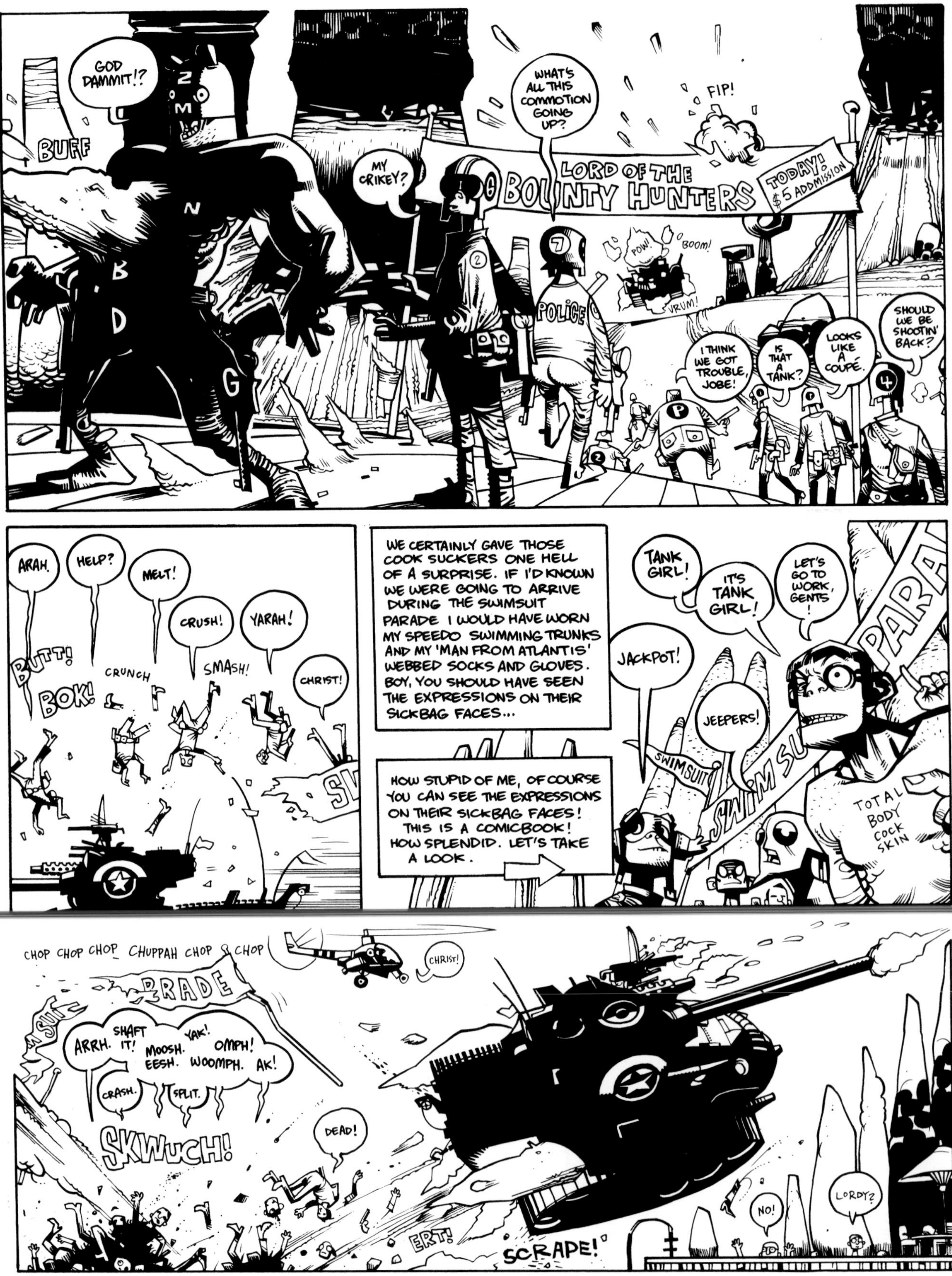

GOD DAMMIT!?
Z
M
BUFF
N
B
D
G
MY CRIKEY?
WHAT'S ALL THIS COMMOTION GOING UP?
FIP!
LORD OF THE BOUNTY HUNTERS
TODAY! $5 ADDMISSION
POW!
BOOM!
VRUM!
POLICE
I THINK WE GOT TROUBLE, JOBE!
IS THAT A TANK?
LOOKS LIKE A COUPÉ.
SHOULD WE BE SHOOTIN' BACK?
ARAH.
HELP?
MELT!
CRUSH!
YARAH!
BUTT!
BOK!
CRUNCH
SMASH!
CHRIST!
WE CERTAINLY GAVE THOSE COOK SUCKERS ONE HELL OF A SURPRISE. IF I'D KNOWN WE WERE GOING TO ARRIVE DURING THE SWIMSUIT PARADE I WOULD HAVE WORN MY SPEEDO SWIMMING TRUNKS AND MY 'MAN FROM ATLANTIS' WEBBED SOCKS AND GLOVES. BOY, YOU SHOULD HAVE SEEN THE EXPRESSIONS ON THEIR SICKBAG FACES...
HOW STUPID OF ME, OF COURSE YOU CAN SEE THE EXPRESSIONS ON THEIR SICKBAG FACES! THIS IS A COMICBOOK! HOW SPLENDID. LET'S TAKE A LOOK.
TANK GIRL!
IT'S TANK GIRL!
LET'S GO TO WORK, GENTS!
JACKPOT!
JEEPERS!
SWIMSUIT
SWIM SU
PARA
TOTAL BODY COCK SKIN
CHOP CHOP CHOP CHUPPAH CHOP CHOP
CHRIST!
PARADE
ARRH. SHAFT IT! MOOSH. EESH. YAK! OMPH! WOOMPH. AK!
CRASH.
SPLIT.
SKWUCH!
DEAD!
ERT!
SCRAPE!
NO!
LORDY?

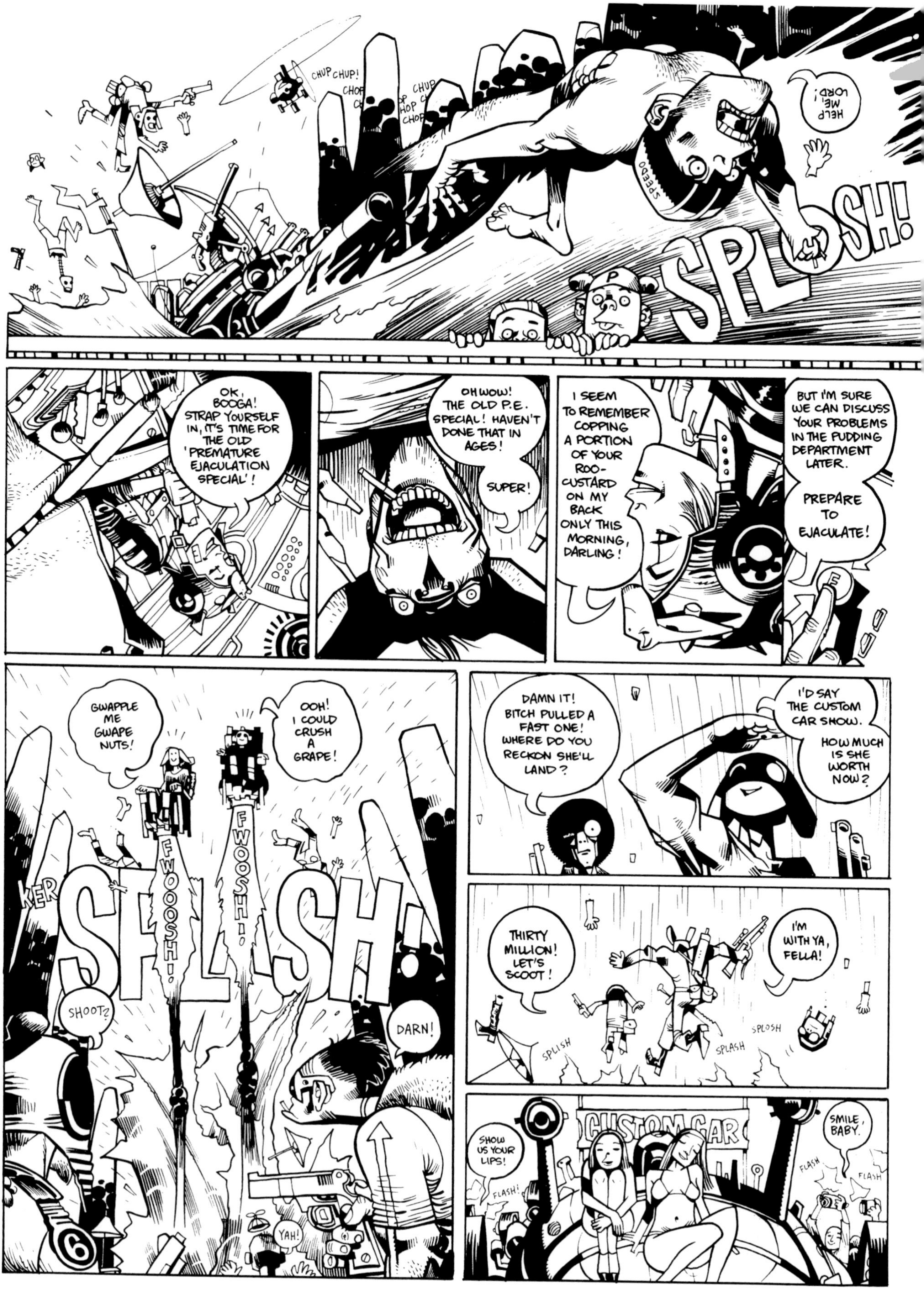
CHUP CHUP!
CHOP CHOP CHOP CHOP
HELP ME, LORD!
SPEEDO
SPLOSH!
OK, BOOGA! STRAP YOURSELF IN, IT'S TIME FOR THE OLD 'PREMATURE EJACULATION SPECIAL'!
OH WOW! THE OLD P.E. SPECIAL! HAVEN'T DONE THAT IN AGES!
SUPER!
I SEEM TO REMEMBER COPPING A PORTION OF YOUR ROO-CUSTARD ON MY BACK ONLY THIS MORNING, DARLING!
BUT I'M SURE WE CAN DISCUSS YOUR PROBLEMS IN THE PUDDING DEPARTMENT LATER.
PREPARE TO EJACULATE!
GWAPPLE ME GWAPE NUTS!
OOH! I COULD CRUSH A GRAPE!
KER SPLASH!
FWOOOSH!
FWOOSH!
SHOOT!
DARN!
YAH!
DAMN IT! BITCH PULLED A FAST ONE! WHERE DO YOU RECKON SHE'LL LAND?
I'D SAY THE CUSTOM CAR SHOW.
HOW MUCH IS SHE WORTH NOW?
THIRTY MILLION! LET'S SCOOT!
I'M WITH YA, FELLA!
SPLISH
SPLASH
SPLOSH
CUSTOM CAR
SHOW US YOUR LIPS!
SMILE, BABY.
FLASH!
FLASH
FLASH

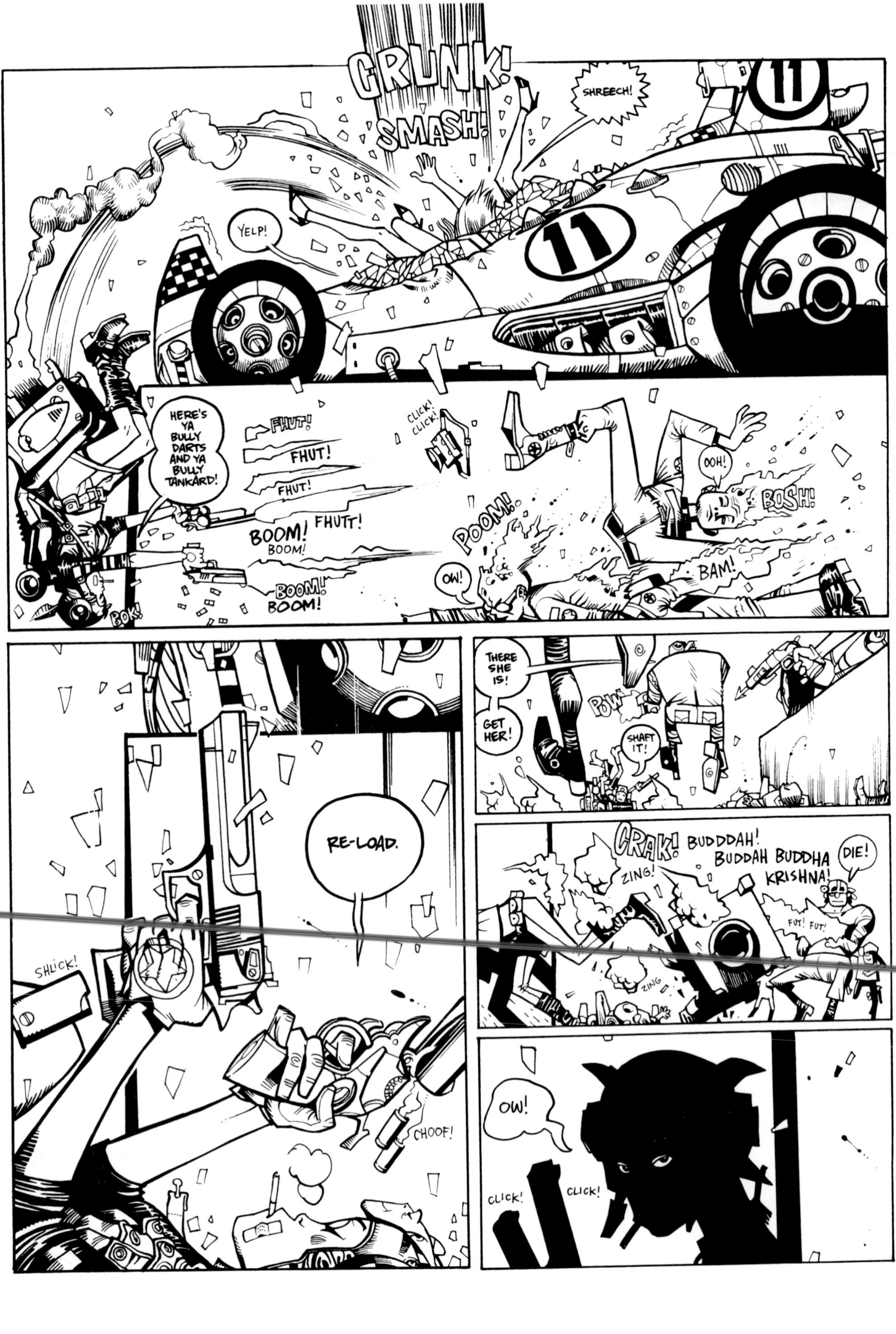
GRUNK!
SMASH!
SHREECH!
YELP!
HERE'S YA BULLY DARTS AND YA BULLY TANKARD!
FHUT!
FHUT!
FHUT!
FHUTT!
BOOM!
BOOM!
BOOM!
BOOM!
CLICK! CLICK!
POOM!
OOH!
BOSH!
OW!
BAM!
BOK!
RE-LOAD.
SHLICK!
CHOOF!
THERE SHE IS!
GET HER!
POW
SHAFT IT!
CRAK!
BUDDDAH! BUDDAH BUDDHA KRISHNA!
DIE!
ZING!
FUT! FUT!
ZING
OW!
CLICK!
CLICK!

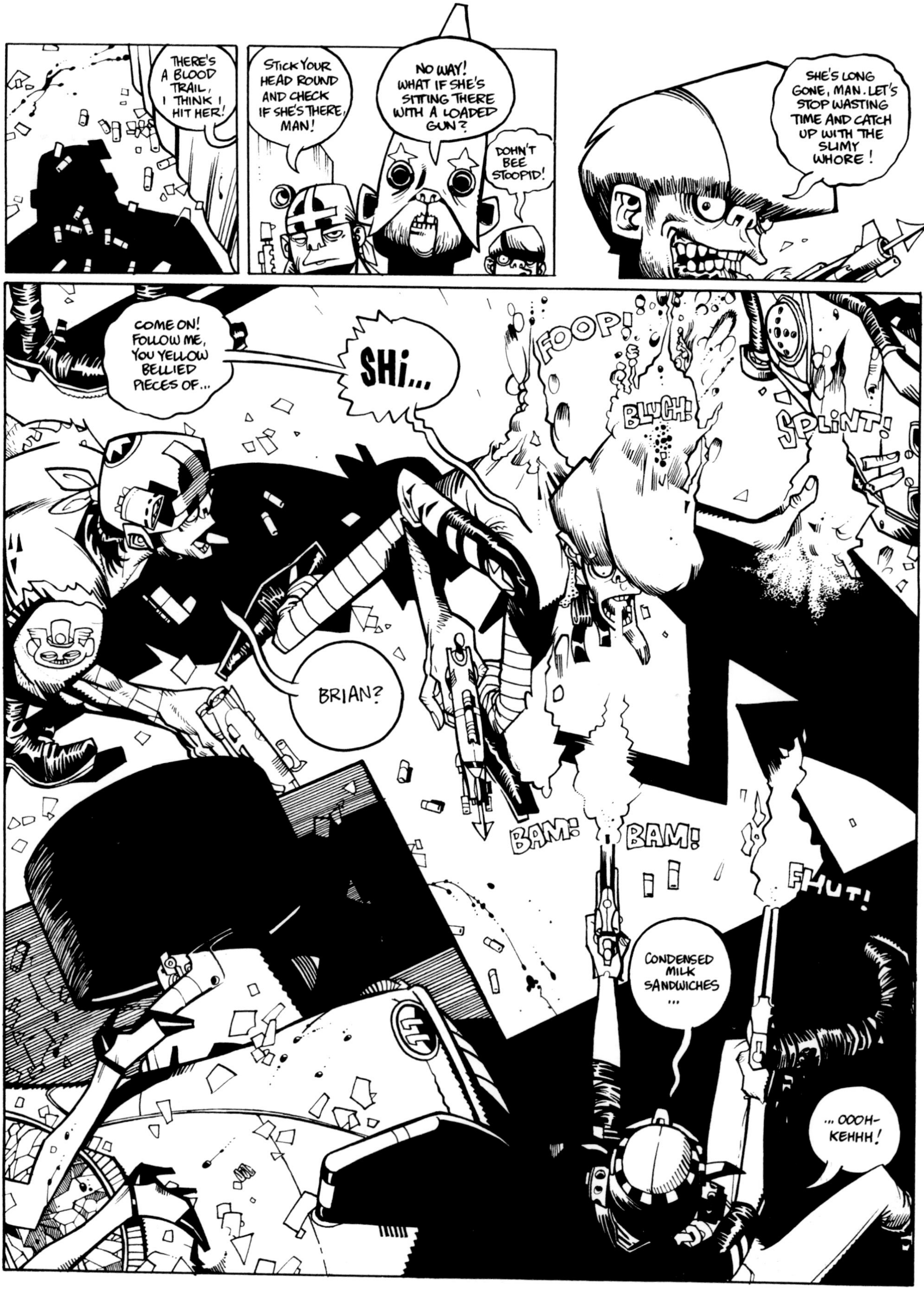

THERE'S A BLOOD TRAIL, I THINK I HIT HER!
STICK YOUR HEAD ROUND AND CHECK IF SHE'S THERE, MAN!
NO WAY! WHAT IF SHE'S SITTING THERE WITH A LOADED GUN?
DOHN'T BEE STOOPID!
SHE'S LONG GONE, MAN. LET'S STOP WASTING TIME AND CATCH UP WITH THE SLIMY WHORE!
COME ON! FOLLOW ME, YOU YELLOW BELLIED PIECES OF...
SHi...
FOOP!
BLUCH!
SPLINT!
BRIAN?
BAM!
BAM!
FHUT!
CONDENSED MILK SANDWICHES ...
... OOOH-KEHHH!

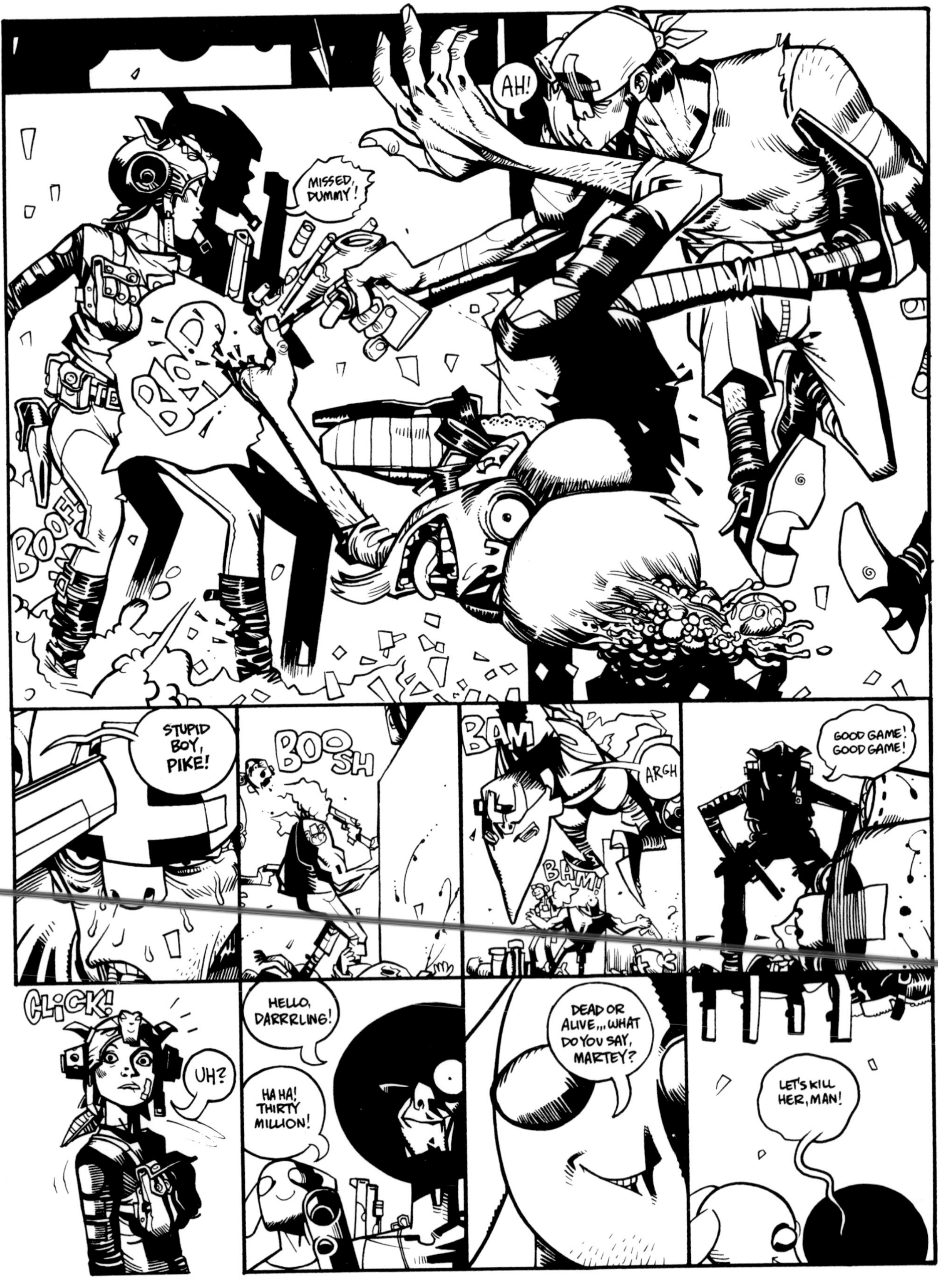
AH!
MISSED, DUMMY!
BLAP!
BOOSH
STUPID BOY, PIKE!
BOOSH
BAM
ARGH
BAM!
GOOD GAME! GOOD GAME!
CLICK!
UH?
HELLO, DARRRLING!
HA HA! THIRTY MILLION!
DEAD OR ALIVE,,, WHAT DO YOU SAY, MARTEY?
LET'S KILL HER, MAN!

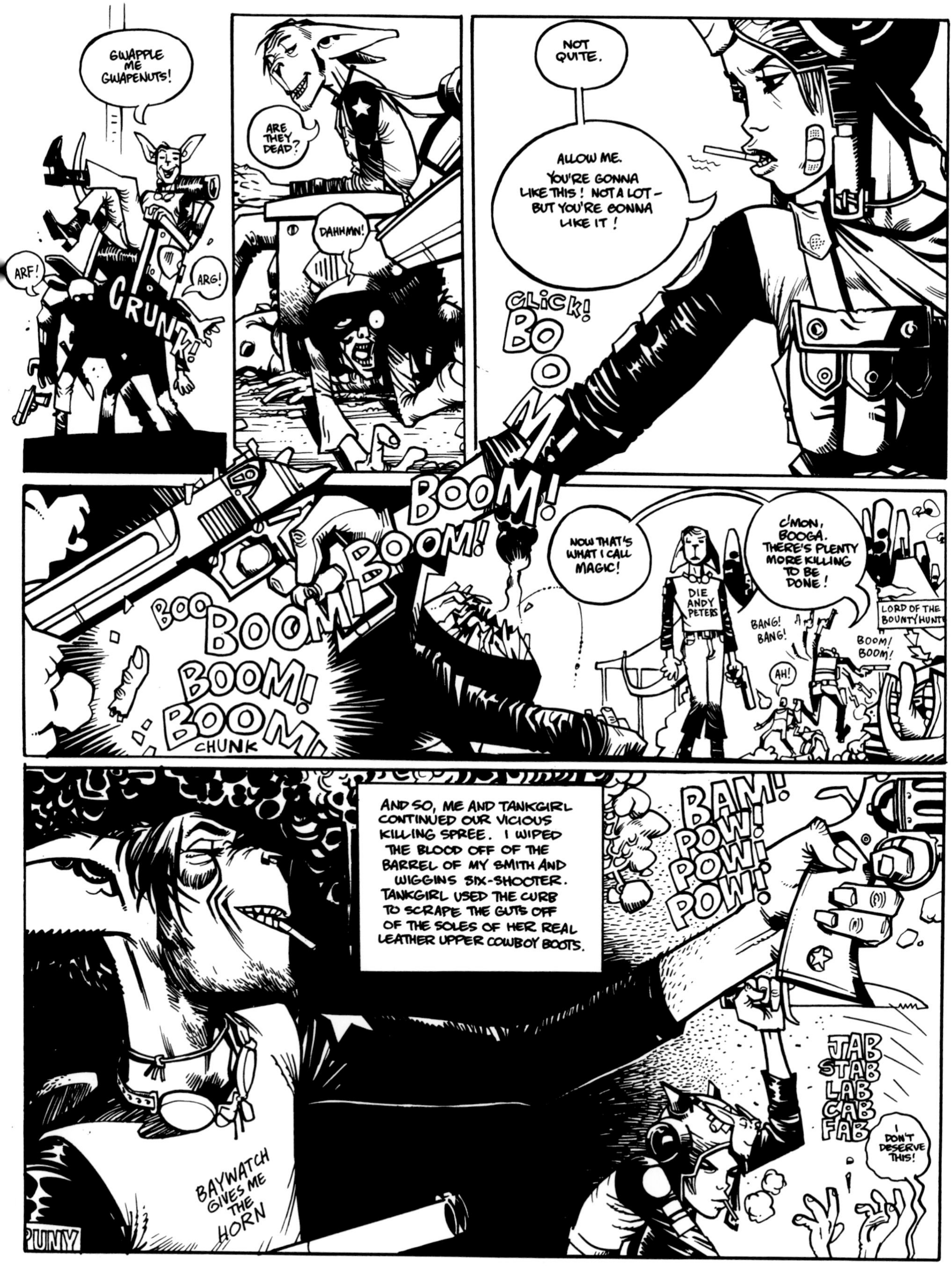
GWAPPLE ME GWAPENUTS!
ARF!
ARG!
CRUNK!
ARE THEY DEAD?
DAHHMN!
NOT QUITE.
ALLOW ME. YOU'RE GONNA LIKE THIS! NOT A LOT - BUT YOU'RE GONNA LIKE IT!
CLICK!
BOOM!
BOOM!
BOOM!
BOO BOOM!
BOOM!
BOOM!
CHUNK
NOW THAT'S WHAT I CALL MAGIC!
C'MON, BOOGA. THERE'S PLENTY MORE KILLING TO BE DONE!
DIE ANDY PETERS
BANG! BANG!
AH!
BOOM! BOOM!
AND SO, ME AND TANKGIRL CONTINUED OUR VICIOUS KILLING SPREE. I WIPED THE BLOOD OFF OF THE BARREL OF MY SMITH AND WIGGINS SIX-SHOOTER. TANKGIRL USED THE CURB TO SCRAPE THE GUTS OFF OF THE SOLES OF HER REAL LEATHER UPPER COWBOY BOOTS.
BAM! POW! POW! POW!
JAB STAB LAB CAB FAB
I DON'T DESERVE THIS!
BAYWATCH GIVES ME THE HORN
PUNY

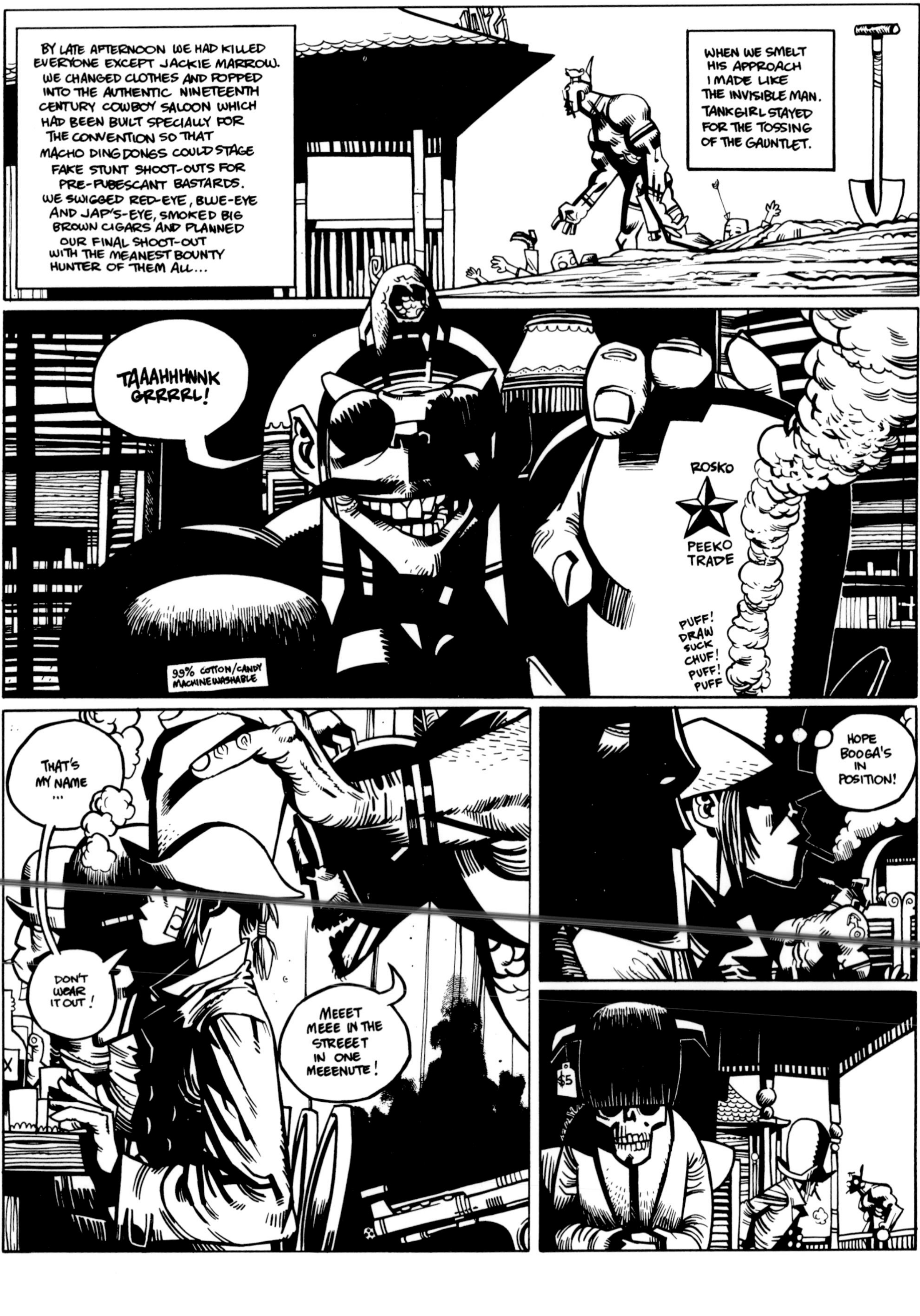

BY LATE AFTERNOON WE HAD KILLED EVERYONE EXCEPT JACKIE MARROW. WE CHANGED CLOTHES AND POPPED INTO THE AUTHENTIC NINETEENTH CENTURY COWBOY SALOON WHICH HAD BEEN BUILT SPECIALLY FOR THE CONVENTION SO THAT MACHO DING DONGS COULD STAGE FAKE STUNT SHOOT-OUTS FOR PRE-PUBESCANT BASTARDS. WE SWIGGED RED-EYE, BLUE-EYE AND JAP'S-EYE, SMOKED BIG BROWN CIGARS AND PLANNED OUR FINAL SHOOT-OUT WITH THE MEANEST BOUNTY HUNTER OF THEM ALL...
WHEN WE SMELT HIS APPROACH I MADE LIKE THE INVISIBLE MAN. TANKGIRL STAYED FOR THE TOSSING OF THE GAUNTLET.
TAAAHHHNNK GRRRRL!
ROSKO
PEEKO TRADE
99% COTTON/CANDY MACHINEWASHABLE
PUFF! DRAW SUCK CHUF! PUFF! PUFF
THAT'S MY NAME ...
DON'T WEAR IT OUT!
MEEET MEEE IN THE STREEET IN ONE MEEENUTE!
HOPE BOOGA'S IN POSITION!
$5

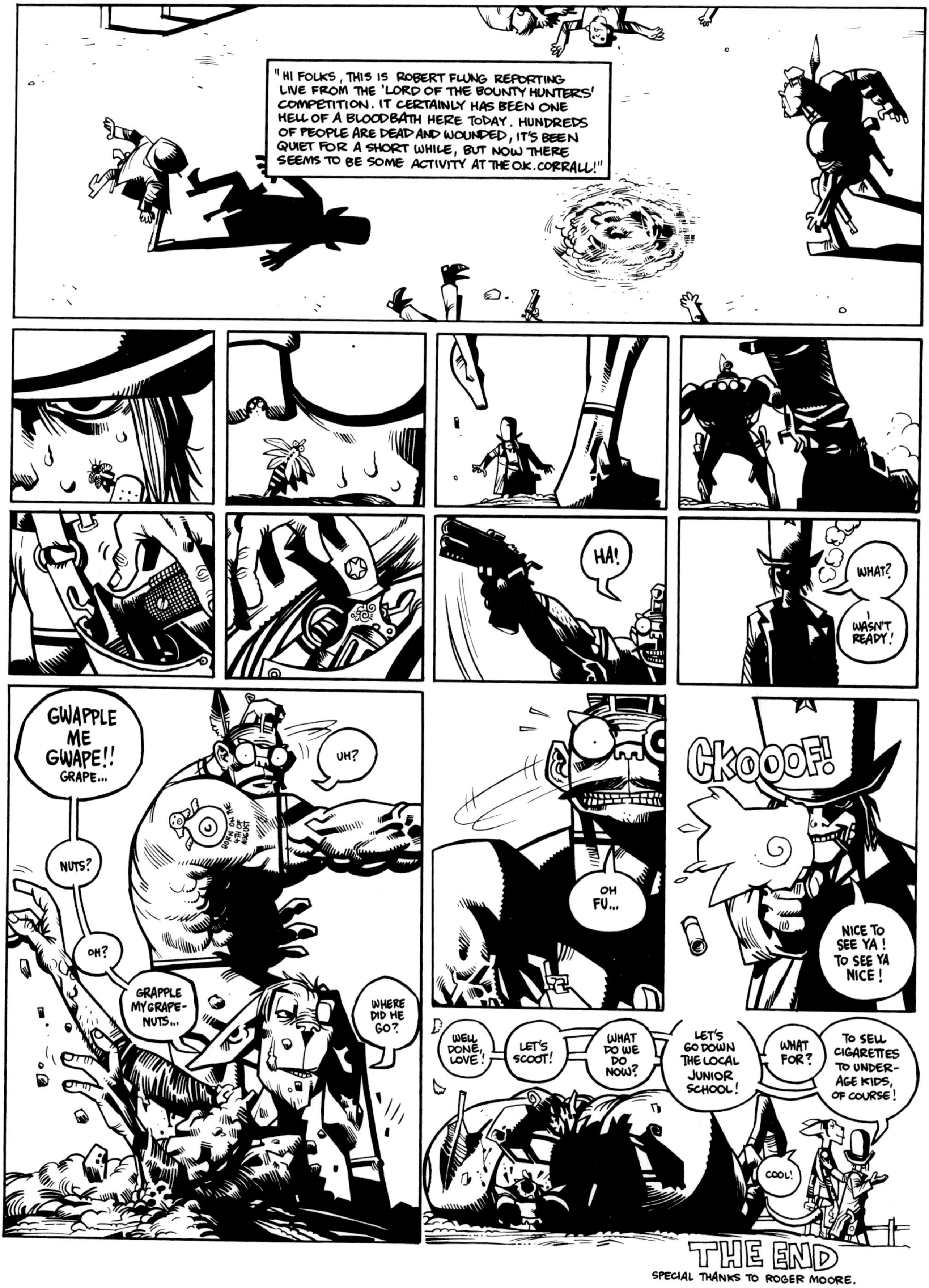
"HI FOLKS, THIS IS ROBERT FLUNG REPORTING LIVE FROM THE 'LORD OF THE BOUNTY HUNTERS' COMPETITION. IT CERTAINLY HAS BEEN ONE HELL OF A BLOODBATH HERE TODAY. HUNDREDS OF PEOPLE ARE DEAD AND WOUNDED, IT'S BEEN QUIET FOR A SHORT WHILE, BUT NOW THERE SEEMS TO BE SOME ACTIVITY AT THE O.K. CORRALL!"
HA!
WHAT?
I WASN'T READY!
GWAPPLE ME GWAPE!! GRAPE...
NUTS?
OH?
GRAPPLE MY GRAPE-NUTS...
UH?
BORN ON THE 4TH OF AUGUST
WHERE DID HE GO?
CKOOOF!
OH FU...
NICE TO SEE YA! TO SEE YA NICE!
WELL DONE, LOVE!
LET'S SCOOT!
WHAT DO WE DO NOW?
LET'S GO DOWN THE LOCAL JUNIOR SCHOOL!
WHAT FOR?
TO SELL CIGARETTES TO UNDER-AGE KIDS, OF COURSE!
COOL!

THE END

SPECIAL THANKS TO ROGER MOORE.

TANK GIRL IN BUSHMAN TUCKER
BY HEWLETT + MARTIN
DEDICATED TO THE LATE BILL HICKS.
HELLO READERS, FUCK YOU, FUCK ALL OF YOU, FUCK OFF! WE'RE NOT FEELING TOO GOOD THIS MONTH, WE'VE BEEN EATING NOTHING BUT CRISPS AND FAGS FOR THE PAST THREE YEARS, SO WE'VE DECIDED TO GO IN SEARCH OF CULINARY ENLIGHTENMENT.
BEEP BEEP!
COME ON! LET'S GO!
I'M COMING, YOU FAT GOB!!
IF WE'RE GOING IN SEARCH OF CULINARY ENLIGHTENMENT MAYBE WE SHOULD GIVE UP SMOKING FOR A WHILE TO REFRESH OUR TASTE BUDS?
DON'T BE A BLITHERING TOSSPOT, BOOGA, NOBODY SHOULD GIVE UP SMOKING, AND PEOPLE WHO DON'T SMOKE SHOULD START. SMOKING'S BY FAR THE BEST AND SURE ROUTE TO WISDOM AND PERSONAL ACHIEVEMENT.
MONTE CARLO OR FUCK OFF!
AND SO WE SET OFF ON OUR QUEST FOR GOOD FOOD, FINE WINE AND STRONG FAGS. FIRST STOP THE TECH COLLEGE, WHERE I HAD ENROLLED BOOGA ON A TWO YEAR CATERING COURSE.
VRUM!
ERT!
EXCELSIOR! I'VE ALWAYS WANTED TO LIVE THE COLLEGE LIFE, I CAN ALREADY HEAR THE ROAR OF THE DRAGSTER ENGINES AS I BURN UP THE QUARTER MILE WITH FELLOW TEAM MATES FROM THE FOOTBALL CLUB; THE SCREAM OF CHEERLEADERS; THE SMELL OF YOUNG HAIR PIE ON PROM NIGHT!
BUGGINS COLLEGE 'WE CATER FOR EVERYONE'
NKOTB
LISTEN, BOOGA, EVERYBODY KNOWS THAT TECH STUDENTS ARE CUNTS. YOU'RE GOING TO SPEND TWO YEARS SHAGGING SUSAN-TULLY-LOOK-A-LIKES; LISTENING TO DIRE STRAITS AND WATCHING TOP GUN.
SHE'S RIGHT.

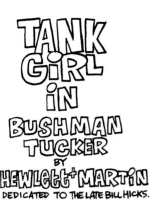

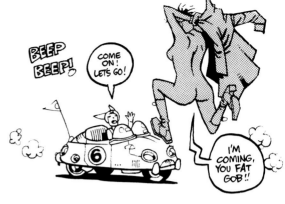

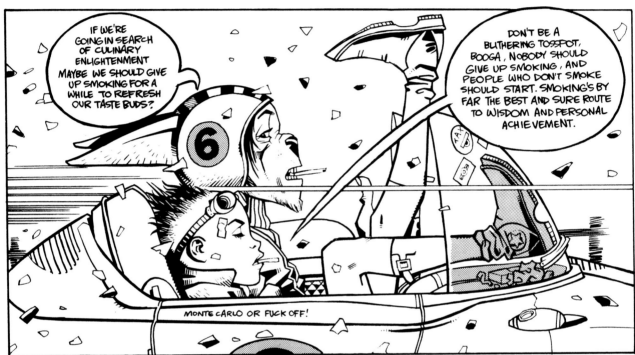

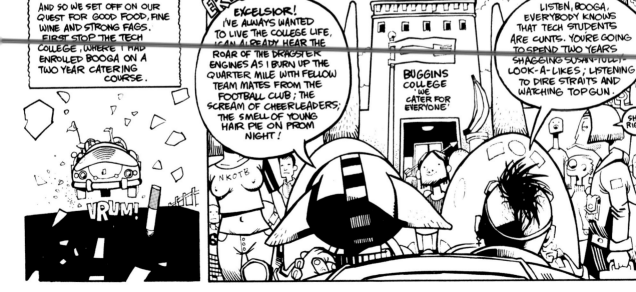

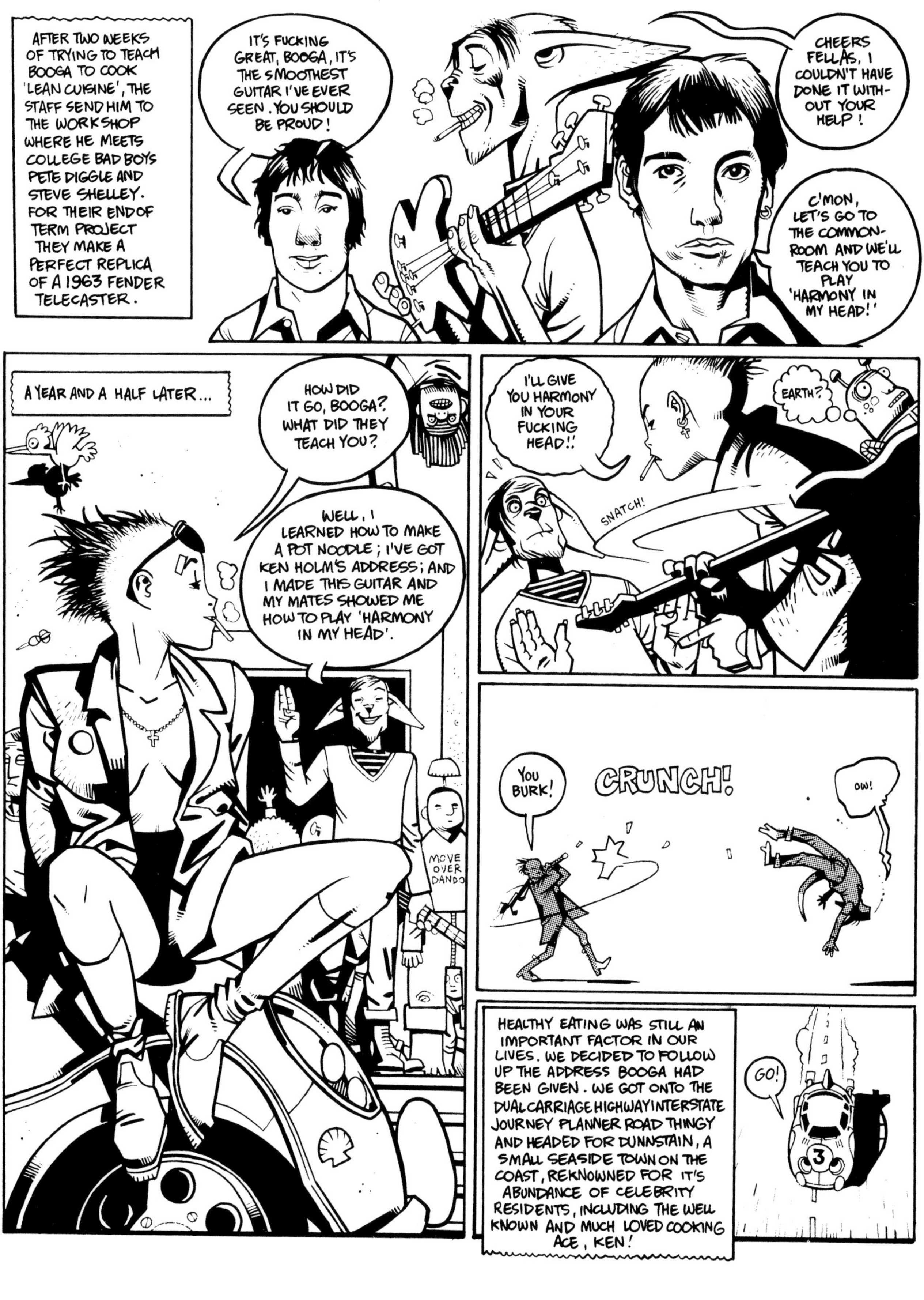

AFTER TWO WEEKS OF TRYING TO TEACH BOOGA TO COOK 'LEAN CUISINE', THE STAFF SEND HIM TO THE WORKSHOP WHERE HE MEETS COLLEGE BAD BOYS PETE DIGGLE AND STEVE SHELLEY. FOR THEIR END OF TERM PROJECT THEY MAKE A PERFECT REPLICA OF A 1963 FENDER TELECASTER.
IT'S FUCKING GREAT, BOOGA, IT'S THE SMOOTHEST GUITAR I'VE EVER SEEN. YOU SHOULD BE PROUD!
CHEERS FELLAS, I COULDN'T HAVE DONE IT WITH-OUT YOUR HELP!
C'MON, LET'S GO TO THE COMMON-ROOM AND WE'LL TEACH YOU TO PLAY 'HARMONY IN MY HEAD!'
A YEAR AND A HALF LATER...
HOW DID IT GO, BOOGA? WHAT DID THEY TEACH YOU?
WELL, I LEARNED HOW TO MAKE A POT NOODLE; I'VE GOT KEN HOLM'S ADDRESS; AND I MADE THIS GUITAR AND MY MATES SHOWED ME HOW TO PLAY 'HARMONY IN MY HEAD'.
MOVE OVER DANDO
I'LL GIVE YOU HARMONY IN YOUR FUCKING HEAD!!
EARTH?
SNATCH!
YOU BURK!
CRUNCH!
OW!
HEALTHY EATING WAS STILL AN IMPORTANT FACTOR IN OUR LIVES. WE DECIDED TO FOLLOW UP THE ADDRESS BOOGA HAD BEEN GIVEN. WE GOT ONTO THE DUAL CARRIAGE HIGHWAY INTERSTATE JOURNEY PLANNER ROAD THINGY AND HEADED FOR DUNNSTAIN, A SMALL SEASIDE TOWN ON THE COAST, REKNOWNED FOR IT'S ABUNDANCE OF CELEBRITY RESIDENTS, INCLUDING THE WELL KNOWN AND MUCH LOVED COOKING ACE, KEN!
GO!
3

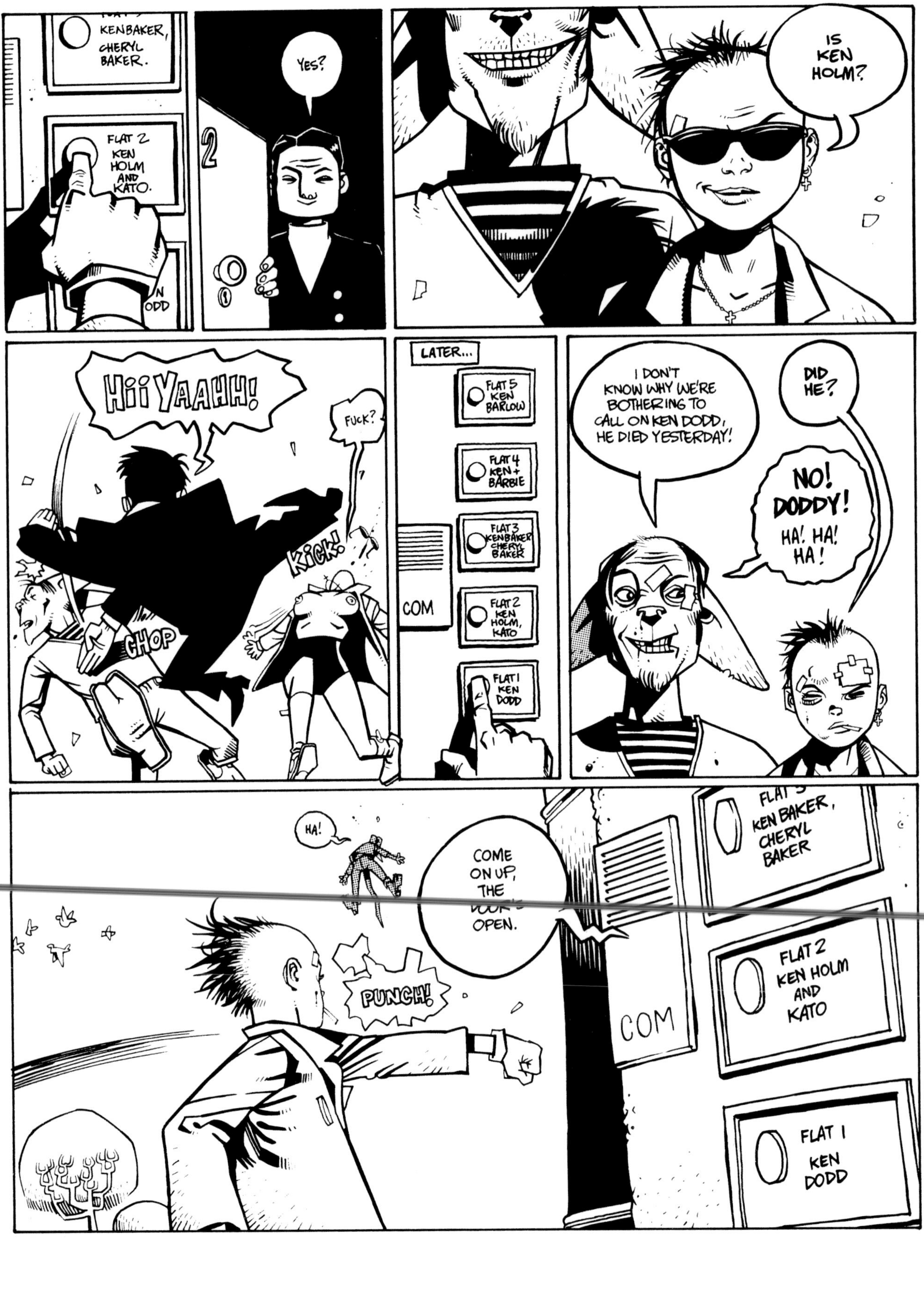
KEN BAKER, CHERYL BAKER.
FLAT 2 KEN HOLM AND KATO.
2
YES?
IS KEN HOLM?
HiiYAAHH!
FUCK?
KICK!
CHOP
LATER...
FLAT 5 KEN BARLOW
FLAT 4 KEN + BARBIE
FLAT 3 KEN BAKER CHERYL BAKER
COM
FLAT 2 KEN HOLM, KATO
FLAT 1 KEN DODD
I DON'T KNOW WHY WE'RE BOTHERING TO CALL ON KEN DODD, HE DIED YESTERDAY!
DID HE?
NO! DODDY! HA! HA! HA!
HA!
COME ON UP, THE DOOR'S OPEN.
PUNCH!
KEN BAKER, CHERYL BAKER
COM
FLAT 2 KEN HOLM AND KATO
FLAT 1 KEN DODD

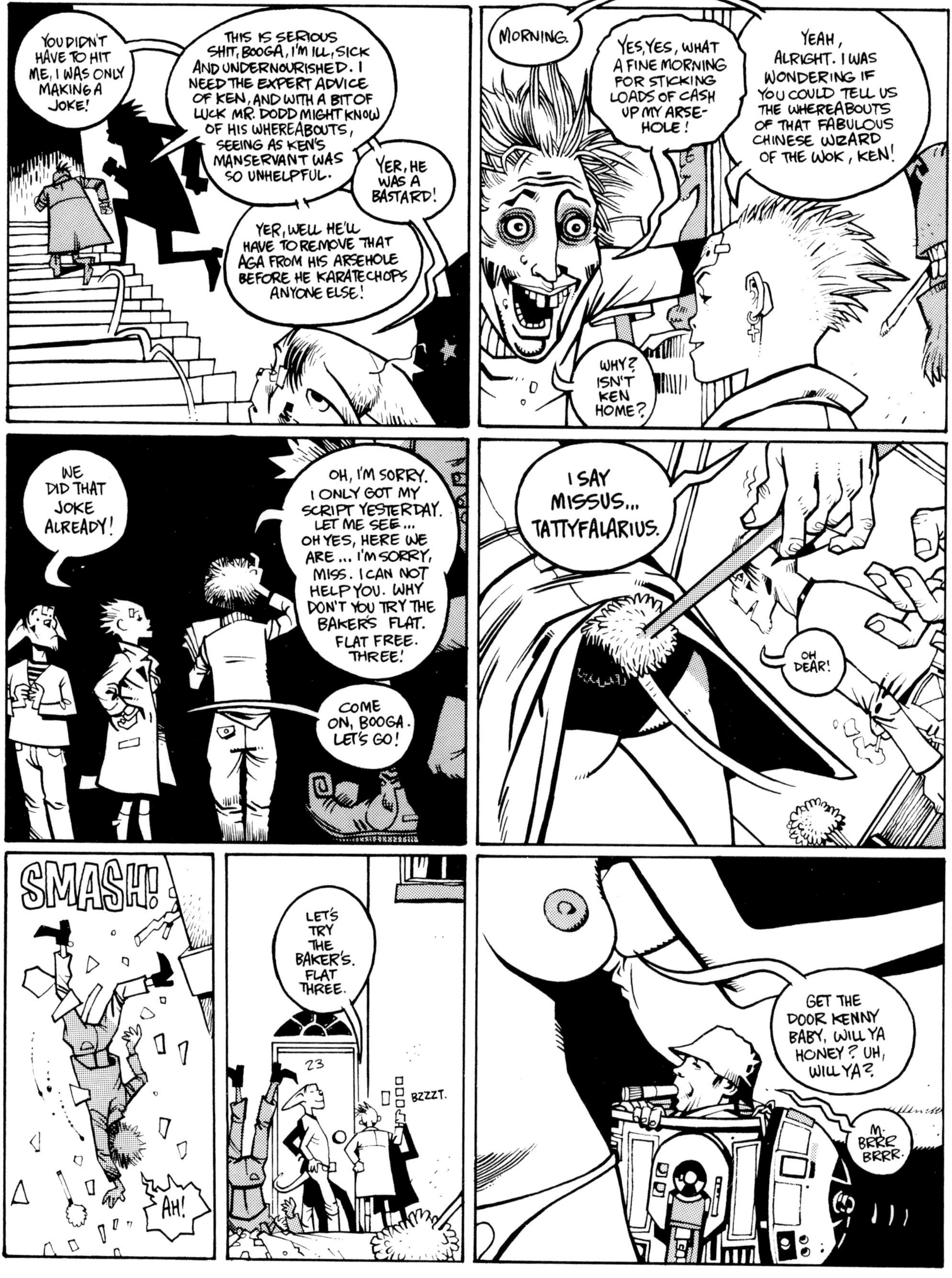

YOU DIDN'T HAVE TO HIT ME, I WAS ONLY MAKING A JOKE!
THIS IS SERIOUS SHIT, BOOGA, I'M ILL, SICK AND UNDERNOURISHED. I NEED THE EXPERT ADVICE OF KEN, AND WITH A BIT OF LUCK MR. DODD MIGHT KNOW OF HIS WHEREABOUTS, SEEING AS KEN'S MANSERVANT WAS SO UNHELPFUL.
YER, HE WAS A BASTARD!
YER, WELL HE'LL HAVE TO REMOVE THAT AGA FROM HIS ARSEHOLE BEFORE HE KARATECHOPS ANYONE ELSE!
MORNING.
YES, YES, WHAT A FINE MORNING FOR STICKING LOADS OF CASH UP MY ARSE-HOLE!
YEAH, ALRIGHT. I WAS WONDERING IF YOU COULD TELL US THE WHEREABOUTS OF THAT FABULOUS CHINESE WIZARD OF THE WOK, KEN!
WHY? ISN'T KEN HOME?
WE DID THAT JOKE ALREADY!
OH, I'M SORRY. I ONLY GOT MY SCRIPT YESTERDAY. LET ME SEE... OH YES, HERE WE ARE... I'M SORRY, MISS. I CAN NOT HELP YOU. WHY DON'T YOU TRY THE BAKER'S FLAT. FLAT FREE. THREE!
COME ON, BOOGA. LET'S GO!
I SAY MISSUS... TATTYFALARIUS.
OH DEAR!
SMASH!
AH!
LET'S TRY THE BAKER'S. FLAT THREE.
23
BZZZT.
GET THE DOOR KENNY BABY, WILL YA HONEY? UH, WILL YA?
M. BRRR BRRR.

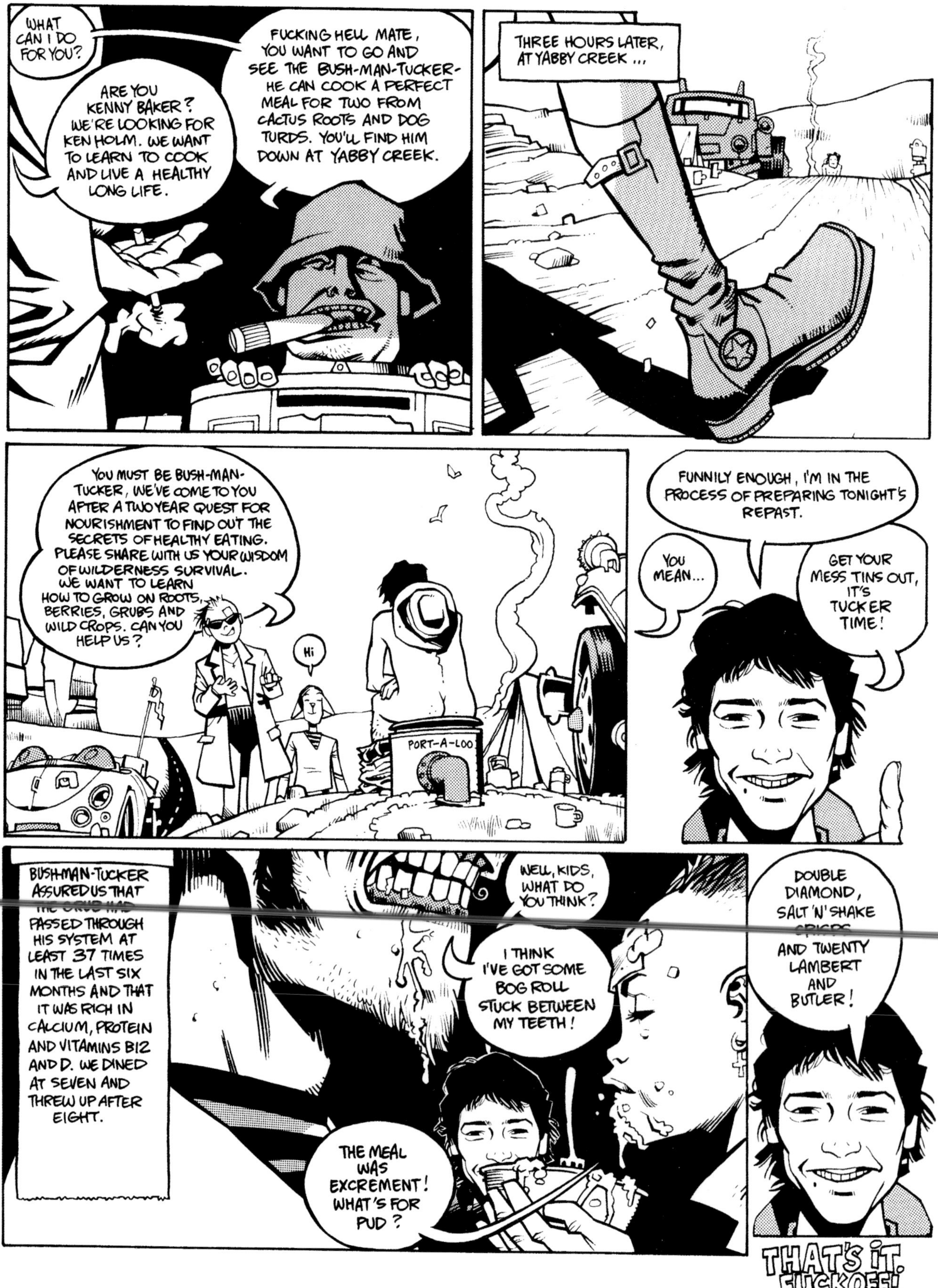
WHAT CAN I DO FOR YOU?
ARE YOU KENNY BAKER? WE'RE LOOKING FOR KEN HOLM. WE WANT TO LEARN TO COOK AND LIVE A HEALTHY LONG LIFE.
FUCKING HELL MATE, YOU WANT TO GO AND SEE THE BUSH-MAN-TUCKER- HE CAN COOK A PERFECT MEAL FOR TWO FROM CACTUS ROOTS AND DOG TURDS. YOU'LL FIND HIM DOWN AT YABBY CREEK.
THREE HOURS LATER, AT YABBY CREEK ...
YOU MUST BE BUSH-MAN-TUCKER, WE'VE COME TO YOU AFTER A TWO YEAR QUEST FOR NOURISHMENT TO FIND OUT THE SECRETS OF HEALTHY EATING. PLEASE SHARE WITH US YOUR WISDOM OF WILDERNESS SURVIVAL. WE WANT TO LEARN HOW TO GROW ON ROOTS, BERRIES, GRUBS AND WILD CROPS. CAN YOU HELP US?
HI
PORT-A-LOO
FUNNILY ENOUGH, I'M IN THE PROCESS OF PREPARING TONIGHT'S REPAST.
YOU MEAN...
GET YOUR MESS TINS OUT, IT'S TUCKER TIME!
BUSH-MAN-TUCKER ASSURED US THAT THE GRUB HAD PASSED THROUGH HIS SYSTEM AT LEAST 37 TIMES IN THE LAST SIX MONTHS AND THAT IT WAS RICH IN CALCIUM, PROTEIN AND VITAMINS B12 AND D. WE DINED AT SEVEN AND THREW UP AFTER EIGHT.
WELL, KIDS, WHAT DO YOU THINK?
I THINK I'VE GOT SOME BOG ROLL STUCK BETWEEN MY TEETH!
THE MEAL WAS EXCREMENT! WHAT'S FOR PUD?
DOUBLE DIAMOND, SALT 'N' SHAKE CRISPS AND TWENTY LAMBERT AND BUTLER!
THAT'S IT. FUCKOFF!

the IMMORTALIST

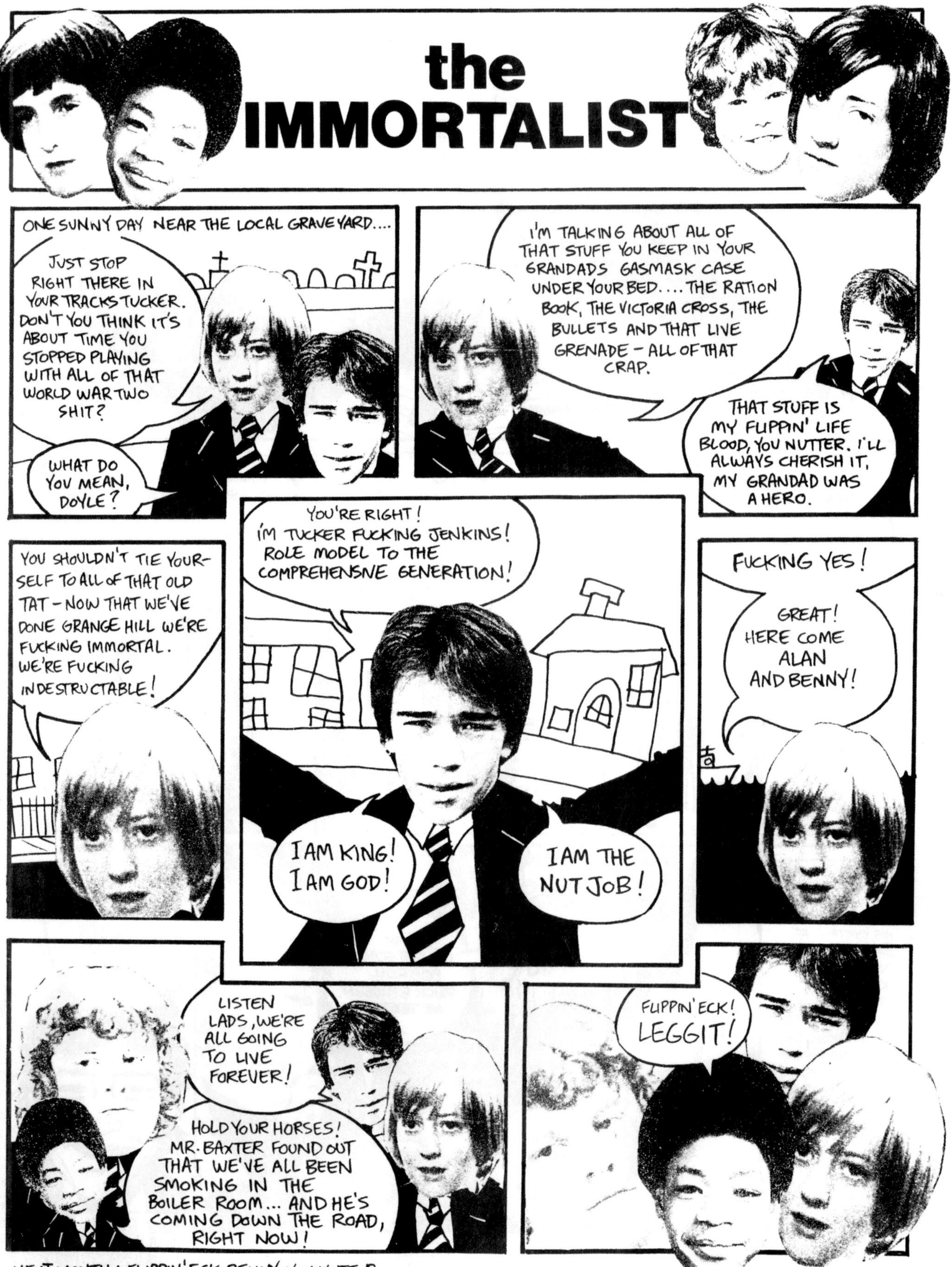
ONE SUNNY DAY NEAR THE LOCAL GRAVEYARD....
JUST STOP RIGHT THERE IN YOUR TRACKS TUCKER. DON'T YOU THINK IT'S ABOUT TIME YOU STOPPED PLAYING WITH ALL OF THAT WORLD WAR TWO SHIT?
WHAT DO YOU MEAN, DOYLE?
I'M TALKING ABOUT ALL OF THAT STUFF YOU KEEP IN YOUR GRANDADS GASMASK CASE UNDER YOUR BED.... THE RATION BOOK, THE VICTORIA CROSS, THE BULLETS AND THAT LIVE GRENADE – ALL OF THAT CRAP.
THAT STUFF IS MY FLIPPIN' LIFE BLOOD, YOU NUTTER. I'LL ALWAYS CHERISH IT, MY GRANDAD WAS A HERO.
YOU SHOULDN'T TIE YOURSELF TO ALL OF THAT OLD TAT – NOW THAT WE'VE DONE GRANGE HILL WE'RE FUCKING IMMORTAL. WE'RE FUCKING INDESTRUCTABLE!
YOU'RE RIGHT! I'M TUCKER FUCKING JENKINS! ROLE MODEL TO THE COMPREHENSIVE GENERATION!
I AM KING! I AM GOD!
I AM THE NUT JOB!
FUCKING YES!
GREAT! HERE COME ALAN AND BENNY!
LISTEN LADS, WE'RE ALL GOING TO LIVE FOREVER!
HOLD YOUR HORSES! MR. BAXTER FOUND OUT THAT WE'VE ALL BEEN SMOKING IN THE BOILER ROOM... AND HE'S COMING DOWN THE ROAD, RIGHT NOW!
FLIPPIN' ECK! LEGGIT!

NEXT MONTH: FLIPPIN' ECK BENNY YOU NUTJOB.

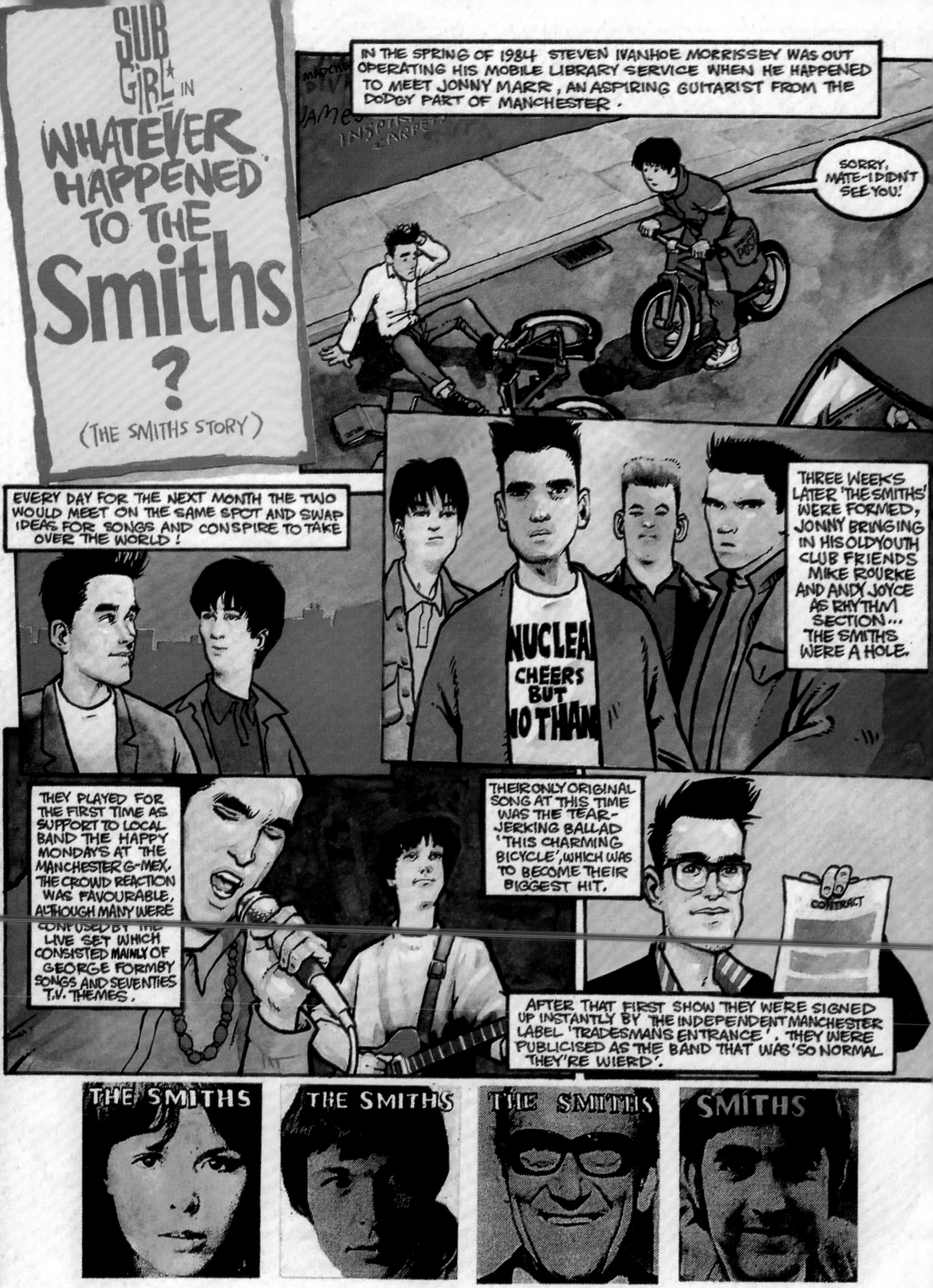
SUB GIRL IN
WHATEVER HAPPENED TO THE Smiths ?
(THE SMITHS STORY)
IN THE SPRING OF 1984 STEVEN IVANHOE MORRISSEY WAS OUT OPERATING HIS MOBILE LIBRARY SERVICE WHEN HE HAPPENED TO MEET JONNY MARR, AN ASPIRING GUITARIST FROM THE DODGY PART OF MANCHESTER.
SORRY, MATE-I DIDN'T SEE YOU!
POST
EVERY DAY FOR THE NEXT MONTH THE TWO WOULD MEET ON THE SAME SPOT AND SWAP IDEAS FOR SONGS AND CONSPIRE TO TAKE OVER THE WORLD!
THREE WEEKS LATER 'THE SMITHS' WERE FORMED, JONNY BRINGING IN HIS OLD YOUTH CLUB FRIENDS MIKE ROURKE AND ANDY JOYCE AS RHYTHM SECTION... THE SMITHS WERE A HOLE.
NUCLEA CHEERS BUT NO THAN
THEY PLAYED FOR THE FIRST TIME AS SUPPORT TO LOCAL BAND THE HAPPY MONDAYS AT THE MANCHESTER G-MEX. THE CROWD REACTION WAS FAVOURABLE, ALTHOUGH MANY WERE CONFUSED BY THE LIVE SET WHICH CONSISTED MAINLY OF GEORGE FORMBY SONGS AND SEVENTIES T.V. THEMES.
THEIR ONLY ORIGINAL SONG AT THIS TIME WAS THE TEAR-JERKING BALLAD 'THIS CHARMING BICYCLE', WHICH WAS TO BECOME THEIR BIGGEST HIT.
CONTRACT
AFTER THAT FIRST SHOW THEY WERE SIGNED UP INSTANTLY BY THE INDEPENDENT MANCHESTER LABEL 'TRADESMANS ENTRANCE'. THEY WERE PUBLICISED AS THE BAND THAT WAS 'SO NORMAL THEY'RE WIERD'.
THE SMITHS
THE SMITHS
THE SMITHS
SMITHS

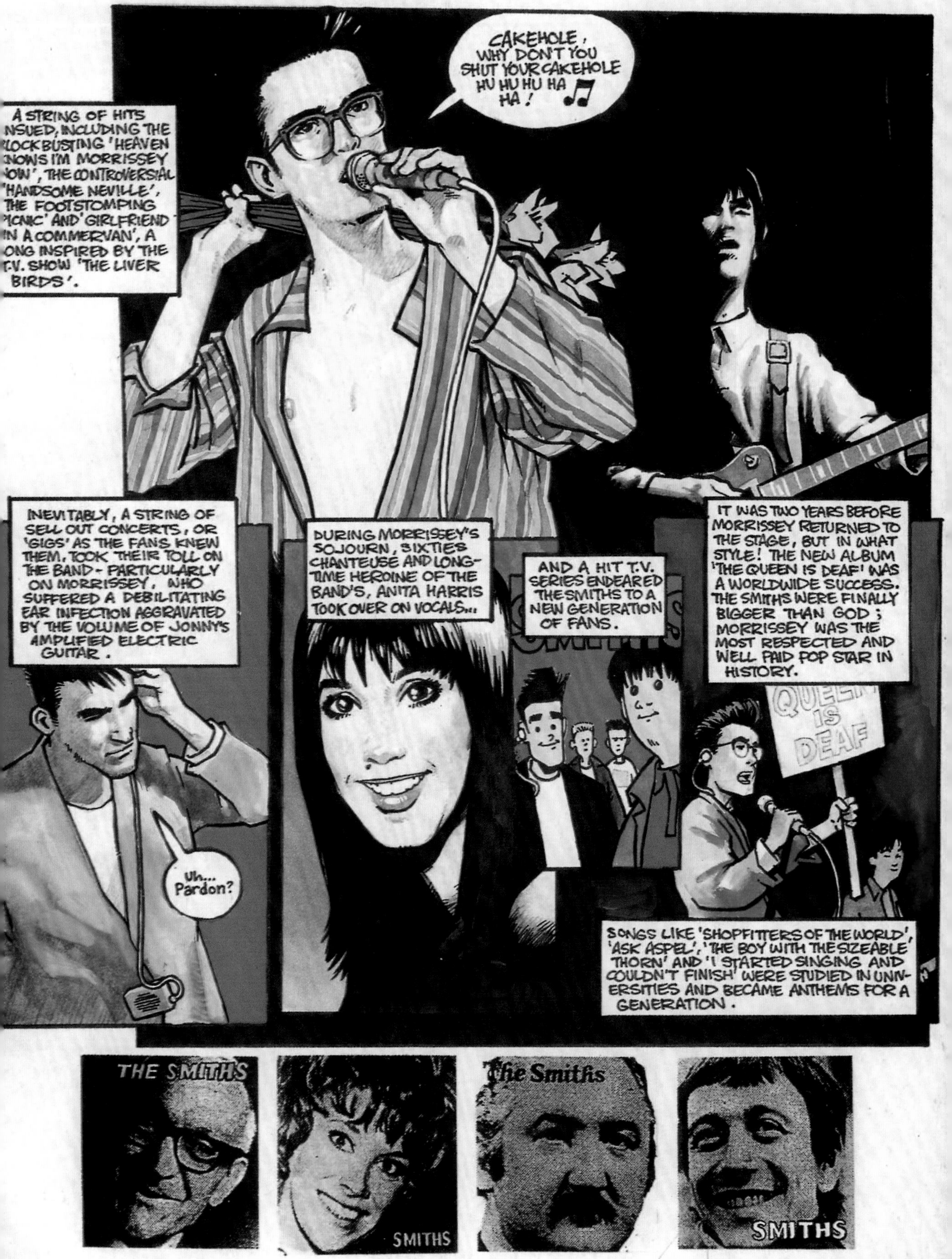

A STRING OF HITS ENSUED, INCLUDING THE BLOCKBUSTING 'HEAVEN KNOWS I'M MORRISSEY NOW', THE CONTROVERSIAL 'HANDSOME NEVILLE', THE FOOTSTOMPING 'PICNIC' AND 'GIRLFRIEND IN A COMMERVAN', A SONG INSPIRED BY THE T.V. SHOW 'THE LIVER BIRDS'.
CAKEHOLE, WHY DON'T YOU SHUT YOUR CAKEHOLE HU HU HU HA HA!
INEVITABLY, A STRING OF SELL OUT CONCERTS, OR 'GIGS' AS THE FANS KNEW THEM, TOOK THEIR TOLL ON THE BAND - PARTICULARLY ON MORRISSEY, WHO SUFFERED A DEBILITATING EAR INFECTION AGGRAVATED BY THE VOLUME OF JONNY'S AMPLIFIED ELECTRIC GUITAR.
Uh... Pardon?
DURING MORRISSEY'S SOJOURN, SIXTIES CHANTEUSE AND LONG-TIME HEROINE OF THE BAND'S, ANITA HARRIS TOOK OVER ON VOCALS...
AND A HIT T.V. SERIES ENDEARED THE SMITHS TO A NEW GENERATION OF FANS.
IT WAS TWO YEARS BEFORE MORRISSEY RETURNED TO THE STAGE, BUT IN WHAT STYLE! THE NEW ALBUM 'THE QUEEN IS DEAF' WAS A WORLDWIDE SUCCESS. THE SMITHS WERE FINALLY BIGGER THAN GOD; MORRISSEY WAS THE MOST RESPECTED AND WELL PAID POP STAR IN HISTORY.
IS DEAF
SONGS LIKE 'SHOPFITTERS OF THE WORLD', 'ASK ASPEL', 'THE BOY WITH THE SIZEABLE THORN' AND 'I STARTED SINGING AND COULDN'T FINISH' WERE STUDIED IN UNIVERSITIES AND BECAME ANTHEMS FOR A GENERATION.
THE SMITHS
SMITHS
The Smiths
SMITHS

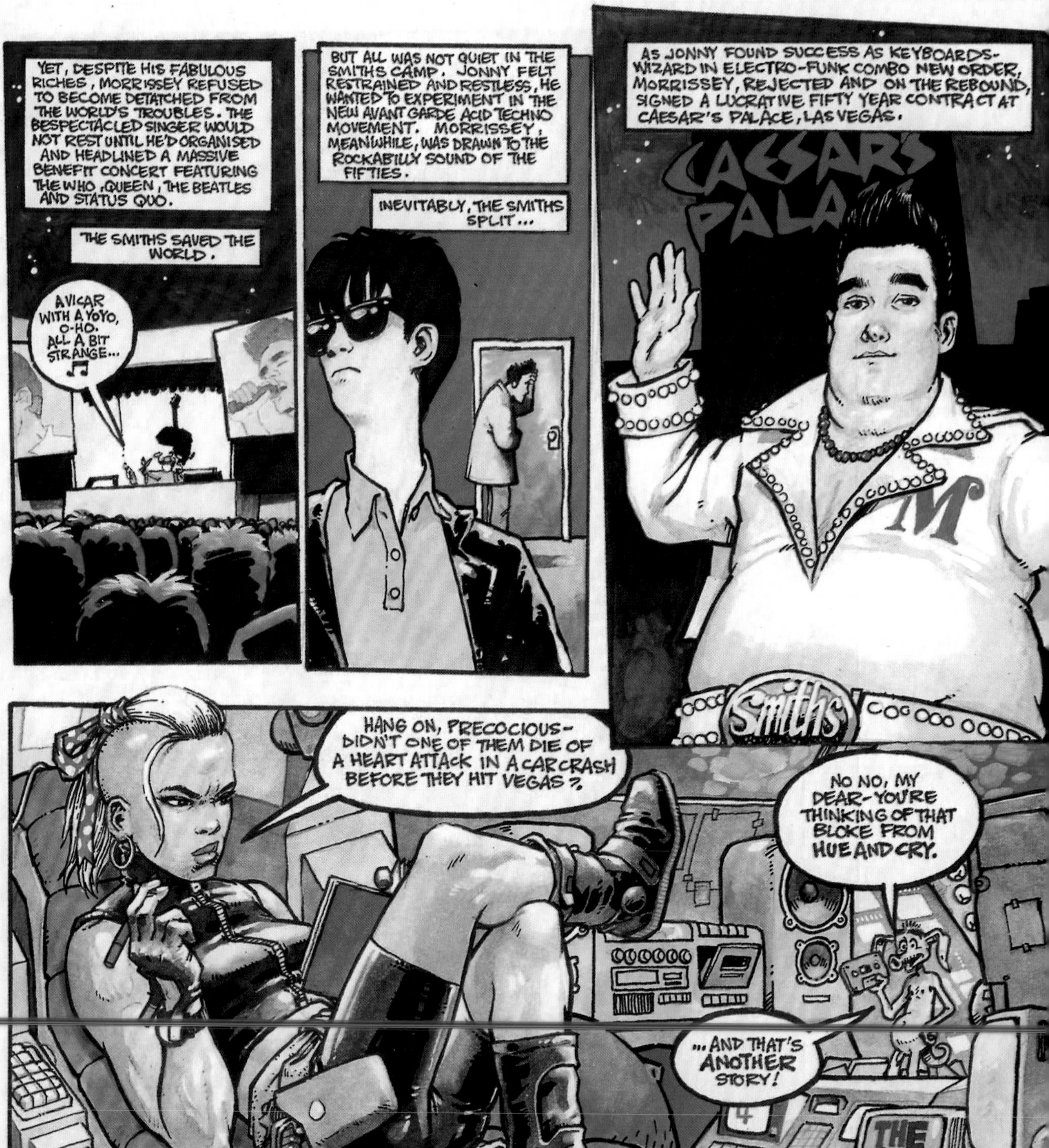
YET, DESPITE HIS FABULOUS RICHES, MORRISSEY REFUSED TO BECOME DETATCHED FROM THE WORLD'S TROUBLES. THE BESPECTACLED SINGER WOULD NOT REST UNTIL HE'D ORGANISED AND HEADLINED A MASSIVE BENEFIT CONCERT FEATURING THE WHO, QUEEN, THE BEATLES AND STATUS QUO.
THE SMITHS SAVED THE WORLD.
A VICAR WITH A YOYO, O-HO. ALL A BIT STRANGE...
BUT ALL WAS NOT QUIET IN THE SMITHS CAMP. JONNY FELT RESTRAINED AND RESTLESS, HE WANTED TO EXPERIMENT IN THE NEW AVANT GARDE ACID TECHNO MOVEMENT. MORRISSEY, MEANWHILE, WAS DRAWN TO THE ROCKABILLY SOUND OF THE FIFTIES.
INEVITABLY, THE SMITHS SPLIT...
AS JONNY FOUND SUCCESS AS KEYBOARDS-WIZARD IN ELECTRO-FUNK COMBO NEW ORDER, MORRISSEY, REJECTED AND ON THE REBOUND, SIGNED A LUCRATIVE FIFTY YEAR CONTRACT AT CAESAR'S PALACE, LAS VEGAS.
CAESAR'S PALA
M
Smiths
HANG ON, PRECOCIOUS- DIDN'T ONE OF THEM DIE OF A HEART ATTACK IN A CAR CRASH BEFORE THEY HIT VEGAS?
NO NO, MY DEAR- YOU'RE THINKING OF THAT BLOKE FROM HUE AND CRY.
...AND THAT'S ANOTHER STORY!
THE END

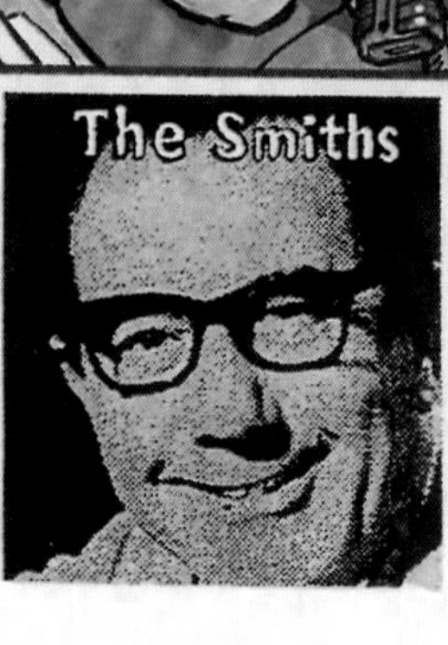
The Smiths

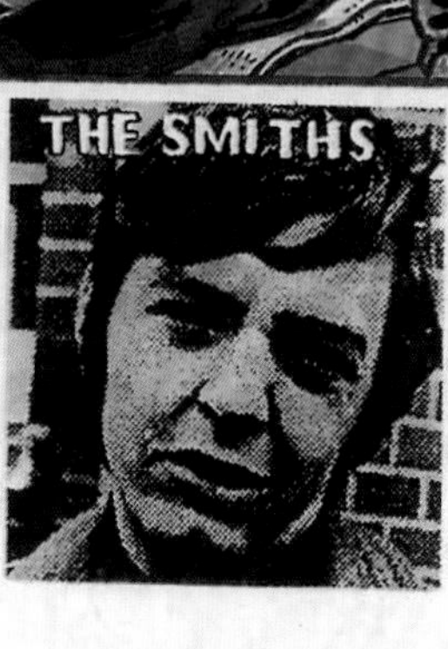
THE SMITHS

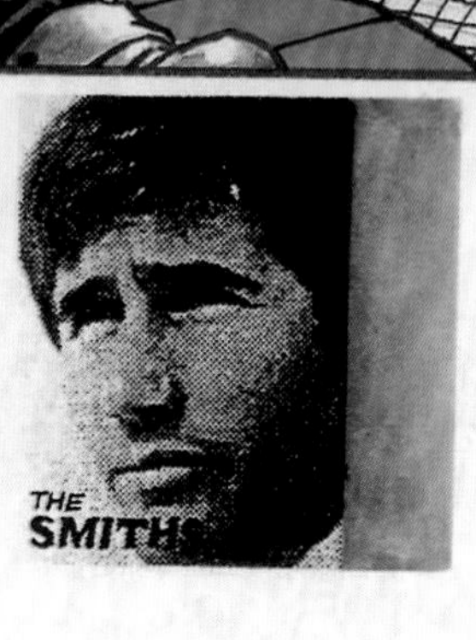
THE SMITHS

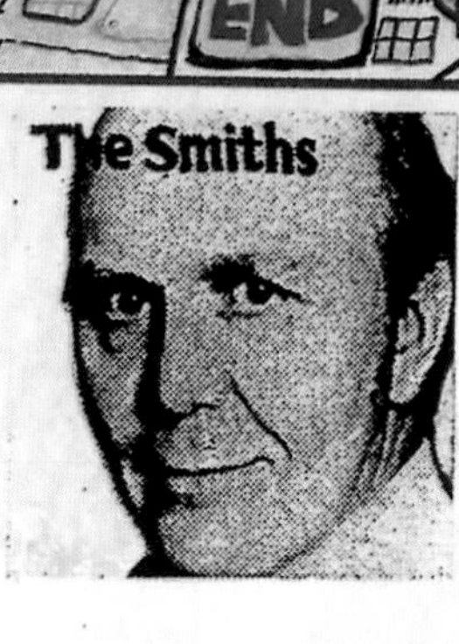
The Smiths

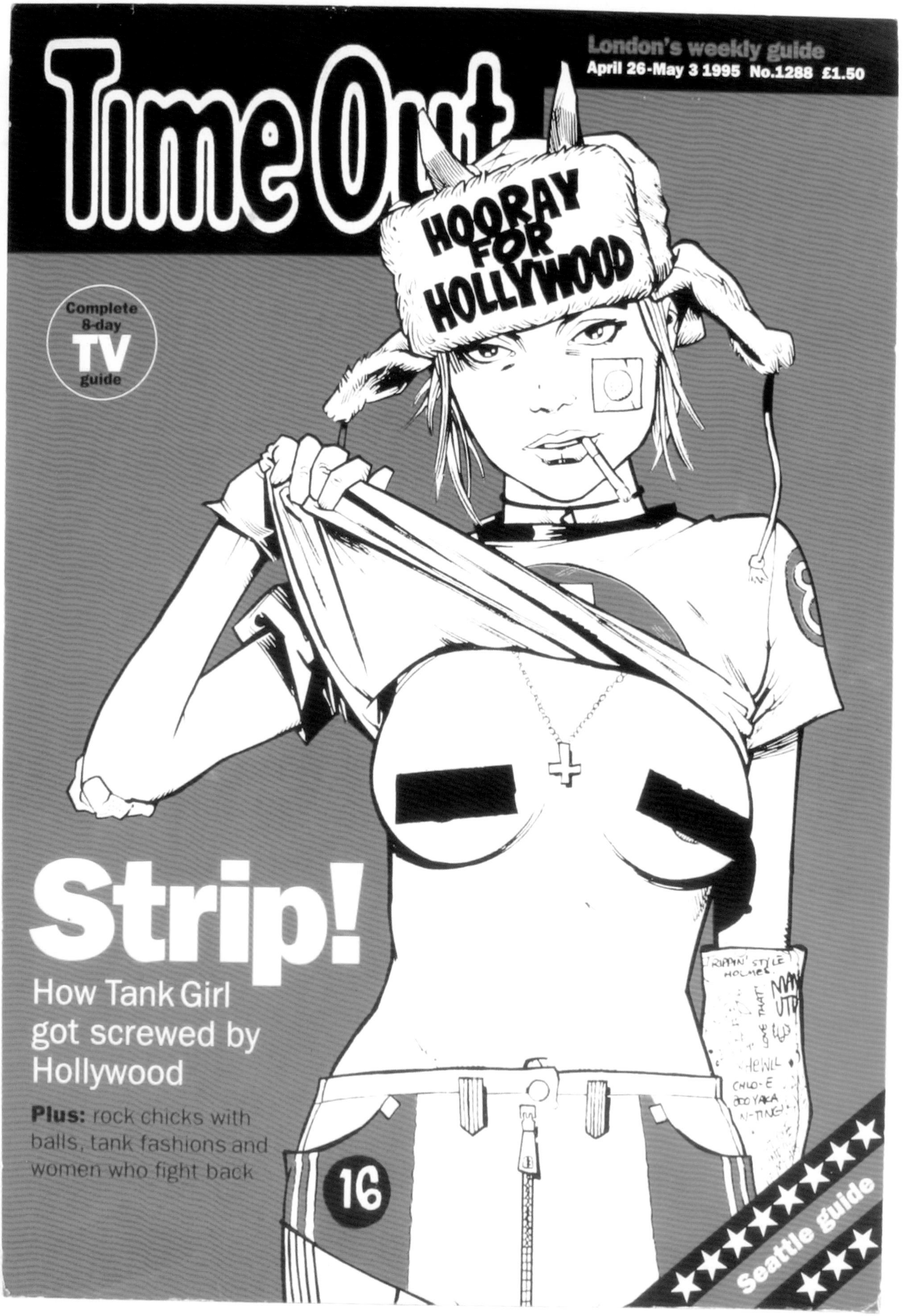
Time Out
London's weekly guide
April 26-May 3 1995 No.1288 £1.50
HOORAY FOR HOLLYWOOD
Complete 8-day TV guide
Strip!
How Tank Girl got screwed by Hollywood
Plus: rock chicks with balls, tank fashions and women who fight back
16
Seattle guide

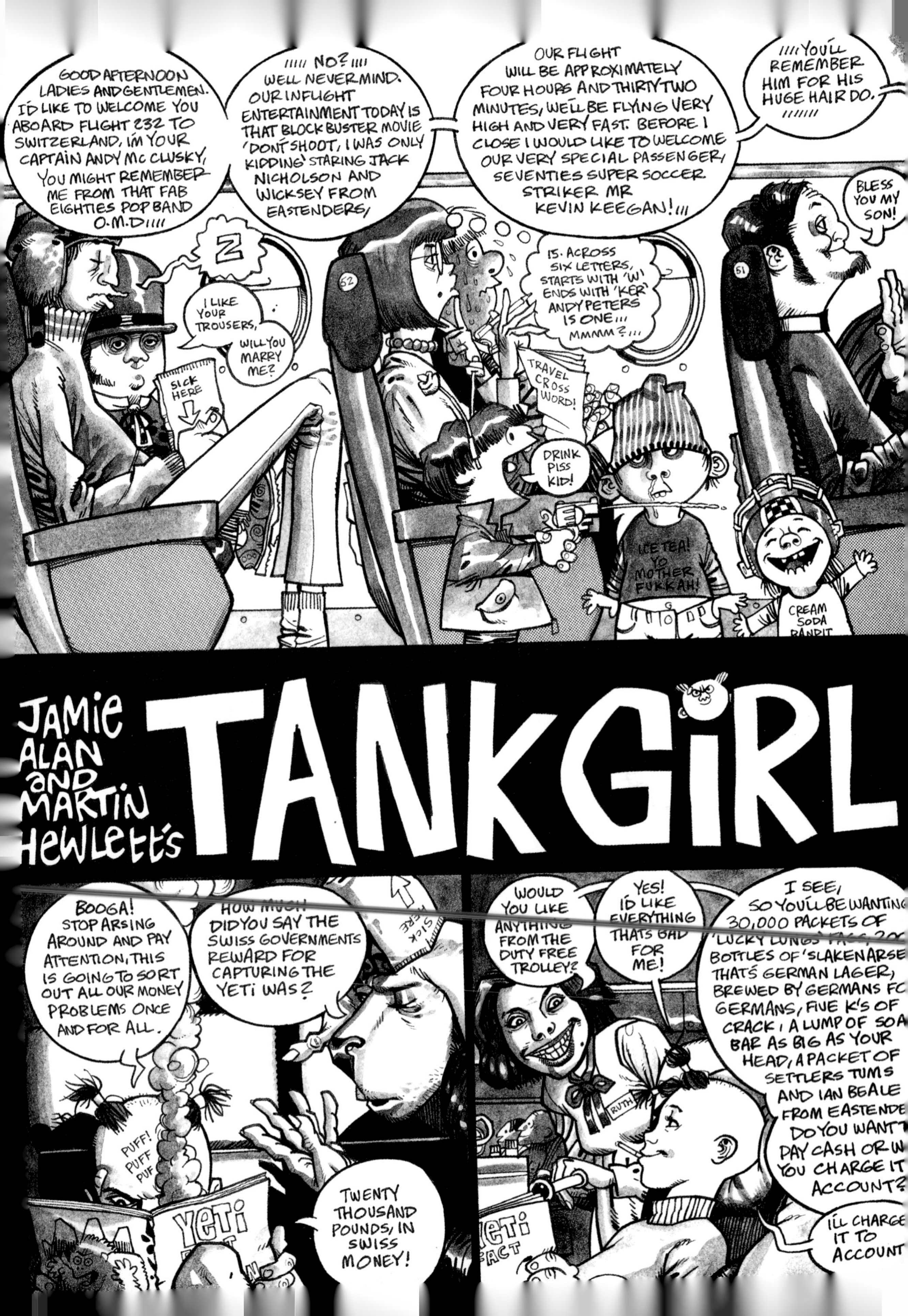
GOOD AFTERNOON LADIES AND GENTLEMEN. I'D LIKE TO WELCOME YOU ABOARD FLIGHT 232 TO SWITZERLAND, I'M YOUR CAPTAIN ANDY MC CLUSKY, YOU MIGHT REMEMBER ME FROM THAT FAB EIGHTIES POP BAND O.M.D
NO? WELL NEVERMIND. OUR INFLIGHT ENTERTAINMENT TODAY IS THAT BLOCK BUSTER MOVIE 'DON'T SHOOT, I WAS ONLY KIDDING' STARING JACK NICHOLSON AND WICKSEY FROM EASTENDERS,
OUR FLIGHT WILL BE APPROXIMATELY FOUR HOURS AND THIRTY TWO MINUTES, WE'LL BE FLYING VERY HIGH AND VERY FAST. BEFORE I CLOSE I WOULD LIKE TO WELCOME OUR VERY SPECIAL PASSENGER, SEVENTIES SUPER SOCCER STRIKER MR KEVIN KEEGAN!
YOU'LL REMEMBER HIM FOR HIS HUGE HAIR DO.
BLESS YOU MY SON!
Z
I LIKE YOUR TROUSERS,
WILL YOU MARRY ME?
SICK HERE
15. ACROSS SIX LETTERS, STARTS WITH 'W' ENDS WITH 'KER' ANDY PETERS IS ONE... MMMM?...
TRAVEL CROSS WORD!
DRINK PISS KID!
ICE TEA! YO MOTHER FUKKAH!
CREAM SODA
JAMIE ALAN AND MARTIN HEWLETT'S
TANK GIRL
BOOGA! STOP ARSING AROUND AND PAY ATTENTION, THIS IS GOING TO SORT OUT ALL OUR MONEY PROBLEMS ONCE AND FOR ALL.
HOW MUCH DID YOU SAY THE SWISS GOVERNMENTS REWARD FOR CAPTURING THE YETI WAS?
PUFF! PUFF PUF
YETI
TWENTY THOUSAND POUNDS, IN SWISS MONEY!
WOULD YOU LIKE ANYTHING FROM THE DUTY FREE TROLLEY?
YES! I'D LIKE EVERYTHING THATS BAD FOR ME!
I SEE, SO YOU'LL BE WANTING 30,000 PACKETS OF 'LUCKY LUNGS' FAGS, 20 BOTTLES OF 'SLAKENARSE' THAT'S GERMAN LAGER, BREWED BY GERMANS FO GERMANS, FIVE K'S OF CRACK, A LUMP OF SOA BAR AS BIG AS YOUR HEAD, A PACKET OF SETTLERS TUMS AND IAN BEALE FROM EASTENDE DO YOU WANT PAY CASH OR W YOU CHARGE IT ACCOUNT?
RUTH
YETI FACT
I'LL CHARGE IT TO ACCOUNT

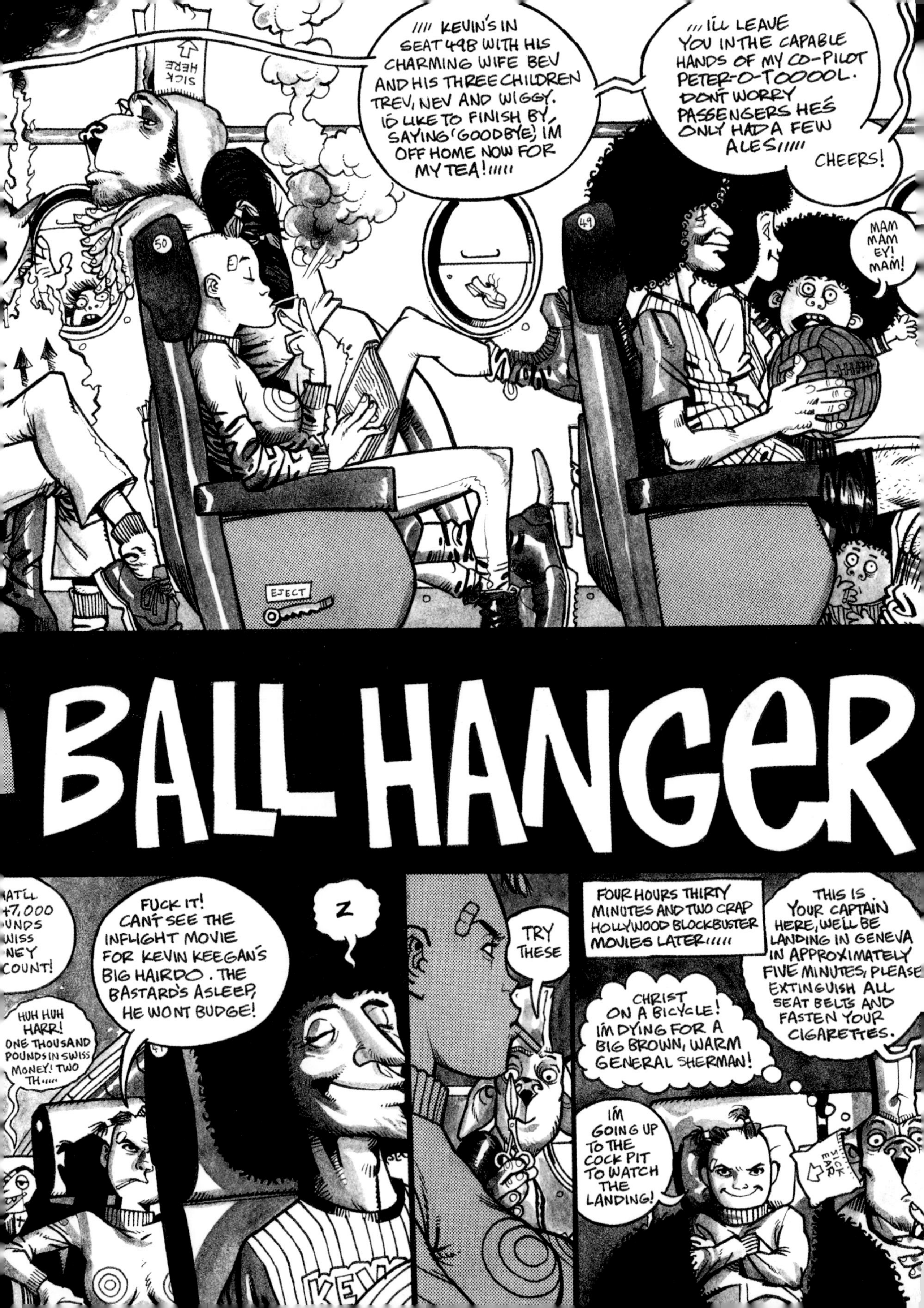
//// KEVIN'S IN SEAT 49B WITH HIS CHARMING WIFE BEV AND HIS THREE CHILDREN TREV, NEV AND WIGGY. I'D LIKE TO FINISH BY, SAYING 'GOODBYE', I'M OFF HOME NOW FOR MY TEA! /////
//// I'LL LEAVE YOU IN THE CAPABLE HANDS OF MY CO-PILOT PETER-O-TOOOOL. DON'T WORRY PASSENGERS HE'S ONLY HAD A FEW ALES /////
CHEERS!
SICK HERE
50
49
MAM MAM EY! MAM!
EJECT
BALL HANGER
FUCK IT! CAN'T SEE THE INFLIGHT MOVIE FOR KEVIN KEEGAN'S BIG HAIRDO. THE BASTARD'S ASLEEP, HE WON'T BUDGE!
Z
HUH HUH HARR! ONE THOUSAND POUNDS IN SWISS MONEY! TWO TH.....
TRY THESE
FOUR HOURS THIRTY MINUTES AND TWO CRAP HOLLYWOOD BLOCKBUSTER MOVIES LATER/////
THIS IS YOUR CAPTAIN HERE, WE'LL BE LANDING IN GENEVA IN APPROXIMATELY FIVE MINUTES, PLEASE EXTINGUISH ALL SEAT BELTS AND FASTEN YOUR CIGARETTES.
CHRIST ON A BICYCLE! I'M DYING FOR A BIG BROWN, WARM GENERAL SHERMAN!
I'M GOING UP TO THE COCK PIT TO WATCH THE LANDING!
SICK EAR

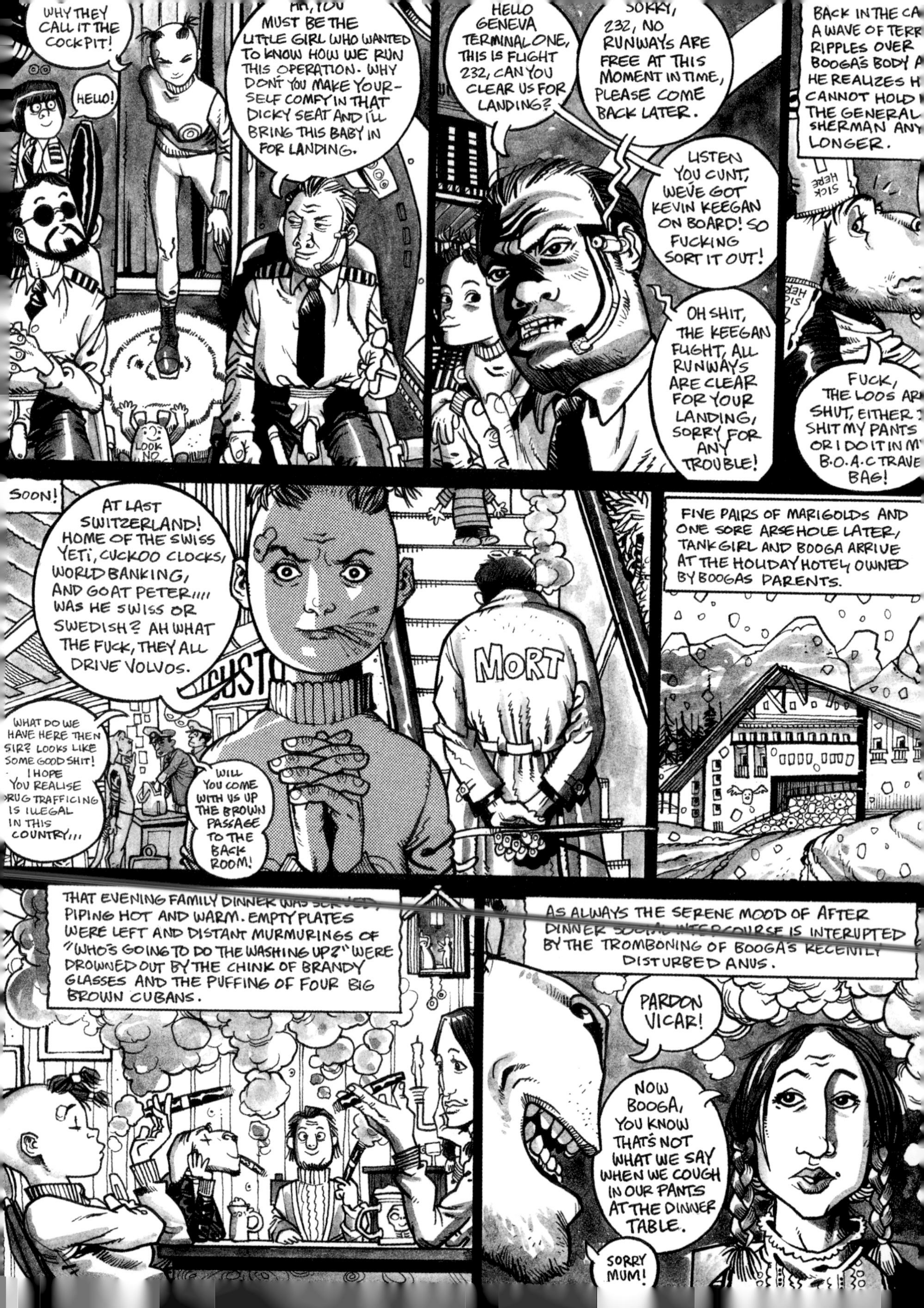
WHY THEY CALL IT THE COCKPIT!
HELLO!
AH, YOU MUST BE THE LITTLE GIRL WHO WANTED TO KNOW HOW WE RUN THIS OPERATION. WHY DON'T YOU MAKE YOURSELF COMFY IN THAT DICKY SEAT AND I'LL BRING THIS BABY IN FOR LANDING.
HELLO GENEVA TERMINAL ONE, THIS IS FLIGHT 232, CAN YOU CLEAR US FOR LANDING?
SORRY, 232, NO RUNWAYS ARE FREE AT THIS MOMENT IN TIME, PLEASE COME BACK LATER.
LISTEN YOU CUNT, WE'VE GOT KEVIN KEEGAN ON BOARD! SO FUCKING SORT IT OUT!
OH SHIT, THE KEEGAN FLIGHT, ALL RUNWAYS ARE CLEAR FOR YOUR LANDING, SORRY FOR ANY TROUBLE!
BACK IN THE CA A WAVE OF TERR RIPPLES OVER BOOGA'S BODY A HE REALIZES H CANNOT HOLD THE GENERAL SHERMAN ANY LONGER.
SICK HERE
FUCK, THE LOOS AR SHUT, EITHER I SHIT MY PANTS OR I DO IT IN M B.O.A.C TRAVE BAG!
SOON!
AT LAST SWITZERLAND! HOME OF THE SWISS YETI, CUCKOO CLOCKS, WORLD BANKING, AND GOAT PETER.... WAS HE SWISS OR SWEDISH? AH WHAT THE FUCK, THEY ALL DRIVE VOLVOS.
CUSTO
MORT
WHAT DO WE HAVE HERE THEN SIR? LOOKS LIKE SOME GOOD SHIT! I HOPE YOU REALISE RUG TRAFFICING IS ILLEGAL IN THIS COUNTRY...
WILL YOU COME WITH US UP THE BROWN PASSAGE TO THE BACK ROOM!
FIVE PAIRS OF MARIGOLDS AND ONE SORE ARSEHOLE LATER, TANKGIRL AND BOOGA ARRIVE AT THE HOLIDAY HOTEL OWNED BY BOOGAS PARENTS.
THAT EVENING FAMILY DINNER WAS SERVED, PIPING HOT AND WARM. EMPTY PLATES WERE LEFT AND DISTANT MURMURINGS OF "WHO'S GOING TO DO THE WASHING UP?" WERE DROWNED OUT BY THE CHINK OF BRANDY GLASSES AND THE PUFFING OF FOUR BIG BROWN CUBANS.
AS ALWAYS THE SERENE MOOD OF AFTER DINNER SOCIAL INTERCOURSE IS INTERUPTED BY THE TROMBONING OF BOOGA'S RECENTLY DISTURBED ANUS.
PARDON VICAR!
NOW BOOGA, YOU KNOW THAT'S NOT WHAT WE SAY WHEN WE COUGH IN OUR PANTS AT THE DINNER TABLE.
SORRY MUM!

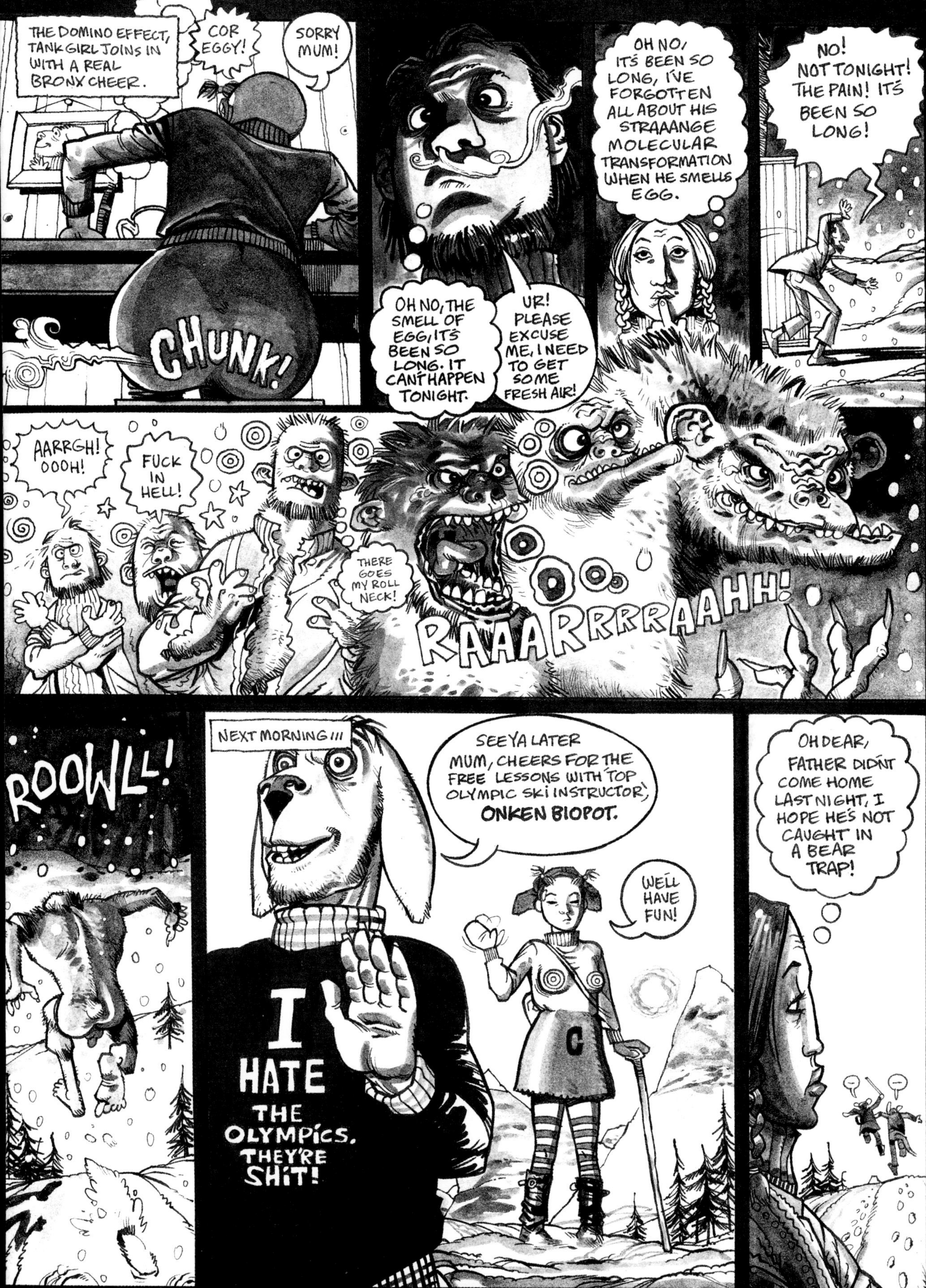
THE DOMINO EFFECT, TANK GIRL JOINS IN WITH A REAL BRONX CHEER.
COR EGGY!
SORRY MUM!
CHUNK!
OH NO, THE SMELL OF EGG, IT'S BEEN SO LONG. IT CAN'T HAPPEN TONIGHT.
UR! PLEASE EXCUSE ME, I NEED TO GET SOME FRESH AIR!
OH NO, IT'S BEEN SO LONG, I'VE FORGOTTEN ALL ABOUT HIS STRAAAANGE MOLECULAR TRANSFORMATION WHEN HE SMELLS EGG.
NO! NOT TONIGHT! THE PAIN! IT'S BEEN SO LONG!
AARRGH! OOOH!
FUCK IN HELL!
THERE GOES MY ROLL NECK!
RAAARRRRRAAHH!
ROOWLL!
NEXT MORNING...
SEEYA LATER MUM, CHEERS FOR THE FREE LESSONS WITH 'TOP OLYMPIC SKI INSTRUCTOR', ONKEN BIOPOT.
I HATE THE OLYMPICS. THEY'RE SHIT!
WE'LL HAVE FUN!
OH DEAR, FATHER DIDN'T COME HOME LAST NIGHT, I HOPE HE'S NOT CAUGHT IN A BEAR TRAP!

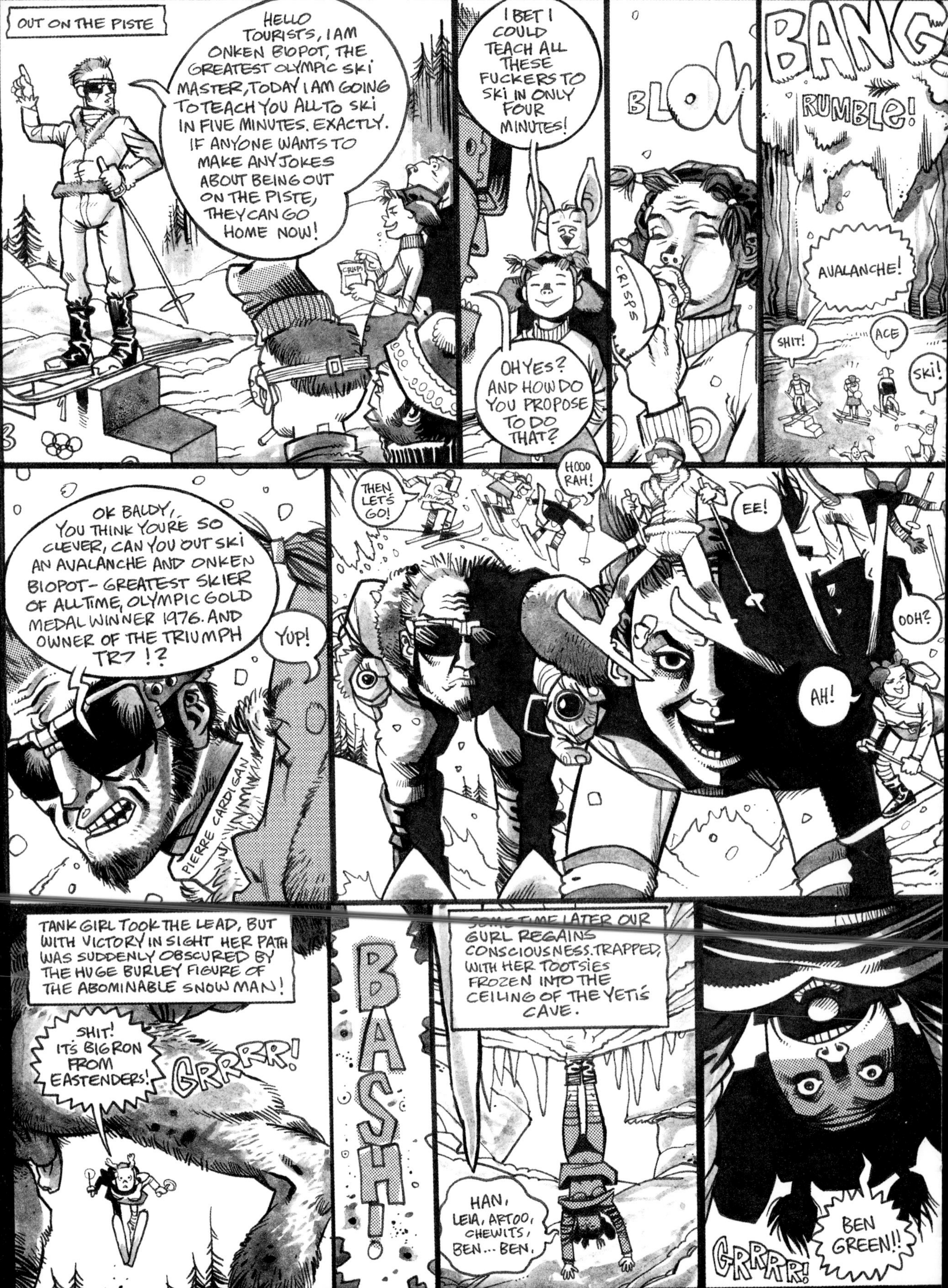
OUT ON THE PISTE
HELLO TOURISTS, I AM ONKEN BIOPOT, THE GREATEST OLYMPIC SKI MASTER, TODAY I AM GOING TO TEACH YOU ALL TO SKI IN FIVE MINUTES. EXACTLY. IF ANYONE WANTS TO MAKE ANY JOKES ABOUT BEING OUT ON THE PISTE, THEY CAN GO HOME NOW!
CRISPS
I BET I COULD TEACH ALL THESE FUCKERS TO SKI IN ONLY FOUR MINUTES!
OH YES? AND HOW DO YOU PROPOSE TO DO THAT?
BLOW
CRISPS
BANG!
RUMBLE!
AVALANCHE!
SHIT!
ACE
SKI!
OK BALDY, YOU THINK YOU'RE SO CLEVER, CAN YOU OUT SKI AN AVALANCHE AND ONKEN BIOPOT- GREATEST SKIER OF ALL TIME, OLYMPIC GOLD MEDAL WINNER 1976. AND OWNER OF THE TRIUMPH TR7 !?
YUP!
PIERRE CARDIGAN
THEN LET'S GO!
HOOO RAH!
EE!
OOH?
AH!
TANK GIRL TOOK THE LEAD, BUT WITH VICTORY IN SIGHT HER PATH WAS SUDDENLY OBSCURED BY THE HUGE BURLEY FIGURE OF THE ABOMINABLE SNOW MAN!
SHIT! IT'S BIG RON FROM EASTENDERS!
GRRRR!
BASH!
SOME TIME LATER OUR GURL REGAINS CONSCIOUSNESS. TRAPPED, WITH HER TOOTSIES FROZEN INTO THE CEILING OF THE YETI'S CAVE.
HAN, LEIA, ARTOO, CHEWITS, BEN... BEN.
GRRRR!
BEN GREEN!!

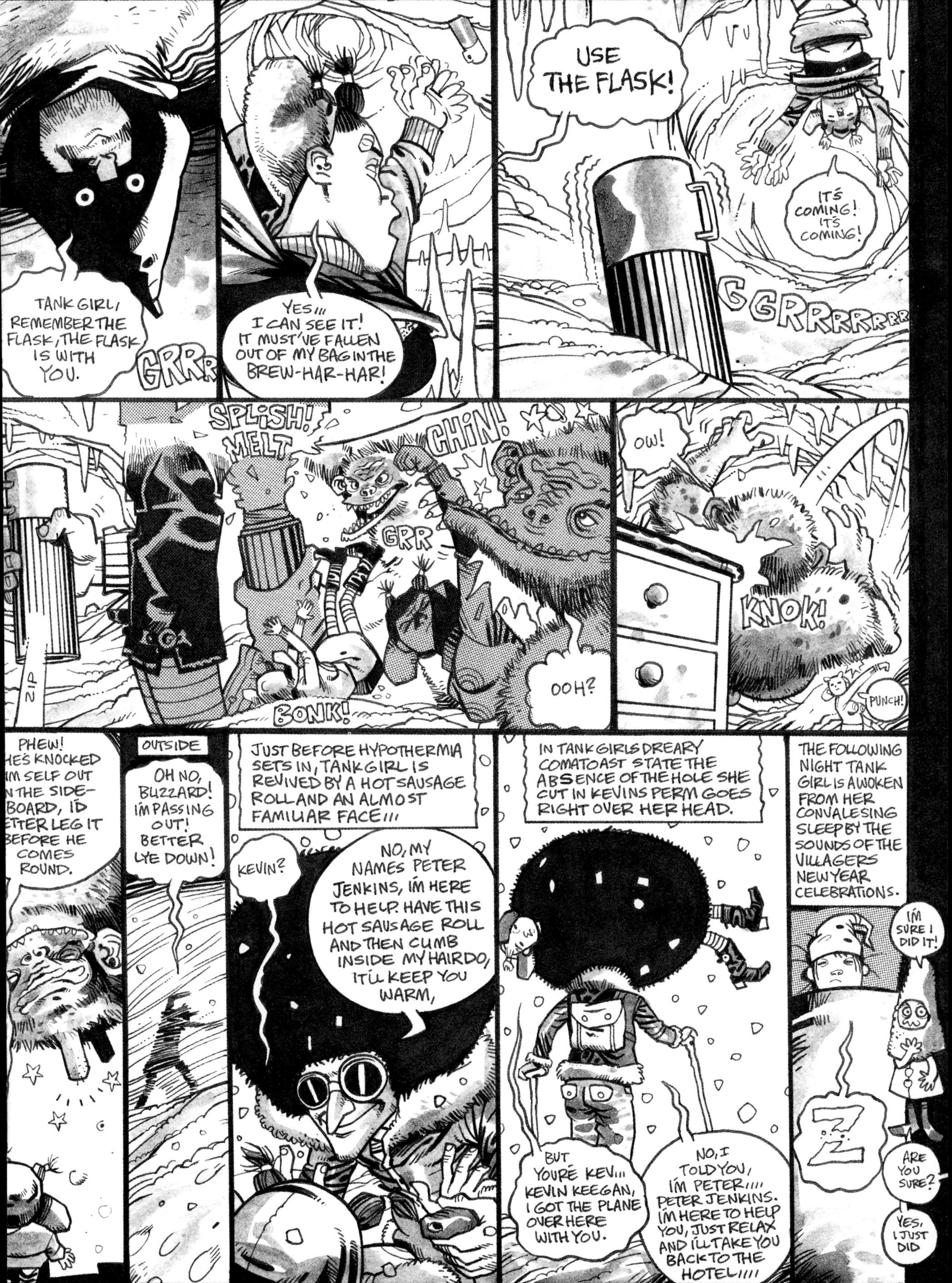
TANK GIRL, REMEMBER THE FLASK, THE FLASK IS WITH YOU.
GRRR
YES... I CAN SEE IT! IT MUST'VE FALLEN OUT OF MY BAG IN THE BREW-HAR-HAR!
USE THE FLASK!
IT'S COMING! IT'S COMING!
GGRRRRRRRR
SPLISH! MELT
CHIN!
GRR
ZIP
BONK!
OOH?
OW!
KNOK!
PUNCH!
PHEW! HE'S KNOCKED HIM SELF OUT ON THE SIDE-BOARD, I'D BETTER LEG IT BEFORE HE COMES ROUND.
OUTSIDE
OH NO, BUZZARD! I'M PASSING OUT! BETTER LYE DOWN!
JUST BEFORE HYPOTHERMIA SETS IN, TANK GIRL IS REVIVED BY A HOT SAUSAGE ROLL AND AN ALMOST FAMILIAR FACE...
KEVIN?
NO, MY NAMES PETER JENKINS, I'M HERE TO HELP. HAVE THIS HOT SAUSAGE ROLL AND THEN CLIMB INSIDE MY HAIRDO, IT'LL KEEP YOU WARM,
IN TANK GIRLS DREARY COMATOAST STATE THE ABSENCE OF THE HOLE SHE CUT IN KEVINS PERM GOES RIGHT OVER HER HEAD.
BUT YOU'RE KEV... KEVIN KEEGAN, I GOT THE PLANE OVER HERE WITH YOU.
NO, I TOLD YOU, I'M PETER.... PETER JENKINS. I'M HERE TO HELP YOU, JUST RELAX AND I'LL TAKE YOU BACK TO THE HOTEL....
THE FOLLOWING NIGHT TANK GIRL IS AWOKEN FROM HER CONVALESING SLEEP BY THE SOUNDS OF THE VILLAGERS NEW YEAR CELEBRATIONS.
I'M SURE I DID IT!
Z
ARE YOU SURE?
YES, I JUST DID

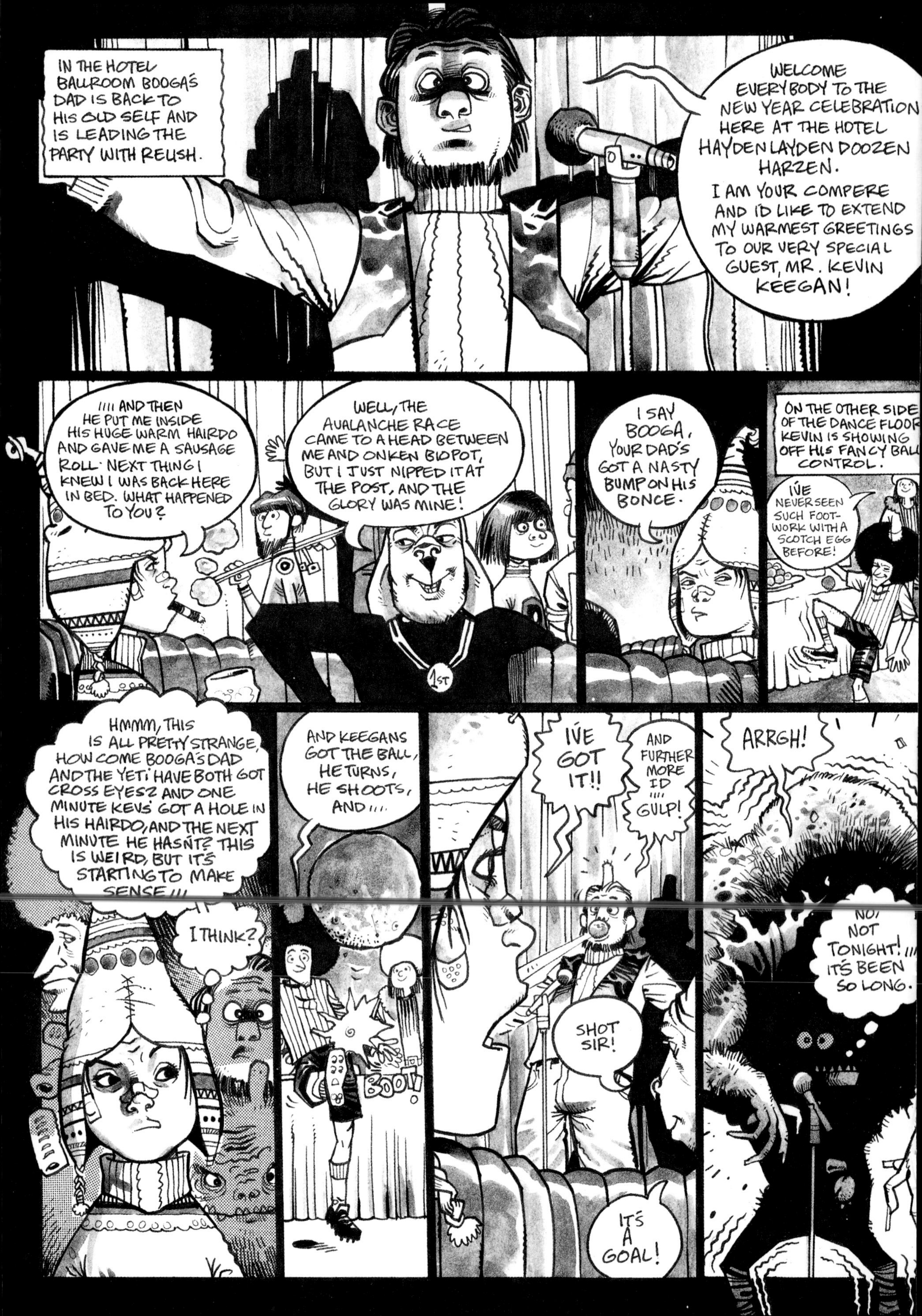
IN THE HOTEL BALLROOM BOOGA'S DAD IS BACK TO HIS OLD SELF AND IS LEADING THE PARTY WITH RELISH.
WELCOME EVERYBODY TO THE NEW YEAR CELEBRATION HERE AT THE HOTEL HAYDEN LAYDEN DOOZEN HARZEN. I AM YOUR COMPERE AND I'D LIKE TO EXTEND MY WARMEST GREETINGS TO OUR VERY SPECIAL GUEST, MR. KEVIN KEEGAN!
.... AND THEN HE PUT ME INSIDE HIS HUGE WARM HAIRDO AND GAVE ME A SAUSAGE ROLL. NEXT THING I KNEW I WAS BACK HERE IN BED. WHAT HAPPENED TO YOU?
WELL, THE AVALANCHE RACE CAME TO A HEAD BETWEEN ME AND ONKEN BIOPOT, BUT I JUST NIPPED IT AT THE POST, AND THE GLORY WAS MINE!
1ST
I SAY BOOGA, YOUR DAD'S GOT A NASTY BUMP ON HIS BONCE.
ON THE OTHER SIDE OF THE DANCE FLOOR KEVIN IS SHOWING OFF HIS FANCY BALL CONTROL.
I'VE NEVER SEEN SUCH FOOT-WORK WITH A SCOTCH EGG BEFORE!
HMMM, THIS IS ALL PRETTY STRANGE, HOW COME BOOGA'S DAD AND THE YETI HAVE BOTH GOT CROSS EYES? AND ONE MINUTE KEV'S GOT A HOLE IN HIS HAIRDO, AND THE NEXT MINUTE HE HASN'T? THIS IS WEIRD, BUT IT'S STARTING TO MAKE SENSE....
I THINK?
AND KEEGANS GOT THE BALL, HE TURNS, HE SHOOTS, AND....
BOOT!
I'VE GOT IT!!
AND FURTHER MORE I'D .... GULP!
SHOT SIR!
IT'S A GOAL!
ARRGH!
NO, NOT TONIGHT! IT'S BEEN SO LONG.

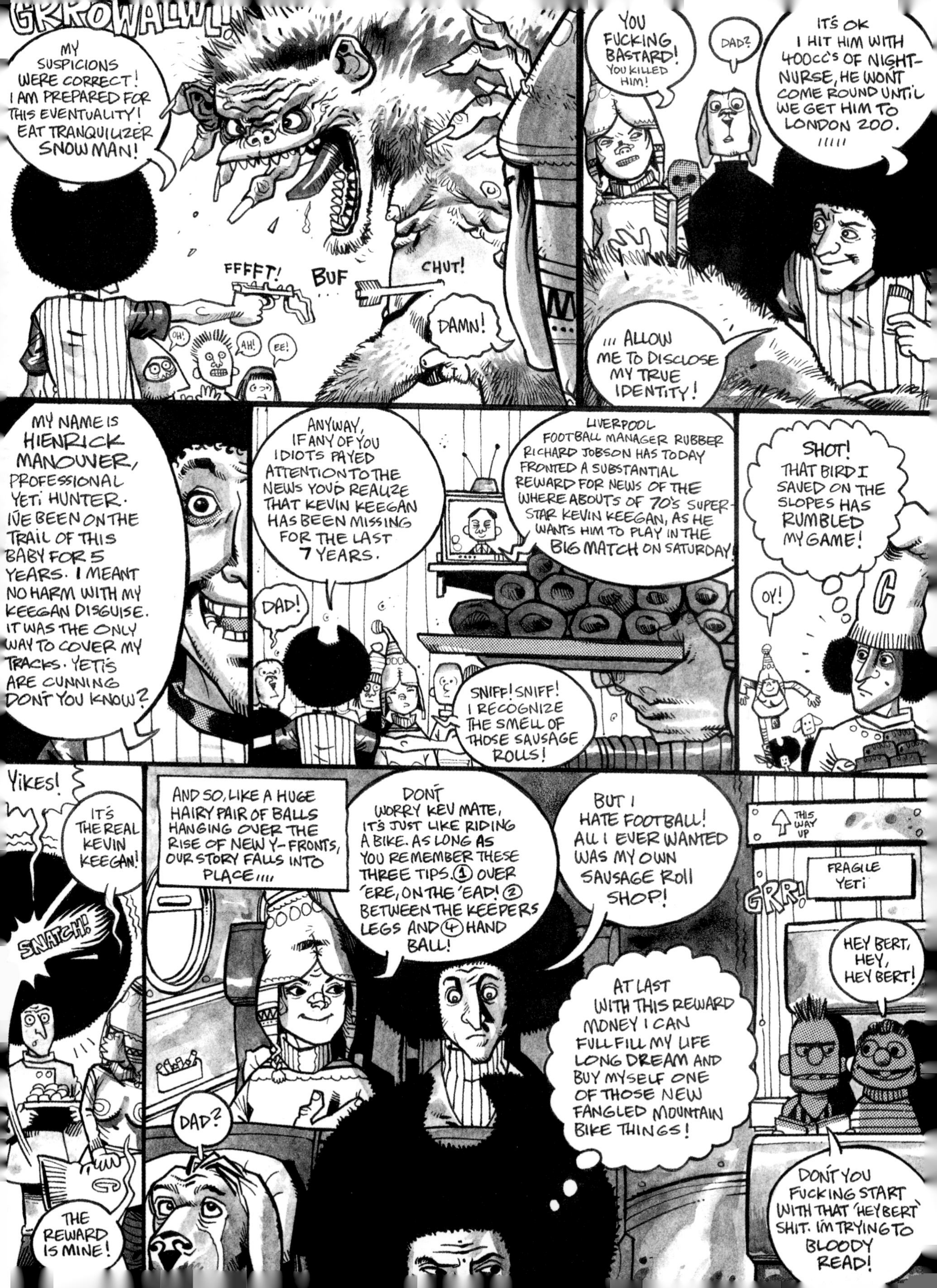

GRROWALWL!
MY SUSPICIONS WERE CORRECT! I AM PREPARED FOR THIS EVENTUALITY! EAT TRANQUILIZER SNOWMAN!
FFFFT!
BUF
CHUT!
OH!
AH!
EE!
DAMN!
YOU FUCKING BASTARD! YOU KILLED HIM!
DAD?
IT'S OK I HIT HIM WITH 400CC'S OF NIGHT-NURSE, HE WON'T COME ROUND UNTIL WE GET HIM TO LONDON ZOO. .....
... ALLOW ME TO DISCLOSE MY TRUE IDENTITY!
MY NAME IS HIENRICK MANOUVER, PROFESSIONAL YETI HUNTER. I'VE BEEN ON THE TRAIL OF THIS BABY FOR 5 YEARS. I MEANT NO HARM WITH MY KEEGAN DISGUISE. IT WAS THE ONLY WAY TO COVER MY TRACKS. YETIS ARE CUNNING DON'T YOU KNOW?
ANYWAY, IF ANY OF YOU IDIOTS PAYED ATTENTION TO THE NEWS YOU'D REALIZE THAT KEVIN KEEGAN HAS BEEN MISSING FOR THE LAST 7 YEARS.
LIVERPOOL FOOTBALL MANAGER RUBBER RICHARD JOBSON HAS TODAY FRONTED A SUBSTANTIAL REWARD FOR NEWS OF THE WHERE ABOUTS OF 70'S SUPER STAR KEVIN KEEGAN, AS HE WANTS HIM TO PLAY IN THE BIG MATCH ON SATURDAY!
DAD!
SNIFF! SNIFF! I RECOGNIZE THE SMELL OF THOSE SAUSAGE ROLLS!
SHOT! THAT BIRD I SAVED ON THE SLOPES HAS RUMBLED MY GAME!
OY!
YIKES!
IT'S THE REAL KEVIN KEEGAN!
SNATCH!
THE REWARD IS MINE!
AND SO, LIKE A HUGE HAIRY PAIR OF BALLS HANGING OVER THE RISE OF NEW Y-FRONTS, OUR STORY FALLS INTO PLACE....
DON'T WORRY KEV MATE, IT'S JUST LIKE RIDING A BIKE. AS LONG AS YOU REMEMBER THESE THREE TIPS. ① OVER 'ERE, ON THE 'EAD! ② BETWEEN THE KEEPERS LEGS AND ④ HAND BALL!
BUT I HATE FOOTBALL! ALL I EVER WANTED WAS MY OWN SAUSAGE ROLL SHOP!
AT LAST WITH THIS REWARD MONEY I CAN FULLFILL MY LIFE LONG DREAM AND BUY MYSELF ONE OF THOSE NEW FANGLED MOUNTAIN BIKE THINGS!
DAD?
THIS WAY UP
FRAGILE YETI
GRR!
HEY BERT, HEY, HEY BERT!
DON'T YOU FUCKING START WITH THAT 'HEY BERT' SHIT. I'M TRYING TO BLOODY READ!

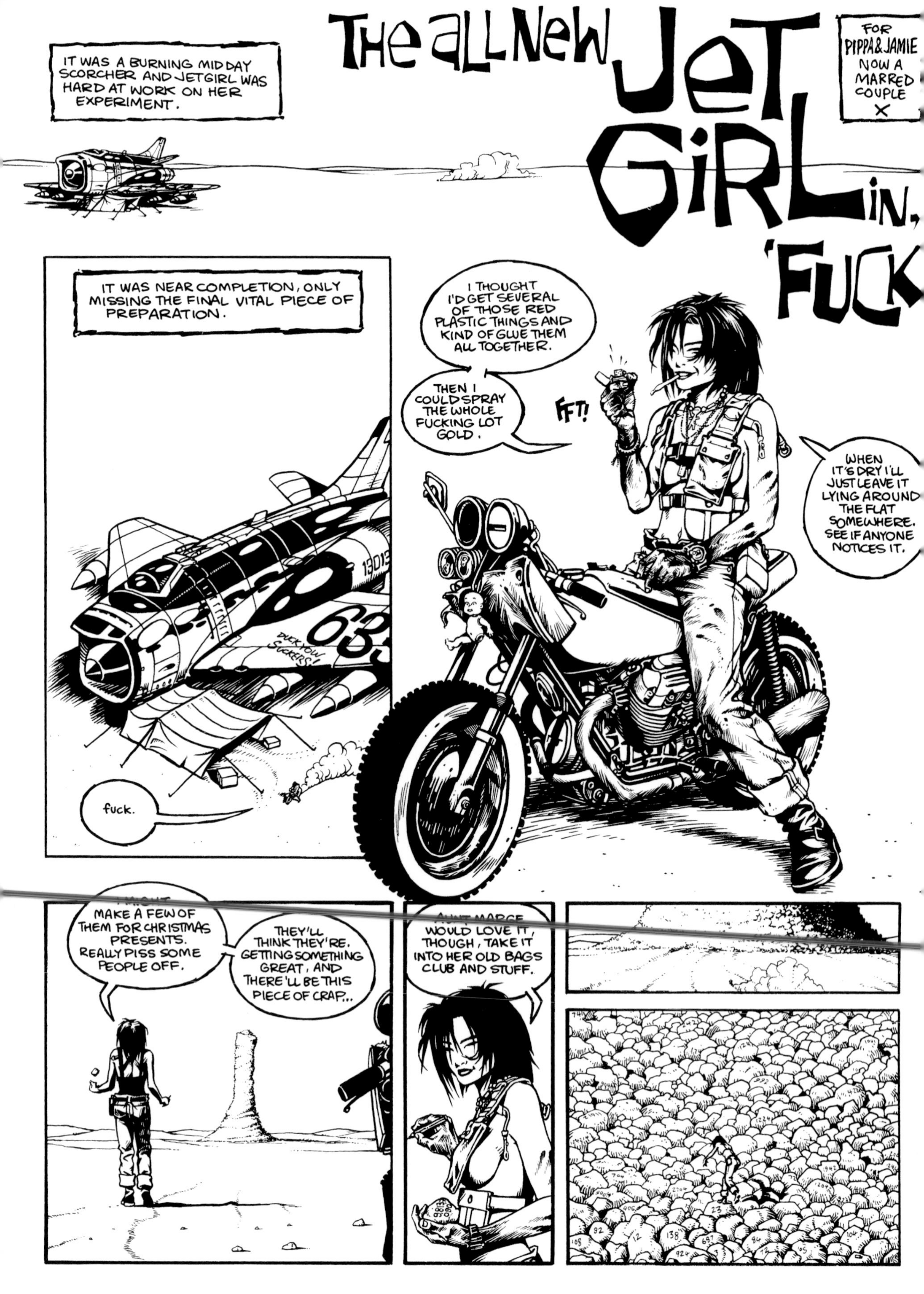
THE ALL NEW JET GIRL IN, 'FUCK
IT WAS A BURNING MID DAY SCORCHER AND JETGIRL WAS HARD AT WORK ON HER EXPERIMENT.
FOR PIPPA & JAMIE NOW A MARRED COUPLE X
IT WAS NEAR COMPLETION, ONLY MISSING THE FINAL VITAL PIECE OF PREPARATION.
DUCK YOU SUCKERS!
fuck.
I THOUGHT I'D GET SEVERAL OF THOSE RED PLASTIC THINGS AND KIND OF GLUE THEM ALL TOGETHER.
THEN I COULD SPRAY THE WHOLE FUCKING LOT GOLD.
FFT!
WHEN IT'S DRY I'LL JUST LEAVE IT LYING AROUND THE FLAT SOMEWHERE. SEE IF ANYONE NOTICES IT.
MAKE A FEW OF THEM FOR CHRISTMAS PRESENTS. REALLY PISS SOME PEOPLE OFF.
THEY'LL THINK THEY'RE. GETTING SOMETHING GREAT, AND THERE'LL BE THIS PIECE OF CRAP...
WOULD LOVE IT, THOUGH, TAKE IT INTO HER OLD BAGS CLUB AND STUFF.

AND THERE IT WAS. THE LAST STONE. EVERYTHING WAS READY.

RIGHT, IF LITTLE DAVID WOULD LIKE TO SIT NEXT TO SUZIE, AND ROWAN CAN GO BETWEEN STUART AND PETER.

HAS EVERYBODY GOT JELLY? CHOW DOWN, KIDS, MUSICAL FISH AFTER THIS.

MAUREEN, I THINK DUNCAN'S PISSED HIMSELF, BUT I CAN'T CATCH HIM. HE KEEPS DIVING BEHIND THE SOFA.

YES, SALLY. THAT'S A LOVELY WOODLOUSE.

IS THAT YOURS? ARE YOU SURE? WELL IT'S NOT MINE. I WOULDN'T BE SEEN DEAD IN THAT.

IT'S FUCKING HORRIBLE. ALL THOSE SHAGGY BITS HANGING OFF THE BOTTOM, AND THE PUFFY SHOULDERS. IT'S GROSS.

IT MUST BE YOURS, YOU SAD OLD FUCK.

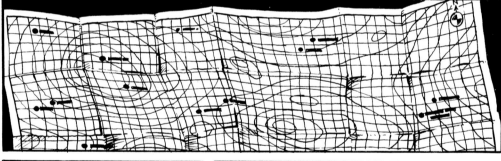

ONE ROCK FROM EACH SECTION ON THE MAP, FORMING A TOWER IN THE CENTER OF THE AREA. THIS WAS HER MISSION. OR WAS IT TESTING FOR RADIOACTIVITY? WHO KNOWS ANYMORE? IT WAS SUCH A LONG TIME AGO. THE BOOZE, DRUGS AND INTENSE HEAT HAD ALL TAKEN THEIR TOLL. NO ONE TO TALK TO BUT HERSELF, THINGS WERE COMING TO A HEAD.

LATER, IN THE JET, THINGS HAD COME TO A HEAD.

FUCK.

YOU'RE FRIENDS WITH ROD STEWART AREN'T YOU? THAT MUST BE REALLY FUCKING COOL.

STAIRS.

I'D LOVE TO MEET HIM. I'VE HEARD ALL OF HIS RECORDS. HE'S REALLY FUCKING COOL.

I LOVE ALL OF THAT OLD SHIT HE SINGS ABOUT.

PUSH

TANK.G

UNDRESS.

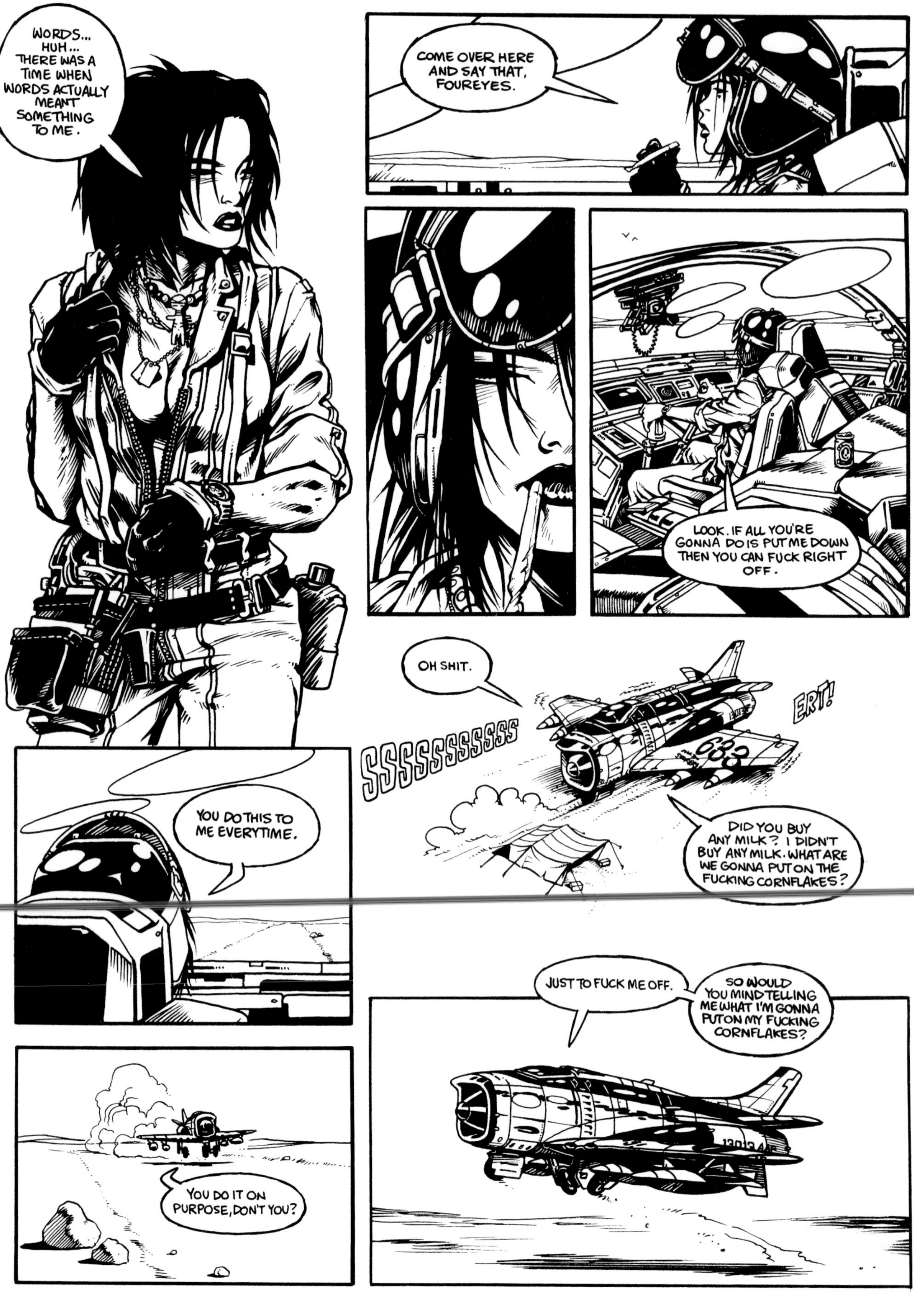
WORDS... HUH... THERE WAS A TIME WHEN WORDS ACTUALLY MEANT SOMETHING TO ME.
COME OVER HERE AND SAY THAT, FOUREYES.
LOOK. IF ALL YOU'RE GONNA DO IS PUT ME DOWN THEN YOU CAN FUCK RIGHT OFF.
YOU DO THIS TO ME EVERYTIME.
OH SHIT.
SSSSSSSSSSS
ERT!
DID YOU BUY ANY MILK? I DIDN'T BUY ANY MILK. WHAT ARE WE GONNA PUT ON THE FUCKING CORNFLAKES?
YOU DO IT ON PURPOSE, DON'T YOU?
JUST TO FUCK ME OFF.
SO WOULD YOU MIND TELLING ME WHAT I'M GONNA PUT ON MY FUCKING CORNFLAKES?

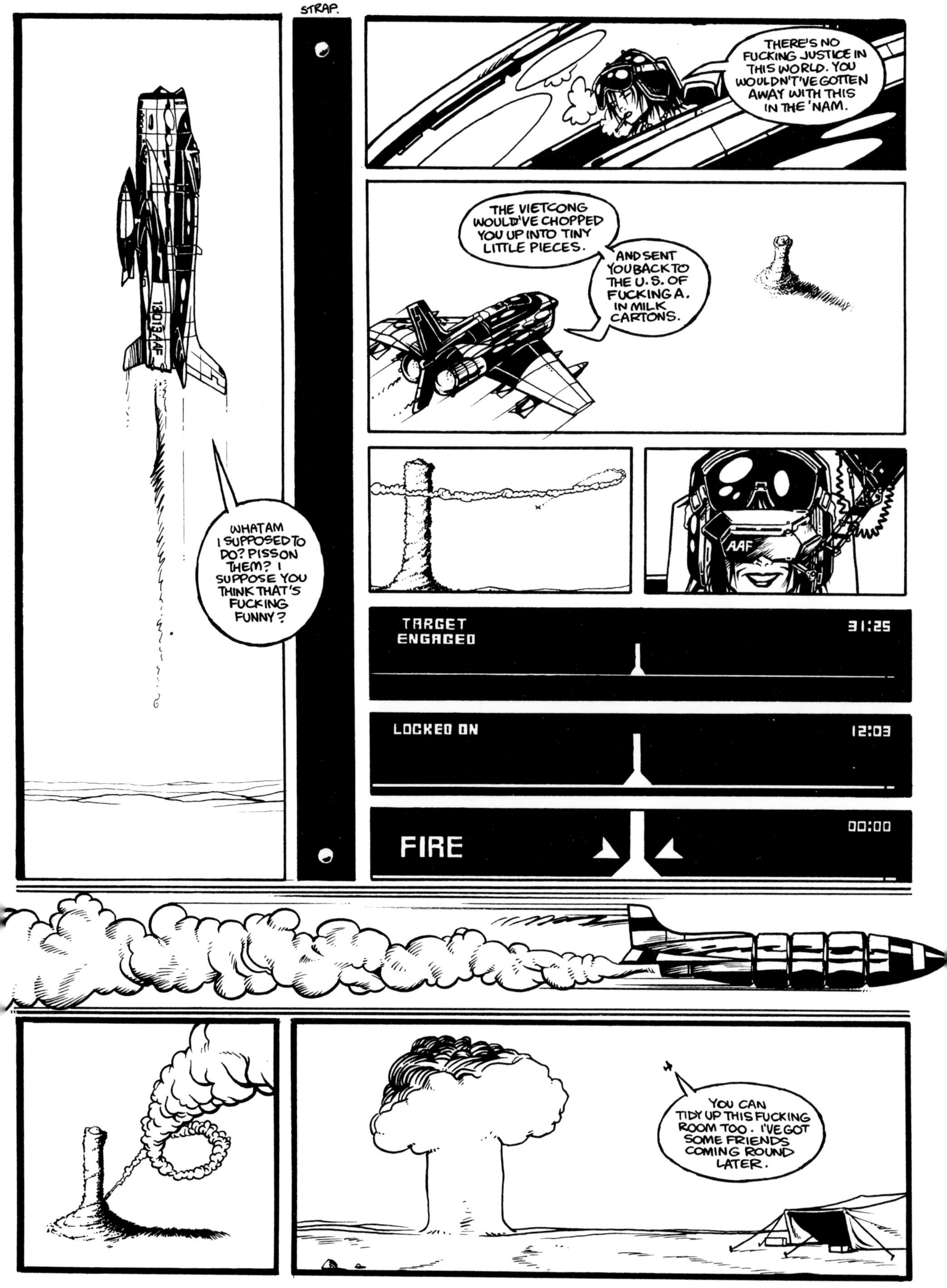
STRAP.
WHAT AM I SUPPOSED TO DO? PISS ON THEM? I SUPPOSE YOU THINK THAT'S FUCKING FUNNY?
THERE'S NO FUCKING JUSTICE IN THIS WORLD. YOU WOULDN'T'VE GOTTEN AWAY WITH THIS IN THE 'NAM.
THE VIETCONG WOULD'VE CHOPPED YOU UP INTO TINY LITTLE PIECES.
AND SENT YOU BACK TO THE U.S. OF FUCKING A. IN MILK CARTONS.
AAF
TARGET ENGAGED
31:25
LOCKED ON
12:03
FIRE
00:00
YOU CAN TIDY UP THIS FUCKING ROOM TOO. I'VE GOT SOME FRIENDS COMING ROUND LATER.

LATER...

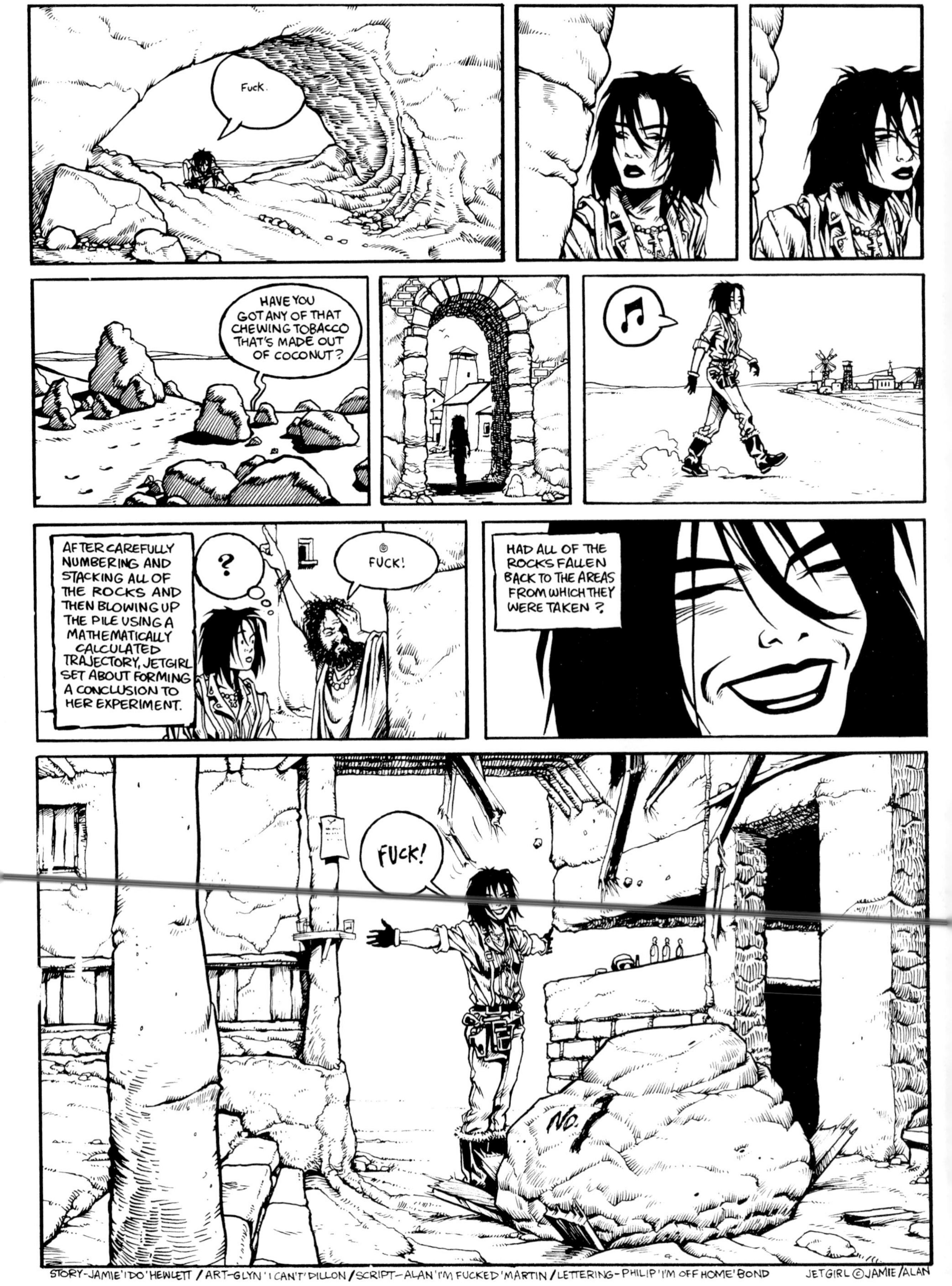
Fuck.
HAVE YOU GOT ANY OF THAT CHEWING TOBACCO THAT'S MADE OUT OF COCONUT?
♪
AFTER CAREFULLY NUMBERING AND STACKING ALL OF THE ROCKS AND THEN BLOWING UP THE PILE USING A MATHEMATICALLY CALCULATED TRAJECTORY, JETGIRL SET ABOUT FORMING A CONCLUSION TO HER EXPERIMENT.
?
FUCK!
HAD ALL OF THE ROCKS FALLEN BACK TO THE AREAS FROM WHICH THEY WERE TAKEN?
FUCK!

STORY-JAMIE 'I DO' HEWLETT / ART-GLYN 'I CAN'T' DILLON / SCRIPT-ALAN 'I'M FUCKED' MARTIN / LETTERING-PHILIP 'I'M OFF HOME' BOND

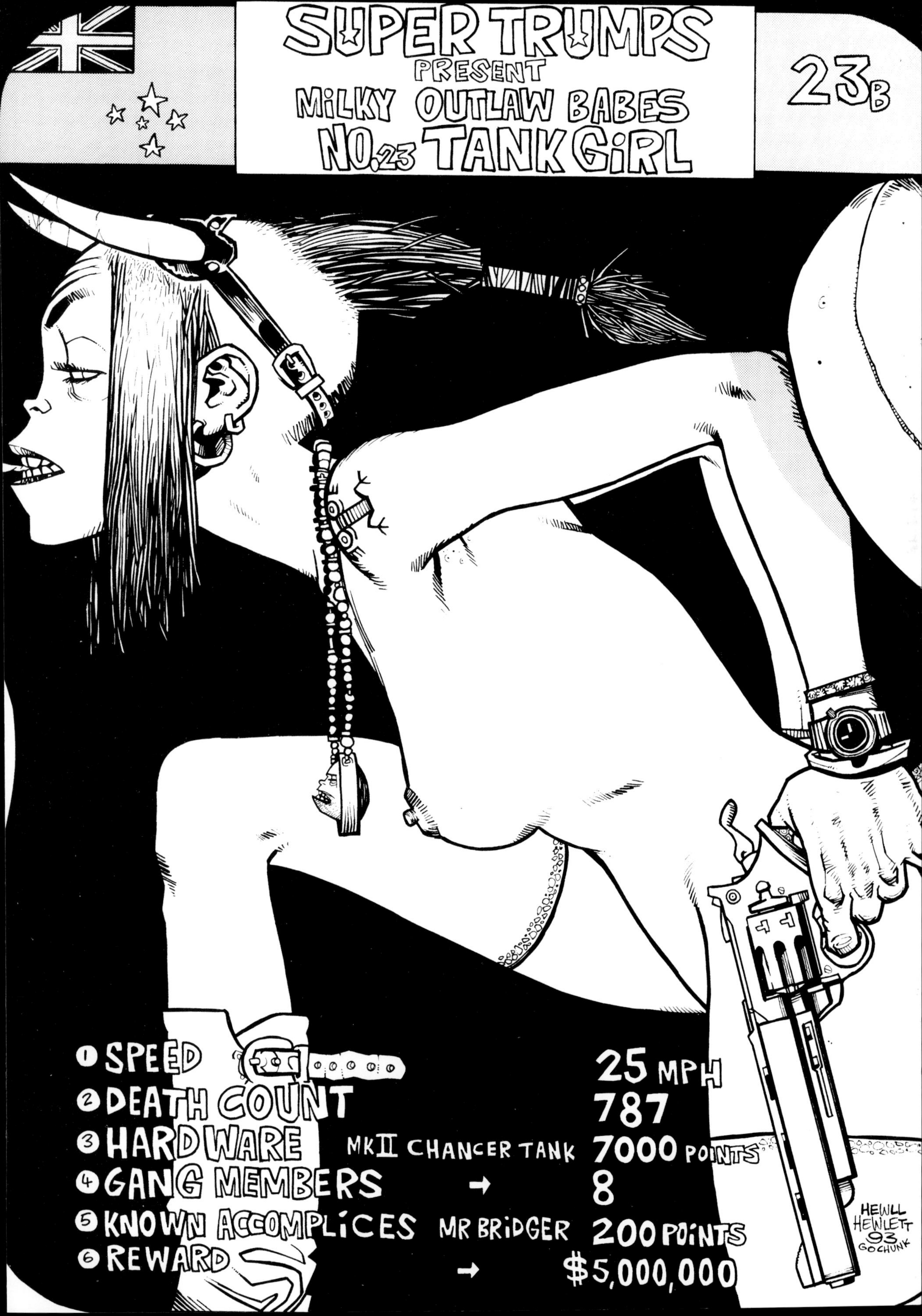
SUPER TRUMPS
PRESENT
MILKY OUTLAW BABES
NO.23 TANK GIRL
23B
1 SPEED 25 MPH
2 DEATH COUNT 787
3 HARDWARE MK II CHANCER TANK 7000 POINTS
4 GANG MEMBERS → 8
5 KNOWN ACCOMPLICES MR BRIDGER 200 POINTS
6 REWARD → $5,000,000
HEWLETT 93

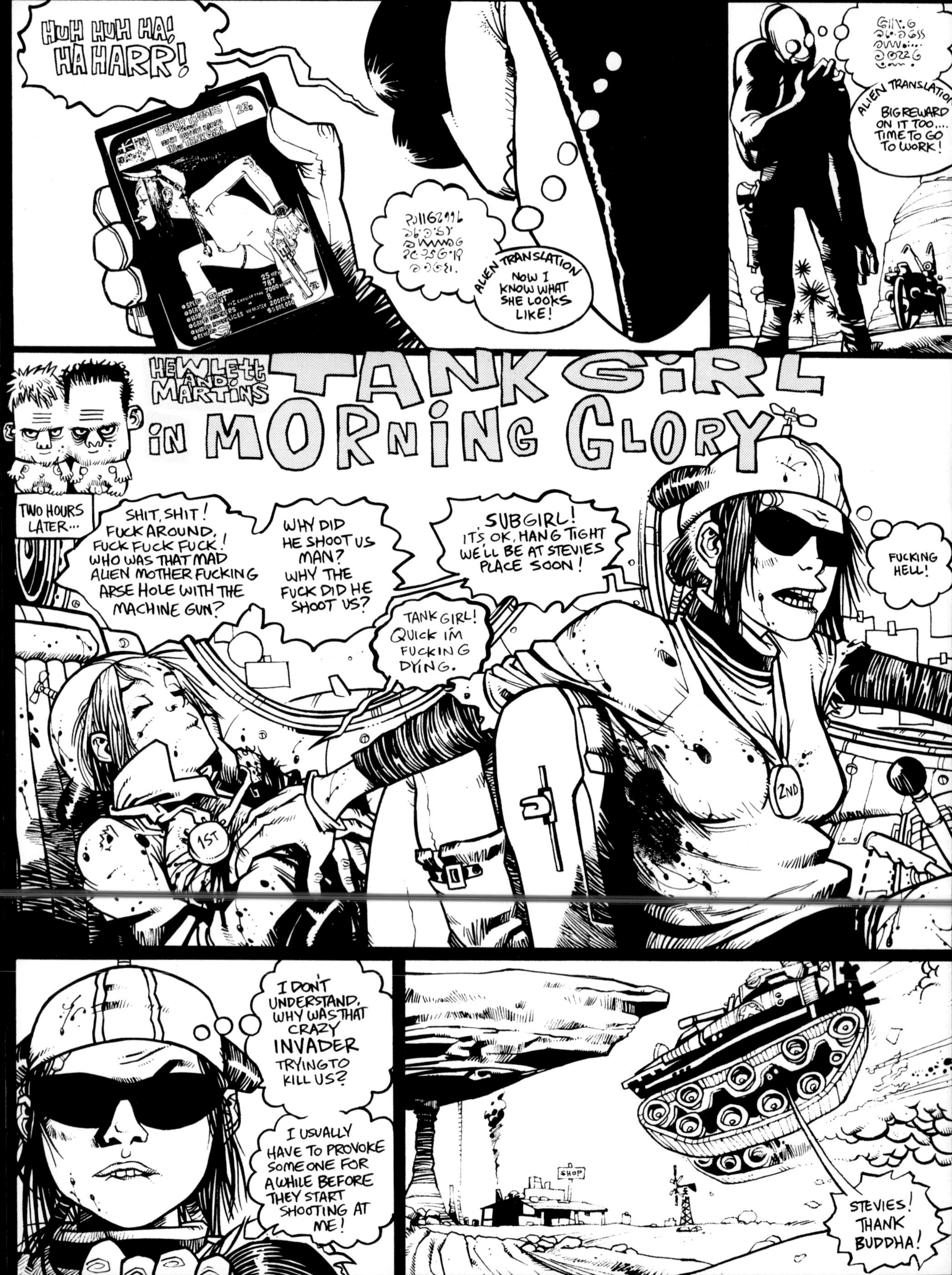

HUH HUH HA! HA HARR!
SUPER TRUMPS
TANK GIRL
23a
ALIEN TRANSLATION
NOW I KNOW WHAT SHE LOOKS LIKE!
ALIEN TRANSLATION
BIG REWARD ON IT TOO.... TIME TO GO TO WORK!
HEWLETT AND MARTINS
TANK GIRL
IN MORNING GLORY
TWO HOURS LATER...
SHIT, SHIT! FUCK AROUND, FUCK FUCK FUCK! WHO WAS THAT MAD ALIEN MOTHER FUCKING ARSE HOLE WITH THE MACHINE GUN?
WHY DID HE SHOOT US MAN? WHY THE FUCK DID HE SHOOT US?
SUBGIRL! IT'S OK, HANG TIGHT WE'LL BE AT STEVIES PLACE SOON!
FUCKING HELL!
TANK GIRL! QUICK I'M FUCKING DYING.
1ST
2ND
I DON'T UNDERSTAND, WHY WAS THAT CRAZY INVADER TRYING TO KILL US?
I USUALLY HAVE TO PROVOKE SOMEONE FOR A WHILE BEFORE THEY START SHOOTING AT ME!
SHOP
STEVIES! THANK BUDDHA!

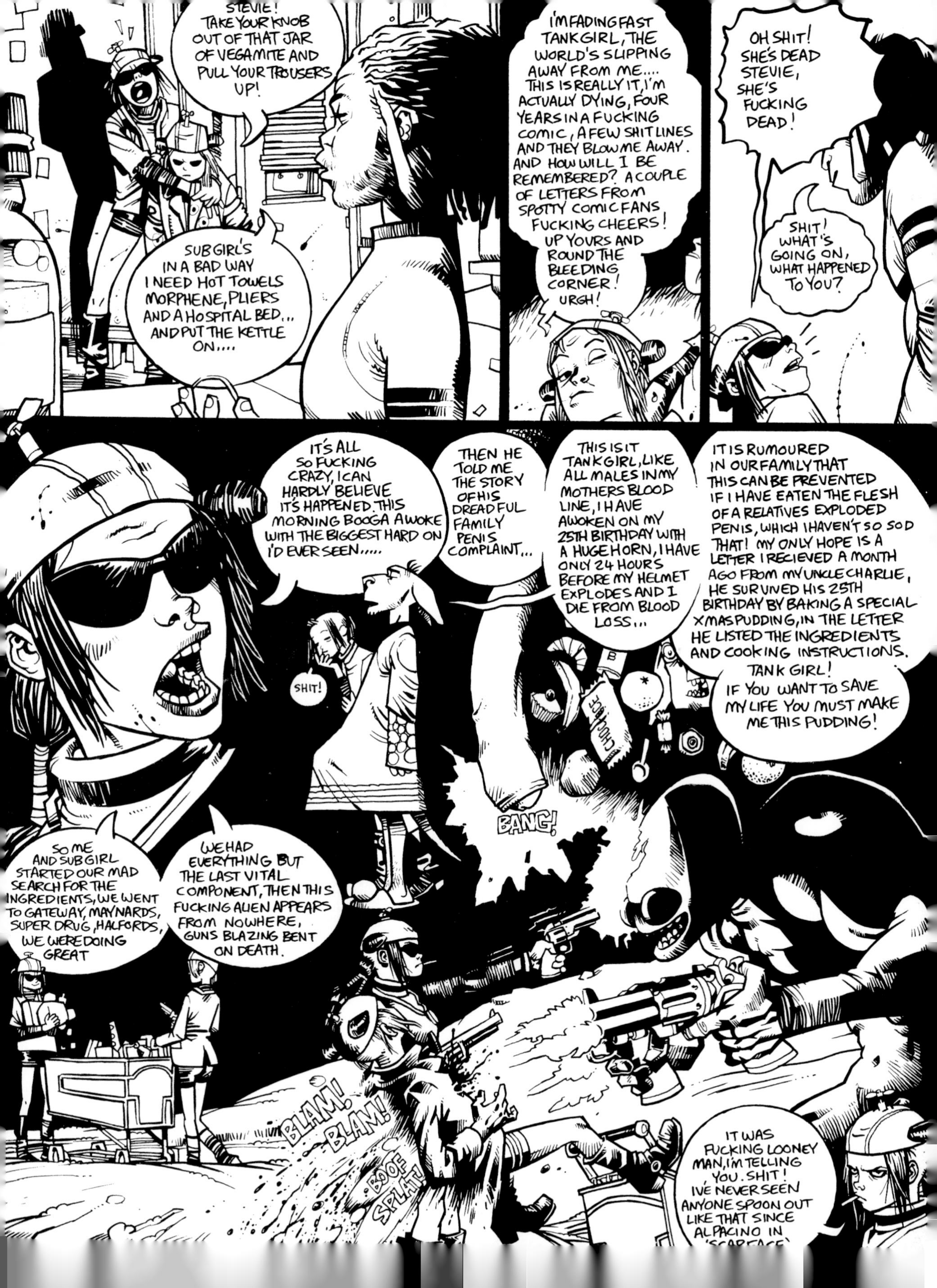
STEVIE! TAKE YOUR KNOB OUT OF THAT JAR OF VEGAMITE AND PULL YOUR TROUSERS UP!
SUBGIRL'S IN A BAD WAY I NEED HOT TOWELS MORPHENE, PLIERS AND A HOSPITAL BED... AND PUT THE KETTLE ON....
I'M FADING FAST TANKGIRL, THE WORLD'S SLIPPING AWAY FROM ME.... THIS IS REALLY IT, I'M ACTUALLY DYING, FOUR YEARS IN A FUCKING COMIC, A FEW SHIT LINES AND THEY BLOW ME AWAY. AND HOW WILL I BE REMEMBERED? A COUPLE OF LETTERS FROM SPOTTY COMIC FANS FUCKING CHEERS! UP YOURS AND ROUND THE BLEEDING CORNER! URGH!
OH SHIT! SHE'S DEAD STEVIE, SHE'S FUCKING DEAD!
SHIT! WHAT'S GOING ON, WHAT HAPPENED TO YOU?
IT'S ALL SO FUCKING CRAZY, I CAN HARDLY BELIEVE IT'S HAPPENED. THIS MORNING BOOGA AWOKE WITH THE BIGGEST HARD ON I'D EVER SEEN.....
SHIT!
THEN HE TOLD ME THE STORY OF HIS DREADFUL FAMILY PENIS COMPLAINT...
THIS IS IT TANKGIRL, LIKE ALL MALES IN MY MOTHERS BLOOD LINE, I HAVE AWOKEN ON MY 25TH BIRTHDAY WITH A HUGE HORN, I HAVE ONLY 24 HOURS BEFORE MY HELMET EXPLODES AND I DIE FROM BLOOD LOSS...
IT IS RUMOURED IN OUR FAMILY THAT THIS CAN BE PREVENTED IF I HAVE EATEN THE FLESH OF A RELATIVES EXPLODED PENIS, WHICH I HAVEN'T SO SOD THAT! MY ONLY HOPE IS A LETTER I RECIEVED A MONTH AGO FROM MY UNCLE CHARLIE, HE SURVIVED HIS 25TH BIRTHDAY BY BAKING A SPECIAL XMAS PUDDING, IN THE LETTER HE LISTED THE INGREDIENTS AND COOKING INSTRUCTIONS.
TANK GIRL! IF YOU WANT TO SAVE MY LIFE YOU MUST MAKE ME THIS PUDDING!
BANG!
SO ME AND SUBGIRL STARTED OUR MAD SEARCH FOR THE INGREDIENTS, WE WENT TO GATEWAY, MAYNARDS, SUPER DRUG, HALFORDS, WE WERE DOING GREAT
WE HAD EVERYTHING BUT THE LAST VITAL COMPONENT, THEN THIS FUCKING ALIEN APPEARS FROM NOWHERE, GUNS BLAZING BENT ON DEATH.
BLAM! BLAM!
BOOF
SPLAT
IT WAS FUCKING LOONEY MAN, I'M TELLING YOU. SHIT! I'VE NEVER SEEN ANYONE SPOON OUT LIKE THAT SINCE ALPACINO IN

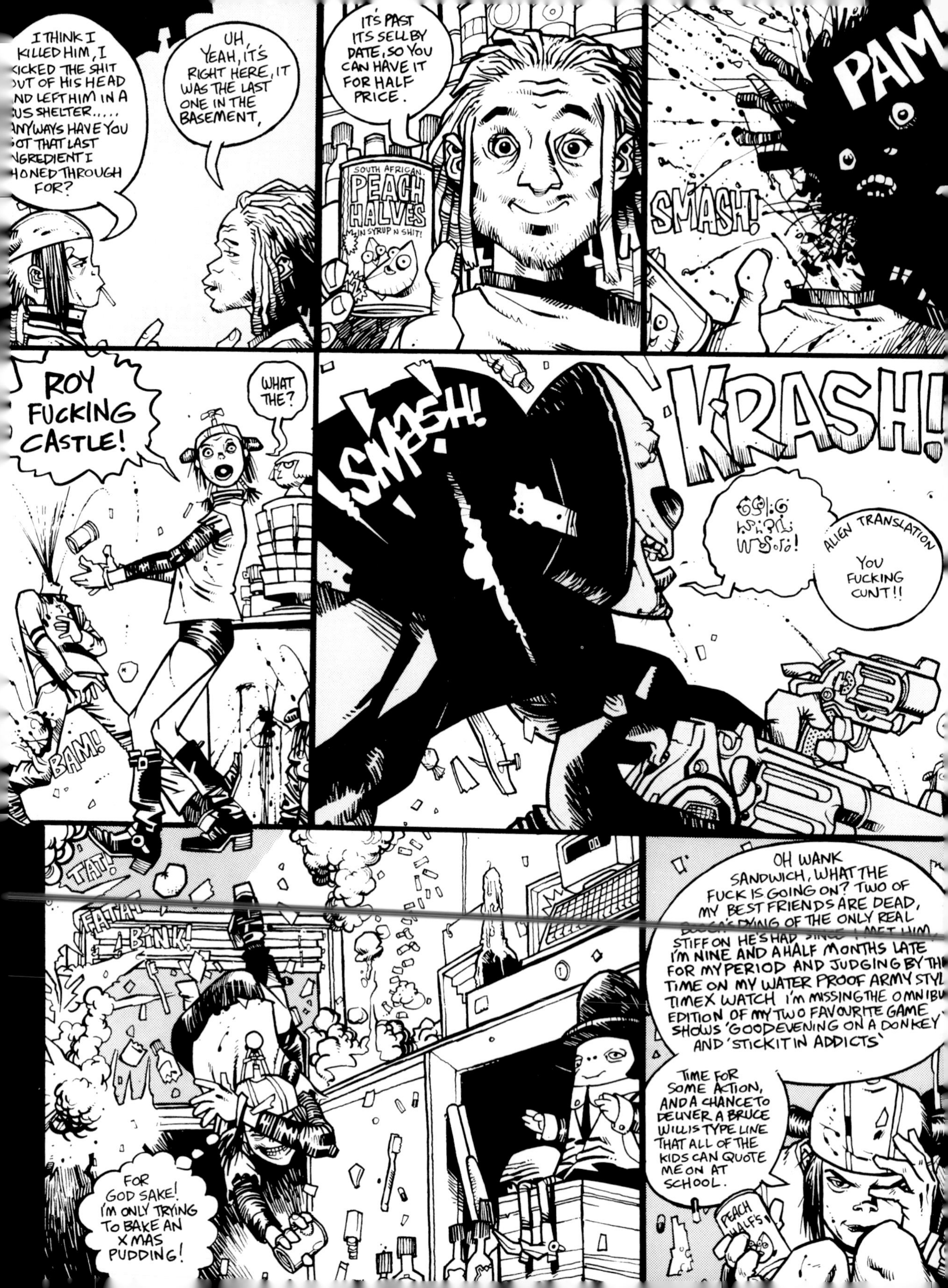
I THINK I KILLED HIM, I KICKED THE SHIT OUT OF HIS HEAD AND LEFT HIM IN A BUS SHELTER..... ANYWAYS HAVE YOU GOT THAT LAST INGREDIENT I PHONED THROUGH FOR?
UH, YEAH, IT'S RIGHT HERE, IT WAS THE LAST ONE IN THE BASEMENT,
IT'S PAST ITS SELL BY DATE, SO YOU CAN HAVE IT FOR HALF PRICE.
SOUTH AFRICAN PEACH HALVES IN SYRUP N SHIT!
PAM
SMASH!
ROY FUCKING CASTLE!
WHAT THE?
BAM!
SMASH!
KRASH!
ALIEN TRANSLATION
YOU FUCKING CUNT!!
TAT!
FATAL
BINK!
OH WANK SANDWICH, WHAT THE FUCK IS GOING ON? TWO OF MY BEST FRIENDS ARE DEAD, BOOGA'S DYING OF THE ONLY REAL STIFF ON HE'S HAD SINCE I MET HIM, I'M NINE AND A HALF MONTHS LATE FOR MY PERIOD AND JUDGING BY THE TIME ON MY WATER PROOF ARMY STYLE TIMEX WATCH I'M MISSING THE OMNIBUS EDITION OF MY TWO FAVOURITE GAME SHOWS 'GOODEVENING ON A DONKEY' AND 'STICKIT IN ADDICTS'
TIME FOR SOME ACTION, AND A CHANCE TO DELIVER A BRUCE WILLIS TYPE LINE THAT ALL OF THE KIDS CAN QUOTE ME ON AT SCHOOL.
FOR GOD SAKE! I'M ONLY TRYING TO BAKE AN X MAS PUDDING!
PEACH HALFS

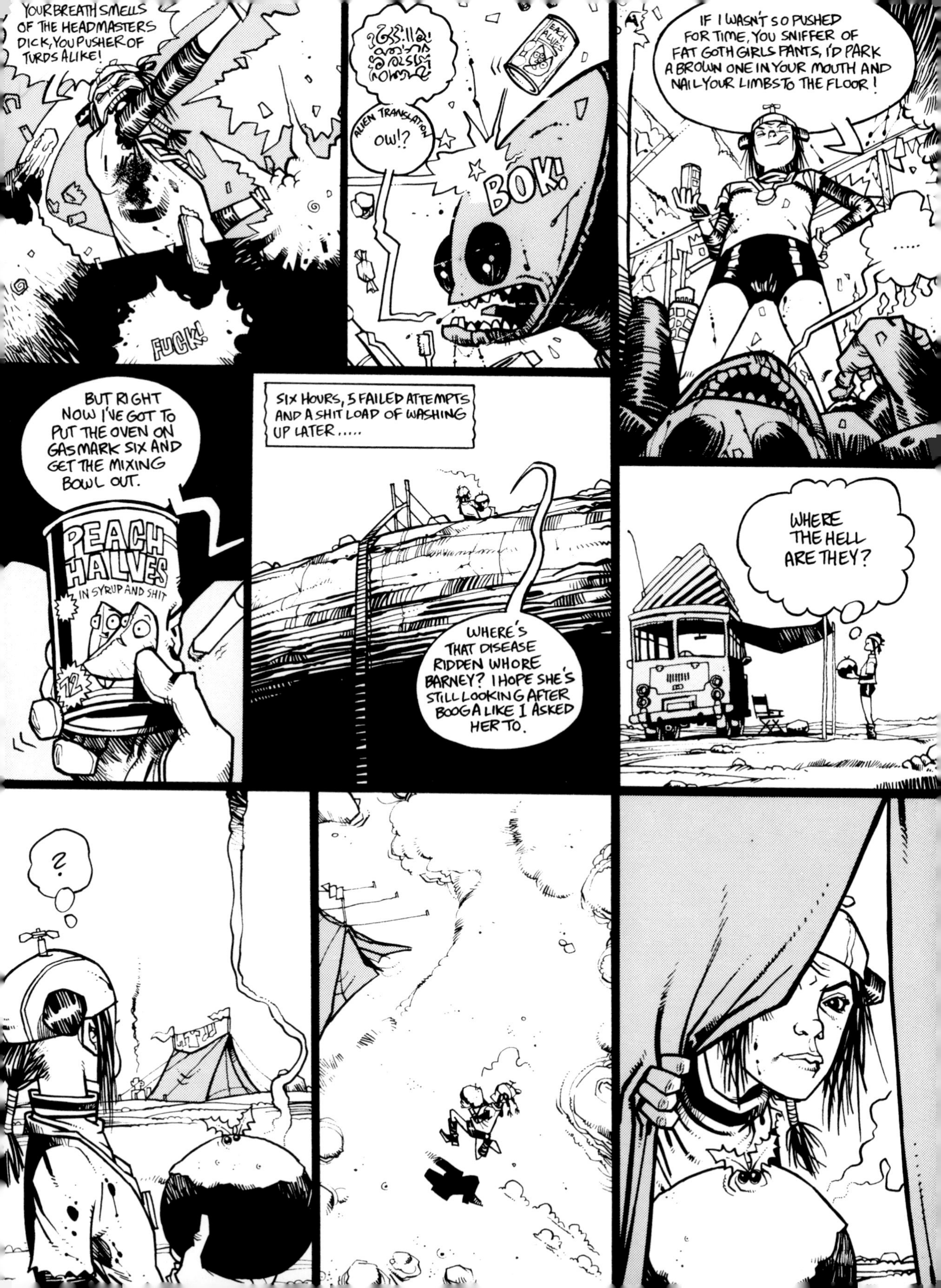
YOUR BREATH SMELLS OF THE HEADMASTERS DICK, YOU PUSHER OF TURDS ALIKE!
FUCK!
PEACH HALVES
ALIEN TRANSLATION
OW!?
BOK!
IF I WASN'T SO PUSHED FOR TIME, YOU SNIFFER OF FAT GOTH GIRLS PANTS, I'D PARK A BROWN ONE IN YOUR MOUTH AND NAIL YOUR LIMBS TO THE FLOOR!
.....
BUT RIGHT NOW I'VE GOT TO PUT THE OVEN ON GASMARK SIX AND GET THE MIXING BOWL OUT.
PEACH HALVES
IN SYRUP AND SHIT
SIX HOURS, 5 FAILED ATTEMPTS AND A SHIT LOAD OF WASHING UP LATER.....
WHERE'S THAT DISEASE RIDDEN WHORE BARNEY? I HOPE SHE'S STILL LOOKING AFTER BOOGA LIKE I ASKED HER TO.
WHERE THE HELL ARE THEY?
?

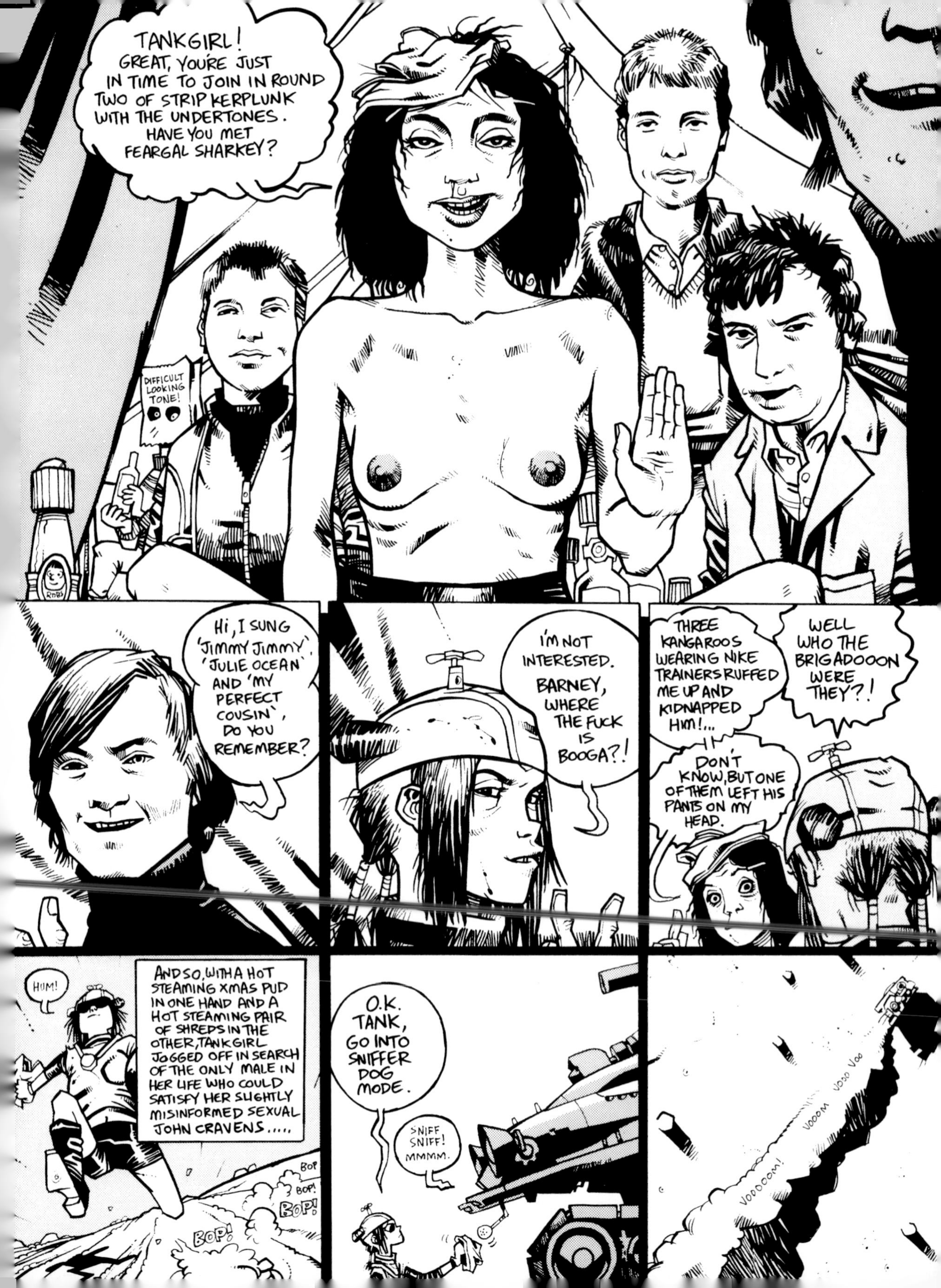
TANKGIRL! GREAT, YOU'RE JUST IN TIME TO JOIN IN ROUND TWO OF STRIP KERPLUNK WITH THE UNDERTONES. HAVE YOU MET FEARGAL SHARKEY?
DIFFICULT LOOKING TONE!
Hi, I SUNG 'JIMMY JIMMY', 'JULIE OCEAN' AND 'MY PERFECT COUSIN', DO YOU REMEMBER?
I'M NOT INTERESTED. BARNEY, WHERE THE FUCK IS BOOGA?!
THREE KANGAROOS WEARING NIKE TRAINERS RUFFED ME UP AND KIDNAPPED HIM!...
WELL WHO THE BRIGADOOON WERE THEY?!
DON'T KNOW, BUT ONE OF THEM LEFT HIS PANTS ON MY HEAD.
HUM!
AND SO, WITH A HOT STEAMING XMAS PUD IN ONE HAND AND A HOT STEAMING PAIR OF SHREDS IN THE OTHER, TANKGIRL JOGGED OFF IN SEARCH OF THE ONLY MALE IN HER LIFE WHO COULD SATISFY HER SLIGHTLY MISINFORMED SEXUAL JOHN CRAVENS.....
BOP
BOP!
BOP!
BOP!
O.K. TANK, GO INTO SNIFFER DOG MODE.
SNIFF SNIFF! MMMM.
VOOOOM!
VOOOM
VOOO VOO

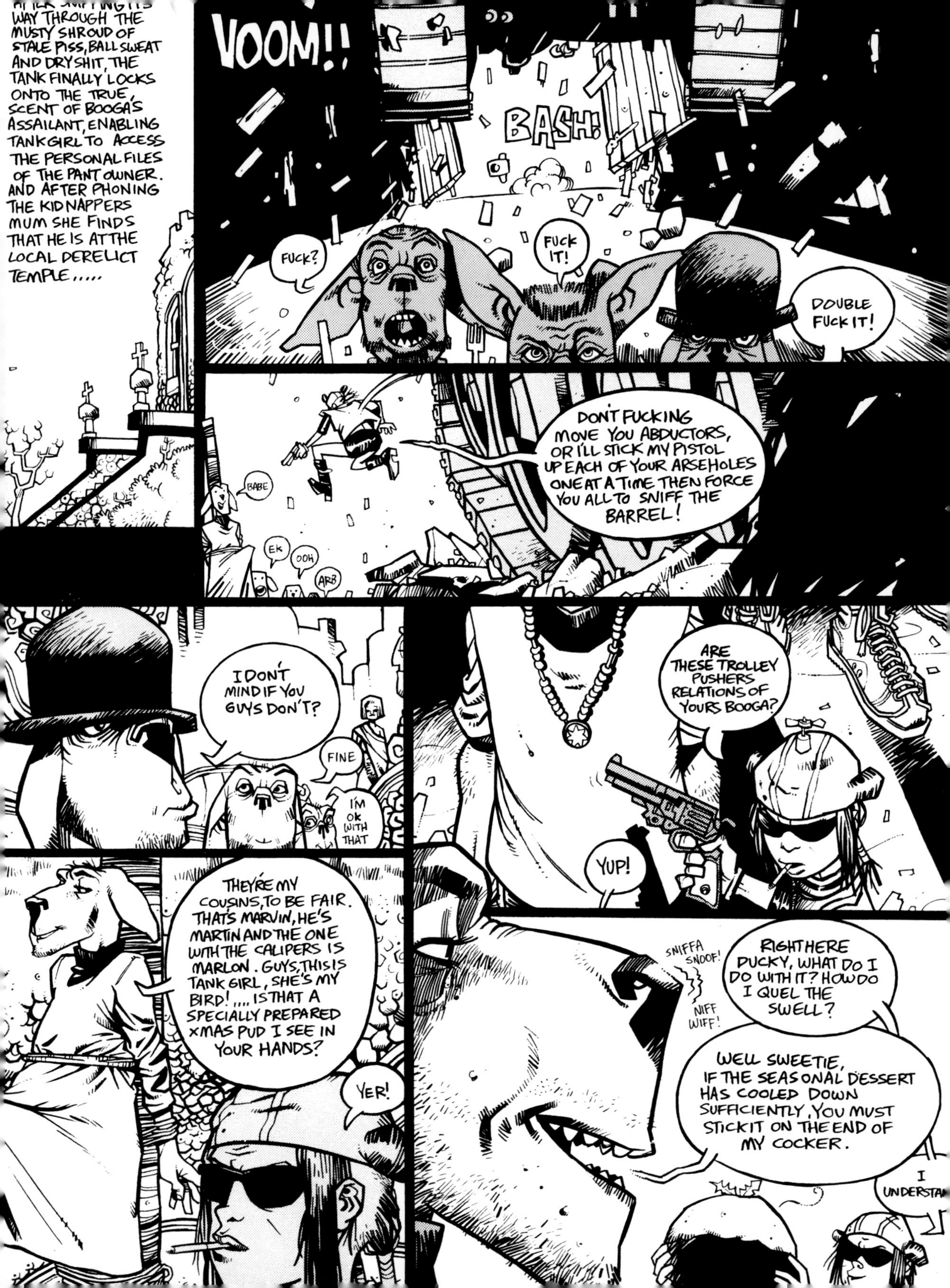
WAY THROUGH THE MUSTY SHROUD OF STALE PISS, BALL SWEAT AND DRY SHIT, THE TANK FINALLY LOCKS ONTO THE TRUE, SCENT OF BOOGA'S ASSAILANT, ENABLING TANK GIRL TO ACCESS THE PERSONAL FILES OF THE PANT OWNER. AND AFTER PHONING THE KIDNAPPERS MUM SHE FINDS THAT HE IS AT THE LOCAL DERELICT TEMPLE.....
VOOM!!
BASH!
FUCK?
FUCK IT!
DOUBLE FUCK IT!
DON'T FUCKING MOVE YOU ABDUCTORS, OR I'LL STICK MY PISTOL UP EACH OF YOUR ARSEHOLES ONE AT A TIME THEN FORCE YOU ALL TO SNIFF THE BARREL!
BABE
EK
OOH
ARB
I DON'T MIND IF YOU GUYS DON'T?
FINE
I'M OK WITH THAT
ARE THESE TROLLEY PUSHERS RELATIONS OF YOURS BOOGA?
YUP!
THEY'RE MY COUSINS, TO BE FAIR. THAT'S MARVIN, HE'S MARTIN AND THE ONE WITH THE CALIPERS IS MARLON. GUYS, THIS IS TANK GIRL, SHE'S MY BIRD! .... IS THAT A SPECIALLY PREPARED XMAS PUD I SEE IN YOUR HANDS?
YER!
SNIFFA SNOOF!
NIFF WIFF!
RIGHT HERE DUCKY, WHAT DO I DO WITH IT? HOW DO I QUEL THE SWELL?
WELL SWEETIE, IF THE SEASONAL DESSERT HAS COOLED DOWN SUFFICIENTLY, YOU MUST STICK IT ON THE END OF MY COCKER.

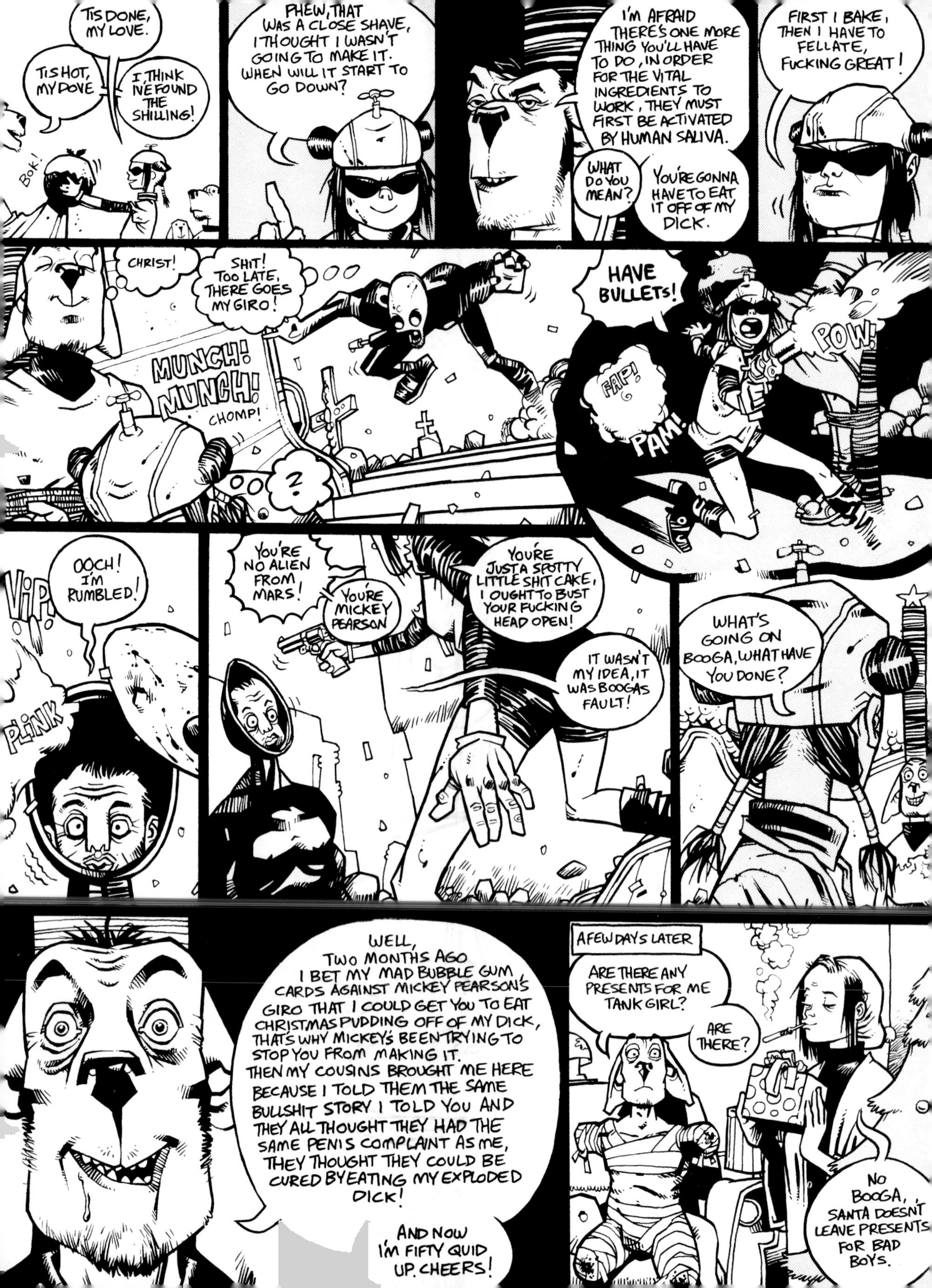
TIS DONE, MY LOVE.
TIS HOT, MY DOVE
I THINK I'VE FOUND THE SHILLING!
BOK!
PHEW, THAT WAS A CLOSE SHAVE, I THOUGHT I WASN'T GOING TO MAKE IT. WHEN WILL IT START TO GO DOWN?
I'M AFRAID THERE'S ONE MORE THING YOU'LL HAVE TO DO, IN ORDER FOR THE VITAL INGREDIENTS TO WORK, THEY MUST FIRST BE ACTIVATED BY HUMAN SALIVA.
WHAT DO YOU MEAN?
YOU'RE GONNA HAVE TO EAT IT OFF OF MY DICK.
FIRST I BAKE, THEN I HAVE TO FELLATE, FUCKING GREAT!
CHRIST!
SHIT! TOO LATE, THERE GOES MY GIRO!
MUNCH! MUNCH!
CHOMP!
?
HAVE BULLETS!
POW!
FAP!
PAM!
VIP!
OOCH! I'M RUMBLED!
PLINK
YOU'RE NO ALIEN FROM MARS!
YOU'RE MICKEY PEARSON
YOU'RE JUST A SPOTTY LITTLE SHIT CAKE, I OUGHT TO BUST YOUR FUCKING HEAD OPEN!
IT WASN'T MY IDEA, IT WAS BOOGAS FAULT!
WHAT'S GOING ON BOOGA, WHAT HAVE YOU DONE?
WELL, TWO MONTHS AGO I BET MY MAD BUBBLE GUM CARDS AGAINST MICKEY PEARSON'S GIRO THAT I COULD GET YOU TO EAT CHRISTMAS PUDDING OFF OF MY DICK, THAT'S WHY MICKEY'S BEEN TRYING TO STOP YOU FROM MAKING IT. THEN MY COUSINS BROUGHT ME HERE BECAUSE I TOLD THEM THE SAME BULLSHIT STORY I TOLD YOU AND THEY ALL THOUGHT THEY HAD THE SAME PENIS COMPLAINT AS ME, THEY THOUGHT THEY COULD BE CURED BY EATING MY EXPLODED DICK!
AND NOW I'M FIFTY QUID UP. CHEERS!
A FEW DAYS LATER
ARE THERE ANY PRESENTS FOR ME TANK GIRL?
ARE THERE?
NO BOOGA, SANTA DOESN'T LEAVE PRESENTS FOR BAD BOYS.

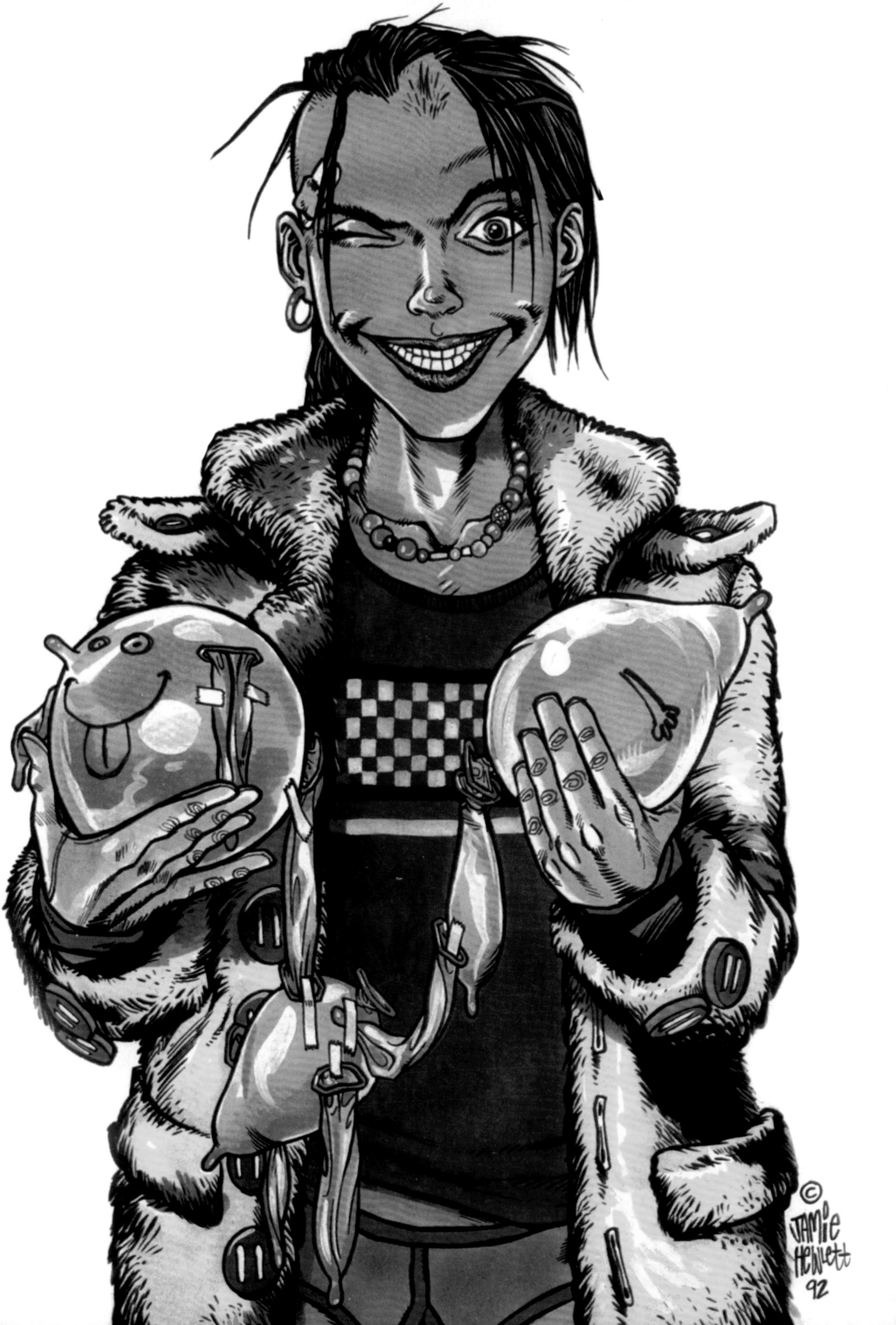
© JAMIE HEWLETT 92

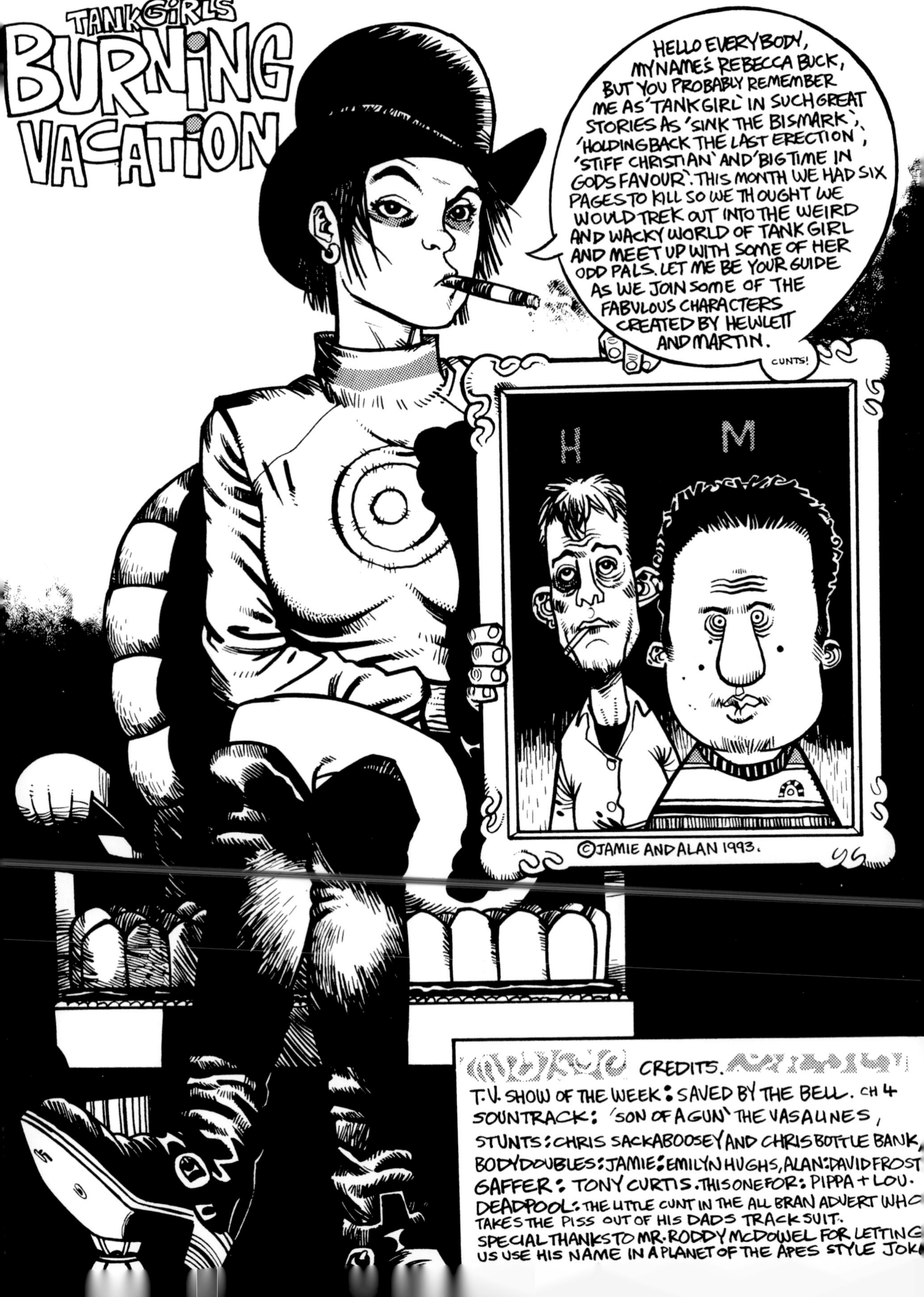
TANK GIRL'S BURNING VACATION
HELLO EVERYBODY, MY NAME'S REBECCA BUCK, BUT YOU PROBABLY REMEMBER ME AS 'TANK GIRL' IN SUCH GREAT STORIES AS 'SINK THE BISMARK', 'HOLDING BACK THE LAST ERECTION', 'STIFF CHRISTIAN' AND 'BIG TIME IN GODS FAVOUR'. THIS MONTH WE HAD SIX PAGES TO KILL SO WE THOUGHT WE WOULD TREK OUT INTO THE WEIRD AND WACKY WORLD OF TANK GIRL AND MEET UP WITH SOME OF HER ODD PALS. LET ME BE YOUR GUIDE AS WE JOIN SOME OF THE FABULOUS CHARACTERS CREATED BY HEWLETT AND MARTIN.
CUNTS!
H
M
©JAMIE AND ALAN 1993.
CREDITS.
T.V. SHOW OF THE WEEK: SAVED BY THE BELL. CH 4
SOUNTRACK: 'SON OF A GUN' THE VASALINES,
STUNTS: CHRIS SACKABOOSEY AND CHRIS BOTTLE BANK,
BODY DOUBLES: JAMIE: EMILYN HUGHS, ALAN: DAVID FROST
GAFFER: TONY CURTIS. THIS ONE FOR: PIPPA + LOU.
DEADPOOL: THE LITTLE CUNT IN THE ALL BRAN ADVERT WHO TAKES THE PISS OUT OF HIS DADS TRACK SUIT.
SPECIAL THANKS TO MR. RODDY McDOWEL FOR LETTING US USE HIS NAME IN A PLANET OF THE APES STYLE JOK

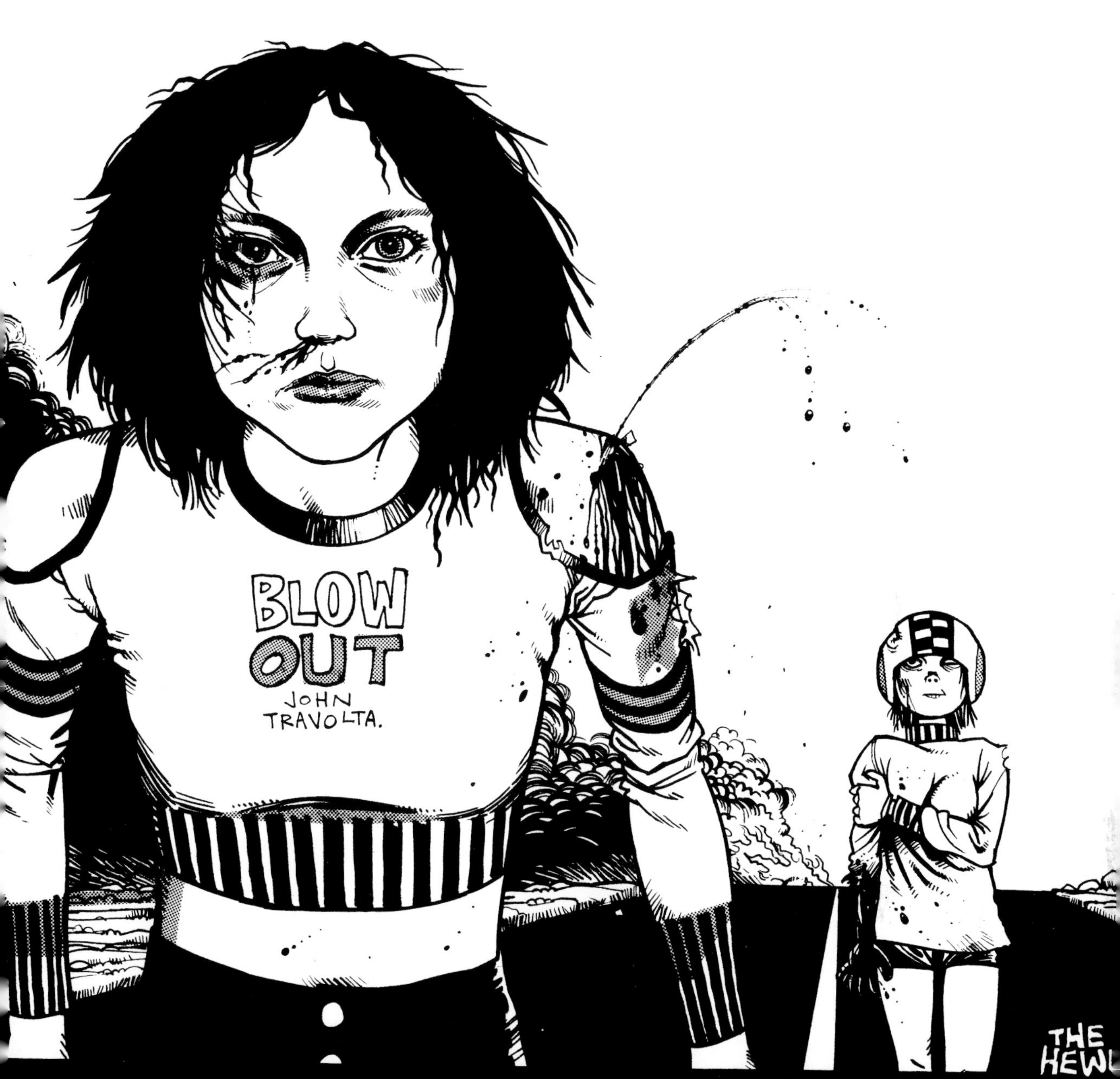
BLOW OUT
JOHN TRAVOLTA.
THE HEWL

STARTSMOKING.

IY FRIEND BARNEY IS A FUCKING HEAD CASE, I MET HER
N A MENTAL HOSPITAL. SHE LIKES TO STEEL CARS AND
RIVES LIKE A FUCKING IDIOT. ONE OF THESE DAYS SHE'LL
END UP IN STOKE MANDEVILLE SMOKING CIGAR BUTTS
VITH JIMMY SAVILLE. I FEEL CLOSE TO HER, WE'VE HAD SO
MANY NEAR DEATH EXPERIENCES TOGETHER, WE'VE
BONDED ON A VERY STRANGE LEVEL OF CONSCIOUSNESS.
MOST OF THE TIME SHE HANGS OUT WITH ALL OF OUR MATES
ND SMOKES POT, BUT SOMETIMES SHE SINGLES ME OUT FOR
NE OF HER TRIPS. I ALWAYS GO. HER FAVE FOOD IS TEA AND HER
AVE FILM STAR IS JAMES DEAN. SHE'S NOT RIGHT IN THE HEAD,
HAT'S WHY SHE'S NEVER BEEN FUCKED.

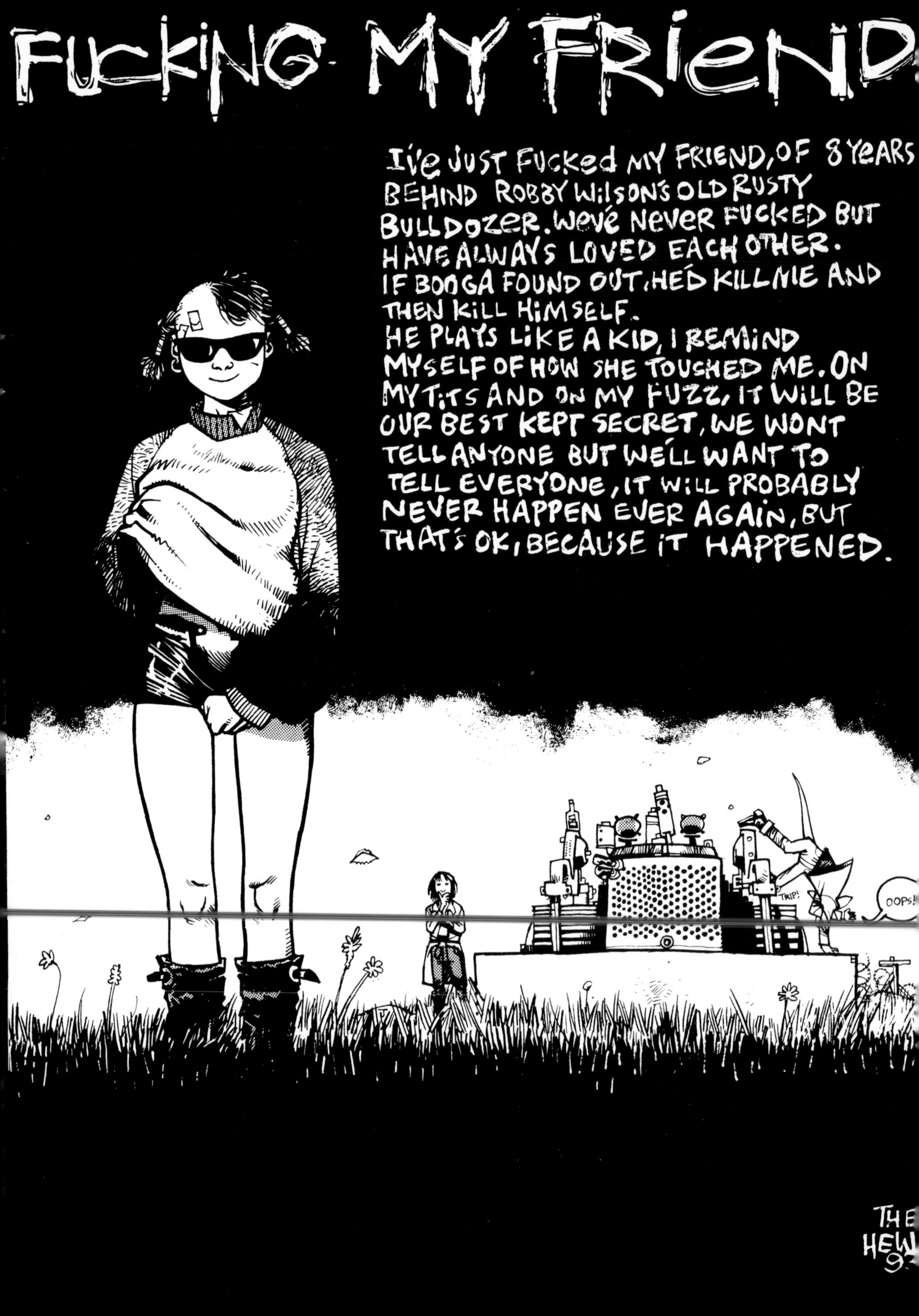
FUCKING MY FRIEND
I'VE JUST FUCKED MY FRIEND, OF 8 YEARS BEHIND ROBBY WILSON'S OLD RUSTY BULLDOZER. WE'VE NEVER FUCKED BUT HAVE ALWAYS LOVED EACH OTHER. IF BOOGA FOUND OUT, HE'D KILL ME AND THEN KILL HIMSELF. HE PLAYS LIKE A KID, I REMIND MYSELF OF HOW SHE TOUCHED ME. ON MY TITS AND ON MY FUZZ, IT WILL BE OUR BEST KEPT SECRET, WE WONT TELL ANYONE BUT WE'LL WANT TO TELL EVERYONE, IT WILL PROBABLY NEVER HAPPEN EVER AGAIN, BUT THAT'S OK, BECAUSE IT HAPPENED.
TRIP!
OOPS!
THE HEW 93

JAVIN THE FLEABAG!

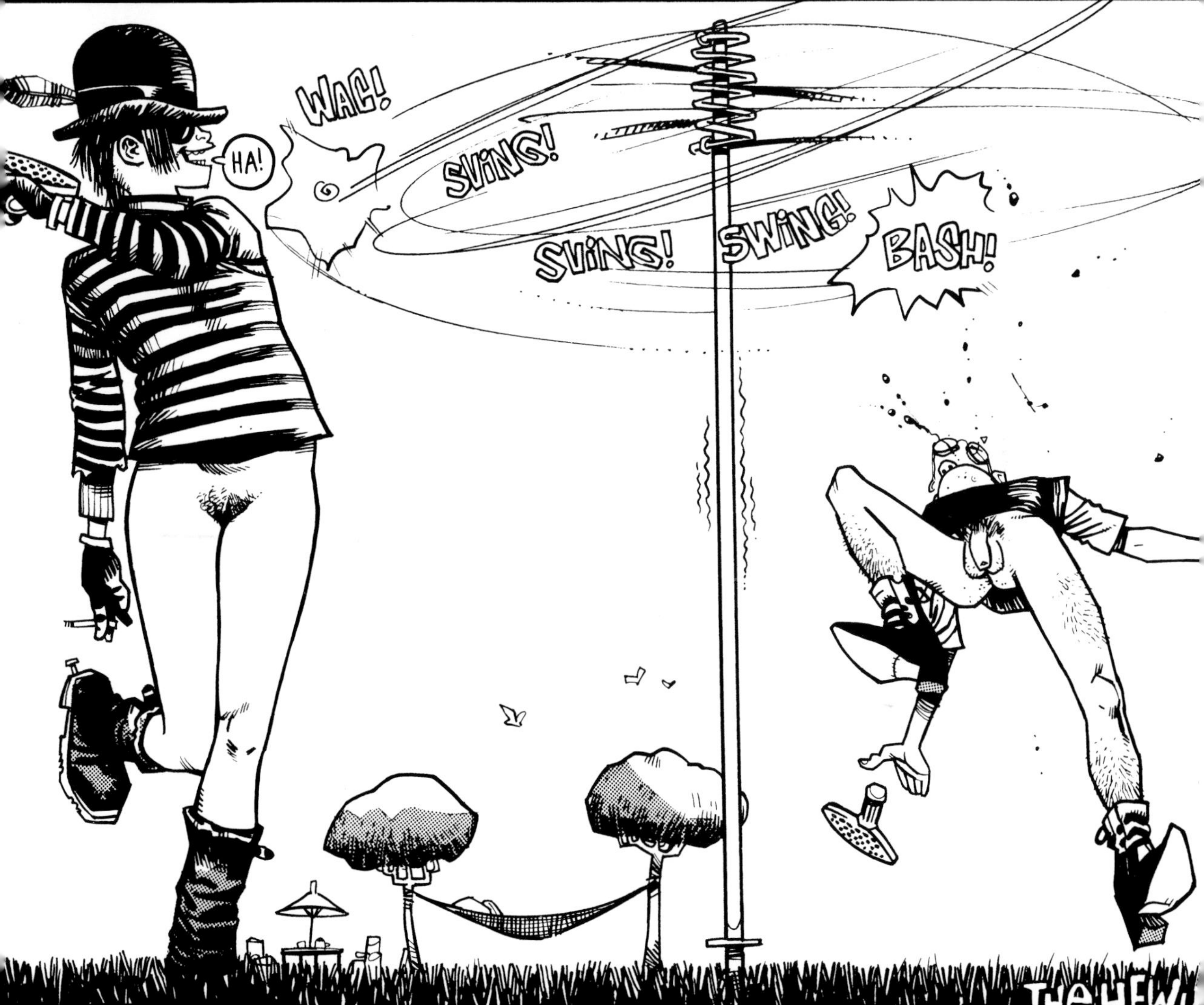

WAG!
HA!
SWING!
SWING!
SWING!
BASH!
THE HEWL

I DO SOMETHING SPECIAL ON FRIDAY AFTERNOONS. THE REST OF THE WEEK I HANG AROUND WITH THE GANG, WE RIDE OUR BIKES ON THE PAVEMENT, SET LIGHT TO OUR PUBES, STEAL, LIE, BREAK THINGS, SMOKE FAGS DOWN TO THE BUTT, DRAW NOBS ON MODELS IN SKY MAGAZINE, PUNCH PEOPLE AND SOMETIMES WE CRUISE INTO THE McDRIVE-IN OF McDONALDS AND ORDER A McSPUNK SHAKE, THEN WE CALL THEM McCUNTS AND McPETROL BOMB THE McFUCKING JOINT. BUT ON FRIDAY AFTERNOON I GO AND PLAY WITH MY FRIEND 'GAVIN THE FLEABAG'. I NEVER TELL ANYONE WHERE I AM, SOMETIMES I SAY I'M GOING TO SEE MY GYNAECOLOGIST, THEN NO ONE PROBES ME BECAUSE SOMETHING SMELLS FISHY. MY SPECIAL TIME WITH GAVIN IS SPENT PRESSING FLOWERS, PRANCING, PLAYING DOCTORS AND NURSES, MENDING THINGS, LISTENING TO 'THE LAMB LIES DOWN ON BROADWAY' BY GENESIS, CRYING, PLAYING BLOW FOOTBALL AND SOMETIMES WE GO OUT TO THE BACK GARDEN WITH NO PANTS ON AND JUMP OVER THE GARDEN SPRINKLER. WHEN I'M WITH MY FRIENDS AND I SEE GAVIN, I BLANK HIM.

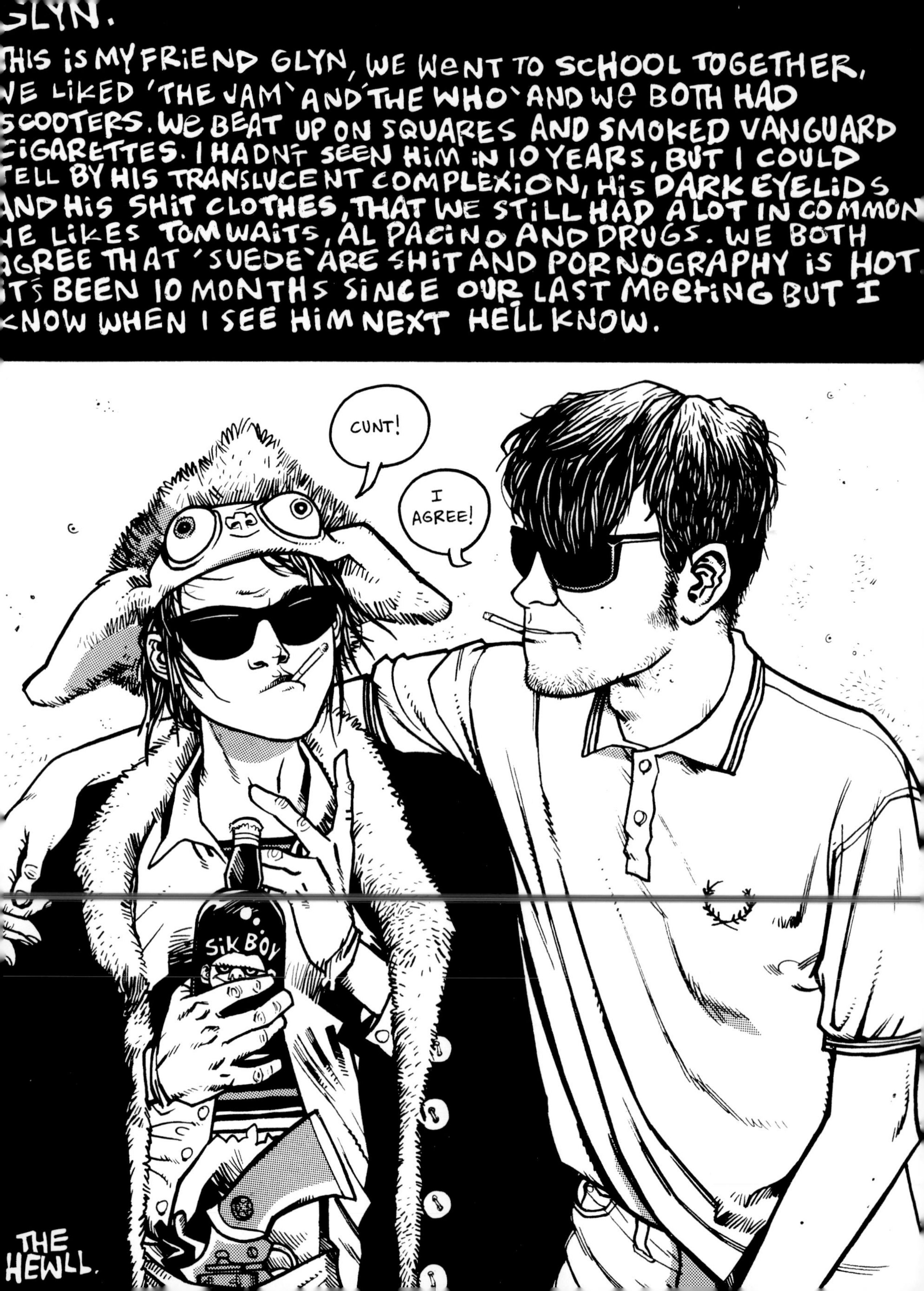
GLYN.
THIS IS MY FRIEND GLYN, WE WENT TO SCHOOL TOGETHER, WE LIKED 'THE JAM' AND 'THE WHO' AND WE BOTH HAD SCOOTERS. WE BEAT UP ON SQUARES AND SMOKED VANGUARD CIGARETTES. I HADN'T SEEN HIM IN 10 YEARS, BUT I COULD TELL BY HIS TRANSLUCENT COMPLEXION, HIS DARK EYELIDS AND HIS SHIT CLOTHES, THAT WE STILL HAD A LOT IN COMMON. HE LIKES TOM WAITS, AL PACINO AND DRUGS. WE BOTH AGREE THAT 'SUEDE' ARE SHIT AND PORNOGRAPHY IS HOT. IT'S BEEN 10 MONTHS SINCE OUR LAST MEETING BUT I KNOW WHEN I SEE HIM NEXT HE'LL KNOW.
CUNT!
I AGREE!
SIK BOY
THE HEWLL.

PARTNERS.

WHEN I FIRST SAW BOOGA HE TRIED IT ON, SO I SAID, "DON'T YOU COME WALKING OVER TO ME LOOKING LIKE AN UNDERAGE RODDY McDOWEL." HE HAD'NT HAD MUCH EXPIERIENCE WITH GIRLS. I THINK I WAS HIS FIRST GIRLFRIEND AND THAT REALLY FREAKED HIM OUT. I TRIED TO KILL HIM ONCE BUT IT DIDN'T WORK. HE DOESN'T TALK ABOUT THAT MUCH, HE PRETENDS IT'S COOL. SOMETIMES I THINK WE HAVE A TELEPATHIC LINK. HE KNOWS TO DUCK WHEN I THROW A WOBBLER. HE KNOWS HOW TO MAKE MY TEA JUST RIGHT. HE'S GOOD AT SQUAT THRUSTS AND RUNNING. AND HE PLAYS A CUNNING GAME OF OTHELLO.

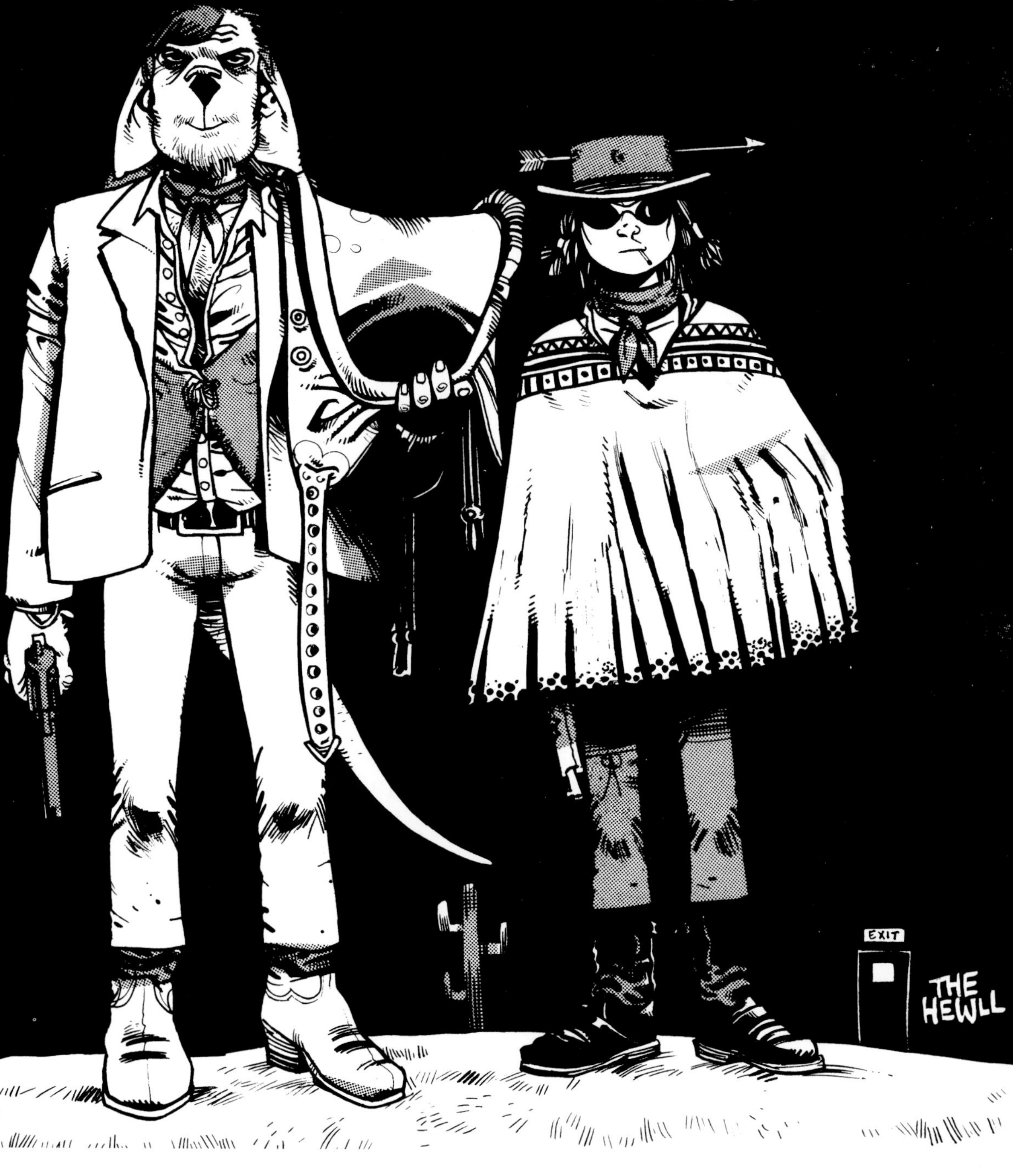
EXIT
THE HEWLL

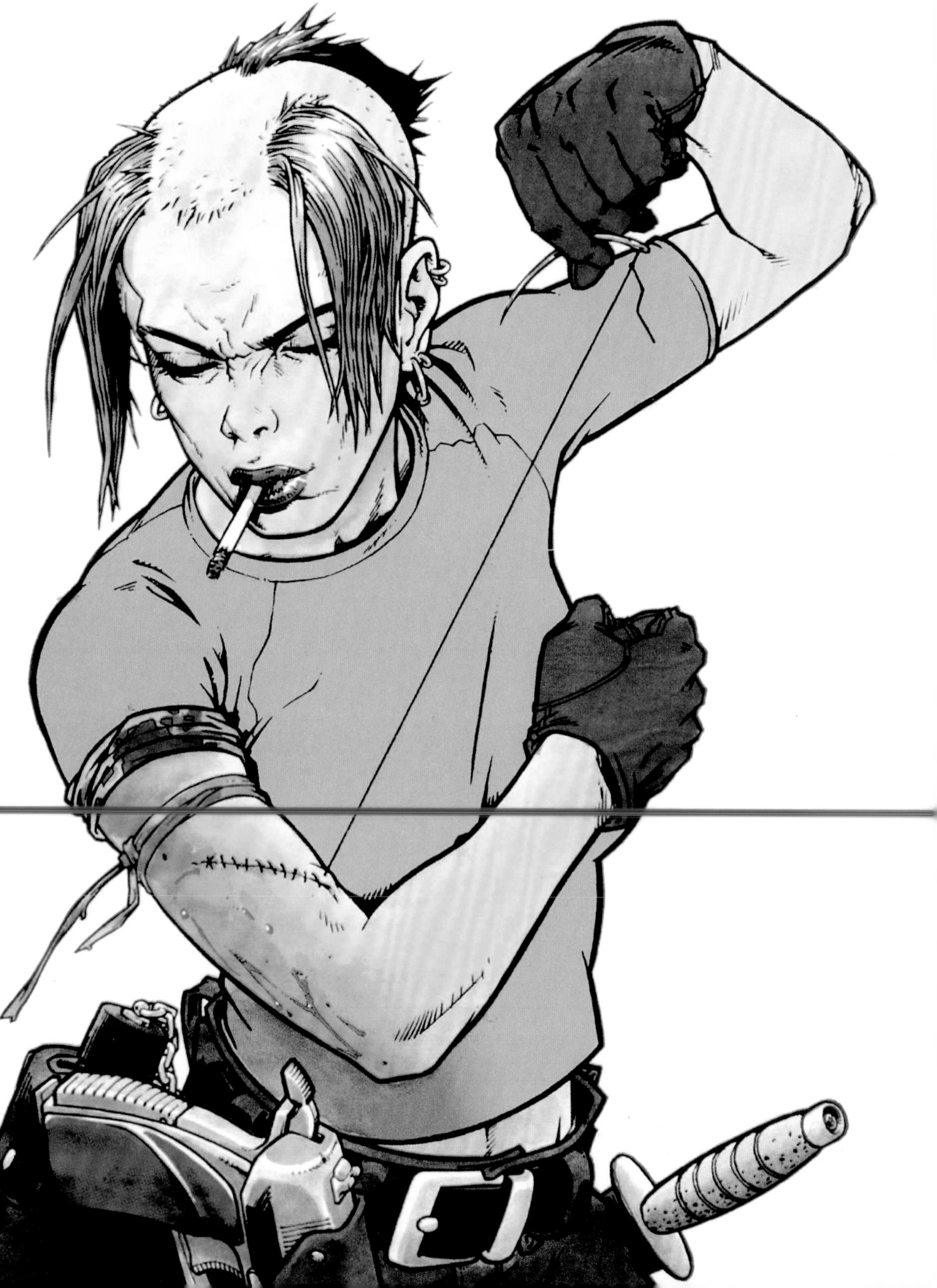

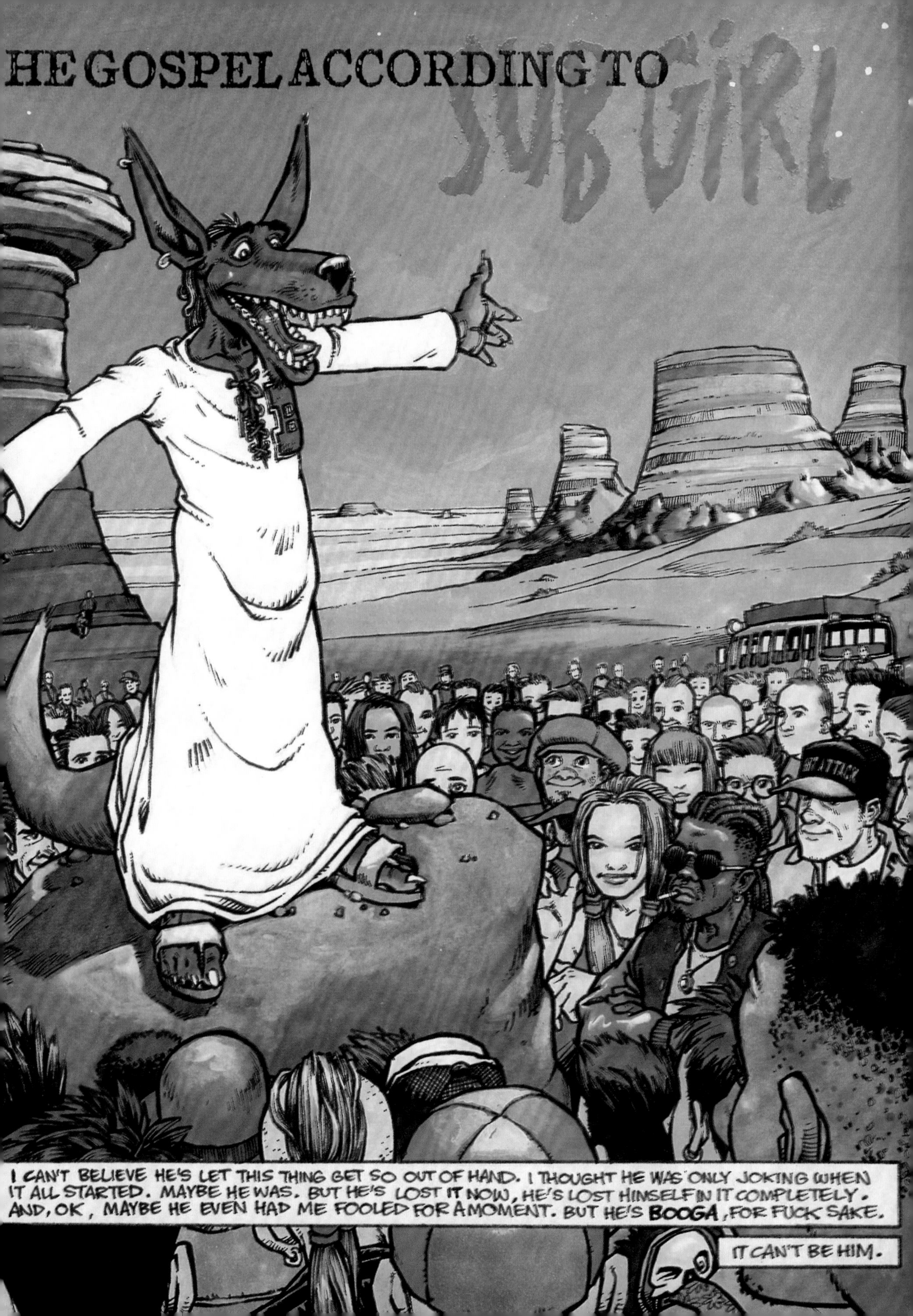
HE GOSPEL ACCORDING TO
SUB GIRL
I CAN'T BELIEVE HE'S LET THIS THING GET SO OUT OF HAND. I THOUGHT HE WAS ONLY JOKING WHEN IT ALL STARTED. MAYBE HE WAS. BUT HE'S LOST IT NOW, HE'S LOST HINSELF IN IT COMPLETELY. AND, OK, MAYBE HE EVEN HAD ME FOOLED FOR A MOMENT. BUT HE'S **BOOGA**, FOR FUCK SAKE.
IT CAN'T BE HIM.

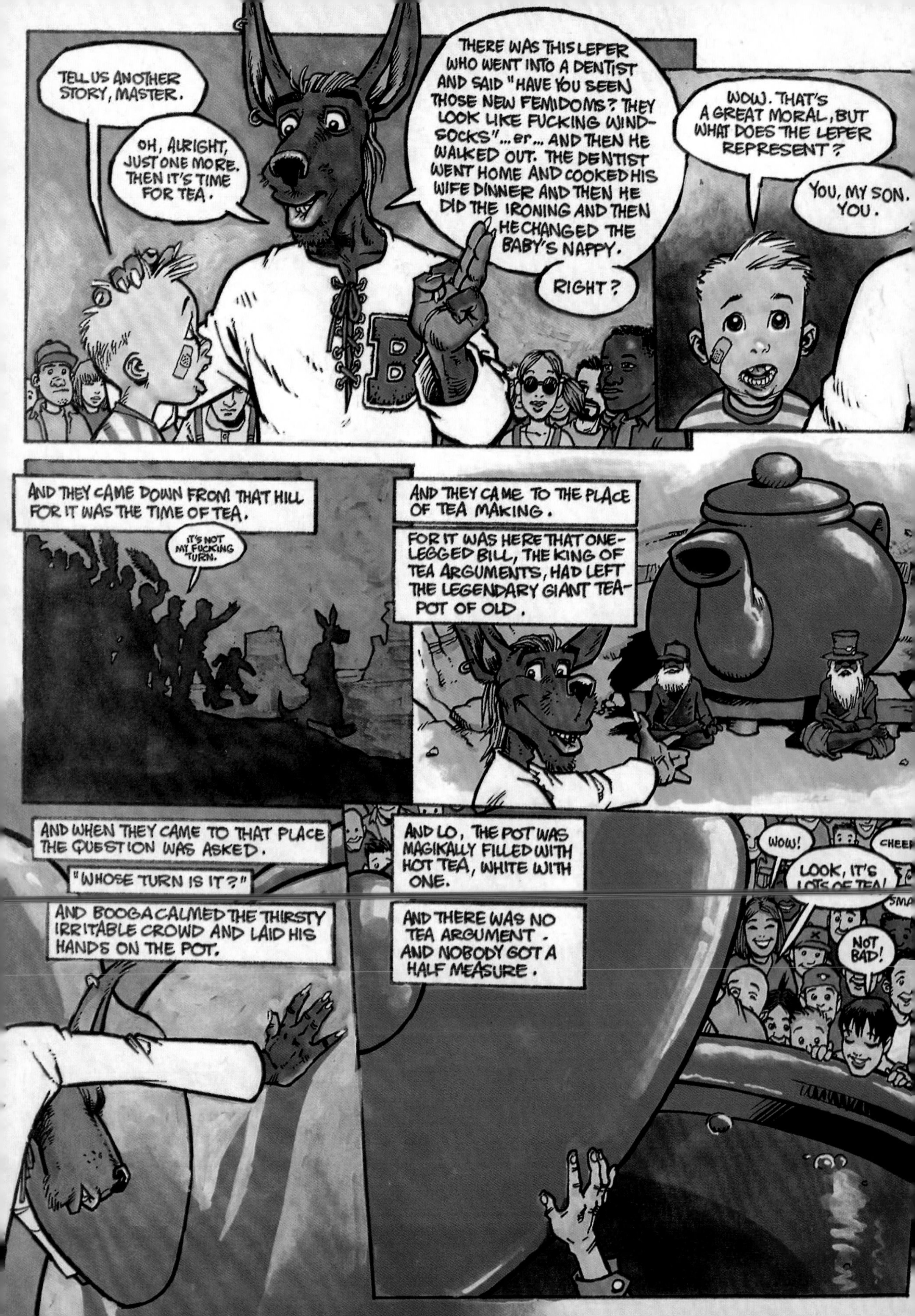
TELL US ANOTHER STORY, MASTER.
OH, ALRIGHT, JUST ONE MORE. THEN IT'S TIME FOR TEA.
THERE WAS THIS LEPER WHO WENT INTO A DENTIST AND SAID "HAVE YOU SEEN THOSE NEW FEMIDOMS? THEY LOOK LIKE FUCKING WIND-SOCKS"... er... AND THEN HE WALKED OUT. THE DENTIST WENT HOME AND COOKED HIS WIFE DINNER AND THEN HE DID THE IRONING AND THEN HE CHANGED THE BABY'S NAPPY.
RIGHT?
WOW. THAT'S A GREAT MORAL, BUT WHAT DOES THE LEPER REPRESENT?
YOU, MY SON. YOU.
AND THEY CAME DOWN FROM THAT HILL FOR IT WAS THE TIME OF TEA.
IT'S NOT MY FUCKING TURN.
AND THEY CAME TO THE PLACE OF TEA MAKING.
FOR IT WAS HERE THAT ONE-LEGGED BILL, THE KING OF TEA ARGUMENTS, HAD LEFT THE LEGENDARY GIANT TEA-POT OF OLD.
AND WHEN THEY CAME TO THAT PLACE THE QUESTION WAS ASKED.
"WHOSE TURN IS IT?"
AND BOOGA CALMED THE THIRSTY IRRITABLE CROWD AND LAID HIS HANDS ON THE POT.
AND LO, THE POT WAS MAGIKALLY FILLED WITH HOT TEA, WHITE WITH ONE.
AND THERE WAS NO TEA ARGUMENT. AND NOBODY GOT A HALF MEASURE.
WOW!
NOT BAD!

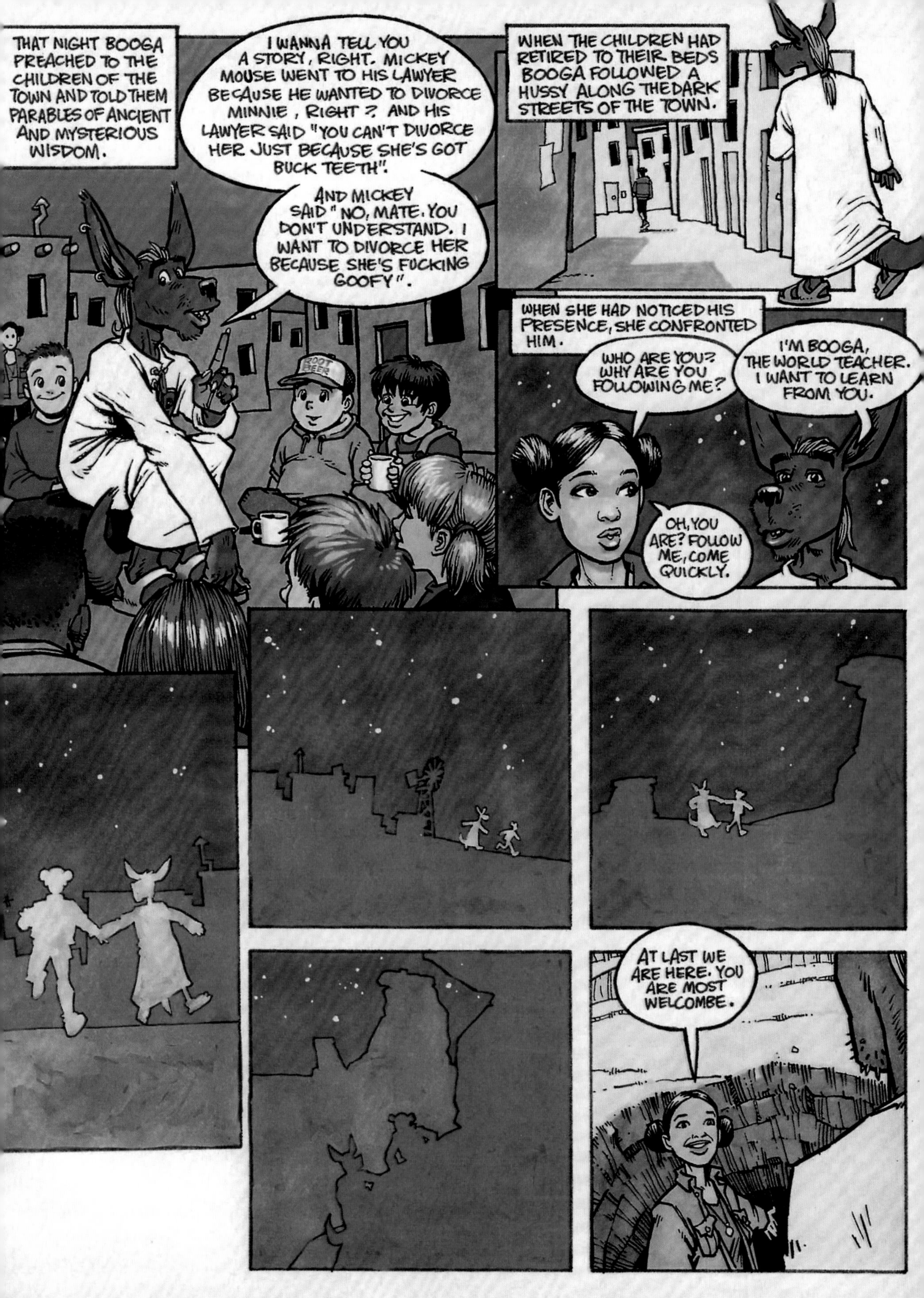
THAT NIGHT BOOGA PREACHED TO THE CHILDREN OF THE TOWN AND TOLD THEM PARABLES OF ANCIENT AND MYSTERIOUS WISDOM.
I WANNA TELL YOU A STORY, RIGHT. MICKEY MOUSE WENT TO HIS LAWYER BECAUSE HE WANTED TO DIVORCE MINNIE, RIGHT? AND HIS LAWYER SAID "YOU CAN'T DIVORCE HER JUST BECAUSE SHE'S GOT BUCK TEETH".
AND MICKEY SAID "NO, MATE. YOU DON'T UNDERSTAND. I WANT TO DIVORCE HER BECAUSE SHE'S FUCKING GOOFY".
ROOT BEER
WHEN THE CHILDREN HAD RETIRED TO THEIR BEDS BOOGA FOLLOWED A HUSSY ALONG THE DARK STREETS OF THE TOWN.
WHEN SHE HAD NOTICED HIS PRESENCE, SHE CONFRONTED HIM.
WHO ARE YOU? WHY ARE YOU FOLLOWING ME?
I'M BOOGA, THE WORLD TEACHER. I WANT TO LEARN FROM YOU.
OH, YOU ARE? FOLLOW ME, COME QUICKLY.
AT LAST WE ARE HERE. YOU ARE MOST WELCOMBE.

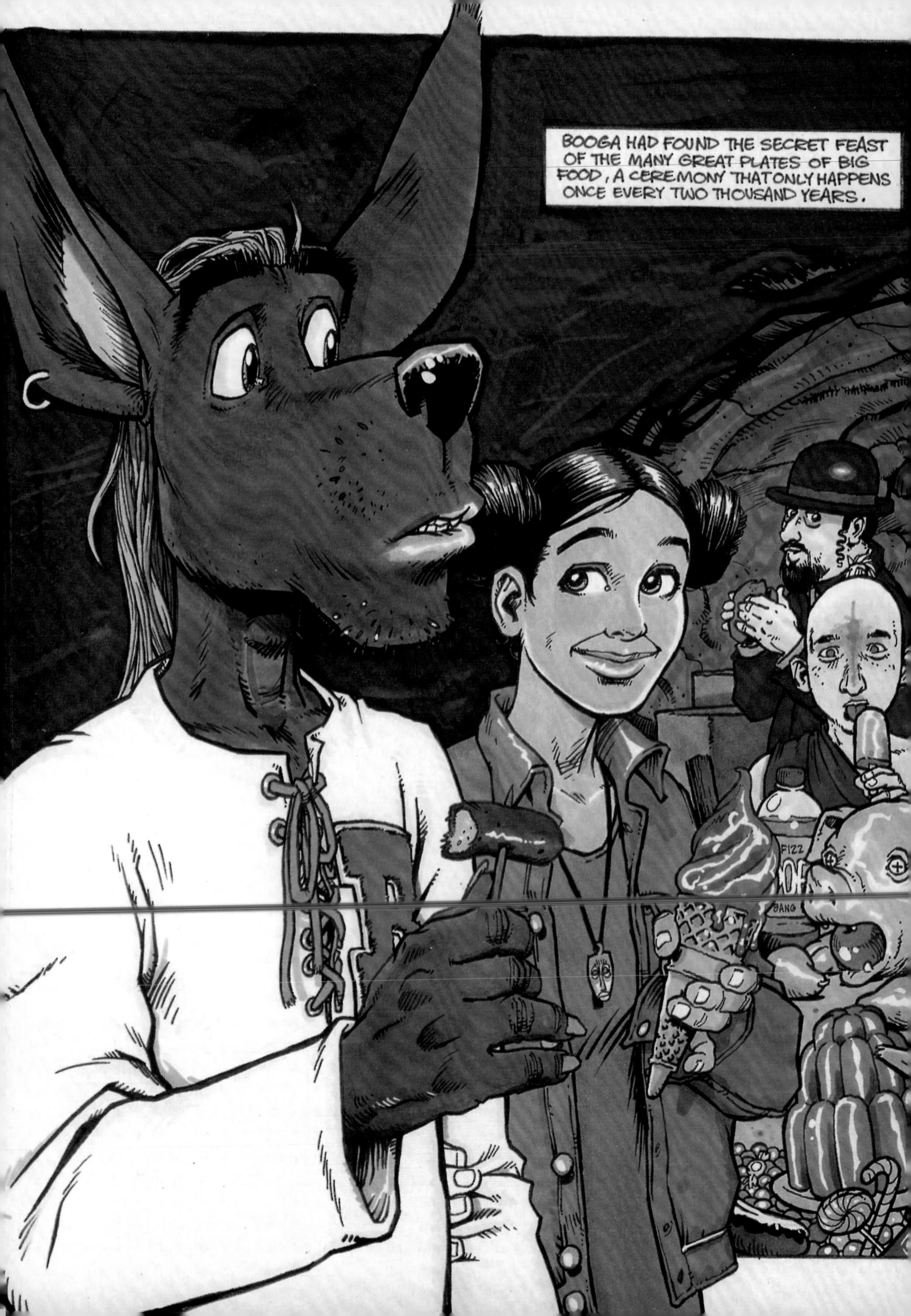
BOOGA HAD FOUND THE SECRET FEAST OF THE MANY GREAT PLATES OF BIG FOOD, A CEREMONY THAT ONLY HAPPENS ONCE EVERY TWO THOUSAND YEARS.
FIZZ
BANG

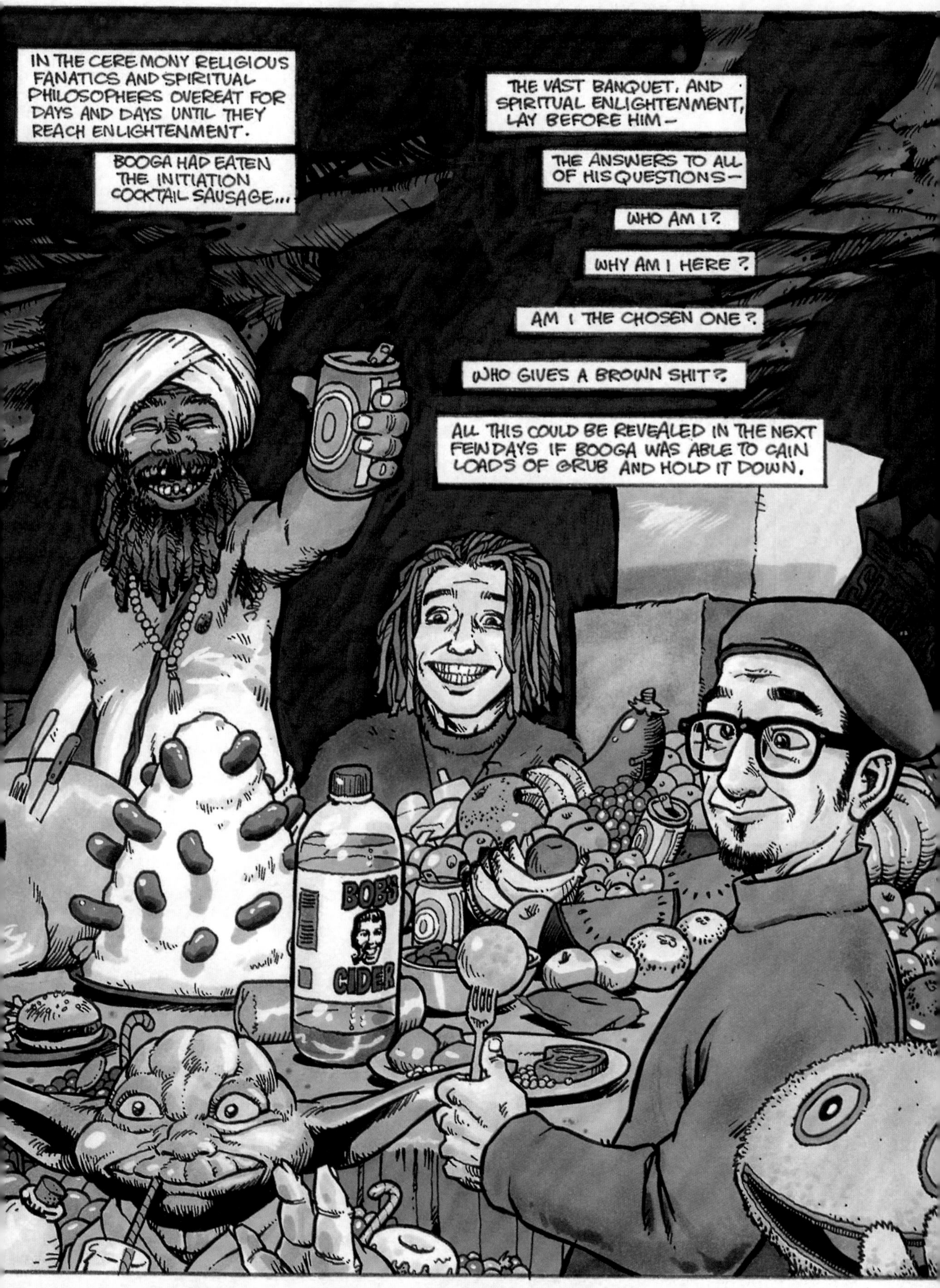

IN THE CEREMONY RELIGIOUS FANATICS AND SPIRITUAL PHILOSOPHERS OVEREAT FOR DAYS AND DAYS UNTIL THEY REACH ENLIGHTENMENT.
BOOGA HAD EATEN THE INITIATION COCKTAIL SAUSAGE...
THE VAST BANQUET, AND SPIRITUAL ENLIGHTENMENT, LAY BEFORE HIM–
THE ANSWERS TO ALL OF HIS QUESTIONS–
WHO AM I?
WHY AM I HERE?
AM I THE CHOSEN ONE?
WHO GIVES A BROWN SHIT?
ALL THIS COULD BE REVEALED IN THE NEXT FEW DAYS IF BOOGA WAS ABLE TO CAIN LOADS OF GRUB AND HOLD IT DOWN.
BOB'S CIDER

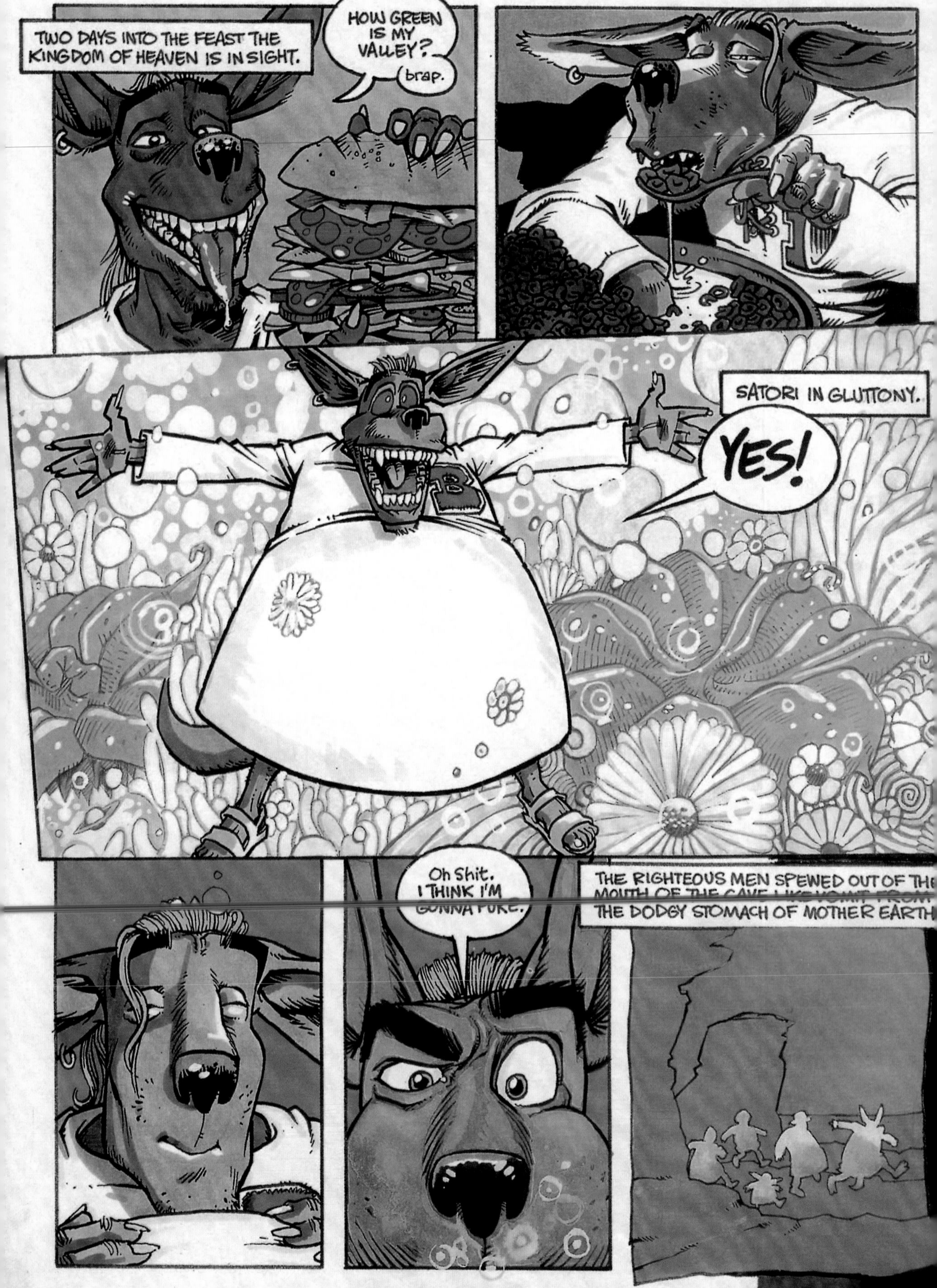
TWO DAYS INTO THE FEAST THE KINGDOM OF HEAVEN IS IN SIGHT.
HOW GREEN IS MY VALLEY?
brap.
SATORI IN GLUTTONY.
YES!
Oh Shit. I THINK I'M GONNA PUKE.
THE RIGHTEOUS MEN SPEWED OUT OF THE MOUTH OF THE CAVE LIKE VOMIT FROM THE DODGY STOMACH OF MOTHER EARTH

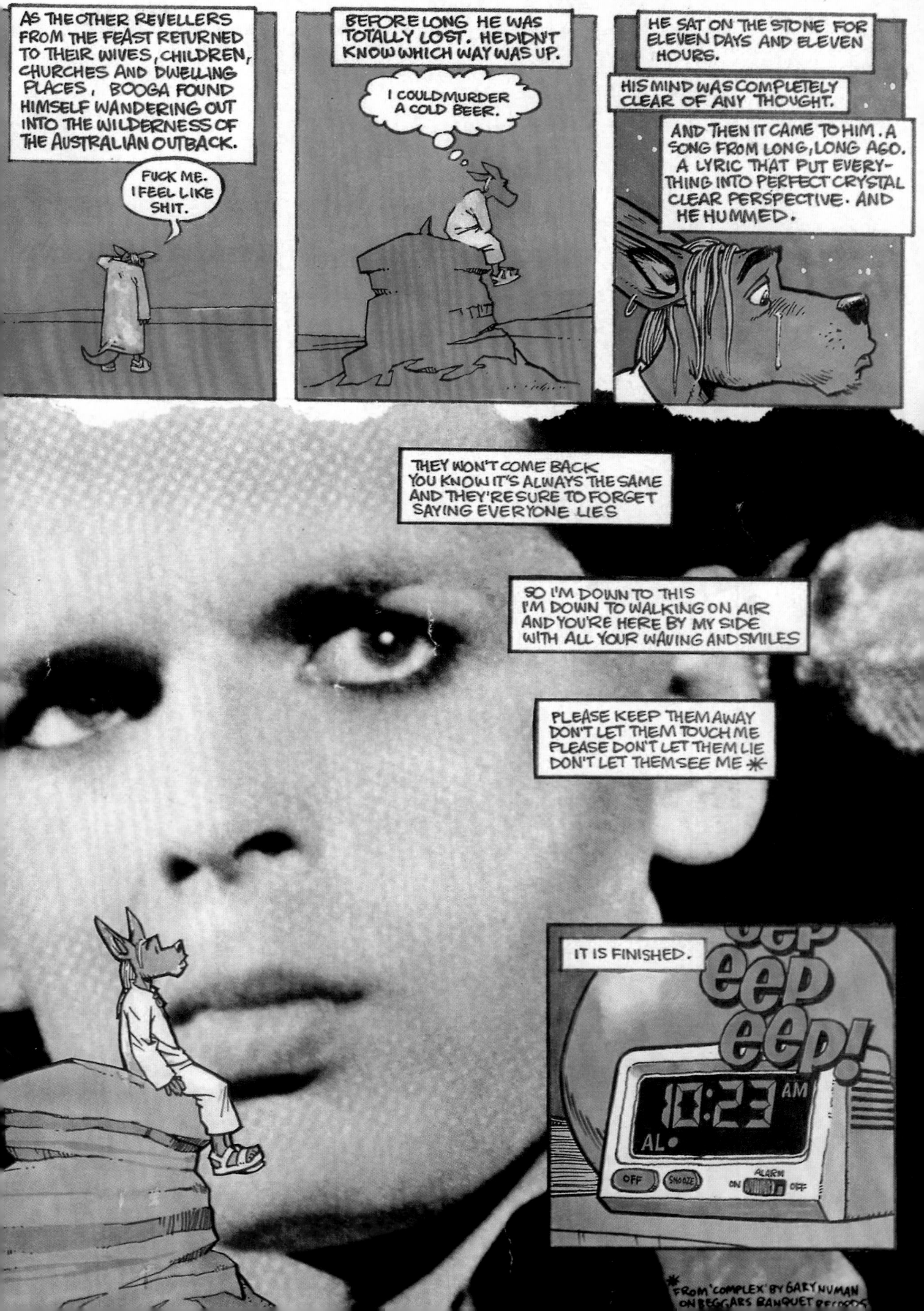
AS THE OTHER REVELLERS FROM THE FEAST RETURNED TO THEIR WIVES, CHILDREN, CHURCHES AND DWELLING PLACES, BOOGA FOUND HIMSELF WANDERING OUT INTO THE WILDERNESS OF THE AUSTRALIAN OUTBACK.
FUCK ME. I FEEL LIKE SHIT.
BEFORE LONG HE WAS TOTALLY LOST. HE DIDN'T KNOW WHICH WAY WAS UP.
I COULD MURDER A COLD BEER.
HE SAT ON THE STONE FOR ELEVEN DAYS AND ELEVEN HOURS.
HIS MIND WAS COMPLETELY CLEAR OF ANY THOUGHT.
AND THEN IT CAME TO HIM. A SONG FROM LONG, LONG AGO. A LYRIC THAT PUT EVERYTHING INTO PERFECT CRYSTAL CLEAR PERSPECTIVE. AND HE HUMMED.
THEY WON'T COME BACK
YOU KNOW IT'S ALWAYS THE SAME
AND THEY'RE SURE TO FORGET
SAYING EVERYONE LIES
SO I'M DOWN TO THIS
I'M DOWN TO WALKING ON AIR
AND YOU'RE HERE BY MY SIDE
WITH ALL YOUR WAVING AND SMILES
PLEASE KEEP THEM AWAY
DON'T LET THEM TOUCH ME
PLEASE DON'T LET THEM LIE
DON'T LET THEM SEE ME *
IT IS FINISHED.
eep
eep!
10:23 AM
AL
OFF
SNOOZE
ALARM
ON
OFF
* FROM 'COMPLEX' BY GARY NUMAN
ON BEGGARS BANQUET

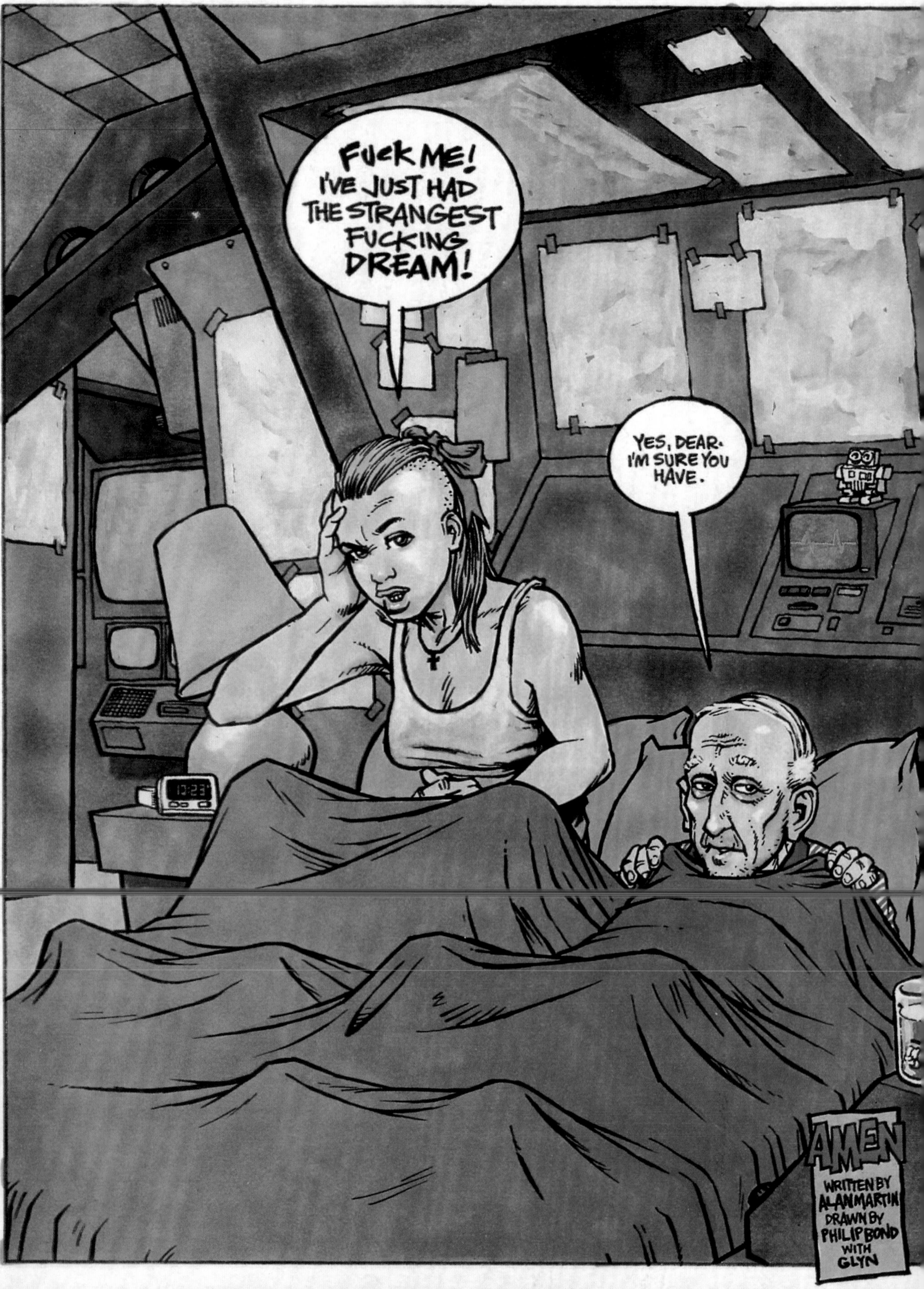
FUCK ME! I'VE JUST HAD THE STRANGEST FUCKING DREAM!
YES, DEAR. I'M SURE YOU HAVE.
AMEN
WRITTEN BY ALAN MARTIN
DRAWN BY PHILIP BOND WITH GLYN

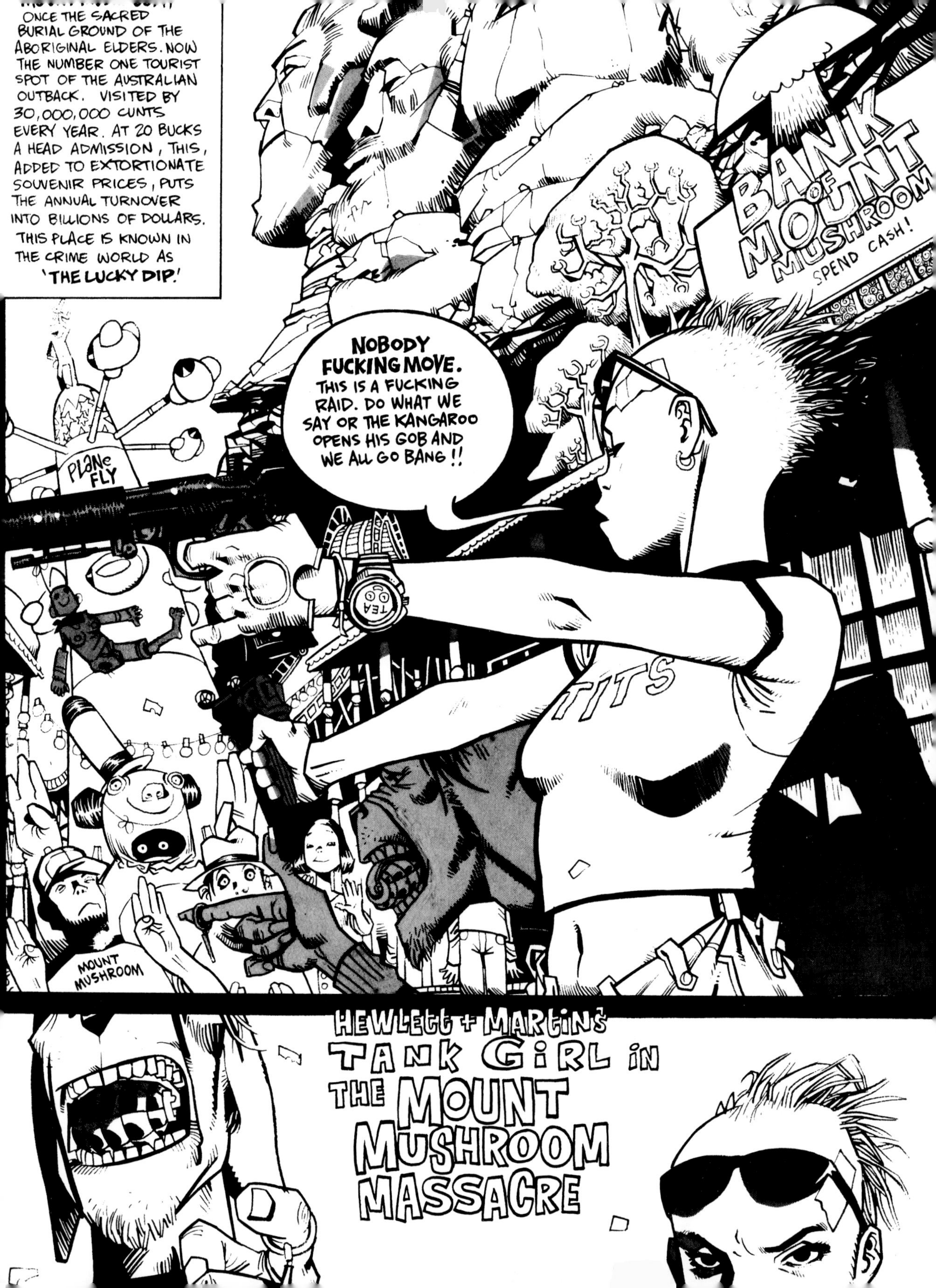
ONCE THE SACRED BURIAL GROUND OF THE ABORIGINAL ELDERS. NOW THE NUMBER ONE TOURIST SPOT OF THE AUSTRALIAN OUTBACK. VISITED BY 30,000,000 CUNTS EVERY YEAR. AT 20 BUCKS A HEAD ADMISSION, THIS, ADDED TO EXTORTIONATE SOUVENIR PRICES, PUTS THE ANNUAL TURNOVER INTO BILLIONS OF DOLLARS. THIS PLACE IS KNOWN IN THE CRIME WORLD AS 'THE LUCKY DIP.'
BANK OF MOUNT MUSHROOM
SPEND CASH!
PLANE FLY
NOBODY FUCKING MOVE. THIS IS A FUCKING RAID. DO WHAT WE SAY OR THE KANGAROO OPENS HIS GOB AND WE ALL GO BANG!!
TEA
TITS
MOUNT MUSHROOM
HEWLETT + MARTIN'S
TANK GIRL IN
THE MOUNT MUSHROOM MASSACRE

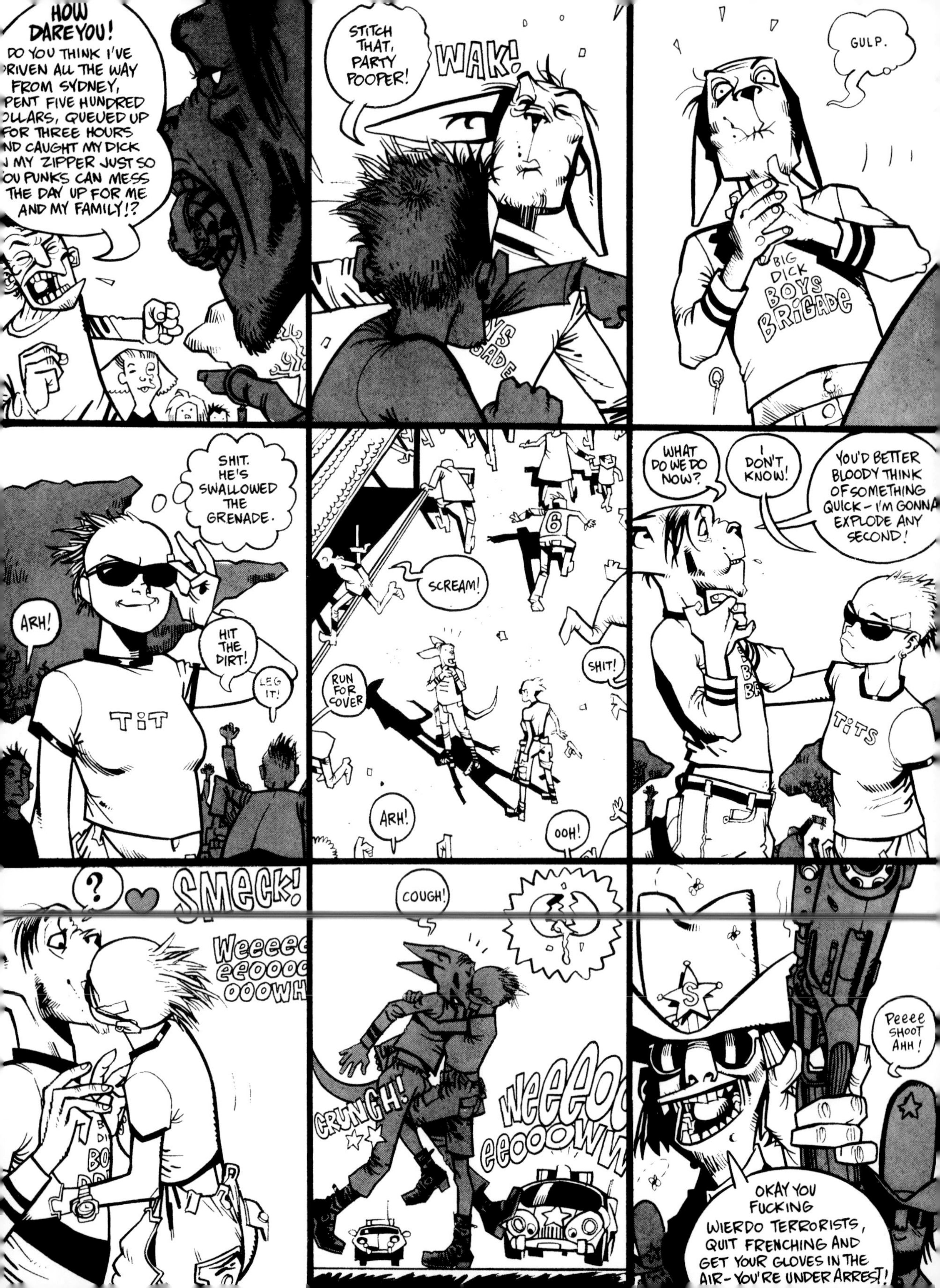
HOW DARE YOU! DO YOU THINK I'VE DRIVEN ALL THE WAY FROM SYDNEY, SPENT FIVE HUNDRED DOLLARS, QUEUED UP FOR THREE HOURS AND CAUGHT MY DICK IN MY ZIPPER JUST SO YOU PUNKS CAN MESS THE DAY UP FOR ME AND MY FAMILY!?
STITCH THAT, PARTY POOPER!
WAK!
GULP.
BIG DICK BOYS BRIGADE
SHIT. HE'S SWALLOWED THE GRENADE.
ARH!
HIT THE DIRT!
LEG IT!
TIT
SCREAM!
RUN FOR COVER
SHIT!
ARH!
OOH!
WHAT DO WE DO NOW?
I DON'T KNOW!
YOU'D BETTER BLOODY THINK OF SOMETHING QUICK - I'M GONNA EXPLODE ANY SECOND!
TITS
?
SMECK!
Weeeee eeoooo ooowh
COUGH!
CRUNCH!
weeoo eeooowu
Peeee SHOOT AHH!
OKAY YOU FUCKING WIERDO TERRORISTS, QUIT FRENCHING AND GET YOUR GLOVES IN THE AIR - YOU'RE UNDER ARREST!

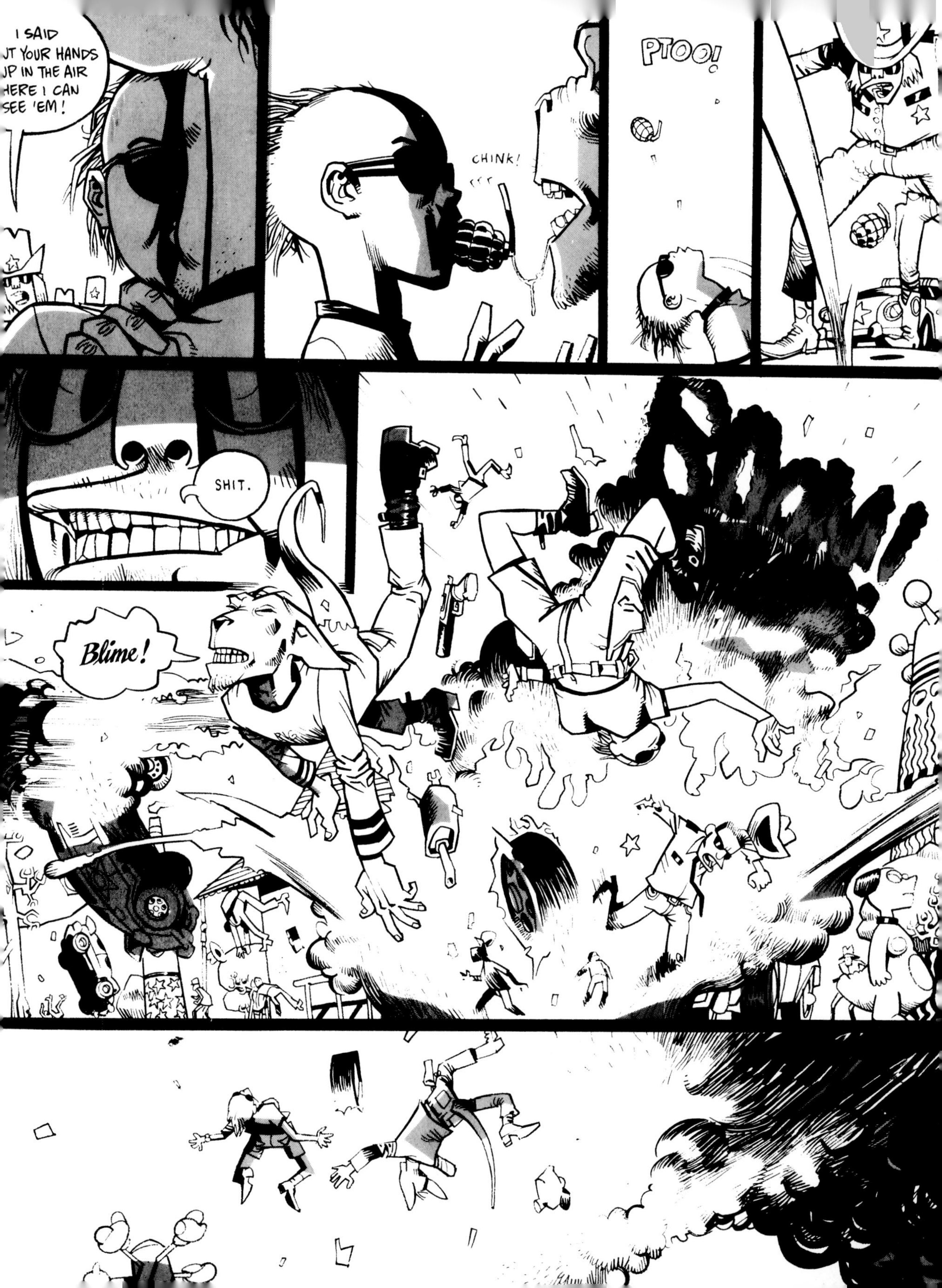

I SAID
UT YOUR HANDS
UP IN THE AIR
HERE I CAN
SEE 'EM!
CHINK!
PTOO!
SHIT.
Blime!

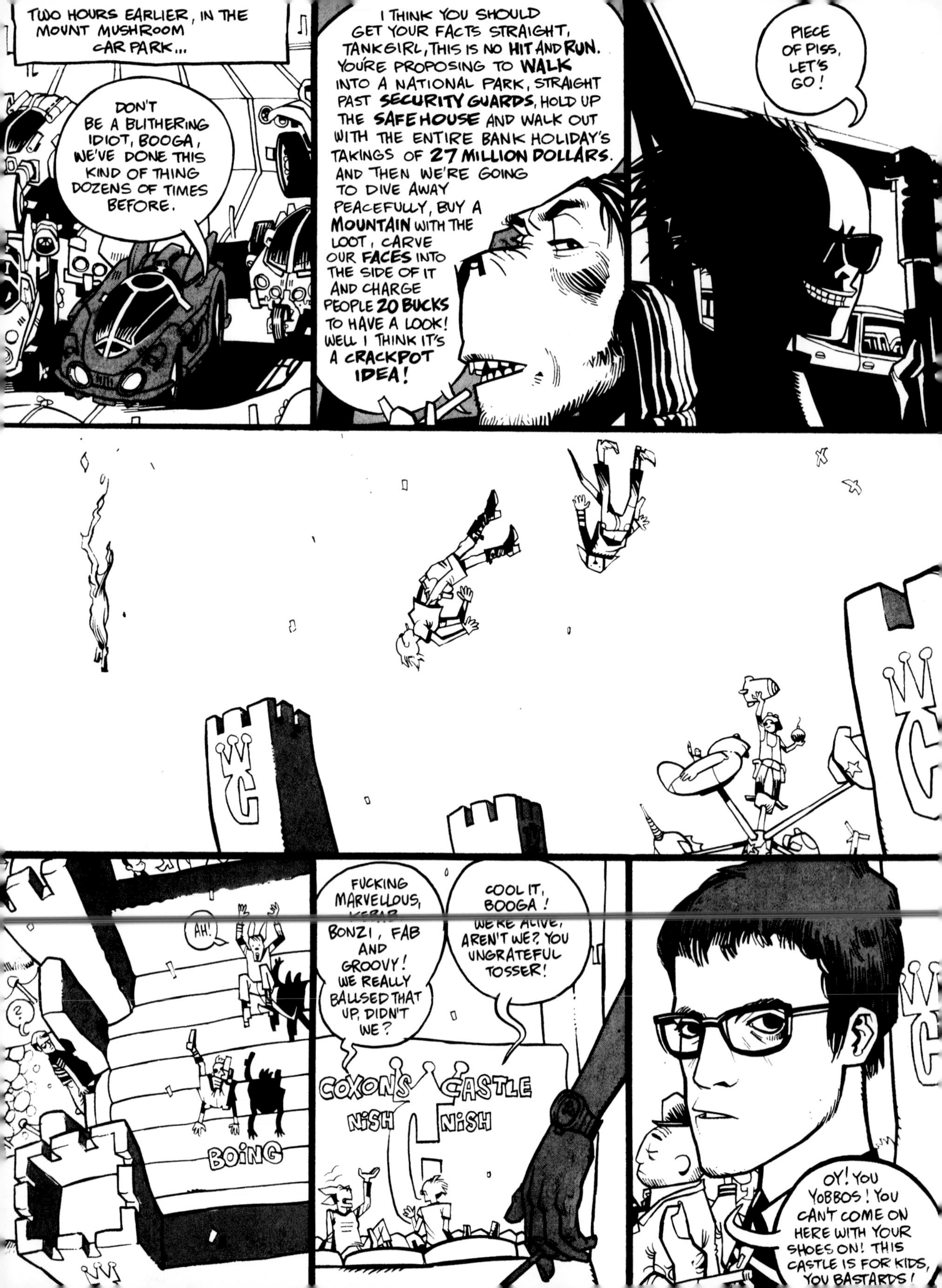
TWO HOURS EARLIER, IN THE MOUNT MUSHROOM CAR PARK...
DON'T BE A BLITHERING IDIOT, BOOGA, WE'VE DONE THIS KIND OF THING DOZENS OF TIMES BEFORE.
I THINK YOU SHOULD GET YOUR FACTS STRAIGHT, TANKGIRL, THIS IS NO HIT AND RUN. YOU'RE PROPOSING TO WALK INTO A NATIONAL PARK, STRAIGHT PAST SECURITY GUARDS, HOLD UP THE SAFE HOUSE AND WALK OUT WITH THE ENTIRE BANK HOLIDAY'S TAKINGS OF 27 MILLION DOLLARS. AND THEN WE'RE GOING TO DIVE AWAY PEACEFULLY, BUY A MOUNTAIN WITH THE LOOT, CARVE OUR FACES INTO THE SIDE OF IT AND CHARGE PEOPLE 20 BUCKS TO HAVE A LOOK! WELL I THINK IT'S A CRACKPOT IDEA!
PIECE OF PISS, LET'S GO!
AH!
?
BOING
FUCKING MARVELLOUS, BONZI, FAB AND GROOVY! WE REALLY BALLSED THAT UP, DIDN'T WE?
COOL IT, BOOGA! WE'RE ALIVE, AREN'T WE? YOU UNGRATEFUL TOSSER!
COXON'S CASTLE
NISH NISH
OY! YOU YOBBOS! YOU CAN'T COME ON HERE WITH YOUR SHOES ON! THIS CASTLE IS FOR KIDS, YOU BASTARDS!

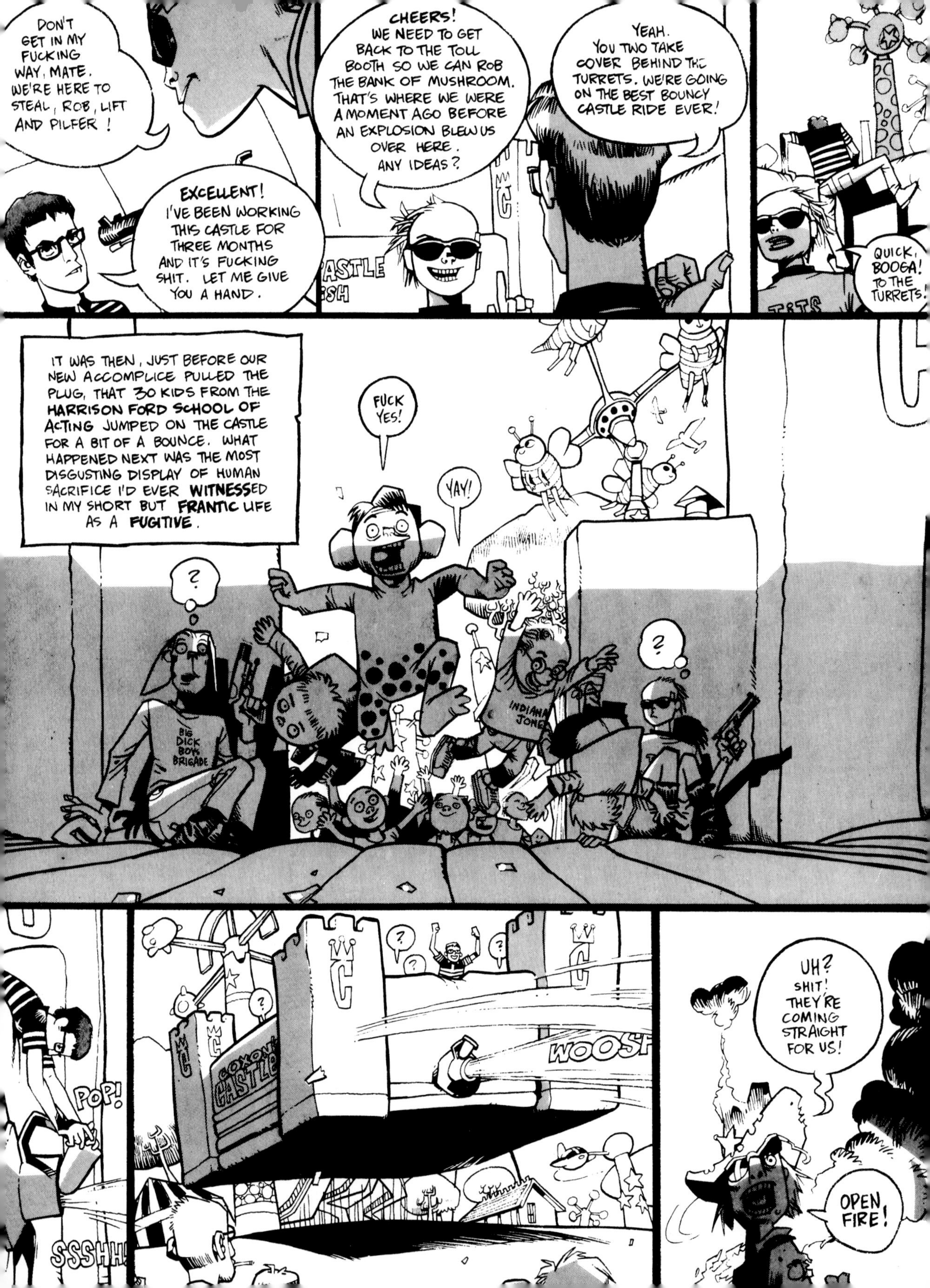
DON'T GET IN MY FUCKING WAY, MATE. WE'RE HERE TO STEAL, ROB, LIFT AND PILFER!
EXCELLENT! I'VE BEEN WORKING THIS CASTLE FOR THREE MONTHS AND IT'S FUCKING SHIT. LET ME GIVE YOU A HAND.
CHEERS! WE NEED TO GET BACK TO THE TOLL BOOTH SO WE CAN ROB THE BANK OF MUSHROOM. THAT'S WHERE WE WERE A MOMENT AGO BEFORE AN EXPLOSION BLEW US OVER HERE. ANY IDEAS?
YEAH. YOU TWO TAKE COVER BEHIND THE TURRETS. WE'RE GOING ON THE BEST BOUNCY CASTLE RIDE EVER!
QUICK, BOOGA! TO THE TURRETS!
IT WAS THEN, JUST BEFORE OUR NEW ACCOMPLICE PULLED THE PLUG, THAT 30 KIDS FROM THE HARRISON FORD SCHOOL OF ACTING JUMPED ON THE CASTLE FOR A BIT OF A BOUNCE. WHAT HAPPENED NEXT WAS THE MOST DISGUSTING DISPLAY OF HUMAN SACRIFICE I'D EVER WITNESSED IN MY SHORT BUT FRANTIC LIFE AS A FUGITIVE.
FUCK YES!
YAY!
?
?
BIG DICK BOYS BRIGADE
INDIANA JONE
POP!
SSSHH!
?
?
?
?
WOOSH
UH? SHIT! THEY'RE COMING STRAIGHT FOR US!
OPEN FIRE!

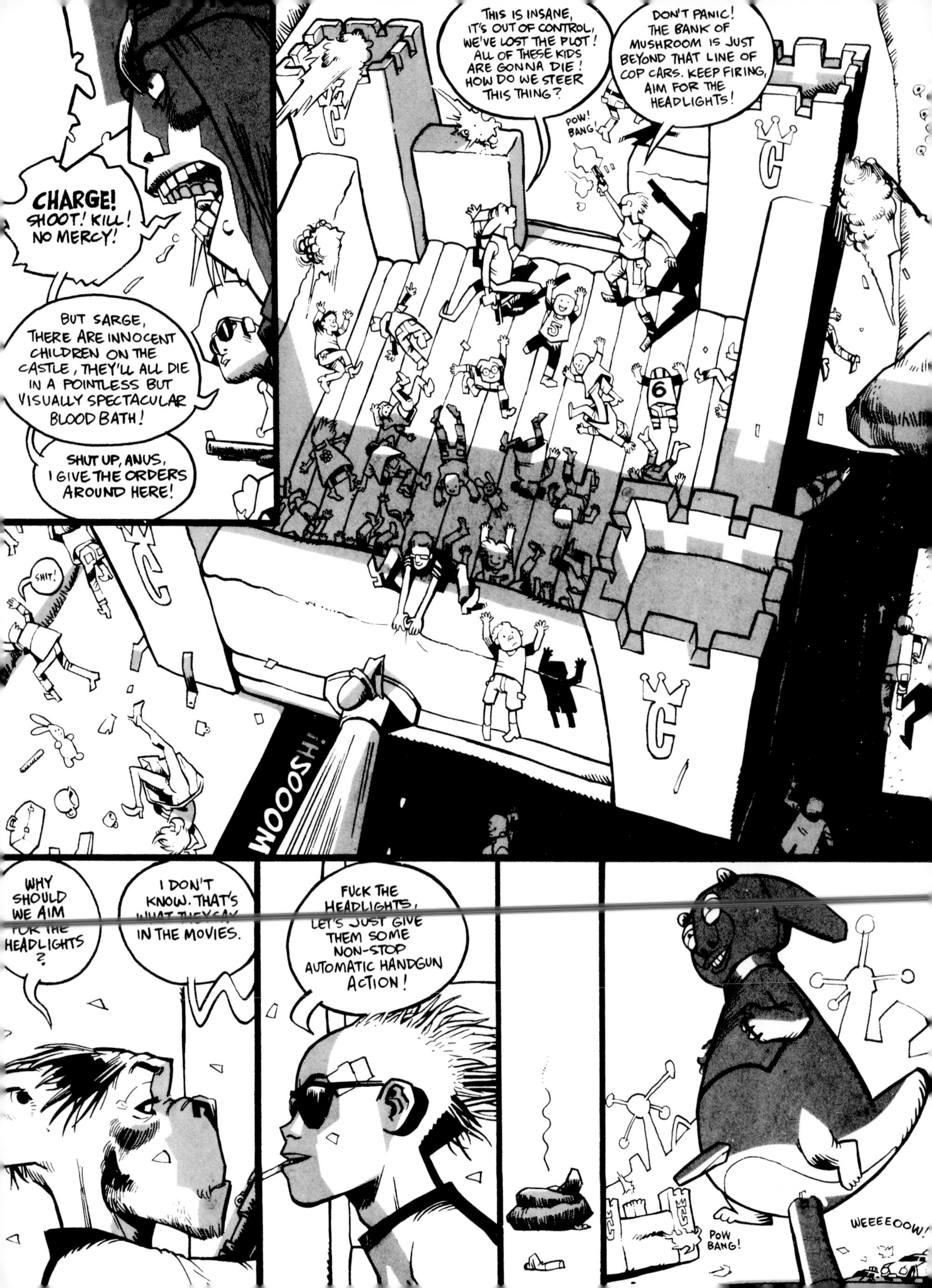
CHARGE! SHOOT! KILL! NO MERCY!
BUT SARGE, THERE ARE INNOCENT CHILDREN ON THE CASTLE, THEY'LL ALL DIE IN A POINTLESS BUT VISUALLY SPECTACULAR BLOOD BATH!
SHUT UP, ANUS, I GIVE THE ORDERS AROUND HERE!
THIS IS INSANE, IT'S OUT OF CONTROL, WE'VE LOST THE PLOT! ALL OF THESE KIDS ARE GONNA DIE! HOW DO WE STEER THIS THING?
DON'T PANIC! THE BANK OF MUSHROOM IS JUST BEYOND THAT LINE OF COP CARS. KEEP FIRING, AIM FOR THE HEADLIGHTS!
POW! BANG!
SHIT!
WOOOSH!
WHY SHOULD WE AIM FOR THE HEADLIGHTS?
I DON'T KNOW. THAT'S WHAT THEY SAY IN THE MOVIES.
FUCK THE HEADLIGHTS, LET'S JUST GIVE THEM SOME NON-STOP AUTOMATIC HANDGUN ACTION!
POW BANG!
WEEEEOOW!

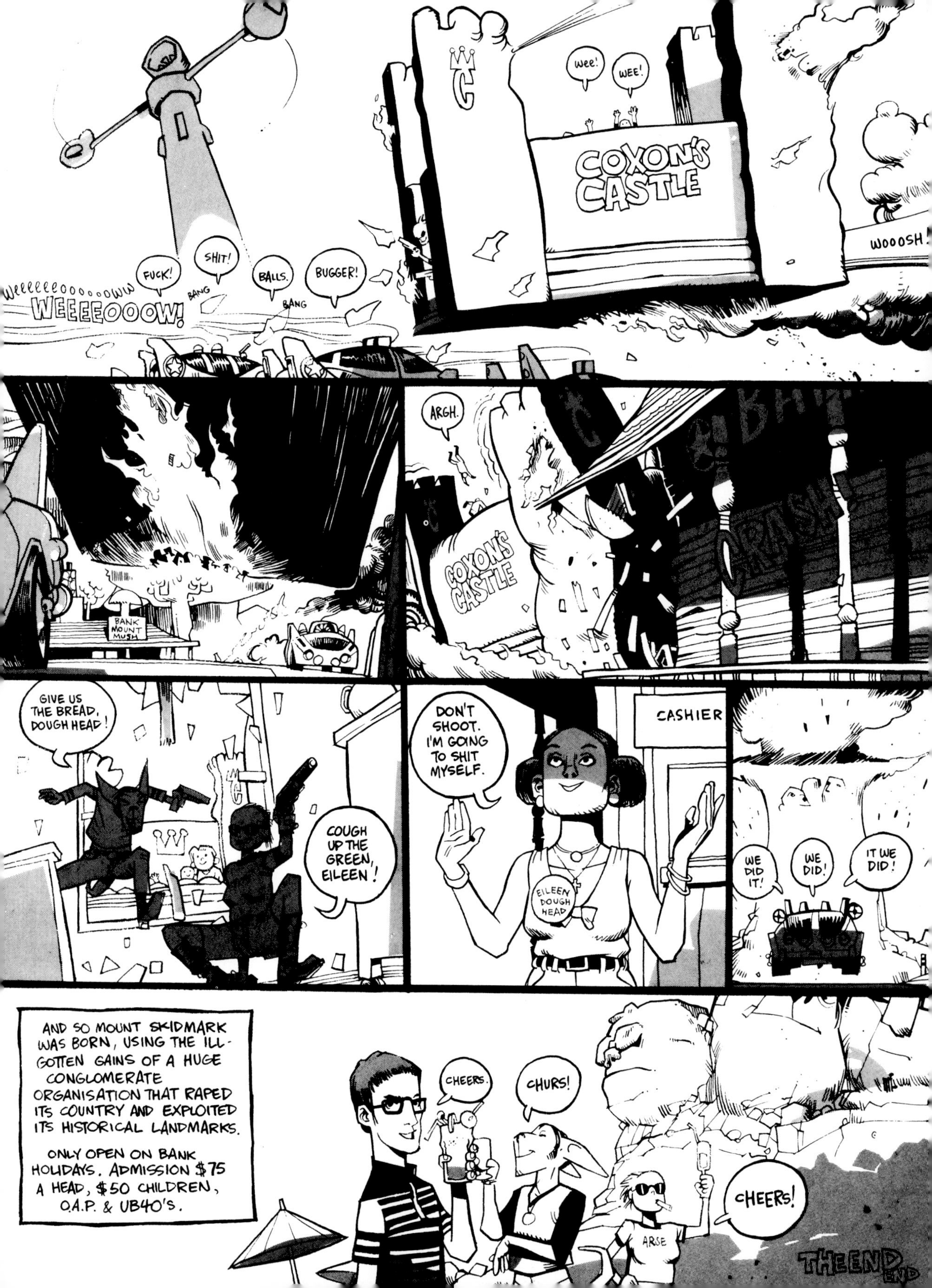
WEE!
WEE!
COXON'S CASTLE
WOOOSH!
WEEEEEOOOOW!
WEELLLLLOOOOOOWW
FUCK!
SHIT!
BANG
BALLS.
BANG
BUGGER!
BANK MOUNT MUSH
ARGH.
COXON'S CASTLE
GIVE US THE BREAD, DOUGH HEAD!
COUGH UP THE GREEN, EILEEN!
DON'T SHOOT. I'M GOING TO SHIT MYSELF.
CASHIER
EILEEN DOUGH HEAD
WE DID IT!
WE DID!
IT WE DID!
AND SO MOUNT SKIDMARK WAS BORN, USING THE ILL-GOTTEN GAINS OF A HUGE CONGLOMERATE ORGANISATION THAT RAPED ITS COUNTRY AND EXPLOITED ITS HISTORICAL LANDMARKS.
ONLY OPEN ON BANK HOLIDAYS. ADMISSION $75 A HEAD, $50 CHILDREN, O.A.P. & UB40'S.
CHEERS.
CHURS!
ARSE
CHEERS!
THE END

TANK GIRL

1994 ALMANAC

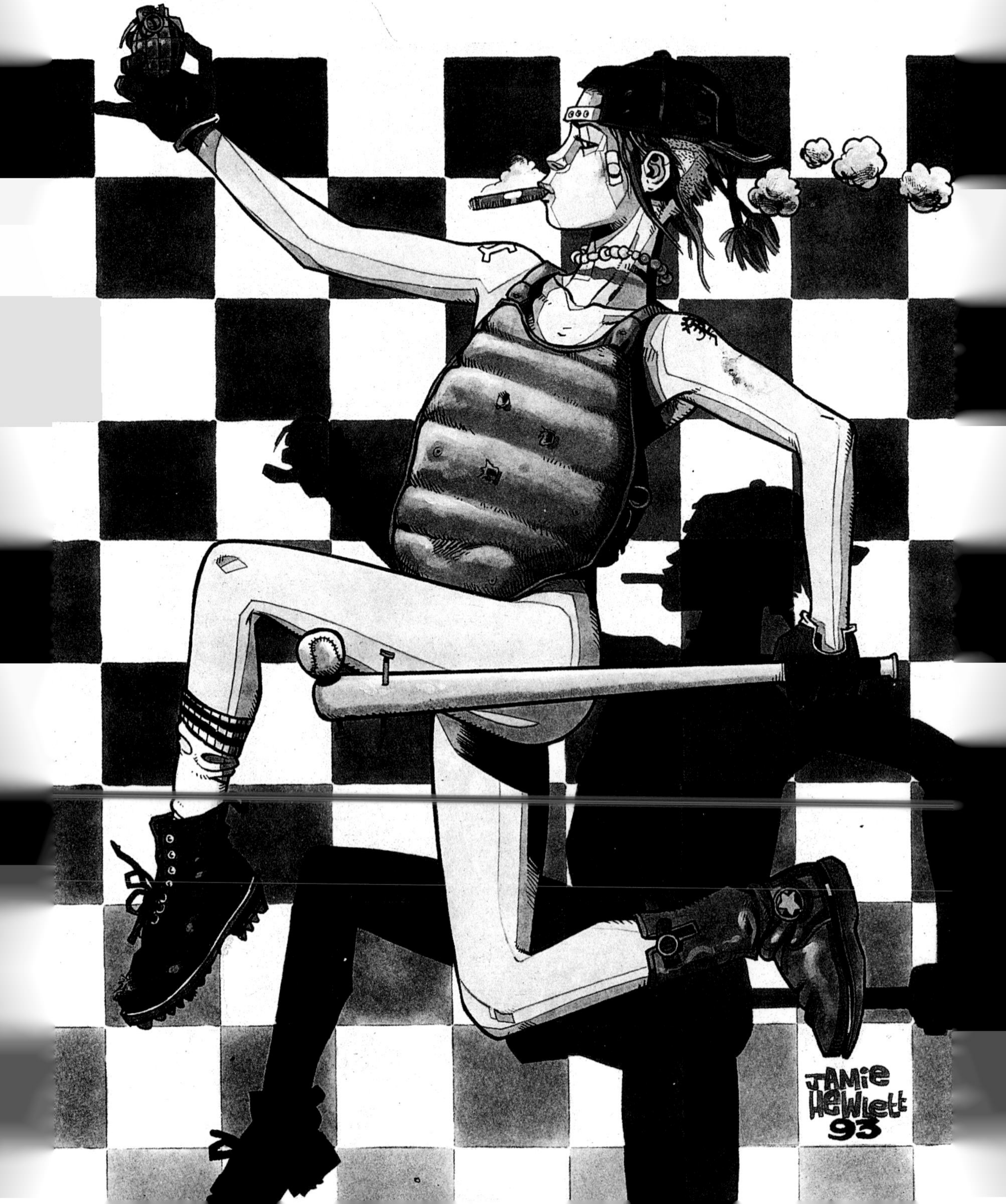
JAMIE HEWLETT 93

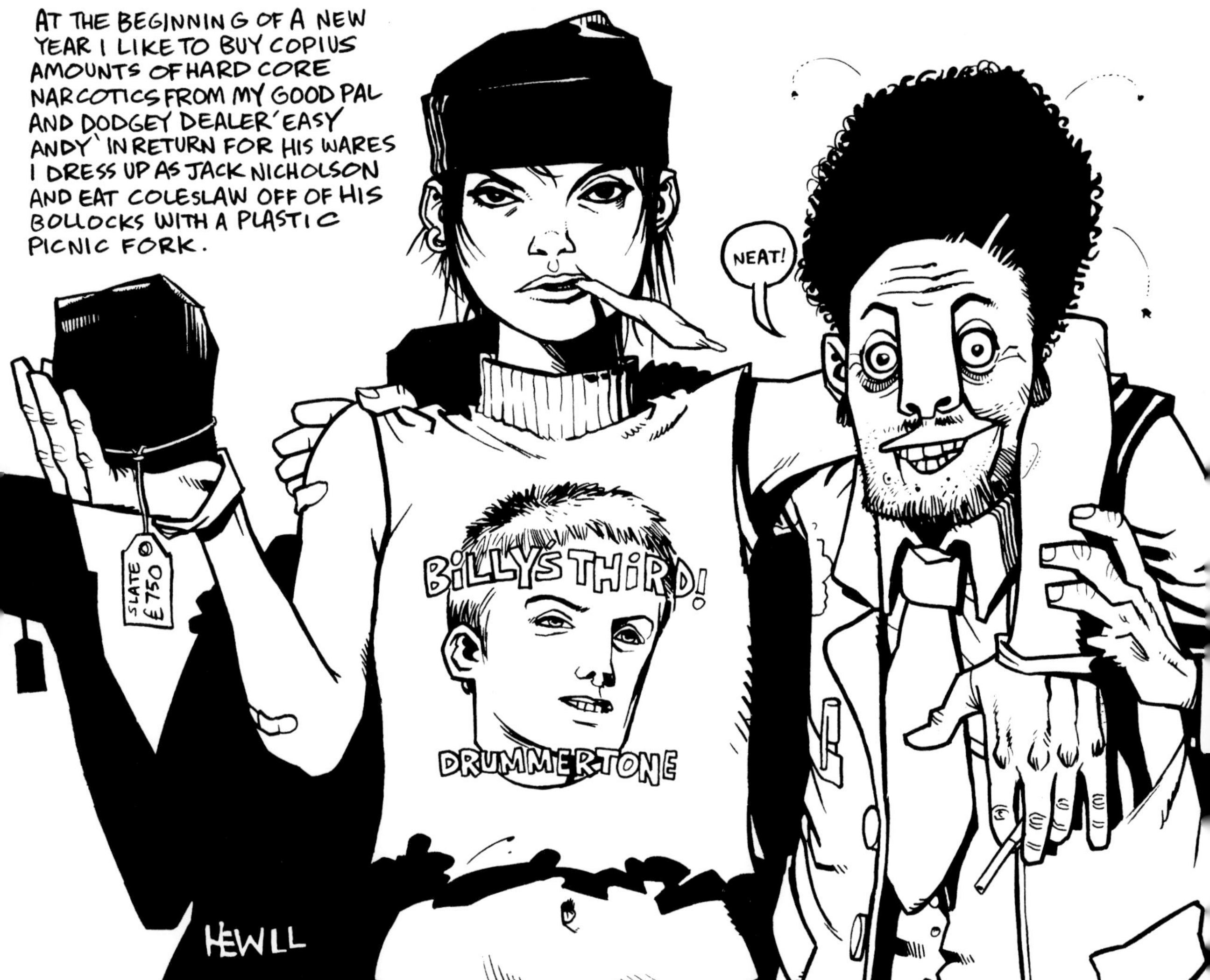
AT THE BEGINNING OF A NEW YEAR I LIKE TO BUY COPIUS AMOUNTS OF HARD CORE NARCOTICS FROM MY GOOD PAL AND DODGEY DEALER 'EASY ANDY' IN RETURN FOR HIS WARES I DRESS UP AS JACK NICHOLSON AND EAT COLESLAW OFF OF HIS BOLLOCKS WITH A PLASTIC PICNIC FORK.
SLATE £750
BILLY'S THIRD!
DRUMMERTONE
NEAT!
HEWLL

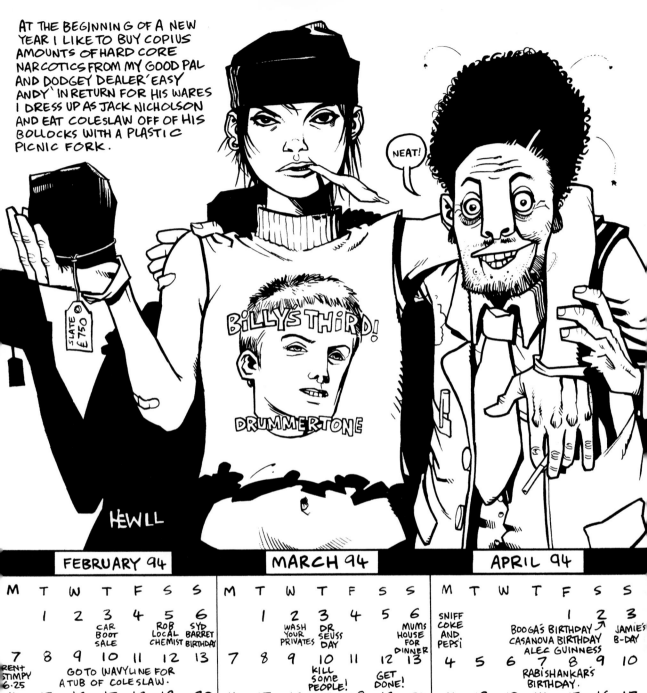

FEBRUARY 94

M	T	W	T	F	S	S
	1	2	3 CAR BOOT SALE	4	5 ROB LOCAL CHEMIST	6 SYD BARRET BIRTHDAY
7 RENT STIMPY 6.25	8	9	10 GO TO WAVYLINE FOR A TUB OF COLESLAW.	11	12	13
14	15	16	17	18	19	20 SIDNEY POITIERS BIRTHDAY
21	22 KENNETH WILLIAMS BIRTHDAY	23 FUCK OFF DAY!	24	25 GEORGE HAMILTON DAY	26	27
28						

NOTES: DENTIST FOR INJECTIONS IN MY GUMS! CHEERS!

MARCH 94

M	T	W	T	F	S	S
	1	2 WASH YOUR PRIVATES	3 DR SEUSS DAY	4	5	6 MUMS HOUSE FOR DINNER
7	8	9	10 KILL SOME PEOPLE!	11	12 GET DONE!	13
14 MIKE CAINE DAY	15 GO TO LONDON	16 IN LONDON	17 BACK FROM LONDON	18 BE ILL	19	20
21	22 STEVE DILLONS BIRTHDAY	23	24 STEVE McQUEENS BIRTHDAY.	25	26	27
28	29	30	31			

NOTES: DON'T PAY ANY RENT TO ANYONE, AND SHOOT THE LANDLORD!

APRIL 94

M	T	W	T	F	S	S
SNIFF COKE AND PEPSI				1	2 BOOGA'S BIRTHDAY CASANOVA BIRTHDAY ALEC GUINNESS	3 JAMIE'S B-DAY
4	5	6	7 RABISHANKAR'S BIRTHDAY.	8	9	10
11	12	13	14 JULIE CHRISTIE	15	16 HOFMANN'S BIKE TRIP	17
18	19	20 HITLER HAROLD LLOYD LESLIE PHILLIPS BIRTHDAY	21	22	23	24
25 AL PACINOS BIRTHDAY	26	27	28 JACK NICHOLSONS BIRTH DAY!	29	30	

SEX SEASON

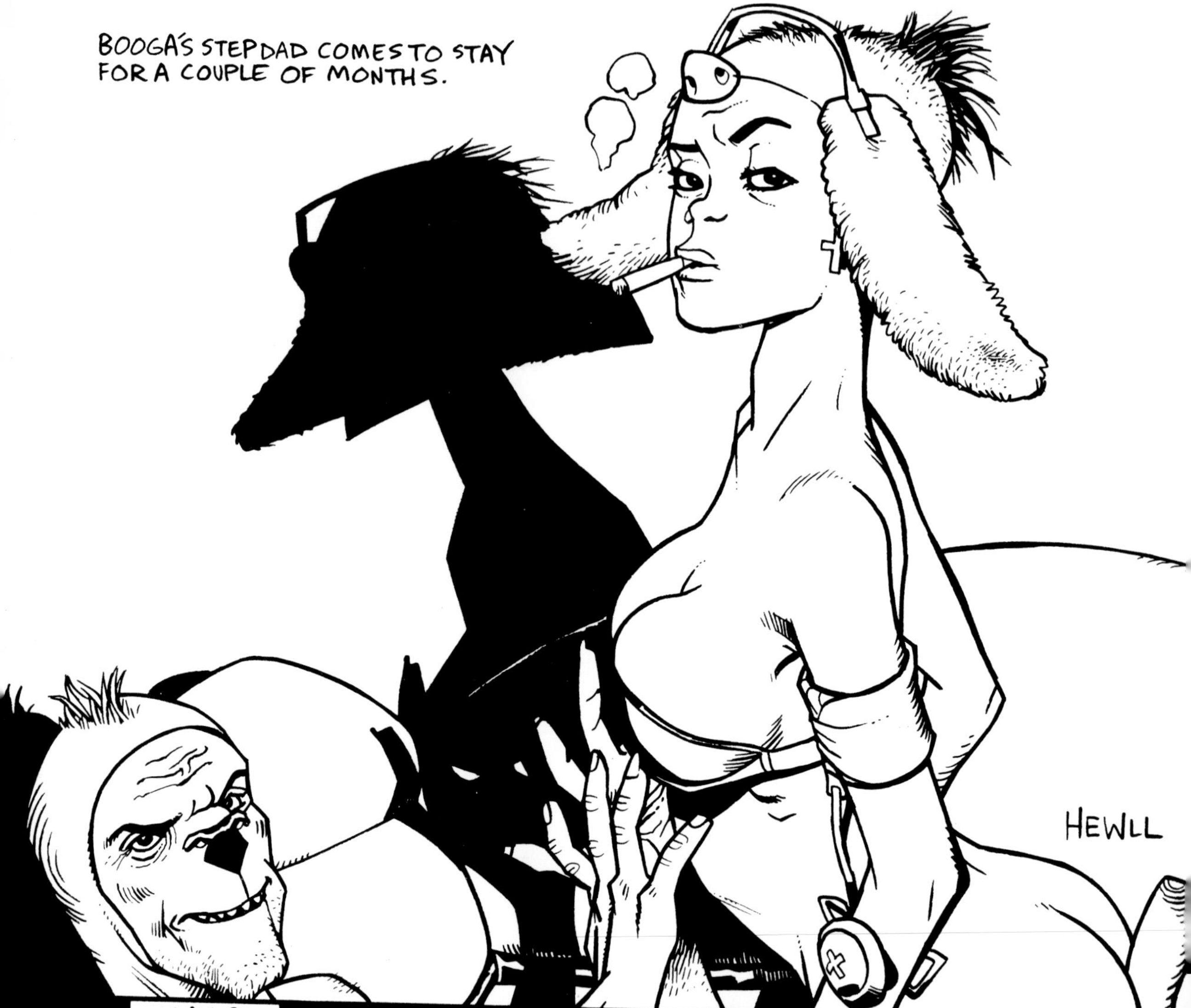

BOOGA'S STEPDAD COMES TO STAY FOR A COUPLE OF MONTHS.
HEWLL

MAY 94

M T W T F S S

1 JOANNA LUMLEY DAY

2 O ALLIS ATE
3
4 AUDREY HEPBURM BIRTHDAY
5 LOUS B-DAY
6
7
8 SID JAMES BIRTH

9 LBERT INNEY
10
11
12
13 CAPTAIN SCARLET BBC2 6.00
14
15 FRANK BAUM DATE

6
17 GLYN AND DENNIS HOPPERS B-DAY. "IT'S TWINS!"
18
19 PETE TOWNSHEND DAY
20
21
22 GEORGE BEST BIRTHDAY

23
24 JONATHAN RICHMANS B-DAY
25
26
27
28 IAN FLEMING BIRTH!
29

30
31 DENHOLM

JUNE 94

M T W T F S S

1
2 CHARLIE WATTS
3 GINSBERGS BIRTH
4
5

6
7
8 PICNIC ON HANGING ROCK
9
10
11 JAQUES COUSTEAU DATE.
12

13 JOHNNY MORRIS B-DAY
14
15 SIMON CALLOW DAY
16 JAMES BOLAM DATE
17
18
19

20 BRIAN WILSON'S BIRTHDAY
21
22
23 OPTICIAN'S 1.00
24
25 PETER BLAKE AND ORWELL
26

27
28
29
30 NOT FEELING TOO WELL!

JULY 94

M T W T F S S

1 AMY JOHNSON FLYGIRL
2
3 KEN RUSSEL

4
5
6
7
8 BIRTHDAY FOR BILL ODDIE
9
10

11 FILIP BONDS DAY
12
13 HAN SOLO DATE
14 WOODY GUTHRIE BIRTH
15
16
17 DON SUTHERLAND B-DAY

18
19
20 BUZZ PISSES PANTS
21
22
23
24

25
26
27 CHRIS DEAN (ICEMAN)
28
29
30
31 BILL BERRY BIRTH

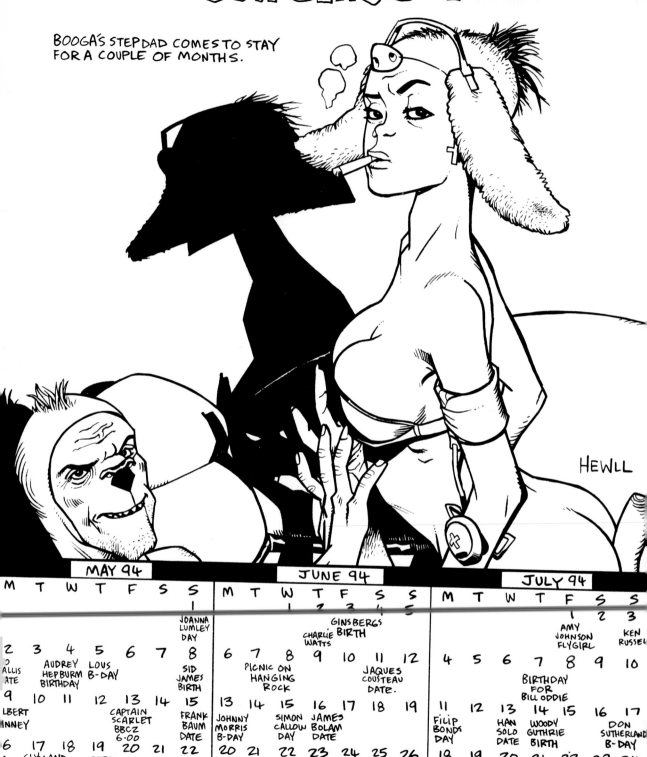

THE MEAN SEASON

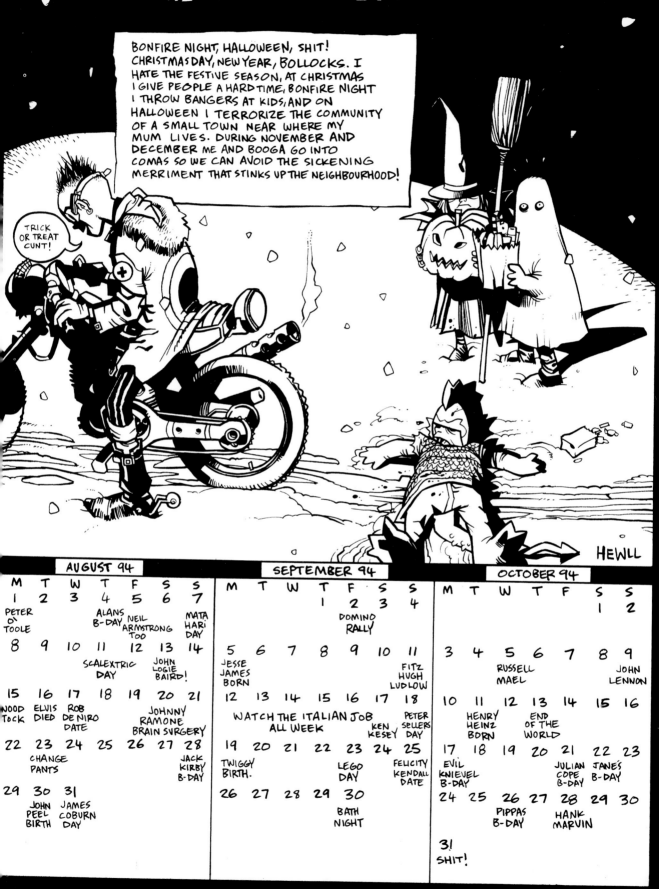

BONFIRE NIGHT, HALLOWEEN, SHIT! CHRISTMAS DAY, NEW YEAR, BOLLOCKS. I HATE THE FESTIVE SEASON, AT CHRISTMAS I GIVE PEOPLE A HARD TIME, BONFIRE NIGHT I THROW BANGERS AT KIDS, AND ON HALLOWEEN I TERRORIZE THE COMMUNITY OF A SMALL TOWN NEAR WHERE MY MUM LIVES. DURING NOVEMBER AND DECEMBER ME AND BOOGA GO INTO COMAS SO WE CAN AVOID THE SICKENING MERRIMENT THAT STINKS UP THE NEIGHBOURHOOD!

TRICK OR TREAT CUNT!

HEWLL

AUGUST 94

M	T	W	T	F	S	S
1 PETER O' TOOLE	2	3	4 ALANS B-DAY	5 NEIL ARMSTRONG TOO	6	7 MATA HARI DAY
8	9	10	11 SCALEXTRIC DAY	12 JOHN LOGIE BAIRD!	13	14
15 WOODTOCK	16 ELVIS DIED	17 ROB DE NIRO DATE	18	19	20 JOHNNY RAMONE BRAIN SURGERY	21
22	23 CHANGE PANTS	24	25	26	27	28 JACK KIRBY B-DAY
29	30 JOHN PEEL BIRTH	31 JAMES COBURN DAY				

SEPTEMBER 94

M	T	W	T	F	S	S
			1	2	3 DOMINO RALLY	4
5 JESSE JAMES BORN	6	7	8	9	10 FITZ HUGH LUDLOW	11
12	13	14 WATCH THE ITALIAN JOB ALL WEEK	15	16	17 KEN KESEY	18 PETER SELLERS DAY
19 TWIGGY BIRTH.	20	21	22	23 LEGO DAY	24	25 FELICITY KENDALL DATE
26	27	28	29	30 BATH NIGHT		

OCTOBER 94

M	T	W	T	F	S	S
					1	2
3	4	5 RUSSELL MAEL	6	7	8	9 JOHN LENNON
10	11 HENRY HEINZ BORN	12	13 END OF THE WORLD	14	15	16
17	18	19	20	21 EVIL KNIEVEL B-DAY	22 JULIAN COPE B-DAY	23 JANES B-DAY
24	25	26 PIPPAS B-DAY	27	28 HANK MARVIN	29	30
31 SHIT!						

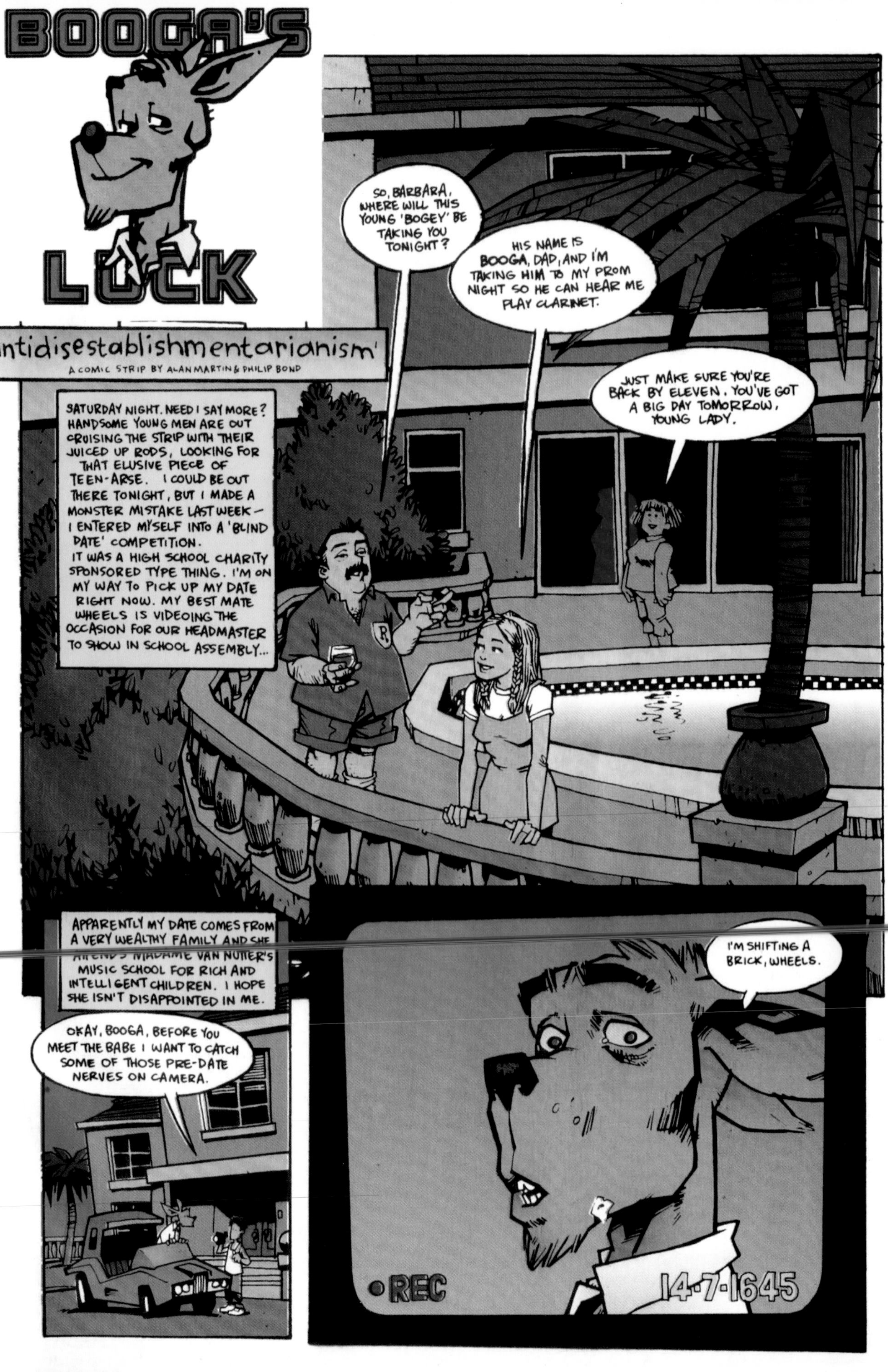
BOOGA'S LUCK
'antidisestablishmentarianism'
A COMIC STRIP BY ALAN MARTIN & PHILIP BOND
SATURDAY NIGHT. NEED I SAY MORE? HANDSOME YOUNG MEN ARE OUT CRUISING THE STRIP WITH THEIR JUICED UP RODS, LOOKING FOR THAT ELUSIVE PIECE OF TEEN-ARSE. I COULD BE OUT THERE TONIGHT, BUT I MADE A MONSTER MISTAKE LAST WEEK – I ENTERED MYSELF INTO A 'BLIND DATE' COMPETITION. IT WAS A HIGH SCHOOL CHARITY SPONSORED TYPE THING. I'M ON MY WAY TO PICK UP MY DATE RIGHT NOW. MY BEST MATE WHEELS IS VIDEOING THE OCCASION FOR OUR HEADMASTER TO SHOW IN SCHOOL ASSEMBLY...
SO, BARBARA, WHERE WILL THIS YOUNG 'BOGEY' BE TAKING YOU TONIGHT?
HIS NAME IS BOOGA, DAD, AND I'M TAKING HIM TO MY PROM NIGHT SO HE CAN HEAR ME PLAY CLARINET.
JUST MAKE SURE YOU'RE BACK BY ELEVEN. YOU'VE GOT A BIG DAY TOMORROW, YOUNG LADY.
APPARENTLY MY DATE COMES FROM A VERY WEALTHY FAMILY AND SHE ATTENDS MADAME VAN NUTTER'S MUSIC SCHOOL FOR RICH AND INTELLIGENT CHILDREN. I HOPE SHE ISN'T DISAPPOINTED IN ME.
OKAY, BOOGA, BEFORE YOU MEET THE BABE I WANT TO CATCH SOME OF THOSE PRE-DATE NERVES ON CAMERA.
I'M SHIFTING A BRICK, WHEELS.
● REC
14·7·1645

WHAT IF SHE DOESN'T LIKE MY SHOES?

DON'T WORRY, MAN. YOU LOOK COOL. EVERYTHING IS GONNA WORK OUT FINE.

YOU'RE RIGHT, WHEELS. I SHOULD CHILL OUT. IT'S ONLY A DATE WITH A RICH SMART BIRD AFTER ALL. WHAT COULD GO WRONG?

BING BONG

GOOD EVENING TO YOU. I AM BOOGA AND THIS IS MY CAMERAMAN FOR THE NIGHT, MISTER J.F. 'WHEELS' SKIDLEY.

HELLO BOYS. MY NAME'S BARBARA, BUT YOU CAN CALL ME BABS. SHALL WE SPLIT TO THE PROM?

GREAT! LET'S TAKE THE SKIDMOBILE!

DON'T BE LATE!

WILL DO!

CHEERS!

SHIFT!

I HEAR YOU ENJOY A BIT OF MUSIC, BABS. WOULD YOU LIKE TO HEAR SOME OF MY HARDCORE BELGIAN TECHNO COLLECTION?

WELL, I... ER...

SORTED.

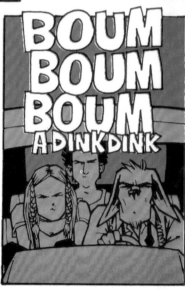

BOUM BOUM BOUM A DINK DINK

BOUM BOUM A DINK DINK

I'D FORGOTTEN WHAT A CONVERSATION KILLER HARDCORE RAVE MUSIC CAN BE. DEFINITELY NOT A GOOD IDEA FOR A FIRST DATE.

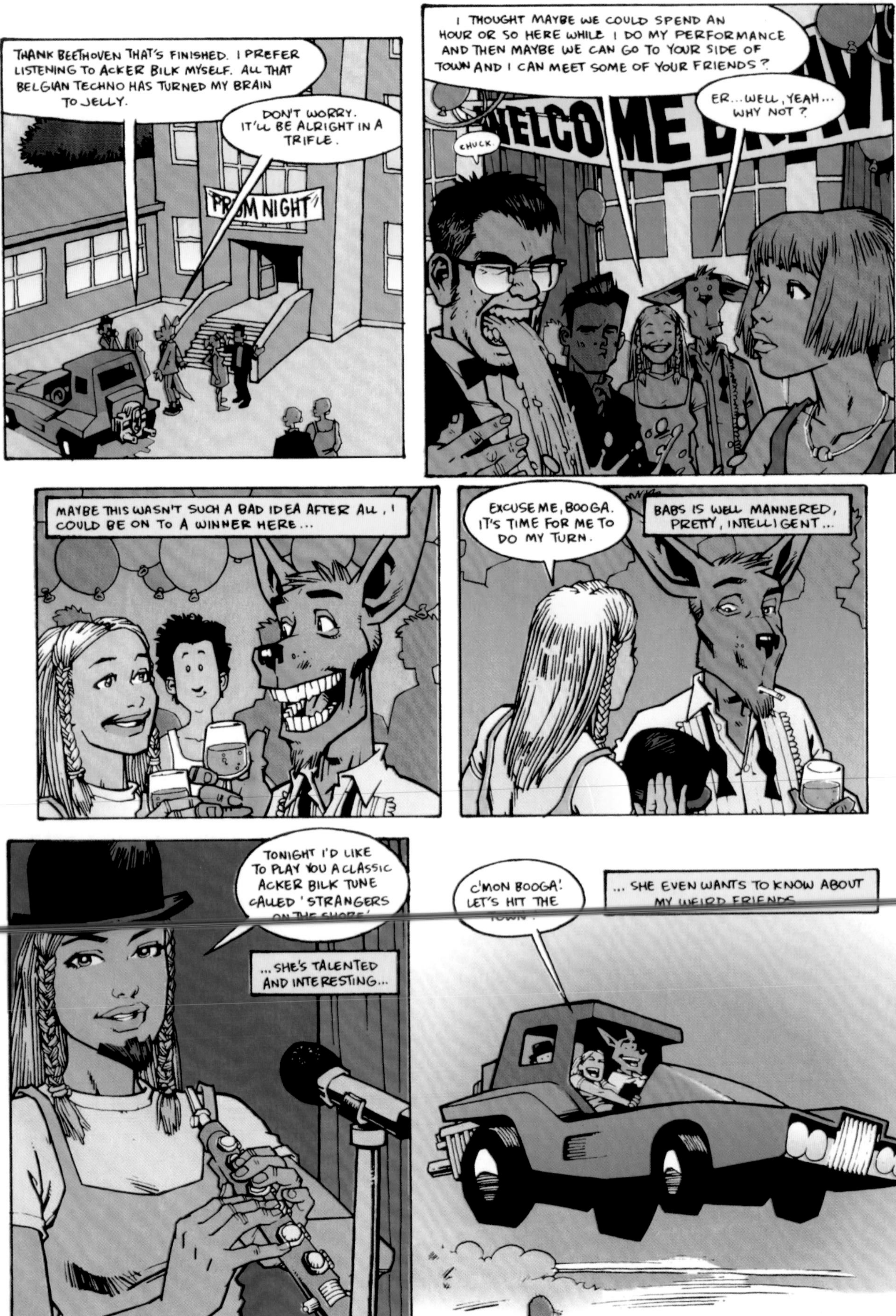
THANK BEETHOVEN THAT'S FINISHED. I PREFER LISTENING TO ACKER BILK MYSELF. ALL THAT BELGIAN TECHNO HAS TURNED MY BRAIN TO JELLY.
DON'T WORRY. IT'LL BE ALRIGHT IN A TRIFLE.
PROM NIGHT
I THOUGHT MAYBE WE COULD SPEND AN HOUR OR SO HERE WHILE I DO MY PERFORMANCE AND THEN MAYBE WE CAN GO TO YOUR SIDE OF TOWN AND I CAN MEET SOME OF YOUR FRIENDS?
CHUCK.
ER... WELL, YEAH... WHY NOT?
MAYBE THIS WASN'T SUCH A BAD IDEA AFTER ALL, I COULD BE ON TO A WINNER HERE...
EXCUSE ME, BOOGA. IT'S TIME FOR ME TO DO MY TURN.
BABS IS WELL MANNERED, PRETTY, INTELLIGENT...
TONIGHT I'D LIKE TO PLAY YOU A CLASSIC ACKER BILK TUNE CALLED 'STRANGERS ON THE SHORE'.
...SHE'S TALENTED AND INTERESTING...
C'MON BOOGA! LET'S HIT THE TOWN!
... SHE EVEN WANTS TO KNOW ABOUT MY WEIRD FRIENDS.

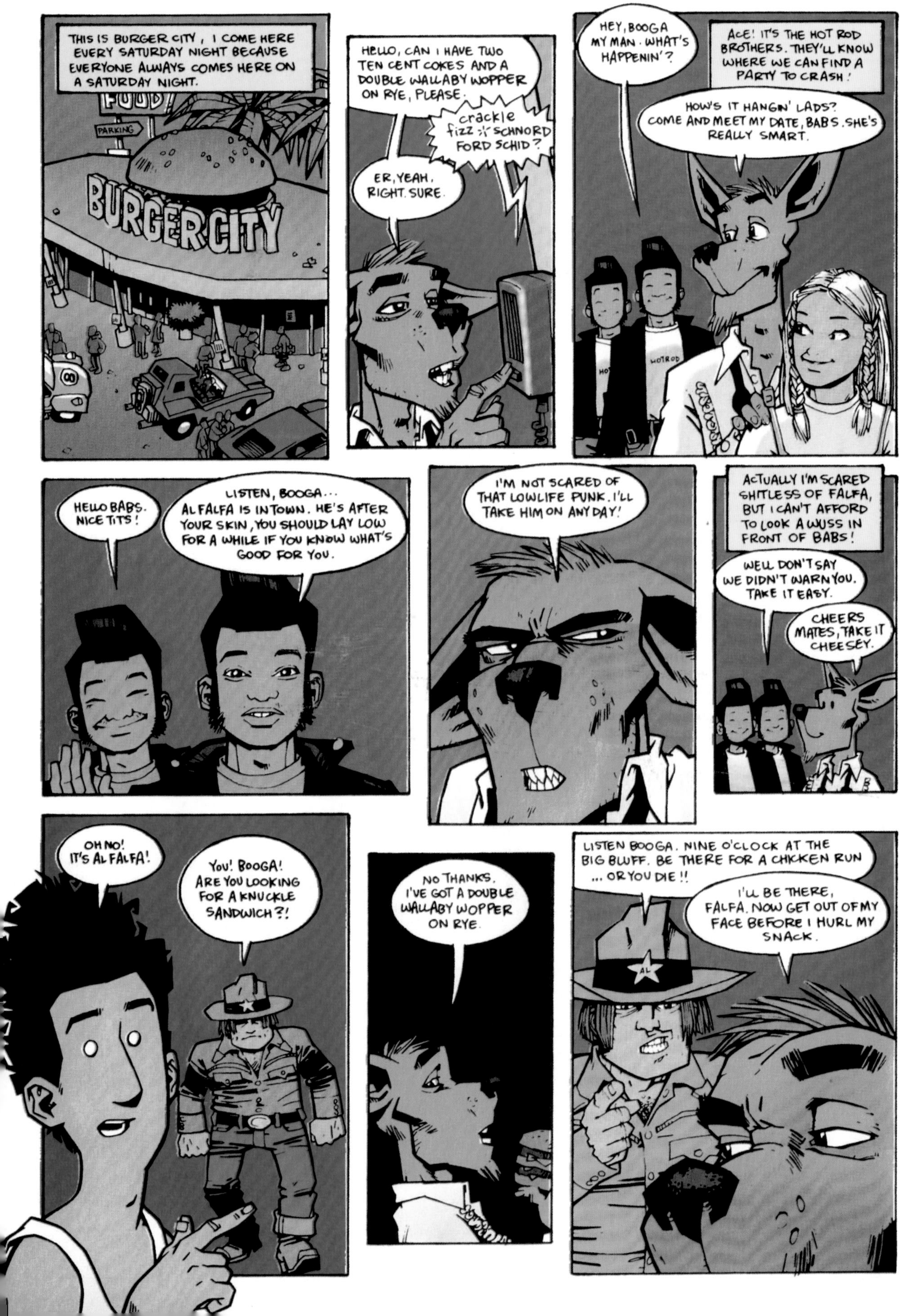

THIS IS BURGER CITY, I COME HERE EVERY SATURDAY NIGHT BECAUSE EVERYONE ALWAYS COMES HERE ON A SATURDAY NIGHT.
FOOD
PARKING
BURGERCITY
HELLO, CAN I HAVE TWO TEN CENT COKES AND A DOUBLE WALLABY WOPPER ON RYE, PLEASE.
crackle fizz SCHNORD FORD SCHID?
ER, YEAH. RIGHT. SURE.
HEY, BOOGA MY MAN. WHAT'S HAPPENIN'?
ACE! IT'S THE HOT ROD BROTHERS. THEY'LL KNOW WHERE WE CAN FIND A PARTY TO CRASH!
HOW'S IT HANGIN' LADS? COME AND MEET MY DATE, BABS. SHE'S REALLY SMART.
HOTROD
HELLO BABS. NICE TITS!
LISTEN, BOOGA... AL FALFA IS IN TOWN. HE'S AFTER YOUR SKIN, YOU SHOULD LAY LOW FOR A WHILE IF YOU KNOW WHAT'S GOOD FOR YOU.
I'M NOT SCARED OF THAT LOWLIFE PUNK. I'LL TAKE HIM ON ANY DAY!
ACTUALLY I'M SCARED SHITLESS OF FALFA, BUT I CAN'T AFFORD TO LOOK A WUSS IN FRONT OF BABS!
WELL DON'T SAY WE DIDN'T WARN YOU. TAKE IT EASY.
CHEERS MATES, TAKE IT CHEESEY.
OH NO! IT'S AL FALFA!
YOU! BOOGA! ARE YOU LOOKING FOR A KNUCKLE SANDWICH?!
NO THANKS. I'VE GOT A DOUBLE WALLABY WOPPER ON RYE.
LISTEN BOOGA. NINE O'CLOCK AT THE BIG BLUFF. BE THERE FOR A CHICKEN RUN ... OR YOU DIE!!
I'LL BE THERE, FALFA. NOW GET OUT OF MY FACE BEFORE I HURL MY SNACK.
AL

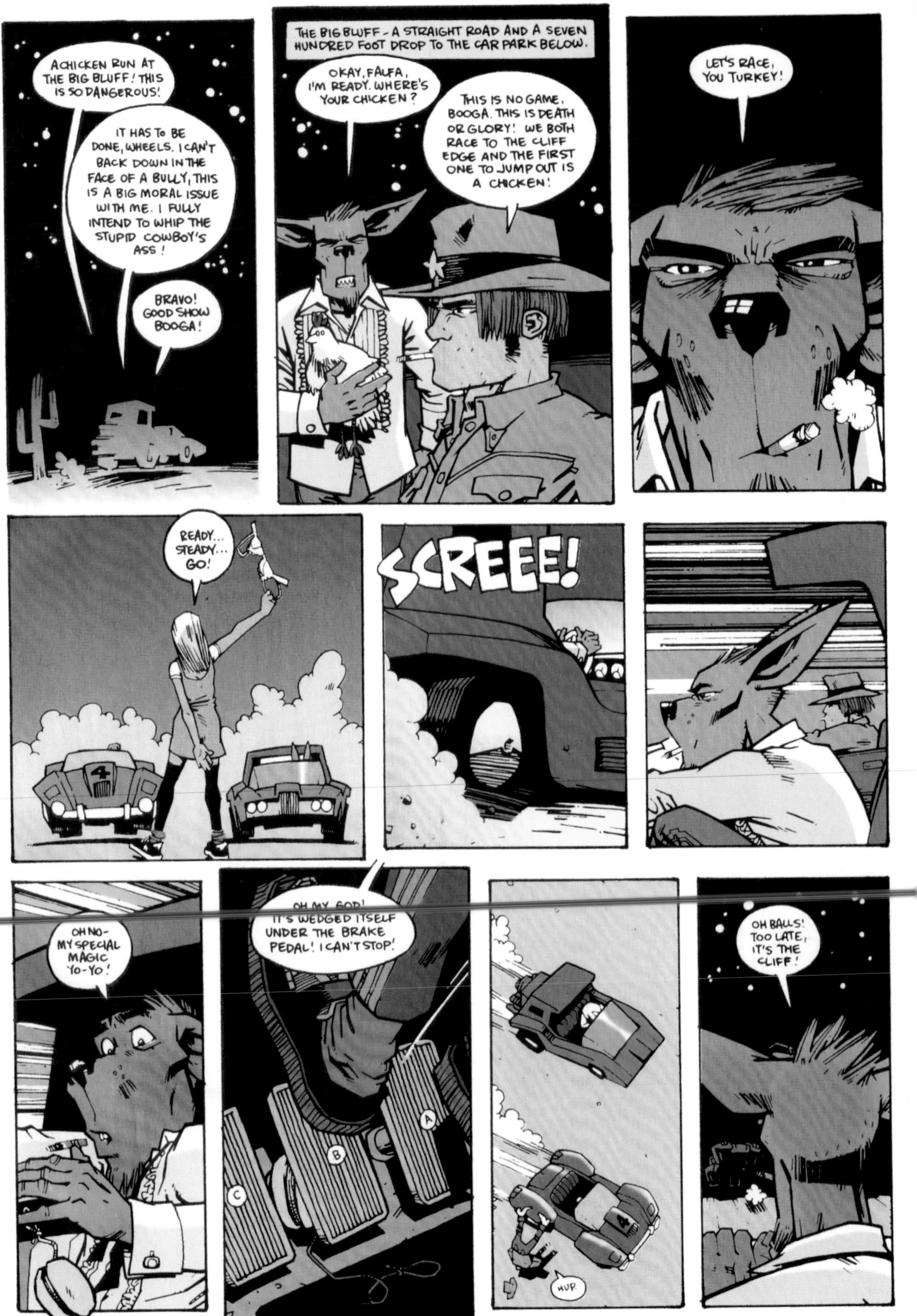
A CHICKEN RUN AT THE BIG BLUFF! THIS IS SO DANGEROUS!
IT HAS TO BE DONE, WHEELS. I CAN'T BACK DOWN IN THE FACE OF A BULLY, THIS IS A BIG MORAL ISSUE WITH ME. I FULLY INTEND TO WHIP THE STUPID COWBOY'S ASS!
BRAVO! GOOD SHOW BOOGA!
THE BIG BLUFF - A STRAIGHT ROAD AND A SEVEN HUNDRED FOOT DROP TO THE CAR PARK BELOW.
OKAY, FALFA, I'M READY. WHERE'S YOUR CHICKEN?
THIS IS NO GAME, BOOGA. THIS IS DEATH OR GLORY! WE BOTH RACE TO THE CLIFF EDGE AND THE FIRST ONE TO JUMP OUT IS A CHICKEN!
LET'S RACE, YOU TURKEY!
READY... STEADY... GO!
SCREEE!
OH NO- MY SPECIAL MAGIC YO-YO!
OH MY GOD! IT'S WEDGED ITSELF UNDER THE BRAKE PEDAL! I CAN'T STOP!
A
B
C
HUP.
OH BALLS! TOO LATE, IT'S THE CLIFF!

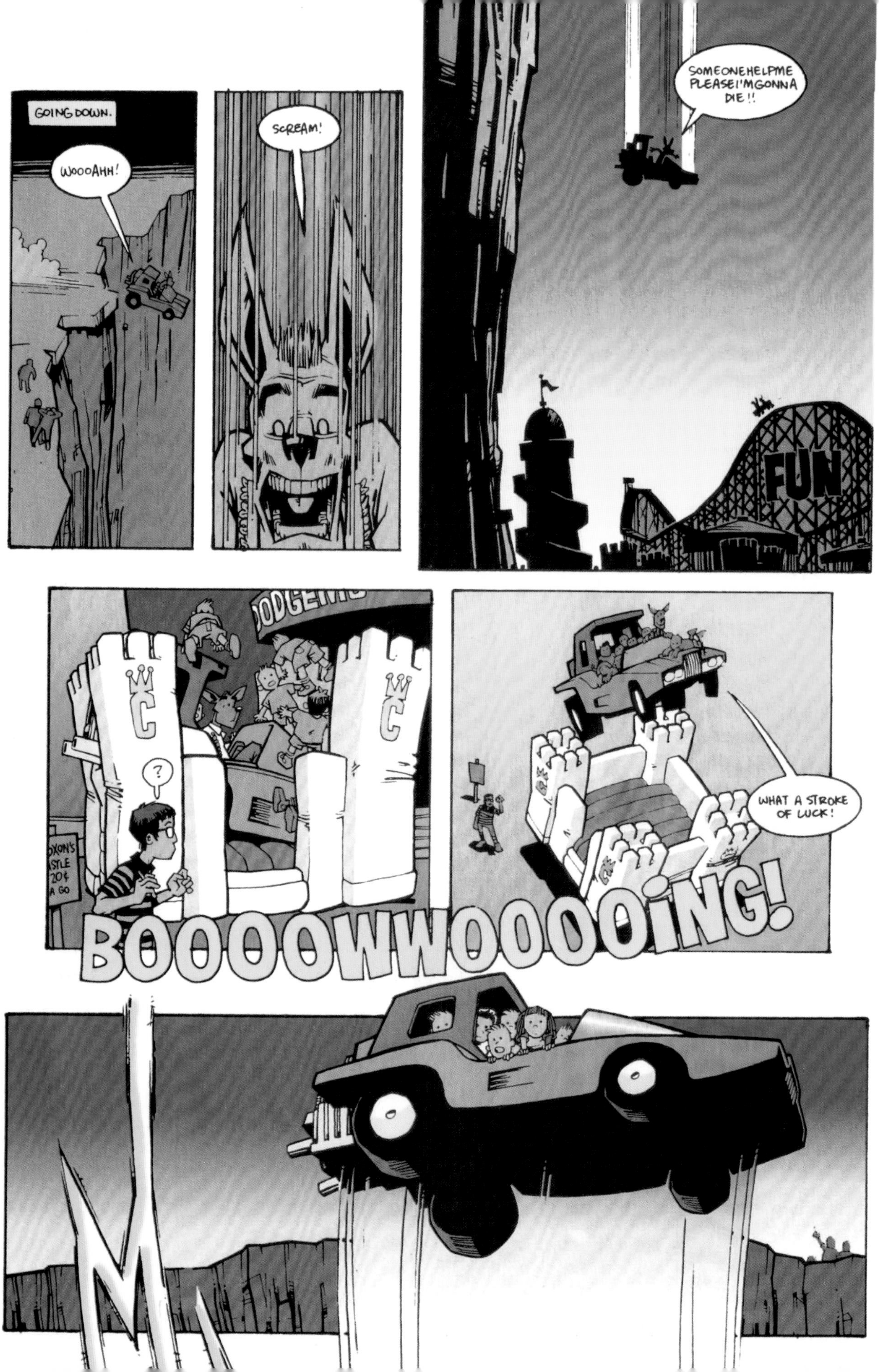
GOING DOWN.
WOOOAHH!
SCREAM!
SOMEONEHELPME PLEASEI'MGONNA DIE!!
FUN
?
WHAT A STROKE OF LUCK!
BOOOOWWOOOOiNG!

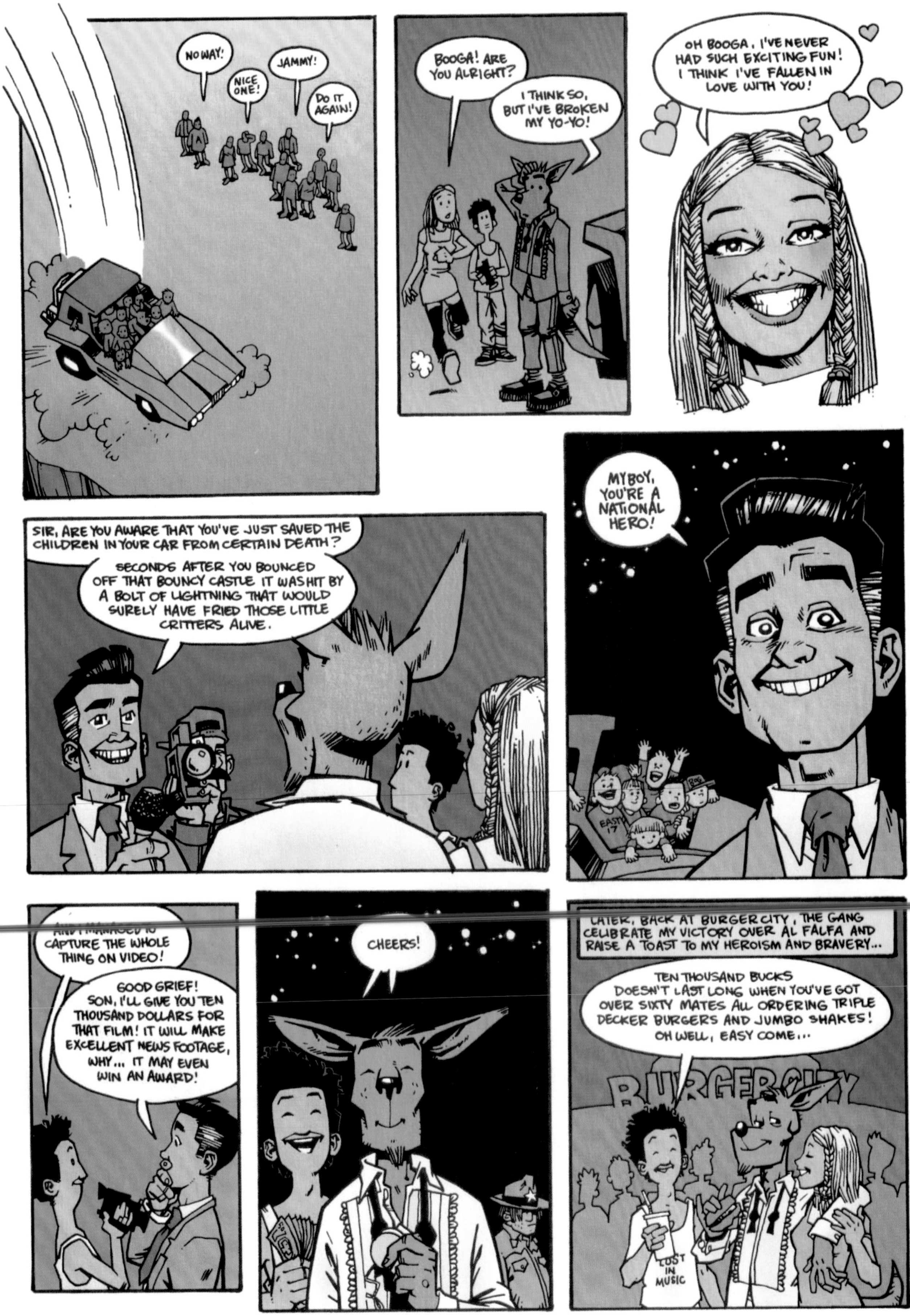
NO WAY!
NICE ONE!
JAMMY!
DO IT AGAIN!
BOOGA! ARE YOU ALRIGHT?
I THINK SO, BUT I'VE BROKEN MY YO-YO!
OH BOOGA, I'VE NEVER HAD SUCH EXCITING FUN! I THINK I'VE FALLEN IN LOVE WITH YOU!
SIR, ARE YOU AWARE THAT YOU'VE JUST SAVED THE CHILDREN IN YOUR CAR FROM CERTAIN DEATH?
SECONDS AFTER YOU BOUNCED OFF THAT BOUNCY CASTLE IT WAS HIT BY A BOLT OF LIGHTNING THAT WOULD SURELY HAVE FRIED THOSE LITTLE CRITTERS ALIVE.
MY BOY, YOU'RE A NATIONAL HERO!
EASY 17
CAPTURE THE WHOLE THING ON VIDEO!
GOOD GRIEF! SON, I'LL GIVE YOU TEN THOUSAND DOLLARS FOR THAT FILM! IT WILL MAKE EXCELLENT NEWS FOOTAGE, WHY... IT MAY EVEN WIN AN AWARD!
CHEERS!
LATER, BACK AT BURGER CITY, THE GANG CELEBRATE MY VICTORY OVER AL FALFA AND RAISE A TOAST TO MY HEROISM AND BRAVERY...
TEN THOUSAND BUCKS DOESN'T LAST LONG WHEN YOU'VE GOT OVER SIXTY MATES ALL ORDERING TRIPLE DECKER BURGERS AND JUMBO SHAKES! OH WELL, EASY COME...
BURGERCITY
LOST IN MUSIC

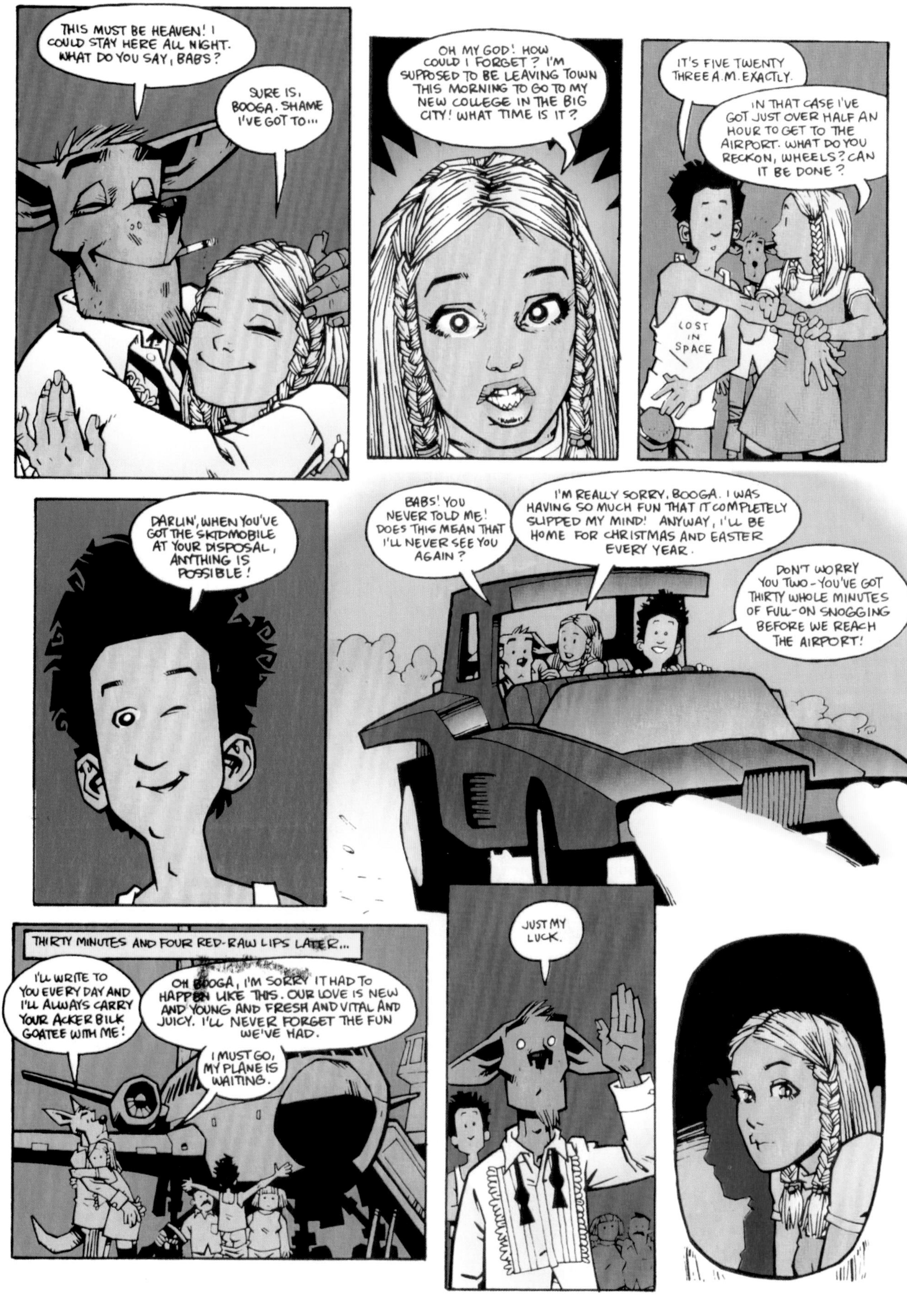
THIS MUST BE HEAVEN! I COULD STAY HERE ALL NIGHT. WHAT DO YOU SAY, BABS?
SURE IS, BOOGA. SHAME I'VE GOT TO...
OH MY GOD! HOW COULD I FORGET? I'M SUPPOSED TO BE LEAVING TOWN THIS MORNING TO GO TO MY NEW COLLEGE IN THE BIG CITY! WHAT TIME IS IT?
IT'S FIVE TWENTY THREE A.M. EXACTLY.
IN THAT CASE I'VE GOT JUST OVER HALF AN HOUR TO GET TO THE AIRPORT. WHAT DO YOU RECKON, WHEELS? CAN IT BE DONE?
LOST IN SPACE
DARLIN', WHEN YOU'VE GOT THE SKIDMOBILE AT YOUR DISPOSAL, ANYTHING IS POSSIBLE!
BABS! YOU NEVER TOLD ME! DOES THIS MEAN THAT I'LL NEVER SEE YOU AGAIN?
I'M REALLY SORRY, BOOGA. I WAS HAVING SO MUCH FUN THAT IT COMPLETELY SLIPPED MY MIND! ANYWAY, I'LL BE HOME FOR CHRISTMAS AND EASTER EVERY YEAR.
DON'T WORRY YOU TWO - YOU'VE GOT THIRTY WHOLE MINUTES OF FULL-ON SNOGGING BEFORE WE REACH THE AIRPORT!
THIRTY MINUTES AND FOUR RED-RAW LIPS LATER...
I'LL WRITE TO YOU EVERY DAY AND I'LL ALWAYS CARRY YOUR ACKER BILK GOATEE WITH ME!
OH BOOGA, I'M SORRY IT HAD TO HAPPEN LIKE THIS. OUR LOVE IS NEW AND YOUNG AND FRESH AND VITAL AND JUICY. I'LL NEVER FORGET THE FUN WE'VE HAD.
I MUST GO, MY PLANE IS WAITING.
JUST MY LUCK.

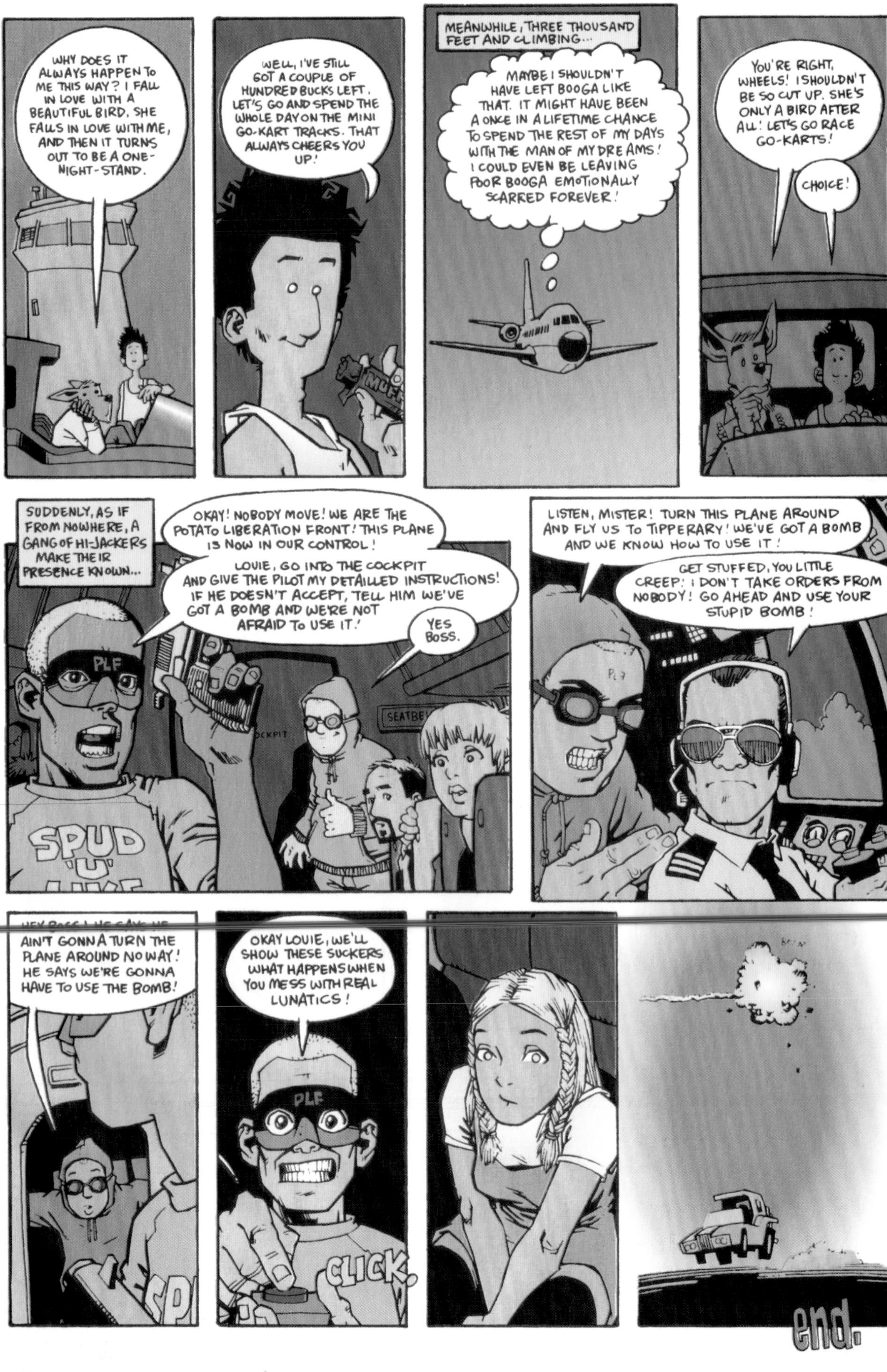

WHY DOES IT ALWAYS HAPPEN TO ME THIS WAY? I FALL IN LOVE WITH A BEAUTIFUL BIRD, SHE FALLS IN LOVE WITH ME, AND THEN IT TURNS OUT TO BE A ONE-NIGHT-STAND.
WELL, I'VE STILL GOT A COUPLE OF HUNDRED BUCKS LEFT. LET'S GO AND SPEND THE WHOLE DAY ON THE MINI GO-KART TRACKS. THAT ALWAYS CHEERS YOU UP!
MEANWHILE, THREE THOUSAND FEET AND CLIMBING...
MAYBE I SHOULDN'T HAVE LEFT BOOGA LIKE THAT. IT MIGHT HAVE BEEN A ONCE IN A LIFETIME CHANCE TO SPEND THE REST OF MY DAYS WITH THE MAN OF MY DREAMS! I COULD EVEN BE LEAVING POOR BOOGA EMOTIONALLY SCARRED FOREVER!
YOU'RE RIGHT, WHEELS! I SHOULDN'T BE SO CUT UP. SHE'S ONLY A BIRD AFTER ALL! LET'S GO RACE GO-KARTS!
CHOICE!
SUDDENLY, AS IF FROM NOWHERE, A GANG OF HI-JACKERS MAKE THEIR PRESENCE KNOWN...
OKAY! NOBODY MOVE! WE ARE THE POTATO LIBERATION FRONT! THIS PLANE IS NOW IN OUR CONTROL!
LOUIE, GO INTO THE COCKPIT AND GIVE THE PILOT MY DETAILLED INSTRUCTIONS! IF HE DOESN'T ACCEPT, TELL HIM WE'VE GOT A BOMB AND WE'RE NOT AFRAID TO USE IT!
YES BOSS.
PLF
SPUD 'U'
LISTEN, MISTER! TURN THIS PLANE AROUND AND FLY US TO TIPPERARY! WE'VE GOT A BOMB AND WE KNOW HOW TO USE IT!
GET STUFFED, YOU LITTLE CREEP! I DON'T TAKE ORDERS FROM NOBODY! GO AHEAD AND USE YOUR STUPID BOMB!
AIN'T GONNA TURN THE PLANE AROUND NO WAY! HE SAYS WE'RE GONNA HAVE TO USE THE BOMB!
OKAY LOUIE, WE'LL SHOW THESE SUCKERS WHAT HAPPENS WHEN YOU MESS WITH REAL LUNATICS!
PLF
CLICK.
end.

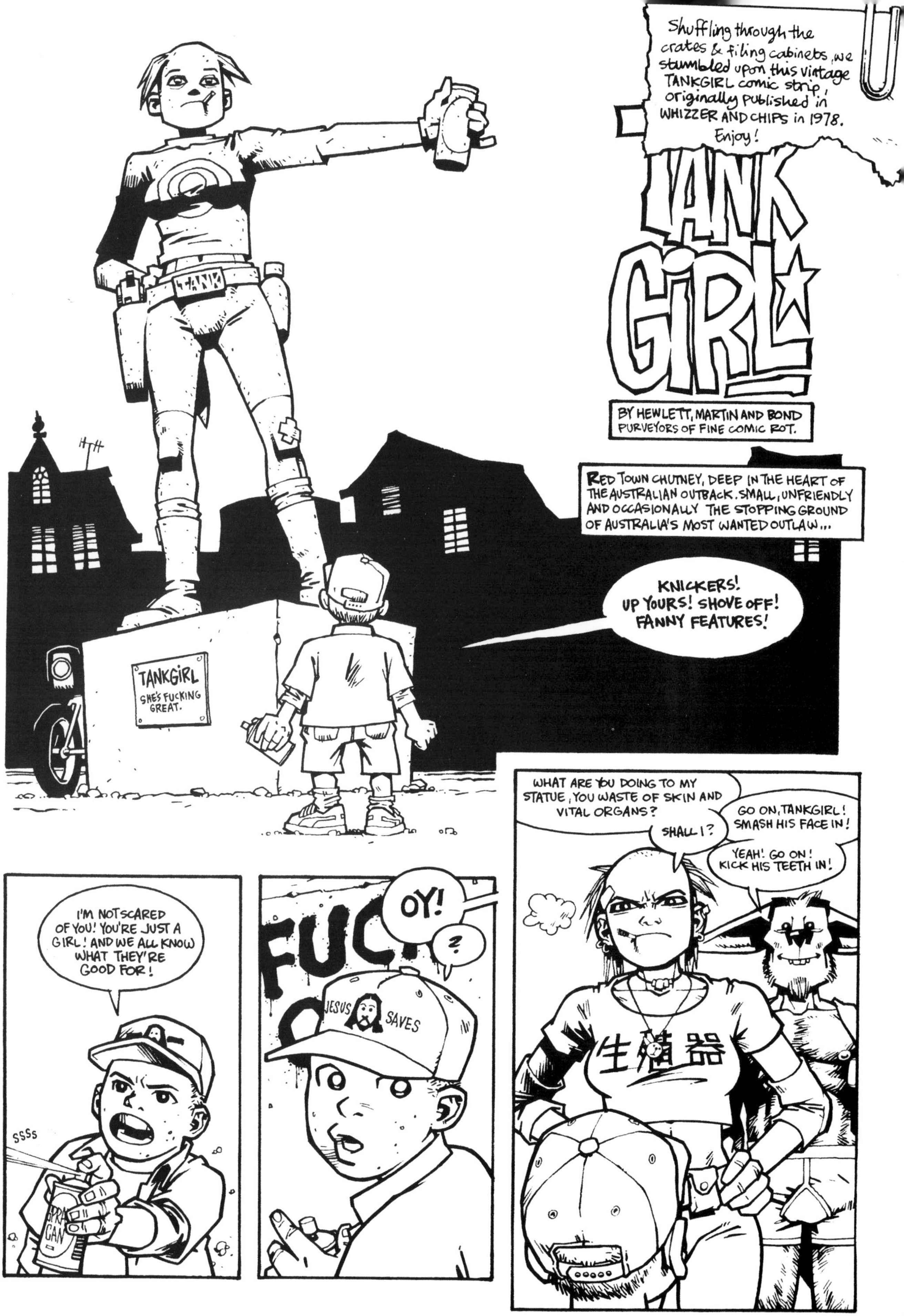

Shuffling through the crates & filing cabinets, we stumbled upon this vintage TANKGIRL comic strip, originally published in WHIZZER AND CHIPS in 1978. Enjoy!
TANK GIRL
BY HEWLETT, MARTIN AND BOND
PURVEYORS OF FINE COMIC ROT.
TANK
RED TOWN CHUTNEY, DEEP IN THE HEART OF THE AUSTRALIAN OUTBACK. SMALL, UNFRIENDLY AND OCCASIONALLY THE STOPPING GROUND OF AUSTRALIA'S MOST WANTED OUTLAW...
KNICKERS! UP YOURS! SHOVE OFF! FANNY FEATURES!
TANKGIRL
SHE'S FUCKING GREAT.
I'M NOT SCARED OF YOU! YOU'RE JUST A GIRL! AND WE ALL KNOW WHAT THEY'RE GOOD FOR!
SSSS
OY!
?
JESUS SAVES
WHAT ARE YOU DOING TO MY STATUE, YOU WASTE OF SKIN AND VITAL ORGANS?
SHALL I?
GO ON, TANKGIRL! SMASH HIS FACE IN!
YEAH! GO ON! KICK HIS TEETH IN!
生殖器

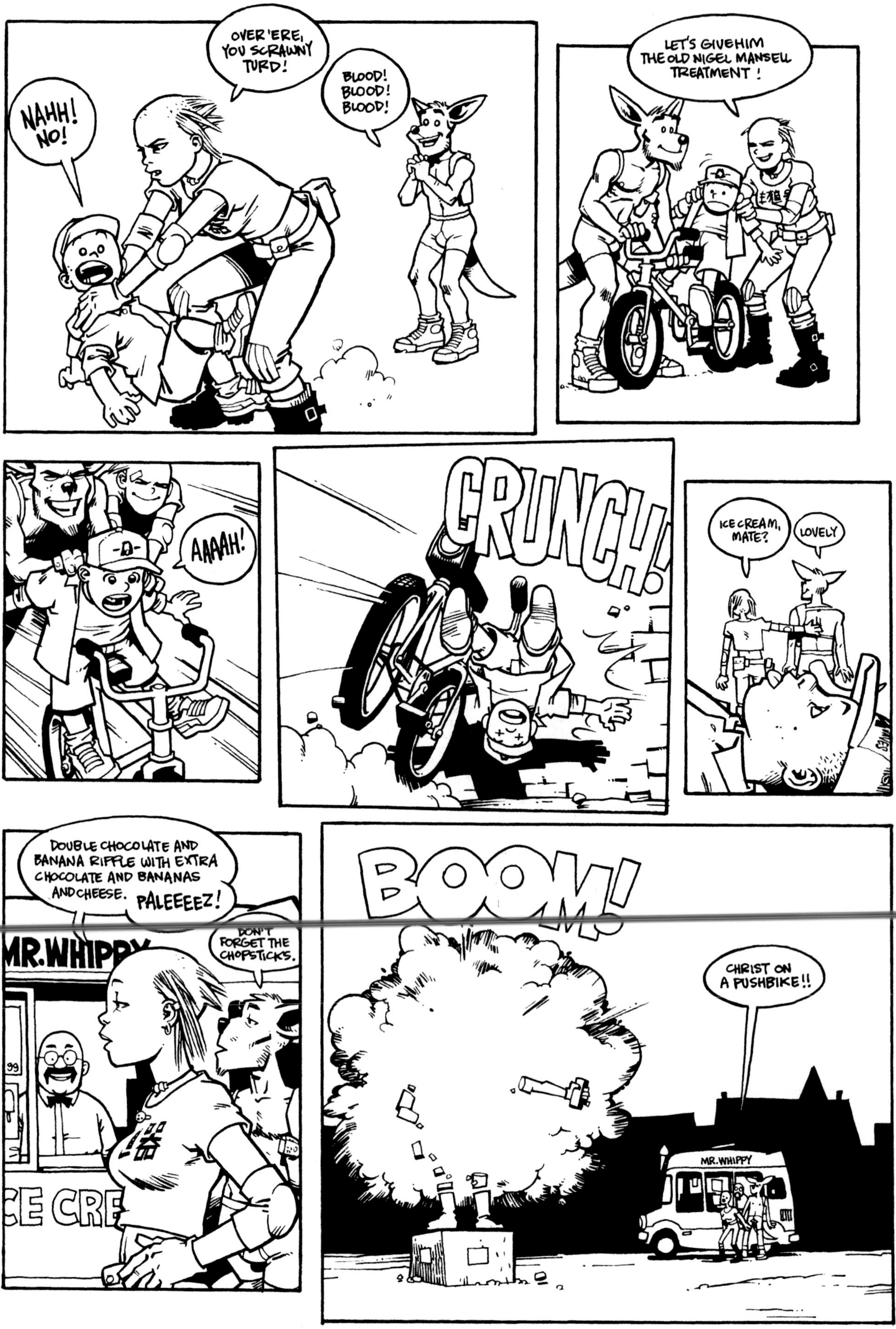
NAHH! NO!
OVER 'ERE, YOU SCRAWNY TURD!
BLOOD! BLOOD! BLOOD!
LET'S GIVEHIM THE OLD NIGEL MANSELL TREATMENT!
AAAAH!
CRUNCH!
ICE CREAM, MATE?
LOVELY
DOUBLE CHOCOLATE AND BANANA RIPPLE WITH EXTRA CHOCOLATE AND BANANAS AND CHEESE.
PALEEEEZ!
DON'T FORGET THE CHOPSTICKS.
MR.WHIPPY
ICE CRE
BOOM!
CHRIST ON A PUSHBIKE!!
MR.WHIPPY

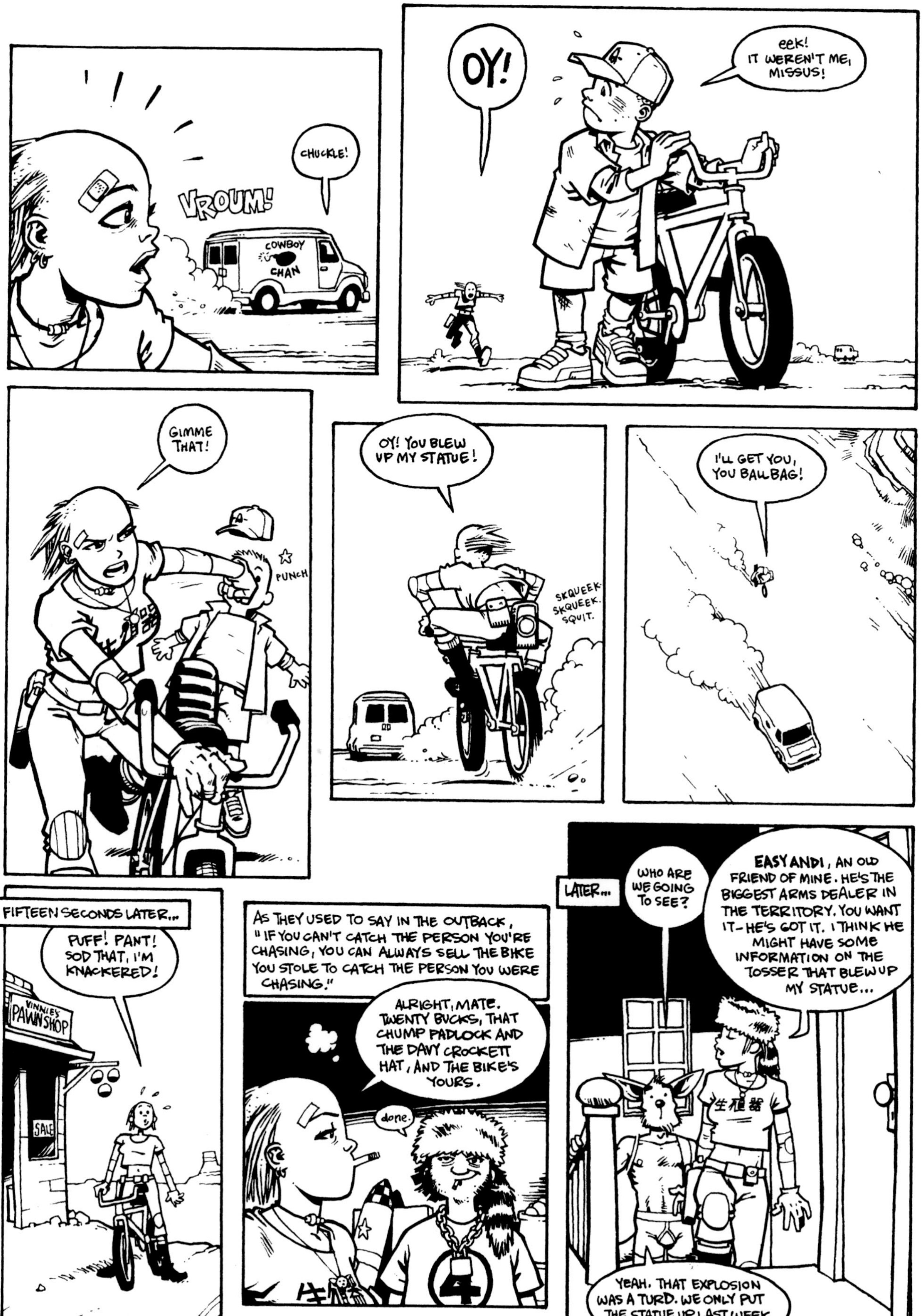
CHUCKLE!
VROUM!
COWBOY CHAN
OY!
eek! IT WEREN'T ME, MISSUS!
GIMME THAT!
PUNCH
OY! YOU BLEW UP MY STATUE!
SKQUEEK. SKQUEEK. SQUIT.
I'LL GET YOU, YOU BALLBAG!
FIFTEEN SECONDS LATER...
PUFF! PANT! SOD THAT, I'M KNACKERED!
VINNIE'S PAWN SHOP
SALE
AS THEY USED TO SAY IN THE OUTBACK, "IF YOU CAN'T CATCH THE PERSON YOU'RE CHASING, YOU CAN ALWAYS SELL THE BIKE YOU STOLE TO CATCH THE PERSON YOU WERE CHASING."
ALRIGHT, MATE. TWENTY BUCKS, THAT CHUMP PADLOCK AND THE DAVY CROCKETT HAT, AND THE BIKE'S YOURS.
done.
LATER...
WHO ARE WE GOING TO SEE?
EASY ANDI, AN OLD FRIEND OF MINE. HE'S THE BIGGEST ARMS DEALER IN THE TERRITORY. YOU WANT IT-HE'S GOT IT. I THINK HE MIGHT HAVE SOME INFORMATION ON THE TOSSER THAT BLEW UP MY STATUE...
YEAH. THAT EXPLOSION WAS A TURD. WE ONLY PUT THE STATUE UP LAST WEEK.

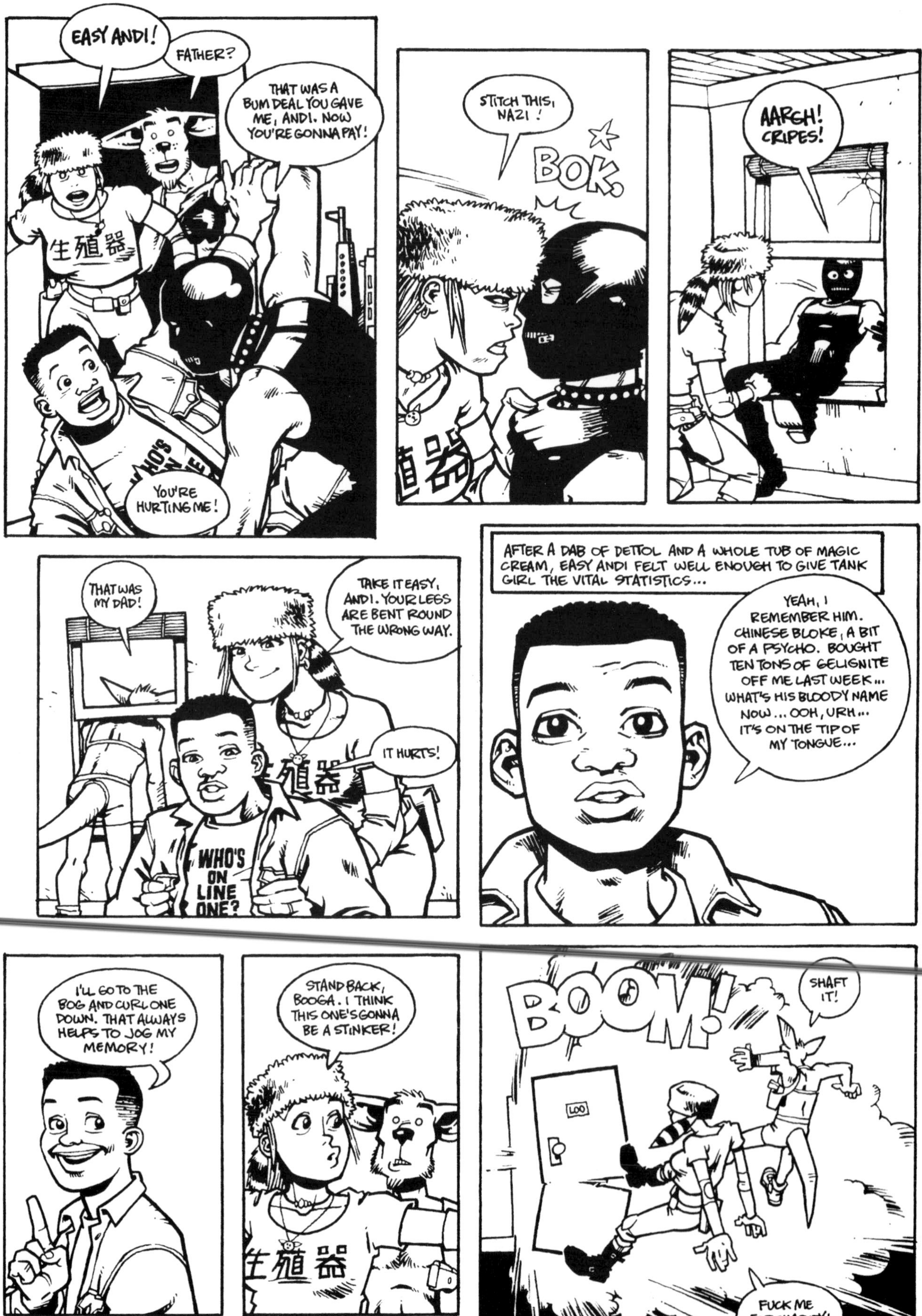
EASY ANDI!
FATHER?
THAT WAS A BUM DEAL YOU GAVE ME, ANDI. NOW YOU'RE GONNA PAY!
生殖器
WHO'S
YOU'RE HURTING ME!
STITCH THIS, NAZI!
BOK.
AARGH! CRIPES!
THAT WAS MY DAD!
TAKE IT EASY, ANDI. YOUR LEGS ARE BENT ROUND THE WRONG WAY.
生殖器
IT HURTS!
WHO'S ON LINE ONE?
AFTER A DAB OF DETTOL AND A WHOLE TUB OF MAGIC CREAM, EASY ANDI FELT WELL ENOUGH TO GIVE TANK GIRL THE VITAL STATISTICS...
YEAH, I REMEMBER HIM. CHINESE BLOKE, A BIT OF A PSYCHO. BOUGHT TEN TONS OF GELIGNITE OFF ME LAST WEEK... WHAT'S HIS BLOODY NAME NOW... OOH, URH... IT'S ON THE TIP OF MY TONGUE...
I'LL GO TO THE BOG AND CURL ONE DOWN. THAT ALWAYS HELPS TO JOG MY MEMORY!
STAND BACK, BOOGA. I THINK THIS ONE'S GONNA BE A STINKER!
生殖器
BOOM!
SHAFT IT!
LOO
FUCK ME FOR CHARITY!

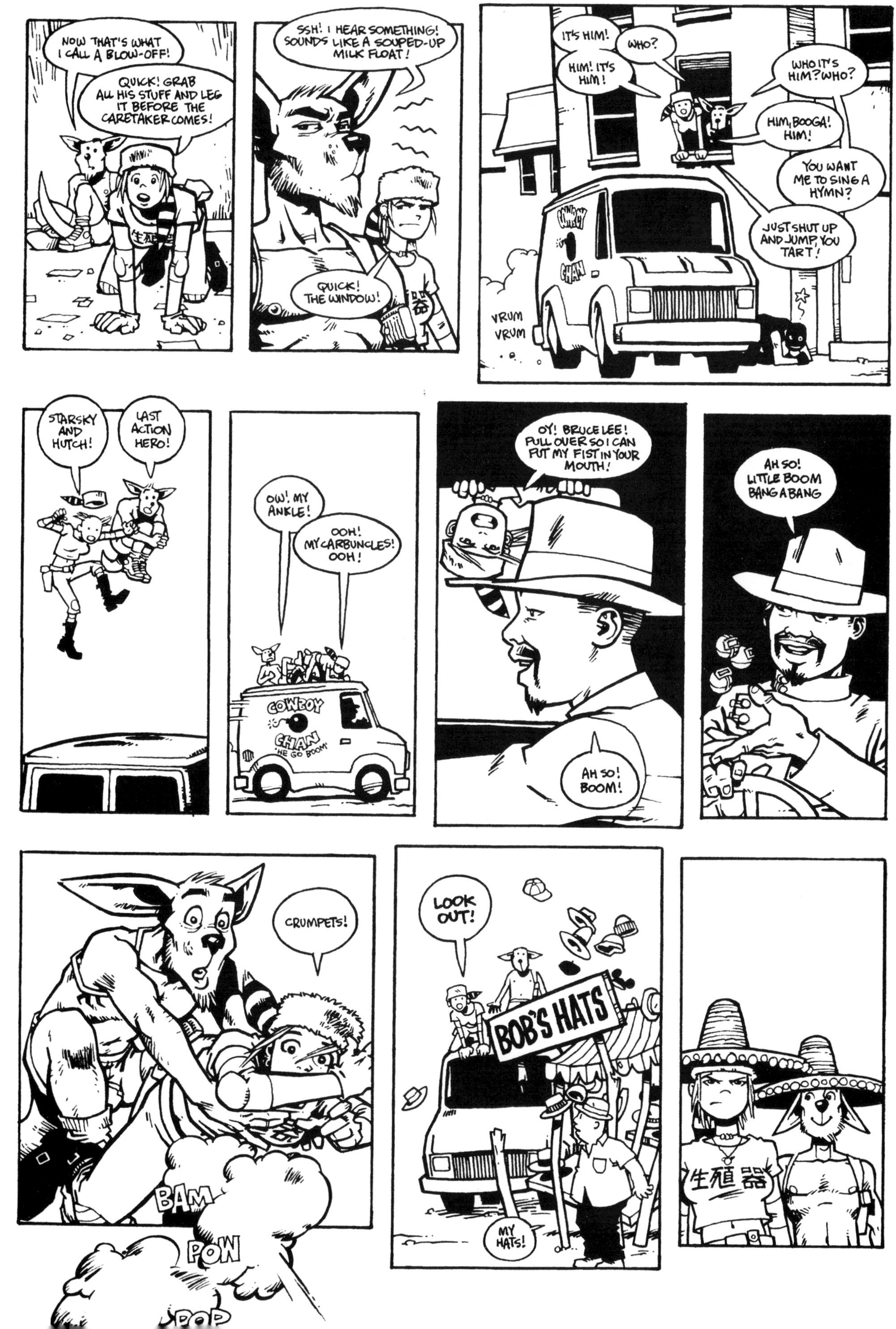
NOW THAT'S WHAT I CALL A BLOW-OFF!
QUICK! GRAB ALL HIS STUFF AND LEG IT BEFORE THE CARETAKER COMES!
SSH! I HEAR SOMETHING! SOUNDS LIKE A SOUPED-UP MILK FLOAT!
QUICK! THE WINDOW!
IT'S HIM!
WHO?
HIM! IT'S HIM!
WHO IT'S HIM? WHO?
HIM, BOOGA! HIM!
YOU WANT ME TO SING A HYMN?
JUST SHUT UP AND JUMP, YOU TART!
VRUM
VRUM
STARSKY AND HUTCH!
LAST ACTION HERO!
OW! MY ANKLE!
OOH! MY CARBUNCLES! OOH!
COWBOY CHAN
'HE GO BOOM'
OY! BRUCE LEE! PULL OVER SO I CAN PUT MY FIST IN YOUR MOUTH!
AH SO! BOOM!
AH SO! LITTLE BOOM BANG A BANG
CRUMPETS!
BAM
POW
POP
LOOK OUT!
BOB'S HATS
MY HATS!
生殖器

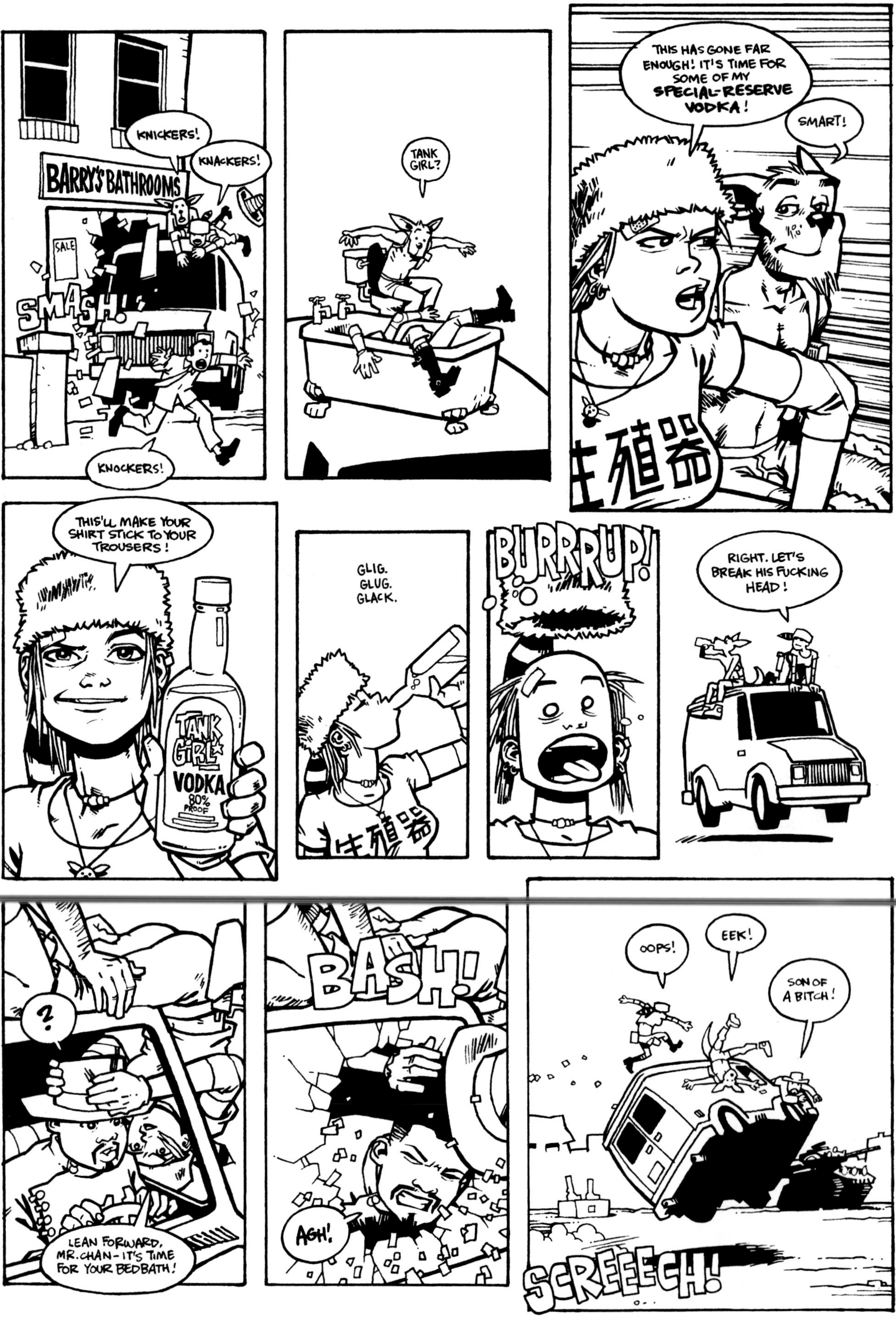
BARRY'S BATHROOMS
SALE
KNICKERS!
KNACKERS!
SMASH!
KNOCKERS!
TANK GIRL?
THIS HAS GONE FAR ENOUGH! IT'S TIME FOR SOME OF MY SPECIAL-RESERVE VODKA!
SMART!
生殖器
THIS'LL MAKE YOUR SHIRT STICK TO YOUR TROUSERS!
TANK GIRL VODKA 80% PROOF
GLIG. GLUG. GLACK.
生殖器
BURRRUP!
RIGHT. LET'S BREAK HIS FUCKING HEAD!
?
LEAN FORWARD, MR. CHAN - IT'S TIME FOR YOUR BEDBATH!
BASH!
AGH!
OOPS!
EEK!
SON OF A BITCH!
SCREEECH!

ADVERTISMENT

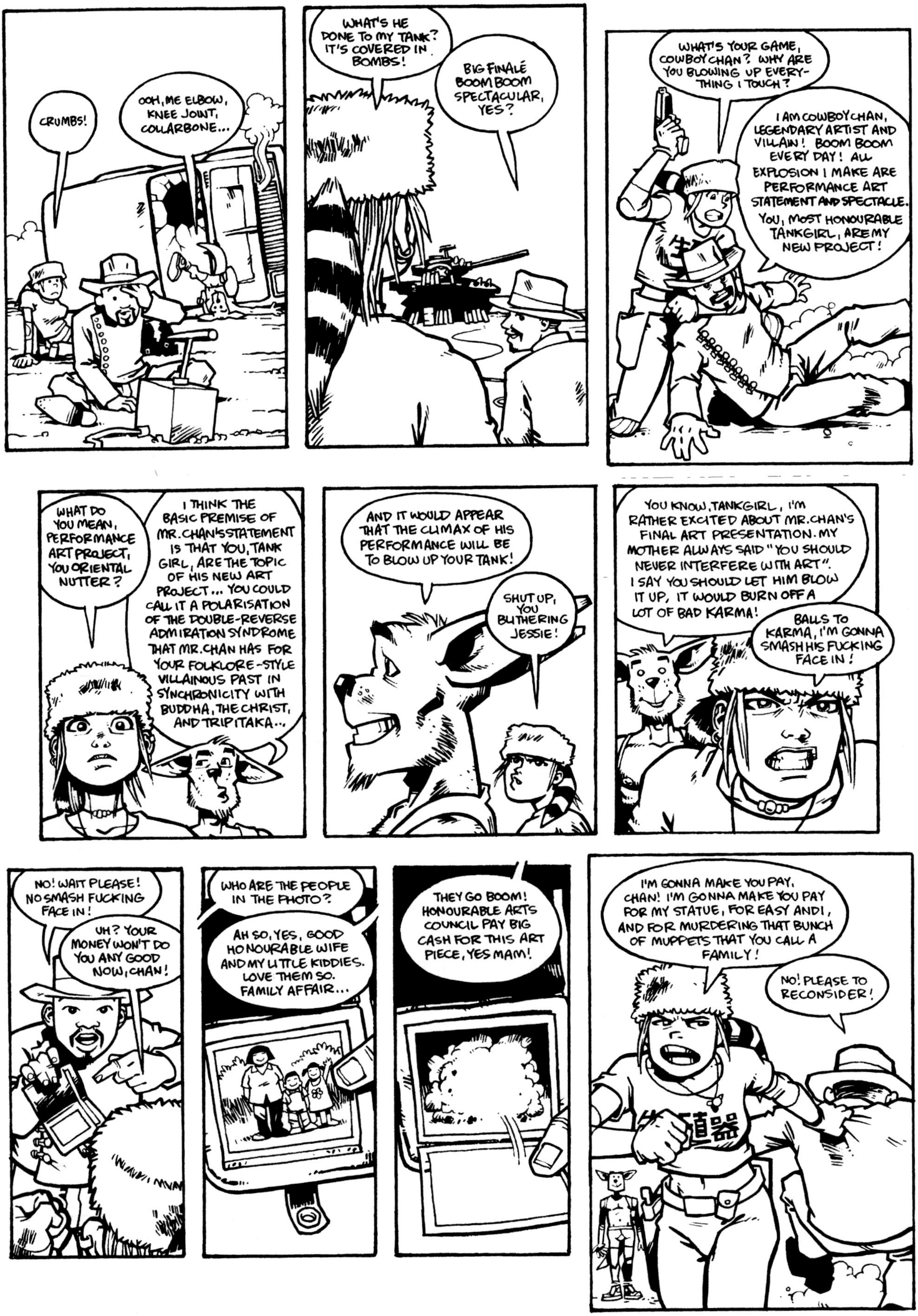
CRUMBS!
OOH, ME ELBOW, KNEE JOINT, COLLARBONE...
WHAT'S HE DONE TO MY TANK? IT'S COVERED IN BOMBS!
BIG FINALÉ BOOM BOOM SPECTACULAR, YES?
WHAT'S YOUR GAME, COWBOY CHAN? WHY ARE YOU BLOWING UP EVERYTHING I TOUCH?
I AM COWBOY CHAN, LEGENDARY ARTIST AND VILLAIN! BOOM BOOM EVERY DAY! ALL EXPLOSION I MAKE ARE PERFORMANCE ART STATEMENT AND SPECTACLE. YOU, MOST HONOURABLE TANKGIRL, ARE MY NEW PROJECT!
WHAT DO YOU MEAN, PERFORMANCE ART PROJECT, YOU ORIENTAL NUTTER?
I THINK THE BASIC PREMISE OF MR. CHAN'S STATEMENT IS THAT YOU, TANK GIRL, ARE THE TOPIC OF HIS NEW ART PROJECT... YOU COULD CALL IT A POLARISATION OF THE DOUBLE-REVERSE ADMIRATION SYNDROME THAT MR. CHAN HAS FOR YOUR FOLKLORE-STYLE VILLAINOUS PAST IN SYNCHRONICITY WITH BUDDHA, THE CHRIST, AND TRIPITAKA...
AND IT WOULD APPEAR THAT THE CLIMAX OF HIS PERFORMANCE WILL BE TO BLOW UP YOUR TANK!
SHUT UP, YOU BLITHERING JESSIE!
YOU KNOW, TANKGIRL, I'M RATHER EXCITED ABOUT MR. CHAN'S FINAL ART PRESENTATION. MY MOTHER ALWAYS SAID "YOU SHOULD NEVER INTERFERE WITH ART". I SAY YOU SHOULD LET HIM BLOW IT UP, IT WOULD BURN OFF A LOT OF BAD KARMA!
BALLS TO KARMA, I'M GONNA SMASH HIS FUCKING FACE IN!
NO! WAIT PLEASE! NO SMASH FUCKING FACE IN!
UH? YOUR MONEY WON'T DO YOU ANY GOOD NOW, CHAN!
WHO ARE THE PEOPLE IN THE PHOTO?
AH SO, YES, GOOD HONOURABLE WIFE AND MY LITTLE KIDDIES. LOVE THEM SO. FAMILY AFFAIR...
THEY GO BOOM! HONOURABLE ARTS COUNCIL PAY BIG CASH FOR THIS ART PIECE, YES MAM!
I'M GONNA MAKE YOU PAY, CHAN! I'M GONNA MAKE YOU PAY FOR MY STATUE, FOR EASY ANDI, AND FOR MURDERING THAT BUNCH OF MUPPETS THAT YOU CALL A FAMILY!
NO! PLEASE TO RECONSIDER!

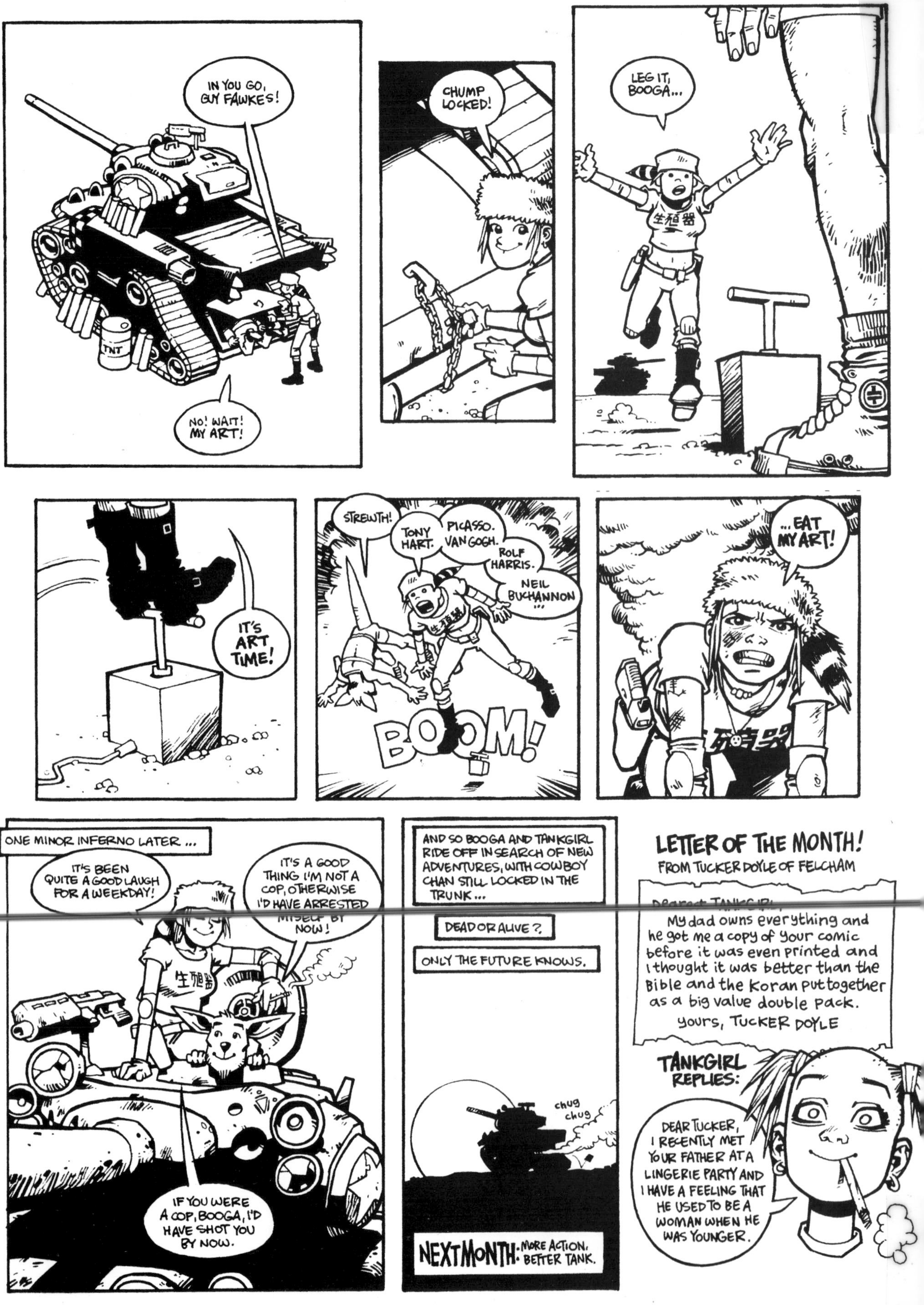

IN YOU GO, GUY FAWKES!
TNT
NO! WAIT! MY ART!
CHUMP LOCKED!
LEG IT, BOOGA...
IT'S ART TIME!
STREWTH!
TONY HART.
PICASSO. VAN GOGH.
ROLF HARRIS.
NEIL BUCHANNON ...
BOOM!
...EAT MY ART!
ONE MINOR INFERNO LATER ...
IT'S BEEN QUITE A GOOD LAUGH FOR A WEEKDAY!
IT'S A GOOD THING I'M NOT A COP, OTHERWISE I'D HAVE ARRESTED MYSELF BY NOW!
IF YOU WERE A COP, BOOGA, I'D HAVE SHOT YOU BY NOW.
AND SO BOOGA AND TANKGIRL RIDE OFF IN SEARCH OF NEW ADVENTURES, WITH COWBOY CHAN STILL LOCKED IN THE TRUNK...
DEAD OR ALIVE?
ONLY THE FUTURE KNOWS.
chug chug
NEXT MONTH: MORE ACTION. BETTER TANK.
LETTER OF THE MONTH!
FROM TUCKER DOYLE OF FELCHAM
Dearest TANKGIRL,
My dad owns everything and he got me a copy of your comic before it was even printed and I thought it was better than the Bible and the Koran put together as a big value double pack.
Yours, TUCKER DOYLE
TANKGIRL REPLIES:
DEAR TUCKER, I RECENTLY MET YOUR FATHER AT A LINGERIE PARTY AND I HAVE A FEELING THAT HE USED TO BE A WOMAN WHEN HE WAS YOUNGER.